McNonwuun

Hills

Of

Exile

Hills Of Exile
First Edition
Copyright 2013 by ©PRINCE MADISON NONWUUN
Publisher: Africtimes Multimedia
Africtimes Multimedia
Cranston Rhode Island
www.africtimes.com
africtimesinfo@africtimes.com

Hills of Exile Book One: The Unknown, by McNonwuun, first publication Fall 2013. This book is a series that is divided into four books. This is book one, published by Africtimes Multimedia and available in paperback copy and eBooks on many platforms, including the iBook Store, Amazon Store (paperback), Kindle, Nook, other eBook readers and at the publisher's website.
www.africtmes.com

You can follow the Author's blog for more interactive contents at:
www.africtimes.com/mcnonwuunblog.com and/or at
http://mcnonwuun.wordpress.com

The Library of Congress has cataloged the print edition as follows:
PRINCE MADISON NONWUUN
Hills Of Exile Book One: The Unknown
ISBN: 978-0-9911093-0-2
EBook ISBN: 978-0-9911093-1-9

Credits

William R. McMunn PH.D, Senior editor
Susan N. Nwokedi, acknowledgement & dedication editor
David Asiamah, Book cover designer

****
****

Table of Contents

Chapters

Part II

Acknowledgement

I wrote with passion, emotion, ignorance and innocence. He made it his duty to suggest some reality so that the world could grasp this deep seated creativity that was about to be born. I was a child with a vision; he was the man with experience. My arts were my children; I feared the cruel existence of the world would dilute them into something I would come to hate. He showed me that my arts needed their own existence, independence and if they were to survive in the cruel world, they would need their umbilical cords detach from my fear. Even more, with graceful utterance he silently taught me that these arts were not just mine, but massages waiting to navigate the world, with the potential to teach, inspire, console, create and sometimes cause relevant confusions and upheaval. They have the potential for revolutions, and to make a man beg for mercy, love, peace, death, sex, wine, hate, or for a good book. Don't be so attached dear author; you are only a vessel through which these arts are to enter into the world. Just like a mother giving birth to a child and the child finding his way through this world, you are the mother to these arts. They are not yours to keep forever.

William R. McMunn, PH.D, is one of a kind, an angel sent to rescue *Hills Of Exile* from its slumber and procrastination. I began working on this book in 2006. It was an off and on endeavor because I was mainly writing for myself. I was also in college and had many personal battles to fight.

Fragile from life's experiences, war in my country, becoming fatherless and questioning my Christian faith, *Hills Of Exile* was born out of this dark and complex place in my life. At its inception, I had many questions at that time that I believed nothing could answer, not even my faith in God. Thus, *Hills Of Exile* was developed as a source to help me overcome those dark times. The book became my escape and my anchor. The one thing I could rely on to answer the questions that raced through my mind; my faith, my pains and nightmares, and what I hoped the future had in store for me. In essence, I was not just writing for comfort but for something to happen (even though I had no clue what that something would be). I just wanted to get a grip on my life or at lest fill this void and darkness of my wandering thoughts that were spiraling out of control. I also held on to this fantasy...yes, the fantasy that writing this book will shed some lights on the darkness that surrounded me. I knew that in *Hills Of Exile*, my fantasy could become my reality and that anything could be possible.

With each page of *Hills Of Exile* I wrote, I felt closer to understanding the man I wanted to become. By trying to understand the man within, Isaac Kline, the lead character of *Hills Of Exile* emerged. Kline would embody all the questions I could ask and all the answers I could not find. I wanted to push him beyond these questions and set him free as his person who is not just living my youthful plight but living as a person with his own problems. He would have his questions about faith, pain, nightmare, loss of a loved one, of loneliness, aloneness, of being loved, and all the other emotions that make us human.

As my lead characters and those around him grew, I too grew. This was when I realized I was not just writing for myself anymore. *Hills Of Exile* had become much bigger than that.   Isaac Kline took on a superior life form more than I ever imagined for him. It became obvious that while my pain was real and my darkness vast, they were nothing compared to what Kline would embark on. He became a man on a journey. His pain, sufferings and challenges shed some lights on my questions.

After searching through several editors for a while to no avail, William R. McMunn PH.D, emerged. William not only helped me edit this book, he ensured the historical part of the story was accurate and authentic. He made quality our priority. He used his expertise to push and challenge me to take *Hills of Exile* to a level I never envisioned. He believed in my vision and helped to ignite the fire in me. For this, I thank you. I am grateful for the many hours you spent perfecting and sharing in my vision. I privileged to have a William McMunn on my side.

-*McNonwuun*

Dedication

Hills of Exile is dedicated to my cousin Aaron Miamen (1975-2004). He died of the Yellow Fever in the spring of 2004. Aaron's death helped me to see how precious life really is. The things we take for granted, the unnecessary complaints that make us lose sight of what's really important. Aaron's death came like a shockwave that forced me to reexamine my life. Such a promising life cut so soon!

Aaron was a man of many talents that rubbed off on me as a youth. Whatever Aaron did, I became fascinated with. I became fascinated with language because of Aaron's love for words. He loved the King James Bible and quoted often from it. He was confident in his God. This too had an effect on me. He was not perfect but believed in the perfect God and in the resurrection.

We were not always the best of buddies but through those difficult times these personalities of his were hard to ignore. Aaron was an imperfect man who believed in his perfect God. He was very confident of going to heaven and talked about it often. But all he saw form me was judgmental eyes. Subconsciously however, all those times I looked at him with judgmental eyes was because I had high regards for him. So when I found him inconsistent with my expectation I always had an opinion. These were perfect times for Aaron to rectify his action and scold me with plenty scriptural WORDS from the King James Bible. He would go on and on and I would get lost in his narratives, and get overtaken by his intriguing tone of reading the King James Bible as if it was his first language.

I did not know how much effects Aaron's ways had on me until after his death. Before Aaron's death, I had already started writing some poems since high school. And after his death I was a sophomore in college and had started *Hills of Exile* vaguely. When I was done weeping with my family over his loss, I found myself alone pondering the idea about life and death—and how one moment you are here and the next you are gone.

We are suddenly alive in this world without knowing the outcome of our lives. We are then taught the moral principles or values of good and bad, wrong and right—but there is so much left to uncover and in the middle of that, tragedies like war, death, social injustice, abandonment so on and so on happens. What do we achieve? What do we know when we lay there at that final stage looking at life almost in a dull state, through the vanishing sight that death holds us in? Do we think about all the good, the bad, these pedagogies (from parents, family, the system, our beliefs) that constantly bombards our lives, forever impacting us with the notions or values of how things should be? Aaron's death took a while for me to accept and even to this day it's one of those experiences that left an eternal scar.

As we go through life, we hope for some tangible rewards; love, laughter, joy, happiness, success and all the things that make life meaningful; and we dread the painful consequences; failing, war, death, social injustice, abandonment and all the things that could make living hell on earth. We are constantly reminded of nagging reality that we must all stare death in the face one day. The lucky ones in that last hour may ponder on their achievements, the life lessons passed down from parents to children, sometimes for many generations.

His death had me questioning many things I could not understand at the time. My life was already slipping from my own grip and now a shocking death of my cousin, strangely, I thought, if ever there was a God and I could stand before him at this moment, I might as well be taken to hell! I was angry, displeased and many other feelings that only times and God knew about. Many wrongs, many rights, faith, hope, resurrection, believes, religions, war, greed, hatred, humanity, humanity, where was I? I had no clue where I fit in to all those things!

The only source of comfort I could find at the time was writing this book. I poured all of my life experiences, my pain, sorrow, and everything in between into this book. For the brief yet important moment of your presence in my life, I dedicate this book to you my dearest cousin Aaron. I dedicate this book to you for the questions I have been asking myself. Questions that eventually became part of this book. Aaron's life, along with my life, became my inspiration for the life of Isaac Kline. I hope we are all searching for balance, chasing some defining moment that will become a true meaning of our existence by the time we reach the unknown time of our final destination.

I have grown, times had changed but I am not the same. Reality and experienced had made me who I am. I will smile, I will get angry, I will write, I will cry, I will talk and I will love... at the appropriate times. But I know every moment of life counts and those we've lost through tragic means, whether war, sickness or any other misfortune of life, we must live for them, smile for them and go one and do positive things to better the world so that the things we know had crippled the humanity for the worst can begin to reduce.

May his (Aaron's) soul rest in peace.

Introduction

When he left the concentration camp near Treblinka to preach on the most violent short of the Zong, Reverend Isaac Kline's countenance was that of a man far removed from his little boy's dream. Due to the sudden upheaval of World War II, the world he thought he knew was altered by so much anguishes and death that his heart filled with remorse left him pondering endlessly about his existence. He was a Nazi soldier before he escaped to Africa, where he joined a group of missionaries called the councilmen. A German raise by a Jews family, he always thought he was a Jew until World War II. But these revelations were the tips of the iceberg. Suffering the sudden loss of his wife to one of the most vile malady on the shore of the west African plain, preaching the gospel to the Zong, or whoever he considered loss was the beginning of a new adventure he had hoped would save him from his past. But the Zong are not so welcoming to any other religion, but their own. The God of Isaac Kline would have to be real to him first, and then show Himself miraculously to the Zong. He was entering the unknown.

BOOK

ONE

The Unknown

Part I

Interlude

The Letter from Sir, Isaac Kline to his son, Isaac Kline studying biomedicine at the university of Munich:

Greeting dear son,

Please do not over-alarm yourself with worries due to the urgency and timing of this letter. It must be considered a relief for the approaching doom hanging over our people. As you are aware by now I hope, all Jews must wear the Star of David. This letter is your escape and we are urging you to open the envelope immediately. You are not a Jew, but a German. Your mother was a German maid in our house. We loved her dearly, and upon your birth, she was overtaken by her infirmities to a point of no return. She died. By then also, your mother and I have been barren, so we took the initiative and adopted you. Furthermore, there was no living relative from your biological mother to claim you. Your mother had a tragic past, which the urgency of this letter does not permit a full detail.

I am in distress son, knowing that this letter is coming to you in shock and will cause you unimaginable pains. But know that we love you and you are our only son in the spirit and in the flesh. We want you to live, go on and be a good man. Multiply and bear us grandchildren even in our absence, that is, we do not know what the war may lead us in the end. Our love for you is something even the yeast-filled grave will allow us to keep.

Son, the next segment of this letter is included for your mother's sake. She was fervent and insisted that I do so. But as we have talked, you know my belief, which I will refrain from infusing further detail in this what I call our eulogy. But as your mother insisted dear son, do not abandon your belief and your God because of this mischief. The God we have shown you is real even if he does not come to rescue us in such a perilous time. It is only our flesh son, but our soul will be with Him. In my field, as a philosopher, I have come to learn that the world does not promise much for the natural man. When you are young, the world seems to be yours. When you are old the world slips slowly from your fragile grip, time runs out. In between, all you find is inconsistencies, fear, failure, disenchantments and uncertainties. However, fortunately it is not always the case, and you can sometimes find joy, love, a purpose and the will to live if you follow your heart and trust in God.

Put your mind to rest dear son and listen to the cry through this note. If you heed, we will unite with you someday in heaven. There was no other way to deliver to you this information. Furthermore, the war is not your fault or ours. Circumstances filled with greed by our current leaders led to this. May you forgive us for keeping so much from you this long, but we urge you to let the God of Israel be your God, and that you find peace as you endeavor.

Momentarily as I, your father Kline writes this to you, we are in the ghetto, and there might not be much time left for me. Today, the old people were rounded up and they never came back. I am just on the edge of that. The next round, I might be considered old. Your mother was taken with the group today. This is the reason I am writing this letter. With her presence it would have been impossible to write you including all I have said now. Oh well. She considered you her son and will die believing in that. Farewell my child and live long; my blessing, your father Isaac Kline.

The Precedents

Munich, Germany 1938. The young and promising Isaac Kline is recruited for an important science research. He is excited. Standing at the train station, a cold winter day, the flat terrain of snow, where the train tracks lay, he awaits impatiently fumbling with his ticket.

Europe and Africa border, five years later, the midpoint of World War II, Isaac Kline is fleeing the country in disguise with some luggage and his wife, Nora. They embark on an unknown cargo ship and head for North Africa. He is last spotted on a desert camel, as a regular tourist heading deeper into the southern hemisphere of Africa.

His life began as a grand and promising journey. Isaac Kline was studying biomedicine at the university of Munich when the letter from his father reached him. By then he was neither a Reverend, nor a man who frequently visited the synagogue, even though he was adopted and raised in a Jewish household. His choice to join the research team in 1938 was a voluntary action in response to the opportunity presented to him. Even though he realized later on, that this opportunity was a deception luring him to become a member of a research team to create deadly poison for the Nazis that was later used on his people, but at the time it was presented, he would have been a fool to reject it.

"You are a part of a greater future, men who destiny is to alter the future for the better," the man who recruited him said to the group of youth standing that late Wednesday afternoon, innocently listening to his empowering rhetoric. This man from whom these words came did not present himself as a threat or a Nazi recruiter yet, he was kind, tall, blonde and with blue eyes. Because the idea of the research was fascinating the Reverend did not investigate further. After all, it was about biomedicine. He would make his father proud, and Nora, who was his newly wedded bride, would thank her God even more for a husband like him.

Three months later, when he returned home to see his wife, the revolution had already begun. Hitler had invaded Portland. In the midst of this unsettling time the letter, along with his original birth certificate arrived from his father. A week later another letter arrived. This time it came from the lab where he had been conducting the research. The lab was dismantled and the research was discontinued.

Kline was suddenly aware that the people who raised him and sent him to school were about to suffer genocide and his educated hand would play some part in it. Furthermore, as the news progressed, the rumor was affirmed.   Some aspects of this research contributed to creating deadly chemicals for the Nazis. Appalled and motivated to see an end to it, he took a job as a soldier, and worked in a few extermination camps hoping to help some Jews escape. This idea, he realized in the end was his worst mistake. Working in these camps he had to obey his superiors and this meant the blood of the innocent must first stain his hand and conscience. Afterward he suffered remorse and self-loathing agony, knowing that the education he gained at the expense of his parents, had helped advance the genocide against them. In the end, Isaac Kline was unsuccessful in saving any life in the extermination camps and on the contrary, he took some. His bitterness increased thereafter and his soul became restless, remorseful and he needed some way for venting and purging.

Chapter One

The Unknown

*E*nduring the reality of the holocaust, Kline was a man hedged in the middle of phenomena he could not control. His fortitude as a normal man was always dissipating and thinning out the morality of his soul, which he must pull out from the great torment of the Nazis (who, he had learned from the birth certificate were, by race, his people), demand for dominance and their strife against humanity. Now, as a Reverend, believing in God was supposed to yield a result in this life, and a crown in the life to come; but being taken at disadvantage to thrive between the foes of his time, wrapped in conflicts of the broiling war between nations, and the mass extinction of his people, the Jew, his life was beginning to unveil what lay at the base of what would be his righteous soul. He had existed on the verge of events unique and distinct from his natural expectations.

Biblically, it is assumed that the eye of the righteous man was most often delicate, hopeful, and free of malice; but being the man he was, none of these attributes were expressed in his face or demeanor. Many choices had led to many regrets and he was a changed man. He was of average weight and size, a five-foot man with hair sprinkled with white and black. It became completely gray by the time his struggle reached its climax, and his pointy large nose and antenna-like ears, oval face; sharp cheekbone and V-chin were his features carrying the scars of his search for redemption. It would be an injustice though to assume that Reverend Isaac Kline was a victim of the holocaust. However, a holocaust lived in him. From all he had seen, heard and done, Isaac Kline perception of reality was sadly altered. His innocence was erased and replaced with images of blood, death, darkness and the unknown. Furthermore, the confusion that arose from his family origin, his ambivalence about being a Jew slammed him against the political unrest of his time—the World War. But who cared to investigate—he looked like a Jew, raised by Jews, he was almost shipped with the Jews if it was not for the document along with a letter, which came from his adopted Jewish parents, giving him the right to claim his status and live as an Arian in a time where many other races were threatened. It would have posed him some difficulties though, if he stayed near Munich because many people there knew him to be a Jew. So he moved further south along with his wife Nora and they established a new identity. There, educated as a doctor before the war, a young promising man during the war, when his innocent heart witnessed these atrocities, he spent many cold and dark nights along with those faithful to the cause of humanity trying to kill the Fuehrer.

After their failed coups and his attempt to save the Jews had failed, he escaped from Germany and by 1946, still in his late twenties, a doctor, he joined the Christian missionaries called "The Councilmen," to wander the world and by passive or spiritual means purge it of its evil, the devil.

Every councilman was required to recite a specific oath before his initiation into the group. The oath stated that a councilman was to preach the good news to the violent world, which, had not yet heard the gospel with every god given energy, strength, might, and even sacrificing their lives if necessary. Reverend Kline excelled at being a preacher, using his medical skills and pondering the most basic questions men have asked since the beginning of time—where am I from? Where am I going? Who created me? Why am I suffering? Why are people evil? Who can quench this agony within? —Whatever we believe, we sometimes find ourselves in this inescapable mire. However, though these questions shook him, but they were part of his nature. There was no telling between him as an individual and the manner through which these thoughts channeled his behaviors. Yet still, he sought after finding meaning to them in maudlin ways as bits and pieces of woes, grief, sorrows, joys, hopes—maybe, the tendency that carried him through? —Don't judge the man! He was no different. The search to quench our darkest voices within can lead us to places—some of which can raise these questions within, some of which can lead to shackles of endless wonderment, some of which can open a way to a new forms interpretations and redemption—some of which can set us high on a pedestal and give us satisfaction. The challenges of life do not always dwell with age, and reality does not discriminate. Nevertheless, time will either render a man hopeless or bind him to something he must believe in and divert his natural eyes from all other matters. Call that religion or sentimentalism, fear or greed, power or politics, hatred or love. Whatever a man cleaves to in his last days as a source of hope, let there be no attempt to separate him from it. It is dangerous for one who tries to convince him otherwise even if the potential of that source of hope proves to have deadly consequences for the beholding individual. An upheaval is born in this prospect. Genocide is created in this light—and who can see into the burrows of the hearts of man and find that which makes him tick, believe, better yet, throw caution to the wind? Let there be no claim, but the heart of man is a mystery and perhaps the darkest place to ever look.

We are on the verge of discovering what lies at the heart of Reverend Isaac Kline. During his days in school, the girl, Nora, gave him her undivided attention, and he married her. Their affection, though filled with love, it was brief and devoid of a lasting enjoyment. In the midst of wandering the world, Nora had to see an early grave. A few weeks later, when the wind of solitude blew, that was when he realized his once hopeful life was shattered and solace was a long way from home. After all he had seen in the war, this was the first time he felt betrayed by his belief—or God. It was surreal. Nora was gone and he was hungry standing in her kitchen with her cooking tools lying about.

On the first anniversary of Nora's death the Reverend sat before his dinner table with a morsel of bread and a cup of coffee. He brightened the lamp a little to better discern his scripture. Outside was dark and noisy from the rain that had not ceased to fall for hours. He should have gone to church for the evening devotion, but detained in the house by the rain he decided to meditate alone. The Reverend suddenly began to shiver violently, like a drowning man in cold icy deep water suffering in the grip of hypothermia. He lifted his eyes lacerated by sorrow and turned to the darkness outside. Lightning blazed through the heavens. Surely now he was alone!

His memory of that gruesome day, when he watched Nora pass away crawled before his eyes. He remembered that day at the little clinic, painted white with dusty porch and zinc roof standing at the entrance of the town, surrounded by a panorama of palm trees. Even the warm wind waving the branches that light sunny afternoon was not comforting. Oh how he prayed to God and called on every scripture necessary to evoke His mercy so that Nora might live. Yet she passed away and there was no remedy in sight from God.

Like the day Nora died this day, too, which he sat to meditate alone showed no difference. Her whispered voice that long ago afternoon seemed like the thunders tonight, brightening the heavens blatantly with lightning glaring across the sky. To him what Nora said, "God giveth, God taketh away…to be absent from the body is to be present with God…" made brief flashes of lightning through his heart. Though her soft voice to his ears was tender, his nerves jerked. The soul of the man he was, these last dying words from his beloved wife, which where intended for comfort was inadequate to steer his soul to believe. He felt that those words were sermons for him who had his spirit and faith intact. He, the Reverend, was just a fragile man wrestling with his existence.

"God giveth, God taketh," these were words he had shut from his World-War ridden brain. Countless times it had been so, "God giveth and God taketh." When will it stop? From the letter and birth certificate sent by his father, which took away the only identity he knew since birth, to the murder of his parents, to the many innocent he watched die by either his hand or the other, God giveth and God taketh? It was an injustice and a sudden calamity that at this point in his life no biblical proclamation was enough to alleviate the sorrow within. Nora was all he had after the escape from Hitler's war. She was the soul that gave him strength. Her love was what kept him intact from everything else alarmingly altering his world. She was the representation of God's goodness and love. She was his guardian angel in the flesh—his romance, the back bone to lain on when troubles, which he seemed to find little answer to struck. And here again, God giveth and God taketh—how damaging!

The Reverend turned his eyes toward heaven. Gazing toward the dark sky from the wind, and flashes of lightning followed his every word. He prayed the same prayer on the day he witnessed Nora's passing.

> "O God let it be your will
> That it shall be well with her soul.
> I know I shall see her again—keep her well.
> My eyes are set on you, now, if indeed you listen,
> Spare me this yoke; spare me this sorrow,
> Spare me this grief; spare me this shadow of solitude;
> My heart is not ripe enough
> To stumble upon the cadaver of my rib
> But O, God, let it be your will.
> As you giveth, so you taketh."

That evening of her death, the Reverend walked back into the room and found her lifeless. From afar, he felt the silence in the room. He paused in a distance and noticed that everyone in the room saw his shocked gaze. It was like a nightmare—Nora was dead. In astonishment, he knelt before her bed and grabbed her lifeless hand and slowly lifted it as if there was hope to rekindle her spirit—or as if his prayer to God had saved her. He pulled her pale hands to his cheek and began to sob softly, like he was talking to her. Nora's eyes were as if she were asleep, peaceful and calmed.

With her dark hair well folded under her head, she was facing up, and wrapped in some woolen napkins to keep the foul smell away. Ebola has taken her away from him.

The Reverend stood upright with his hands to his waist looking up to the ceiling disappointedly, as if he saw something staring back at him. He brought his head down slowly and looked at his fellow councilmen. He walked away, quickly passing everyone.

The town of Bentuh was the place the missionaries or councilmen, had chosen as the Home base. Sitting on the western plain of Africa, Bentuh was opened to the vast ocean and it was conducive enough that the councilmen made it their home. They assumed it was a portal to endless possibilities for the world they perceived warranted redemption.

Nora's death in Bentuh robbed the Reverend of his last smile the atrocity of the war forgot to grab. He felt he had nothing left to live for yet, the questions to understand what his life had been until now kept him restless. Somehow he felt that the answers to these questions would bring him freedom and comfort—and perhaps define the cores of the choices he had made that had led him to his current status as a Reverend. In retrospect, there had been some volatile occurrences in his life that made these questions even more pressing. Mainly, his recollection of that cold winter day of February 1938, when he was recruited for that obscure science experiment, which he later on realized, contributed to the research that helped to create the deadly poisons for the Nazis.

As he rode on that train to the lab that February, it felt like a torture. However, at that time, being motivated by knowledge, he was going to see it through. This reality now, looking back, was grave and propelled his search for understanding beyond just finding mere freedom and comfort from his past and sorrows. It was a war within. A subtle yet, unconsciously internalized anguish to understand the heart of men and the differences between the man with the gun and the man the gun is pointed at—the difference from the man who dreams of atrocities against humanity by devising deadly weapons that made even he, the inventor, vulnerable to his own devices and the timid man that allowed all to happen—and conclusively, bringing the question down to his level, he wanted to know the difference between the man who stood in the name of humanity and confronted the Fuehrer and put his life on the line and the man who did nothing to stop it. Unlike the Reverend, none of these characteristics of men were ever present in his personality even now. He was the guilty witness and the coward, who watched helplessly as his bothers and sisters were tortured and killed. Furthermore, he could not speak freely for even his washed hand still carried the many bloods he spilled at the pulling of the trigger and the hauling of gassed bodies from the gas chamber. He was no different in many ways, though peculiar, but with unique characteristics he was yet to understand.

What he was now was a human maze, an entity that only existed because of time. The past, present and the future all intertwined within him and made these urges, this search for answers or understanding even more demanding and beyond his human comprehension.

Now overwhelmed with all that he had to endure to achieve these answers, he realized that he must first escape the torment of the constant reminder of the grim hand of death that had snatched his wife away. Furthermore, sadly enough, in his present state of mind he knew not how to achieve any of what his thirsty heart longed for to bring him that freedom and comfort he so desperately needed, nor did he have the slightest clue of the depth of the reality he must sort through to understand the hearts of men. But even so, knowing fully well that forfeiting now these pending unexplained chaotic hunger for understanding would have been a rewarding act and perhaps a clean slate to live again, the Reverend refused to abandon his sorrow-filled past. He even hoped that his status as a councilman was the portal and the beginning to the longing quest of his boiling heart that reached a calamitous point since Nora died.

Before Nora's death, the Reverend spent some times enjoying their union. They traveled the shores of the world's continents and they finally came to Bentuh, as his duty as a councilman demanded. The Reverend and other Councilmen found the people of Bentuh to be peaceful and repented quickly of the idol gods. They received the Good News and the Christ readily. However, unknown to the councilmen, there was a greater danger lurking the shores of Bentuh. Men of strange strengths came from beyond the great sea and were worshiped by the natives in Bentuh. These men were called the Zong. Inspiring awe, they had great might and were regarded as gods by the natives. Until the white man came with his power from the fast, painful and quick-kill device the gun, the Zong were the most powerful force the people of Bentuh ever saw. Armed with different forms of arsenals, masks and tones of terror, the Zong were brutal by nature. Every December the Zong came in great steel armors and deadly weapons and invaded the shores of Bentuh. They seized brothers and sisters and took them away in their larger and bigger canoes as slaves. With that looming fear, however, the people of Bentuh concealed these menacing occurrences from the White men and embraced the new conviction, which, somehow, in a strange way, kept their land safe for almost half a decade. Furthermore, the story of the cross was pious and hopeful. And since the land had such a vulnerable foundation, easily susceptible to the invasive and violent Zong, the White men were a source of great peace. Not only did the white men gave them hope, peace and protection, but they also gave them imaginations; something more graceful and humane. Instead of worshiping the god who took their sons and daughters violently every December, they had Jesus, the God, who gave his life for them. This was heartwarming and persuasive. Some, however, kept their idols hidden for fear of enraging the gods who came from below the sea. No one knew or questioned why the Zong had not invaded the shores for such a long time to claim their slaves, but the people of Bentuh were glad to have lived in peace.

When the white men took over, many years elapsed and the Zong refused to resurface from the sea. Some thought the God of the white men had shielded their lives from the might of the Zong; but other natives thought otherwise. The Zong were inevitably coming and would take their slaves according to the years they had missed. And for the protection of the entire land many leaders met in secret and settled it amongst themselves as to who shall take their children or any offensive individual to the shores when the gods from the sea emerge. Nonetheless, many years later, when the gods refused to surface, the people of Bentuh believed even more that the white man's God had shut away all other gods. Many threw away their idols and became great servants of the Almighty. Some joined the native defenders army and God was good until the arrival of a wounded Zong, Basin, which led the councilmen to discover the island of Meheyassahapunawa—the land of the Zong!

Chapter Two

The Ore

*U*ntil now, oblivious to the councilmen, there were lives beating beyond the horizon of the blue and violent ocean. As missionaries, the councilmen have never ventured so deeply into the blue sky that sunk yonder beyond the horizon that merged with the mesmerizing view of the blue ocean. In the past they had tried. The trip became deadly and the bashing oceanic waves and roaring thunders called for a swift return. The blue and beautiful sky had darkened suddenly, as would be a cloudy storm and covered the sun. Lashing rain almost put the fragile woolen ship asunder. Their quest to purge the world of its evil turned into a survival plight. The storm quickly deterred the men from navigating the sea and they returned to Bentuh. At other times the journey on this same ocean, when it was calmed and welcoming, took them swiftly to other lands already redeemed and vibrant with the Good News. After many deadly failed attempts the councilmen concluded that this was the end of the journey and perhaps the world and that there was no more land yonder virgin to the gospel.

Basin's arrival changed their concepts. Though it brought joy to the missionaries, but for the people of Bentuh, fear was renewed. Their gods, the Zong, would emerge from the ocean again, and they panicked over Basin's arrival. On the contrary, Basin was immensely glad to have arrived in one piece from the foaming jaw of the violent ocean; and that he was on shore and free from being the sacrificial lamb for his people. He appeared on shore with broken arm and pleaded for help from the missionaries. Although it took him untold months to travel across the ocean to the white men, it was a miracle. His escape was later known as a Divine Intervention for he came hundreds of miles away from his motherland that had sought to feed him to their snake gods.

When the men parading the shore brought Basin to town with his dead arm swinging about his shoulder filled with mucus and reeking bile, he finally revealed the most profound fear and the secret of the Zong. The secret; the White man—men of strange complexion and ideals would come again to Meheyassahapunawa—the land of the Zong, that dark island beyond the violent and foaming ocean. Basin also told the councilmen about his people and the island and about their violence and vicious protesting against all other beliefs and religions. Imagining the pain and torture he had endured from the hands of his people, Basin's eyes watered with tears and his heart quivered lightly as he showed his dead arm and cried out as evidence of what happens to his dark world, which he believed was isolated from the truth. The Zong had held on to the belief, until now, that the island of Meheyassahapunawa was invisible. The cry of N'Daygmong, the head god centuries ago, shut foreigners away from their shores forever.

Basin needed his arm amputated and buried, for it was useless to let it hang about his shoulder in such an appalling fashion, emitting foul smell and attracting juice-sucking flies. This was a health hazard if the infectious bile reached Basin's heart. They needed him alive to tell more about the people of Meheyassahapunawa. The fact that Basin had lived this long with such a wound still puzzled the missionaries and they called it a miracle. However, as the missionaries searched for ways to ease Basin of his painfully marred arm, there was no surgeon in town to attend to the arm.

The butcher, John Townsend, lived nearby. He was a heavy man with a head that resembled a tiger's head. He had large smile and big teeth. He was an Englishman that had prospered from butchering pigs and cows and hanging the viands in his unclean gibbet to supply the ever persistent missionaries and Englishmen mining gold and other valuable minerals in the area. Rev George Muller, the messenger for the councilmen, was sent to consult the butcher quickly and to devise a way of releasing Basin from his decomposing arm. Basin's life was a torch to the missionaries who had desired him to take them to the land of the Zong. The Zong needed preaching—they needed to hear the Good News. The missionaries had ways of accomplishing this task with enough Bibles to sink a ship.

The butcher stood with a big root in his mouth, eyes stretched out and tongue lashing out profanities at a native for his delinquency. The native had kept the slaughtered animals' blood in the wheelbarrow for many days now; the thick gel-like liquid sat in the slaughter room that had its walls tattooed with bloodstain. The putrid smell of blood that attracted fat flies overwhelmed the butcher so that he spat even more than usual. Standing with his apron soaked in animal fluid and manures, the butcher spat yellow slimes to the ground and chewed his root some more. With his stern and throaty voice, he instilled fear in the native by raising his big arm, almost clobbering the native's head. As the native took the blood out trembling with fear, the butcher turned to Rev Muller. "I have fresh swine hanging in my gibbet, sir, if that is what you need."

"That's very kind of you to refer that sir, but I'm afraid I'm here for a more gravely needed matter."

"Have I killed a native's pig without his consent?" The Butcher took the whetstone and began to sharpen his axe.

"No sir, but we need your help. We, the missionaries, have some work you must do in the name of the Lord."

The butcher paused from sharpening the blade and chew some more on his root. The yellowish liquid from the root had drenched his hairy beard and mustache with crust and stain that the area about his mouth appeared to be growing foreign forms of circular yellowish hair. His lips were as yellow as a bee and his pale complexion even added certain ridiculousness to his face as he chewed and spoke. He spat some more and raised his eyebrows as a question.

"Well, don't be frightened. I am sure, as a butcher, you have experience with what I am about to ask of you. I know you have done it to pork several times, but not to a human." The Reverend paused, rolled his eyes as if to realize the strangeness in his request but then he dismissed the thought and continued. "Anyhow, as you are aware, there is no surgeon at the present moment and we need your tools that you may never use on your pork again, and lend us your hand." The Reverend paused a bit to see the butcher's reaction. The butcher was calm.

"How so," he asked, resuming the sharpening of the blade against the whetstone. The sound was loud and coarse.

"See, I don't want to waste your time. But, there is a man that needs amputation." The Reverend finally breathed as if to have been relieved.

The butcher stopped and squinted with surprise but with somewhat satisfaction. In the past he was known for treating the natives with cruelty. Since the new rule posed by the general prohibited him from such brutality, this was a renewed chance. Furthermore, because the missionaries were new in the land, they were not aware that some natives walked around with scars from the butcher's anger.

"It's going to be the Lord's work...you will be contributing your part of work towards the kingdom," Reverend Muller inferred.

The butcher grimly laughed and cleaned his axe with a rag. "I must say, coming to me is a bit blown out of proportion wouldn't you agree?"

"He is a native that has suffered vicious attacks from his brethren, and has come to the church for help."

"I suppose so…who do you expect to run the shop while I'm gone to slice off arms—angels from heavens?" The butcher was insolent and stern but placed the question with a tease. "I have irresponsible workers who are not able to waste the blood from the slaughter room for weeks." He paused, "How long will I be gone?"

A few hours later the butcher arrived to amputate Basin. His axe was sharp and cleaned with certain oil from the soil that made it glimmer with terror. Basin, perplexed and confused partly from the herb given to him for sedation and partly from the menacing manner the butcher handled the axe, laid his rotten arm on a wooden stool. A few natives held on to him so that some vital organs would not gravitate towards the swinging axe. The butcher swung his axe with pleasure and the dead arm fell to the earth. Those closer to it suddenly jumped away so that they were not in contact with it. All eyes looked upon the arms repulsively for it fell and wetted the ground with bodily fluid and released some foul odor. A pious native completely enamored with his new faith shouted "Halleluiah," and took the reeking arm away. He wrapped it in a piece of sackcloth that hung from the attic.

The butcher had chopped the arm with such a force that the bone cracked in Basin's arm. The men used a saw and chipped out the cracked pieces. Little blood leaked from the opened wound but Basin came close to death. He breathed deep, wailing and searching for comfort and at one point he fainted. But the missionary once more passionate with the message of the Great Commission loved on Basin. Their attentions revived him.

The house, in which Basin lay after they administered some remedies to his wound, was the house of the leader of the Councilmen, Reverend Elton Goodspeid. Inspired by the wisdom of the Great Commission, the councilman was a devout man of great valor. He had gained respect in this part of the world where he and his men have settled and preached the Gospel to the inhabitants. Reverend Goodspeid was shocked to know that an unexplored island virgin to the Gospel still existed. A few months later when Basin was well, Reverend Goodspeid sent a message to the commanding officer, the general of the English army dwelling in Bentuh, requesting immediate dispatch to the new land.

The general was not present when the messenger, Reverend George Muller arrived. Sitting behind his desk writing a paper was the assistant who gave the messenger a reluctant response. "Not many ships are available at the moment. Moreover, the general is not present. I am just an assistant." He lay back in his chair and stared with the bottom of the fountain pen under his chin. He gathered his thoughts and lean forward. "This cause, which you ask, should be approved by the general himself. I am sorry we must wait for the end of the year when the general returns."

The assistant general was more of a soldier than a believer. He worked for the queen. He was also responsible for the lives of the missionaries, which he took seriously. The absence of the general was beyond his control. Furthermore, he thought the idea to approach the Zong with the Gospel, when their guns and ammunitions were insufficient, was a poor call. The matter was not pressing enough to risk his men. Although the request was made for the advancement of the Gospel, however, the assistant realized, venturing into an uncharted world unarmed might lead to unpredictable outcomes for which he was not ready to claim the responsibility. He declined the request.

Basin's arrival had revived the grim reality for the natives. They were preparing themselves for the coming days when their gods, the Zong, would come from below the ocean. Some had gone back on the little mountain outside of the town and lit fire for sacrifice and began chanting strangely with powdered faces. The assistant general had begun receiving complaints of disorganized activities from the natives, where debtors were being pulled out to the shores for punishments.

"Tell Sir Goodspeid that I am greatly sorry," said the assistant general. "But we must deal with matters on hand here now. These people are as savage as the, huh, how do you call them?"

"The Zong," Reverend Muller assisted.

"Hum, huh, the Zong? Anyhow, let us try first to tame the savages here at the moment while we wait." The assistant general returned to his writing. He rolled his eyes into the air searching for words as if the Reverend's presence had interfered with his ability to compose. He brightened his lantern and crouched over the note pad.

The Reverend narrowed his eyelids and stared in disbelief. Without a word he left the room. The councilman walked away discouraged, yet determined. When he arrived a discussion among the leaders led the men to conclude that their expedition must commence soon.

At the shore there were two wooden ships that lay there since 1700s. The first White men who set foot on this land came in these vessels and the ships had been there ever since. Though unused, they were well preserved with canons and old-fashioned weapons. The missionaries had the luxury, in the past, to travel with the English armies in more modern vessels. However, since faced with such urgency, the councilmen reverted to their old ways. Men were sent to inspect the ships. When they returned, words were given out that the ships were reliable. Carpenters and stone carvers were sent to work on the ships about three weeks later. Their two wooden ships, armed with canons and some old fashioned guns, were ready to sail from the harbor to the violent ocean in the coming months.

Chapter Three

Hitler's Victims

Nora was dead two years now. Her bones were now decaying to dust and sand and the tides of sorrow were receding from Reverend Isaac Kline's mind. His last six months were spent in isolation, finding nothing to do. One of his old friends, Reverend John of Cantony, a South African native, and his family often visited him. The visits were well, but time did little to alleviate his spell as a widower.

He carried the guilt that Nora's death was his fault even though it was her idea to travel the world. When they escaped the war in Europe, she was more of a believer than he was. Being raised by Jews, he knew mostly the rituals of the synagogue. Nora's strong faith converted him truly and he believed in her God. As his heart turned inside out, her Christ became his Christ, the cross became his burden, and the urgency of the Great Commission was the message, which led him to take on the status as a Councilman wholeheartedly.

Yet when she died, though it had not reduced his belief in her God, somehow he felt her survival should have come from his lips. And that if he had prayed hard enough and early enough, when the first blemish of the malady began to plough her fragile body before rendering her weak and dehydrated, his prayers should have saved her. However, he had been busy catering to her instead of supplicating to God for a miracle. So, for this reason, he felt that his prayers had not traveled fast or quick enough, and when his prayer, which he envisioned as a white slowly leaking smoke peering through the celestial bodies, it was too late. The malady had run its course. Nora was dead.

Being in the trench of his contemplation he remembered a verse, which came to him as a silent whisper—"for I will never leave you nor forsake you."

"Why, then lord? Why did Nora have to die?" He said out loud staring about his surroundings as if to have directed the question at a living being. His eyes stern in in his head, lips trembling he pushed the bible aside and sat in silence. Then he breathed, "What should I do then, Lord? For I need your saving hand." The Reverend battled himself a bit and could not satisfy the quest within. When he heard of the trip to the land of the Zong, a strange sense of relief beheld him immediately.

"This was the reason she left," he said to himself. "She is watching me from heaven! It is true now. To be absent from the body is to be present with God. Nora left so she could watch me from above. For, the land of the Zong, as I have learned, is a vicious place. My Nora was too fragile to take the trip with me. God took her so she would not suffer. Lord, you want me to suffer for my sins and to grow more in you. I accept the challenge."

Little did the Reverend realize these simple utterances would define the man he was to become. These simple words uttered out of emotion dipped in a fountain of anguish would be a long stretch of testing that he would endure until time itself was to expire. But he sat calmly affirming that these words were truly from his settled mind and not from his World War II ridden mind, that had been altered by experience and unexpected grieves. The plain was now laid out before him. The horizons of indispensable experiences (pain, joy, laughter, and whatever the mind could fathom) now awaited the Reverend to take that leap and dive into what was yet to be explored. It was he versus his voice—or whatever was lurking at his heart to speak of such a challenge. It was his call for duty; his call to understand the nature of his existence, for which he hoped these preceding experiences held the key.

At the next meeting the men discussed who would lead the volunteering soldiers, who mostly consisted of the converted. These converts had now become a part of a larger cause and were believed to have surrendered their idols. Many of these men felt they needed, for once, to take the adventure in the name of their new God. Perhaps, they felt, they would see the land of the Zong—the people who for centuries had sailed the ocean and taken their people as slaves. About five hundred men filled with zeal and determination signed up for the adventure. Now as the men gathered up their gears, they needed a few councilmen to accept the challenge and lead them as the overall voice of the Good News. Among the councilmen at least two had to agree voluntarily for the two ships. However, in reality, none refused yet, none agreed either. It was a daunting task to take on for the news from Basin about the existence of his people made the land of the Zong a place to consider seriously. Basin's detailed description of his homeland was as if it was a different planet or a land forgotten by time, space, creation and morality. It was a place occupied by strange and monstrous beasts, savage animals, venomous reptiles and crawling things that seemed unrealistic to the councilmen. Basin's narration about their nature was the most repulsive that caused curiosity and fear. Even more, the natures of the oceans surrounding the island as described by Basin were alive and behaved at will.

Sitting in the conference rooms now, for many, the true meaning of being a councilman was yet to be tested to the fullest and beyond what they had done until now. Silence ran through the crowd as Reverend Goodspeid posed the question asking for a volunteer councilman. It was obvious to Reverend Kline that this was why he was present at the meeting. He was calm and rose from his seat as the sacrificial lamb. "'For their sake I lay down my life,'" he said, raising his pointy finger. "I am the one to bear the cross of leadership, possibly death, but I choose to lead the people."

They murmured a bit among themselves. Then Rev. Goodspeid questioned the Reverend's motive to be sure.

Reverend Kline was stern in his response, "What have I got to live for but Christ? Amongst you there are married men and loved ones who shall miss their family if the mission turns into a calamity. At least for me, not that I wish to draw pity upon myself, but I am a man who already has all his needs in heaven. This land as we have seen from the people here and Basin, their own native, is a violent place unexplored and mysterious. I am the right candidate for this mission. With my experience as a military doctor, I am fit to lead the people." The Reverend smiled a little as if he heard something amusing. He looked around the room, "Just promise one thing," he said with a smirk, "unless I should die, do not let the people perish. Send more men after us when the general returns. That is, if we fail and have not returned in about a year. Or, if the rapture takes place—which we all await." The Reverend then pointed his finger at the men one by one. "My earthly ghost will hunt you if you fail to do so and we perish. While you eat or drink your fine wine at night, remember that and you will not get fat. Keep your current status and weight, send more men or I will strangle you with your own meal before your glimmering lanterns."

There were a few giggles, but most were quiet and receptive. Reverend Kline's mind was made up. He would take the call.

"Well, then," said Reverend Goodspeid, who had failed to dissuade the Reverend from taking the trip. "Who is the next man, as brave as our faithful friend? Who will lead the second ship?" He concluded searching over the crowd of councilmen.

A few more murmurs, men starring at each other hoping that one of them donate his life now and save the day and relieve the pressure. Rev. John Buchanan rose from his seat. He was new to the land. A young Englishman, he was in his late twenties. He had a young wife and a child and had already made his mark by setting up a fine choir for the church in Bentuh. At times, he went into remote areas and came back with more souls for Christ. Also, his young wife's voice was something everyone loved and enjoyed. After her melodious singing in Sunday morning services, many walked out with pious smiles confidently holding their heads up high with their Bibles under their arms, and eyes filled with spirituality. She was a sweet girl with many beautiful qualities that made her young husband proud. Reverend John Buchanan thought this trip would be an experience of a lifetime. He was not missing out.

"Sir, should you discuss this issue with your wife first?" One of the councilmen who saw the need for the question spoke from his seat.

Rev Buchanan smiled. "It is the work we all are here for. Even her. For me, 'to live is Christ, to die is gain.' My wife and I are in one accord. I appreciate your concern. But don't worry. She is young and beautiful and I am sure one of the fine bachelors here can always make her sing again—that is, if I am gone and have not returned. Of course, and that she had waited at least two centuries." They laughed and applauded. Later they prayed, sang some hymns and were dismissed.

When departure was near, Reverend Kline made a last visit to his dear Nora's grave. Before her grave he talked about the possibility she might be seeing him sooner than he had expected for, his pending voyage to the land of the Zong was dangerous. He might fall ill to some malady, get attacked by some venomous reptile and end his life, or the roaring, massive and violent ocean might swallow him up. His conversation at the grave seemed like a death wish. It was not directed toward heaven and that was a good thing but all he had said was within the boundary of a death wish. As tears streamed from his eyes and his voice trembled, there was certain calmness in his demeanor as he now interpreted the misfortunes that might befall him on this journey. Before him was the white carved stone, inscribed with the name and details of his dear departed wife:

"Here lies Nora Allen Kline
1917-1948
The Beloved wife of
Sir, Dr. Councilman
Rev. Isaac Kline.
'May her soul rest in peace.'
To be absent from the body
Is to be present with God."

The Reverend laid a bouquet of flowers at the grave, kissed it and sat in his wagon loaded with his luggage for the trip. He drove to shore where men were already embarking the ship. It was a crowded site, as converted natives took this opportunity to see the land, which their ancestors had worshiped. For some it was a new experience. The white man had given them the privilege to see the people their ancestors once called gods. For some, with the guns in hands, the Zong must pay for their centuries of violence against their people. For some, still, it was a mystery. None of these reasons a man could fathom appealed to them, but the thrill of such a mysterious journey was mixed with some looming fear.

Basin was in the corner silent, cold and confused as to why he was being sent back to the land he knew was filled with intolerance.

There were men working to load the ship, women and children saying farewell to their loved ones, and on the other side, the main focus of attention was the display of Rev Buchanan's choir led by his wife. With a tone that could calm the merciless ocean and rhythms that could heal a native from his melting intestine due to some unknown illness, they sang with courage and made the men work harder to prepare the ships for departure. The ships were ready by the late hour and the men embarked.

The journey started as a fantasy ride. The mouth of the ocean was peaceful and spilled out little rolls of streaming waves. Then, as the ship melted beyond the horizon, leaving the shore of Bentuh, as the wavers on shore reduced to tiny spectacles of non-sessile entities eventually disappearing into the distant sky, the ocean was awakened from its slumber and rushed against the wooden ship. The clouds darkened at noon and spread their shadows over the billows of the ocean. A gushing wind interrupted their excitement and began to rock the ships. The salty current looked angry and hit hard against the ships and hurled some gallons of waters on board.

Everyone panicked. Lightning struck through the distant sky and sent flashing bolts across the clouds. The beautiful ocean turned to black and disturbed water. For miles the ocean lay empty of land while waves with depths of a valley formed and approached the ships nearly sucking them under in the swirling currents.

Basin cried out and ran to the center of his ship. His feelings were ambivalent. The violent waves clashing against the wooden vessels were expected, but the trauma he had experienced before arriving on the shores of Bentuh was renewed. He was ill equipped to withstand any torture from his people and their gods again. In Basin's eyes, the fists of the gods of the Zong were within the rushing waves and would soon turn the ships into pieces of woods, sinking them below the aggressive and shallow depth of the ocean. Even though this was just in Basin's imagination, the natives on board also remembered their history of how their ancestors once worshiped the mighty Zong before the coming of the white man. And, as they saw darkness when the sun was apparently at the midpoint of the day, some must have lost their faith in the God of the white man and wanted to cry out to the god of the Zong for mercy.

The turbulence from below and now lashing on board, gave them the impression that the gods of the Zong had unleashed their fury upon the intruders. Even the councilmen on board must have held on to their faiths with the grip of their fingernails; and even so, it must have been some supernatural occurrence for the burrows of the ocean where the ship steered through called for natural fear in a natural man.

It was such a long time since they settled in Bentuh. Since then, there had been no challenge as such, where they would venture out to the shores of a foreign lands of strange men to preach the Good News. This trip was to once again revive the meaning of the existence of the group—the councilman. However, at the time this decision was made, Reverend Goodspeid and his fellow leaders underestimated the fragility of the ship and the group. The comfort, free spirit and open arms they got from the people of Bentuh must have blinded them to the reality of the delicate nature of the group. Many of the true councilmen who conquered many violent lands and people had passed on and this was a fairly new and inexperienced group of councilmen. Now that they were on their way to meet the Zong, these realities for the men on board began to dominate their minds. The main concerns were the ships were without proper balance and enough soldiers. The troubles of the journey were too soon and it was too late to turn back. With every rocking of their ships, the sweet moments of their lives flashed before their eyes. Imaginations of what could have been, or what should have been, diminished their urge from joy to regret. Was this how it was supposed to end? Some must have questioned in their minds. However, to voice out any regret was not the nature of a Councilman.

A part of The Council Creed detailed that when they took the oath to council "the world in need of a savior," they had already given up the privilege of a marked grave. And if the end awaited them in the midst of this ocean, it must come in that fashion.

Men on board began to wonder. It was as if the gods of the Zong were sending a message through the storms. Or, perhaps, this trip may have been over-rushed and unapproved by God. Maybe prayer for discernment was not concrete enough and God took His hand away and hid His face from their journey, leaving them to their own devices. Even worse, still, maybe the Zong, through their years of violence, had run out of God's mercy and had inherited hell without hearing the Good News of the cross. If this was the case, then, this trip was irrelevant and doomed. And the waves of the sea were not from the hands of the gods of the Zong rather, from God Himself. Being angry that His sons had disobeyed Him, He decided they must now suffer the consequences. All men on board must then give up and prepare to give themselves in for a slaughter by the foaming ocean. Their bodies would float or sink for the nourishment of the beasts of the ocean, as their ships decay below the dark depth of the ocean.

In all this, Reverend Kline sang in a thundering tone, believing their demise would be a righteous death. He went below the deck alone while the falling utensils from high up on the shelves were missing his head. As he sang, men above struggled to sustain themselves from the lashing waves of water spilling on board. The most curious natives on board could not help but realize, in some odd and cold manner, that they were caught in between the dilemmas of religion. For, the earth was made, and the history of men only lay in bones of those before them.

It was a mutual feeling among the men. A death warrant was ultimately signed when they embarked on this journey. Even Basin, being the man showing the way, trembled to encounter his people once more. By then, he was well. A hardened cyst had grown in the spot where the dead arm was removed. However, the thought of the Zong stirred up his stomach like the violent ocean, and he vomited involuntarily. He tried to use his one hand to catch the gushing puke, but the cream and chunks of food slipped through and dashed to the wooden deck. His unsettling countenance proved to those around him that the Zong were not just common men but savage men with extreme thirst for blood.

The uneasiness, as the ships steered through the ocean to the sea from wide-open bodies of water to the narrowed fjords, and to other forms of watery tributaries of narrowed dark steep pits; and again to the open ocean, made the men's skin crawl. Some parts of the sea seemed so strange that some men began to voluntarily lock in the clips of their bayonets to their old fashioned rifles.

A portion of the ocean looked terrifying, with strange creatures whining and flying all around some wooden materials in a form of a sunken ship, which lay protruding out of the ocean. These protruding wooden objects were so massive and identical to ships that some natives continued to believe in their hearts that the God of the white man had lured them to their early deaths. Others gave in to the realization that their ancestors did worship a real god of the land. Some even repented of their conversions to the White man's Jesus. However, all this was done secretly and in vain for, they were on their way to meet the Zong.

As the ships steered through more secret places, as if going through natural black holes—the sounds of the ocean against the ships, the darker heavens looming above the roaring thunders— death was the last cruel persuasion of the White man to the converts on board. Reverend Kline suddenly surfaced from below to renew the hope of his men. His ship was ahead of Rev Buchanan's who, after perhaps conquering his fear, burst into a song. "It Is Well with My Soul," hoping to relieve his men from the potential calamities ahead.

When peace like river attendeth my way,
When sorrow like sea bellow rolls;
Whatever my lot,

Thou hast thought me to say,
It is well with my soul..."

It is well,
It is well,
With my soul,
With my soul,
It is well; it is well with my soul...

My sin O the bliss of this glorious thought
My sins, not in part but the whole
Is nailed to the cross
And I bear it no more

Praise the Lord!
Praise the Lord!
O my soul.

It is well; it is well, with my soul..."

Basin was within the ship ahead. Overwhelmed with such fear, as Mother Nature puts on her best displays yet with the forces of the waters, and the heavens, the only element a man could not hold on to in the time of need. After Basin heard the strenuous voices of men behind him singing to the heavens below the stormy cloud, he suddenly believed they were drowning already. However, for the men on board with him, the song gave them a sense of relief. With the lashing water against their faces and bodies from the downpour of the nonstop rain, they shouted above nature's calamities:
"It is well,
It is well with my soul!"
Basin, being utterly confused, afraid and overtaken by all he had experienced and would experience again when he met his people, suddenly vanished from their sight. It was not well with his soul, for he knew his people! This song, which now echoed from every mouth wet from the climbing waves and rain on this rocking ship, was for those who had fully experienced the mercy of this God they called Jehovah—Christ— whatever His name was. Yes, the white man was good enough to relieve him of his

dead arm. They fed him and treated him like one of their own. However this, alas, traveling to the land of the Zong for the purpose of the Great Commission was not his idea. He wished he had stayed back in Bentuh until at least, death from a natural cause found him. But no, they convinced him and promised him protection and the liberation of his people from evil.

"What people?" Basin had asked with clenched teeth as he contemplated alone at the dark side of the rocking ship, face drenched with tears and salty water. Were they those—the white man called his people? — Those people who placed his arm between two trees and bent it against its natural flexibility until it snapped and hung loose in the socket? Those were not his people! They were monsters! "Damn you, white man, and your God. I was born with mischief around my neck. Yalashimba—shame on me to be deceived by the white man's provocative yet deceptive language. I am out!"

At first, like a possessed man, he paced to and fro the ship secretly; throwing overboard whatever his one arm could find and lift. By the end of the hour Basin had almost emptied the ship of the stocked goods and valuables the men needed to survive the ocean and the Zong. There he stood at the verge of the ship, staring at the dark horizon intensely letting out shallow airs of exhaustion and watching the ocean waves climb and rise in erratic rhythms. He chanted like a mad man.

When Basin felt contented, he found a rope at the back of the ship and a load heavy enough to sink him. With his one arm, he managed to tie the rope to his neck and onto the load lying beside him. Fighting for almost an hour, he sent the load from the ship and into the beating ocean. Basin had a second thought to save his neck as the rope slowly followed the load. But his one arm was not fast or strong enough to save him. He tried to resist by holding onto something. His neck strained in agony and the rope choked him even harder as he tried to cry for help. The voices of men trying to keep the ship afloat by evoking the power of God, singing and praising, "it is well with my soul," were too loud to hear his wailing, and enough to suppress his screams and Mother Nature's roars.

The load's weight, being heavy for Basin's neck and body, shut out the circulation to his head. Basin was dizzy and the diminished blood circulation shut out his sight. He was pulled away from the deck. Soon, his hand released whatever he had clung to and his neck followed, snapping violently and slamming him against the ship's banister and jerking him down into the raging ocean.

When Basin fully comprehended the reality of his demise, he was overboard descending beneath the fast moving object. Perhaps he regretted as he went down. He had tried to save himself. Yet, it was too late. How could he have seen when his neck was snapped first before his body encountered the salty water and whatever else lurking below? As his legs quivered above the raging waters, the Zong with one arm was gone. The foaming jaw of the ocean had swallowed his deformed body.

The men had worked for hours singing and fighting the storm with prayers and whatever else they saw fit to keep the ship afloat. The deck was drenched with water and the men trembled from days of fighting with the turbulent ocean. When Reverend Kline came up upon the deck, they searched for Basin and eventually realized what had happened to the man who was supposed to lead them. With the missing loads, they put the pieces together to determine the fate of the man. They were on their own.

"Sir, we have lost the, huh, Zong," the native convert, left in charge, approached the Reverend as he emerged from the ship. "We found out that he sank with the sack of ammunition we stashed in the back. The explosives are all gone, sir. We have no means of defense with the heavy artilleries."

"Good Lord," Reverend Kline sighed softly passing the man and staring over the calmer portion of the ocean. The man turned back and slowly opened his mouth, walking towards the Reverend. They all aligned themselves at the front of the ship, staring in astonishment at the distance shore. Slowly, bright fiery lights began lacerating the clouds peering through the heavens and plundering into the ocean. It was fireballs from catapults of armed men standing at the shore of Meheyassahapunawa. The air was hot and filled with black and dense smoke and war cries from the Zong standing on their shores.

This was the land of the Zong! There it was, that sandy beautiful shore, shrouded in clouds of smoke and loaded with warriors on horses and by foot, with weapons ranging from machetes, axes, bows and arrows, spears and other deadly steels. After years of parading the oceans and seas searching for lost souls, this sight was the most terrifying yet to the men now on board the ships, bearing the title of missionaries or councilmen. Never before had they encountered such a sight where a flood of men clustered in unison ready to pour down balls of fire upon them. After all, they were just a group of missionaries on board of peaceful ships. But to the Zong, they must be scorched to ashes by the reign of fire from the catapults. Stunned by such multitude of well shielded men in body armors, steel plates, headgears made out of iron, stones, horns and brass, the missionaries stood for a while silent and appall. Some of the men on shore wore masks so terrifying that a convert on board yelled loudly out of fear and nearly fell into the ocean. Their appearances and technologies caused great dismay for the ships over the horizon. For some converts the dream was now a reality. Stories of the gods from below the sea were now evident before them. Those headgears and armors described by their fathers and mothers at the fireplace were on the men on the shore intensely letting out fireballs through the air.

The Zong had seen the ships from afar and prepared the attack. With their teeth grinding beneath their armors and big arms swinging with blades and maces, the land of the Zong was more than expected. The missionaries were surely aware of the alarming messages echoing through the strange and violent noises that illuminated the sky caused by the swinging catapults.

The open sea lay ahead and the bright afternoon light cast its shadow upon the scene. The sky and shore remained in smoke. The blue water floated ahead, meeting the white sandy shore. Palm trees in dense forests, windy, cool and inviting. Yet, through these wondrous spectacles of nature, came the lashing sounds of fireballs and bows and arrows fiercely against the wind, awakening the beasts that slept there. Birds of the sea and land and other animals dwelling within these natures ran terrifyingly in all directions roaring and complaining of the disturbance in their own fashion.

The ships were on the verge of falling in range of the tumbling fireballs and Reverend Kline immediately called his men to halt the ship. Panic arose on board the ships as they managed to stop before coming near enough for the coming fire to consume them. The speed, due to turbulent waters made the ships speed faster and the men worked even harder and stopped it. The war cries and terrifying sounds from the Zong struck great fear for all on board of the ship that even the trees vibrated. It was as if even the sea was aware of the pending disaster that was about to begin, that its waves almost responded with below of rolls and vibrations beneath the ships. By then, the natives were convinced that the Zong were truly gods; for such powers, almost supernatural, were demonstrated in their stances and fearless war cries. The ship was halted in a distance that the catapults could not reach. The men could somehow see and feel the unwelcoming stances from the Zong.

A convert on board almost out of breath for fear for his life cried out. "Load the cannons!" He ran to a few more men, who already stood stunned and then he shook them with two arms for assistance.

"Load the cannons, Gentlemen," Reverend Kline added to the already shrieking man.

All men ran about the ship, in chaos preparing for what they believed was the worst yet. Reverend Kline soon met Rev. Buchanan and they devised a way that the second ship remained far behind, as a last resort for escape. Though they had been through treacherous waters in the last months, the shore now was a challenge they began to devise a way to conquer. They realized that a sudden decision must be made for nothing appeared certain, not even the night. The shoreline was already loaded with thousands of mini-canoes since the range of the catapults still kept the ships intact. If the morning found them peaceful over this sea, it would be a miracle. As the sunset over the sea even more deadly weapons began to surface unto the shoreline and many soldiers on board shrank in their uniforms, overtaken by fear. The rifles appeared useless in their arms. Their eyes widened in their heads and veins of defeat struck the linings of their faces.

Basin's suicide enhanced the danger facing them now when he sank with the shells for the heavy artilleries. The rattling cries from the shore penetrated their nerves with fear like a sharp, pointy needle, and those who still believed in the white man's God suddenly dropped openly to their knees, with rifles hanging about their necks, and they called out to the smoke-ridden heavens for a miracle.

Even Reverend Kline froze helplessly and paced about the deck like a lost boy searching for his mother. It was World-War II anew. The man he was in the Nazi camps beat at his heart asking for resurrection. There were many bitter days in those camps that he had squandered to oblivion. Yet, now, like a putrid, sour vomit, they climbed up to his throat like raging termites demanding revelation.

His hands trembled and a sudden rush of regret kept his pushed out eyes red and his mind indecisive. There were many atrocities in the dark and oily mud of the extermination camp. Many times he was asked to use his gun on a Jew. Every now and then he was called to shoot. And then he shot. One Jew. Then he shot. Ten Jews. Then he shot. Fifty Jews. Then he shot...He lost the count. He was called again the other day to shoot the dying old man whose skin cleaved to his bone from starvation. The starving old man's eyes, almost unmovable in his head, looked up at him as the gun spat out the hot bullet. The old man was sessile when the gun smoke reduced to thin air. It was not a painful death though, for the old man's tortured body demanded death before it was given to it.

All these murders were blood on his hands. All these unforeseen atrocities; all these screams and cries; the wailings from agony and burning flesh in the crematory; these were all a diversion from his initial plan, which was to become a soldier and help many Jews, his people escape the camp. In retrospect, it was completely the wrong choice, for being a soldier; he could not achieve enough status to preserve any Jew's life. The Reverend was embedded deep in his thought when a convert interrupted, demanding answer. "What should we do, now, sir?"

The Reverend regained his composure from his voyage to the past. He was still indecisive as he looked on the shore and saw the Zong preparing for the night. "We wait," He said unconsciously, moving among the men who were now loading the canons in haste. "We wait! No one fires a single round until I command you," Men with rifles took their positions. "Do not fire yet. I give command here!" Reverend Kline continued to call to his men, "There must be a way to do this. We can get along without a fight. That is our first goal. Remember now you are all Christians. You are here to save lives, not take them. Keep that with you at all time. You are councilmen, before you are soldiers. We don't shoot. We wait. Just stay alert for me." The Reverend spoke louder and sighed beneath his breath as though he was praying or finding a way to resolve the situation at hand. He talked and ran about like a mad man.

The sun went down and the night came. The men were still in position waiting. On shore the zeal from the Zong increased. They made large fires and chanted all night until the next morning. After several hours of instilling fear into the men on the ships, and standing their ground, the vicious throwing of fireballs ceased. No one, the missionaries or the Zong, had made an attempt to land or cross the sea to the ships.

Three days later the two sides still held their positions. No contact. The signal from the shore, which began on the first day with raining fireballs, was still the same. Though the throwing of fireballs had stopped, it was still unsafe to send any delegate for peaceful talk.

Chapter Four

Galaxies of Mystery

*T*he universe is a strange place. With billions of galaxies and debris in space, this mesmerizing commotion of rubbles, some moving as fast as the speed of light, our beautiful blue planet hangs in the midst. We are yet to discover its uniqueness in its entirety. With modern inventions we have acquainted ourselves with some of our planet's behaviors. However, we are still astonished by certain aspects of it, especially the ocean.

Being a vast place, the ocean has continued to intrigue our imaginations within the existence of our world. Humans have to overcome it or, it will continue to turn them into material for consumption—as it did on the shores of Bentuh, which was a legend known to all sailing the ocean.

"Be wary to travel that which you cannot hold with your hands, for it is violent and merciless. You will be engulfed without warning."

The belly of the ocean was filled with the sons of Bentuh, and it continued to be so for modern men as well. Vanishing on the ocean in this part of the world was a common occurrence. Many had wondered where the missing had gone. Had they disappeared into a new world or vanished from the face of our planet? Had they gone onto another world only capable of being seen by the third eye, which, unfortunately man may never acquire? But a Zong will cry out, "Death is the third eye! And only the gods see beyond this dark boundary. Let no man venture and test his ability to look where the eyes were not meant to. He will be a changed man, regretfully!"

However, retracting from the Zong claim and pulling words out of Reverend Kline's mouth, perhaps, death could answer our darkest fear of the mysteries that weigh our world. But for those who believed in the resurrection, this mystery was answered by the emptied sepulcher. For others, however, it could be an unexplained matter—the big bang theory, karma, the endless list goes on. Let the imagination run wild. Searching within this depth, this abyss, where contemplation remains relative or subjective, is it sufficient to simply take away the wonders and emptiness one feels at times? Is it enough for harmony and peace to exist between men on planet earth? Can we find answers to the genetic code that prevents our emotions from flooding our judgment and inflating our greed to give credence to murder, homicide and ultimately genocide?

The common man, if he lacks understanding, searching for meaning, implores men of wisdom, faith, religious prophecy and foreseeing, brilliant scientists, skeptics, sentimentalists, mouths of platitude and those who dream to reduce the discomfort his imagination may instill when he develops the urge for contemplation to reveal the third eye someday. Further inquiries may suggest that there are billions of ways to approach the mysteries of our world. But let the simple and ignorant man step aside.

However dangerous, however mysterious, however adventurous, these mysteries have never stopped men from venturing or endeavoring blindly towards the obscurity of the implacable dark oceanic jaws. On May 9th, 1722, a ship set out from the coast of South Africa bound for Britain, to assist in taming the brawling American revolutionists in Virginia. On board this ship were missionaries, soldiers and dignitaries important to the English quest to conquer the world for the Queen.

These men were of great importance, for their works would have caused the advancement of the Queen's conquest of America. However, somewhere by night over the ocean, they vanished before their journey was completed. No one heard of them again. In fact, their disappearance is a mystery to this date. Communication being scarce then, those who remained behind failed to recognize their disappearance until it was too late to attempt a rescue. Whether Black Holes or not, whatever consumed them, they were gone and never discovered.

Such disasters were considered events that had led great men to fall through the cracks of history. For the world then, and the world now, being vastly unrelated were distinguished by knowledge and idealisms. Once many believed like a child. However, with inventions and technologies available to us now every man, every country and every beast had to search for his own god—a niche, protection. This was essential for survival. And, it being so, the Zong, in the face of the approaching ships, made a show of strength against the strange ships gliding toward the shores.

A week passed. The shores remained quiet. Shocked by the Zong defiance, the missionaries were unsure of their next plan. Surely, no one was foolish to step over the sea for a peaceful talk. Furthermore, their fate was uncertain if the Zong attacked. What they had, though deadly, may not complete their defense against a shore packed with screeching giant men. As cannons emerged on the sides of the ships the men on board were less confident that the battle was to their advantage and so they waited as Reverend Kline had ordered.

These were not so new challenges for Reverend Kline however. For, he saw war in its raw form when he served the Nazis. However, when he escaped the war and joined the Councilmen, he expected all to remain peaceful. When the people of Bentuh welcomed the missionaries and the Englishmen it was with open arms. And the soldiers ventured out to nearby forests searching for more conquests for the Queen. Thereafter, every evening they returned with pieces of stones—diamonds, to be sent back to England.

Then the councilmen preached the good news and talked about the old rugged Calvary rood that saved. This being strange to the people of Bentuh many fell to their knees without hesitation. For the gods they knew until now were men from below the sea and they came only to capture them as slaves. But a God who died for them was heartwarming. This was new and good. So they burst out like a wave of termites and received the new religion.

That was then. Now, on the sea of the Zong, this was a new chapter, a new conquest and a new conversion. But unlike the people of Bentuh, these people were resilient, strong and unwelcoming. Now glancing through the binoculars, for whatever means he could fathom to overcome the defiant Zong, the Reverend thought it must be more than just a conquest. The soldiers were obliged to follow his judgment anyhow for he was their leader. He was hoping to devise a way to make sure everything was well planned out.

"Do not shoot until I tell you!" He had continued announcing to his men at sunrise and at sunset. His echoing voice had been so for almost a week now. At times, he was below the deck searching through his bible as if a revelation would jump out at him. Sometimes he even held on to the bible more tightly trembling and sweating, but then the sun came and set. No answer. The bible still lay on his bed idled. There were other times he descended below and stood at a distance staring at the bible as if it would move in a strange fashion and reveal to him how he must lead the men. But a convert looking up to him for guidance soon interrupted him. Back and forth the Reverend struggled to solve this quest. Somehow, with his clouded judgment, he felt this was a chance for his redemption from all he had done as a soldier in the Nazi camp. He clenched his fist, pacing and reflecting upon it.

All his life he had done nothing right, to this point. In the crematory, his disguise to save lives became a mistake in the end. After he shot the old man it was the end. That night he fell into Nora's arms and wept. Then the choice was simple, yet complicated. He must find a way to leave the camp. For, he could not save the Jews by himself. In five months, countless men and women died at the squeeze of his trigger. This, he assumed, may have been a covert intension by his superior to test his loyalty to the Third Reich, since there was a certain lingering concern that he was a Jew Sympathizer.

A rumor spread that he was raised by Jews and perhaps came to help many escape. From there on his duties continued to cause him deep distress. A week later the gutter was full of rotten corpses. The first few he killed were to show his loyalty, and he hoped the commanding officer would let him roam free. The Reverend first shot three naked men and pretended that he was a true Arian instead of "Jew Sympathizer." However, two days later, he was called again to kill the son of a very old man he had come to like as the replacement of his father Kline. A week later, the wife and daughter of the same old man were pulled from the steaming gas chamber. In the end, the old man wished for death even more. His entire generation was wiped out. As his lifeless form folded under the Reverend's gun, his bitter face longing for the fast bullet. It was given to him in the head. This had been the Reverend's last act of violence against his brothers and sisters. Running home to Nora that night, he was never the same. Thereafter, he disappeared underground and surfaced as a Councilman.

Now, overlooking the horizon, these memories surfaced confusedly in his mind. He feared that he was on the verge once more, to release his hand of sorrow upon the people—the Zong and those he brought under his command. Whatever decision he made now, harm would come to one of the groups.

The Zong seemed comfortable on the shore. He was sure he desired peaceful interaction with them. However, the Reverend had no means of bringing his idea to fruition. There was this strange feeling, which crept through his veins like venom, that he had to do something drastic again as he did during the war. Before he escaped the camp, he took the son of his commanding officer to the white snowy hills, which stood outside of the walls.

The son was a mediocre soldier by the name of Fredrick. He had killed no Jews, but he had not protested against the atrocities of his father either. His father kept him safe as a bodyguard so that he would not be shipped to the violent fronts. But the Reverend, being filled with bitterness, after a few drinks with Fredrick in that cold wintery night convinced him to come up the hill and see views. The voices of men and women being tortured were heard echoing vaguely from above that white snowy mountain. There, he bashed Fredrick's head in considering that he was of no use as a soldier. He first made Fredrick listen to the sorrows echoing from below and he searched Fredrick's face to see his reaction. The Reverend looked into his eyes as the voices echoed below, but Fredrick remained the same, sometimes laughing at their cries. The Reverend turned his back as if to agree with the laughter and then he reached for a stone covered in snow. The stone landed. Fredrick fell to his face and his cracked skull leaked. The Reverend dropped to his knees and threw a few more violent blows. Every hit was a response to the suppressed voices within. Voices that should have echo through the dark air when they ordered him to kill, "No, I refuse to kill the three naked men. No, I decline to pull these corpses from the chambers. No, he has a resemblance to my father let him live. No! No! No!" Fredrick's bashed head sunk in the snow and the Reverend dropped the blood-dripping stone and stood on his feet breathing intensely looking down at Fredrick's battered head. He could feel the cold and brisk wind blowing from the tall empty trees void of life. The obscure dark night echoed terror and solitude. Down at the other end the old station wagon awaited him. Nora was in it ready to flee for the border.

This episode surfaced in the Reverend's memory and sent him into deeper trend of depression. His hands were unclean. Bleak in despair, he could yell on the deck and release his distress. But, he was not alone. And if he broke down now something worse could happen. Unlike the dark nights when he left the crematory and walked down the road into the woods, all alone to the cabin the old man he shot had told him about. In that old wooden cabin he wept for hours and played with his 45mm pistol, several times, pointing the gun to his head contemplating suicide. Then the beautiful face of Nora would appear in an odd fashion and he would strike the pistol into the holster and run home to her. Had the Lord forgiven him then? Have the Jews forgiven him too? Who shall be the victim here? And what role would he play to cause their demise?

Scream Isaac, scream, for even the heavens know you are violent! Wherever you are, your presence shall follow destruction for the people, you worker of iniquity! You later found out that your final result in that research assignment helped to create poison for the war and the gas chamber. Your brilliant mind was fed upon, and your simple input to the mixture of elements created deadly chemicals. When you sat in that lab and you were told that your selection in the research was neutral, you were helping to create that which was used against your people. That ticket you received, as a bonus to join young college students to further your study, you should have torn it and gone the other way.

You quit later, but it was to no avail for, the assailants had already descended upon your people. They said Hitler died with poison streaming in his veins. Fredrick died over the mountains and his blood was absorbed into the snow. You partook in the murders of those poor, innocent Jews gassed and shot. Your father you deserted long ago, the letter he wrote to you about your mother taken from him unexpectedly. Now here you stand again, ready to cause destruction either for the Zong or the men you have on board. Your innocent Nora had already paid the price in your place. Shame on you!

"Lord, have mercy!" The Reverend screamed and all on board stared astonishingly. He was deep into his thoughts and had forgotten his surroundings. "There must be a peaceful way to manage this," he suddenly burst out and bolted for the stairs leading below the deck. "I need some time to pray," He said to his now attentive audience before disappearing below.

The lurid sun set in for bed and casted its colorful shadows beyond the horizon. Birds were coming home to the shore, singing perhaps from the wondrous experiences of chasing flies and bugs. The vines of the distant trees wavered to the oceanic wind. But the beautiful shore was cluttered with Zong. Once again they must go for another day without confronting the Zong.

For the Reverend this was a premonition he approached with distress as he held on to his Bible once more, and crouched to his knees below the deck. A great sense of burden, as if his life was now dwindling into a spiral trench to the coming morning sun, which would find his unaccomplished, un-repented, sin-ridden body lying at the deck with vultures hovering above. The Reverend remembered the night Jesus was crucified. Perhaps this was how it felt as his Lord prayed to the heavens in supplication, hoping that God would relieve him of the cup. But, in the end, He faithfully laid His life down and his prayer concluded that "If it is the Lord's will."

Now Reverend Kline trembled greatly for the coming morning. For some unknown reason, he knew his prayer was the same as Jesus, "I want this cup!" As he had said to Reverend Goodspeid, he will be the sacrificial lamb if the Zong refused to interact peacefully, though without a concrete plan, his spirit was proving him right and that he would surely be the sacrificial lamb one way or the other. The hour appeared to be at hand. Furthermore, the thoughts, which surfaced now were powerful and had to be resolved. Hopelessly, he felt he could not live in such agony of indecisiveness any longer. The Reverend heard his men walking about laughing and playing some games; some discussing the brute nature of the Zong.

"They are only savage men ignorant of the sweet ragged cross, which will calm the raging agony within." Some said. "Huh, huh, after their evil had reached into your soul at night during your slumber—no they must rip your arms from your shoulders like they did to Basin—they will feed him to their snake god—so you boys aren't afraid of those strange cloth wearing men, huh?"

The Reverend laid back slowly from exhaustion and tense nerves. He retired for the night. The morning will be long.

Chapter Five

Souls Of Steel

When the sun peered through the morning clouds and cast its soothing light over the sea, the ships echoed with men cleaning their wounds, and bodies lying over the decks. They had to face the Zong in battle before the morning sun beamed on the deck of the ship. After the dark hours and calmness returned to the sea, the Zong attacked in waves. Being so accustomed to quiet nights, still waiting for the leader, Reverend Kline to give the command, no man on board expected the Zong to climb on board drenched with anger and saltwater.

On the deck, converts and councilmen made warm teas and drank calmly without knowing that their night was on the verge of being altered. The laughing voices, playful and whimsical, were to end with some brethren lying on the deck lifeless with spears and arrows protruding from their bodies. Before the guards looked over the waters, the Zong were already close to the ship with terrifying voices that reached the dark heavens, echoing the most riveting war cries ever heard. A guard facing the main shore opened his mouth to cry for formation but a twelve-foot spear made out of wood thrown by a giant hand, caught him in his neck and shut him up. The wood stuck to the ship and threw the man violently to his back. Soon, men on the shore of Meheyassahapunawa plunged into warfare.

"Attack is upon us! We are being attacked!" A convert on board babbled   his scream, with a face full of fear and determination. "We are being over run by the savages! Every man, get up in the name of our Lord! Let us stand this night in defense for our lives!"

All the men got up and assumed their positions. Canons began to sound and roar at the sides of the ships, followed by unceasing gunfire. Automatic rifles began to turn over the boats, but the Zong were determined and came in waves. As they did, the fight intensified. Bayonets were plunged. Axes were thrown, and many more deadly tools fell on skins. Men cried and screamed from pain. The men in Rev Buchanan's ship watched helplessly and tried to come to assist, but even so, it was too late. The men on board of Reverend Kline's ship overcame the Zong. It was almost a slaughter except for the fifteen converts who fell victim to the attack. By the morning, bodies soaked in blood and saltwater, speared corpses, decapitated carcasses, and some wounded men moaning from their wounds, all lay about the ship.

The Reverend was asleep below the deck when the Zong attacked. By the time he managed to get into the fight, his men were gaining the upper hand. Within ten minutes the fight was over. A sound of trumpets from shore, which sent a rippling wave across the sea and shook the ships and men on board, called all Zong to pull out. The Reverend managed to lay four Zong to the deck with his short hand pistol. The remaining Zong jumped back into the sea and swam away, catching up to their canoes, sailing as fast as possible, while shots rang behind them.

"We should pursue them, they are retreating!" A convert spoke out at the men leaning from the ship with their rifles smoking with rounds at the escaping Zong.

"That will be foolish. You don't know how many people lie awaiting your innocent soul!" Reverend Kline yelled at the convert and let go a round from his pistol. "Stand your ground and keep on firing!"

The men continued firing from the ship until the rounds were incapable of reaching the escaping Zong. When all were receding, the Reverend inspected his wounded men and grieved. Those left unscathed were even more petrified; for the wounds on their brethren made all feel hopeless. The wounds from the blades and machetes, men in agony from arrows struck through their bodies, knives that gashed and left deep open wounds, arms almost falling from hacking by axes, faces bruised from violent slaps by some unknown tools, were overwhelming. Moreover, they lay about making great noises of pain as they tended to their wounds.

By the early morning light, some had already fallen victim to the wounds and their cadavers lay on the deck awfully bleeding out blood and saltwater. Those that remained were already swollen around the wounds. It seemed that the tools used by the Zong had certain poisons that rot the skin in an odd fashion; leaving thick green mucus within the sores. A man who almost had his eyes pulled out lay by with a swollen face. His friend who came to his rescue used his bayonet and plunged it within the ribcage of the giant Zong, who was using his thumbs to gash out the other friend's eyes. His friend, who came with the bayonet and plunged it in the Zong's rib cage was first standing at a distance and had landed four shots into the Zong. But being the giant he was the Zong did not even bulge from the four bullets or the pain. He continued to push his fingers into the man's eyes. And the friend with the gun shooting at the Zong soon realized that if he did nothing his friend's eyes would be removed from his head with violence. So he came with speed, screaming almost as would a crying man, mouth foaming with rage, and he jabbed the bayonet twice before the Zong vomited with blood and lay out on the deck. His friend was now in agony and he used hot water to press on the wounded eyes.

Even the morning sun caused pain for some reason. Its usual beauty, which they enjoyed when they watched the Zong from afar, now irritated them and they moaned in pain. With such pain and the past tedious night, they had to clean the ship and dump the bodies into the sea. Certainly, even their dead brothers were also thrown overboard along with the Zong for fear that corpses rotting on board would bring diseases. They first made prayers for their departed brothers and committed their souls into the hand of the Lord. One by one with sadness and tear-filled eyes they swung them into the sea. Some wept for the rest of the day.

The pile of dead Zong lay slowly leaking with mixed blood and salty water. These corpses would have had a different treatment but Reverend Kline, seeing this as an opportunity to show the Zong that they came in peace demanded that they receive the same consideration as the dear departed brethren.

"Something must be done!" A convert, who was also a councilmen suffering from hypothermia, spoke from his shivering blanket.

"I agree," another spoke looking over the horizon and watching the sandy shore. "These men are the devil himself. They need to be sent back to hell with a fiery mouth of our cannons, and rain of bullets. They are vicious with vile behaviors!"

"Patience, my brothers," Rev. Kline spoke with concern. He narrowed his eyes and looked on shore toward the Zong. "I know something must be done. These men were especially cruel, but they are humans. We shall see how long they shall entertain their wickedness towards us."

"Yes, excuse me sir, but we have waited for almost two weeks now and their violence has not ceased. How long must we wait? Must we all die? We must return with enough ammunition to toast the beach. What is it that keeps us here to die?" The native convert, also a councilman, spoke sternly while looking down at the wounded. The bloody eye native moaned as they pressed his wound with hot water.

The Reverend looked through the binocular towards the shore and noticed the number of Zong arriving was increasing. The shore seemed to be their new home. They made big fires chanting and singing as they cared for their wounded. This time, the shore was more different than they had seen. The Zong changed their formations and more giant-like men in shielded iron armors appeared in view. Their voices and cries were fiercer and defused the confidence of the soldiers on board the ships even more. The war dance created such a menace that a wounded convert yelled out and begged to be taken back to Bentuh.

The arriving night promised no peace as the Zong looked more determined than ever. Women came from the inner-land bringing hearty meals and offering their bodies for pleasure on the banks of the roaring sea in plain sight.

With such casualties and smell of blood on the deck, the missionaries needed access to the shore to look for some cures for their wounded and maintain sanitation for the ship. Looking towards the soft morning light, through this agony, Reverend Kline decided to lecture his men and encourage them on their duties. Like a preacher evoking the devil out of his men, his voice rang out thundering, but was flat to the ears on board. "Men before us have come, in the name of the Lord, but have killed many innocent people instead. If there were earlier conquerors to these shores, I believe they where filled with gluttony and did unimaginable evils in the name of their leaders, kings and queens, but, most appallingly, in the name of Christ. This may be the reason these natives are violent toward us. We must refuse to be like men, written about in the pages of history, with such labels. Sooner or later there has to be some peaceful exchange. We will wait on that time."

The Reverend glared curiously to see his men's reactions. Those working on dead corpses, those cleaning blood, those wounded and lying on the deck and those saved from the attack were all attentive. They were all silent and gave him their undivided attentions. However, most of his men made faces and stared in disbelief. After a night filled with terror and death, those words triggered confusion in the minds of his men. They expected words of hope from their leader, yet he rambled on forever continuing his incoherent and irrelevant lecture.

"We must live close to death to feel life. We will only achieve that when we introduce eternity to the lost or give ourselves to the downtrodden. I believe that time with civil interaction is the essence of change! Change to the land of Meheyassahapunawa!" The Reverend tightened his fist at his already irritated men, "Life for them all!" He walked to the steaming pot and poured a mug of hot water. All eyes followed in confusion. He turned and grimly grinned, "We will act in the name of peace."

The Reverend understood what happens when power was in the hand of the wrong man. The evidence was what he saw when he served the swastika. However, this time he felt it was a second chance to make a difference—to save lives and not to take any. In his mind however, he wished he had a clear vision from the Lord concerning his current challenge. He became emotional as though he had seen something gravely pending to destroy all humanity. And there seemed to be no remedy in sight, not even from him who the solution and the weight of the outcome rested upon. His eyes watered as he left the scene with his men standing and confused wondering what would be his next move.

Before coming to Meheyassahapunawa, a major discussion by Rev

Elton Goodspeid led many to volunteer for this mission. Though, now it was clear to all on board that this trip was premature. It had been expedited due to the persistence of Reverend Kline's demands and verbal persuasions. The Reverend was convinced that the idea of being a councilman overcame all fears, and that ships filled with tenderhearted men ready to preach the Gospel were essential to a world such as the Zong, which he perceived to be shrouded in darkness due to their sins.

"The Good News must be proclaimed!" He announced at the meeting. "As a Great Commission and a greater pleasure, one must give up his life in order to gain it!" The Reverend was persuaded that those men he was accompanying had already given up the luxurious offers of life, and that they were set on their journey to make sure that all men of every creed, race and culture were saved before the second coming of their Lord. "When the time of the rapture arrives—when all who believe are called—the Zong must crawl out of their moldy graves, into the light! And those who are alive and believe in the hope of eternity must be transformed gloriously in heaven. We are the carrier of such chance, such opportunity! Let us make haste and delay no further." At the time when he spoke these words, they were with power and conviction. Furthermore, they were so true to him that he never questioned their origins.

"We must not forget the words of our Lord. Go ye into all the worlds and preach Good News! Even to the violent ones!" This was Reverend Kline's last word at the departure ground even after the assistant general ran from his compound gulping for breath. He had warned them to wait for more sophisticated weapons that were coming from the recently ended World War II.

The Reverend was quick to rebut and discourage the assistant from interfering with the plan. The expedition did not require men in arms, but men filled with the Holy Ghost. It did not require another troop of men seeking conquest for the Queen or politicians sitting in high places from the western world, imposing their wills on people they would never see. "But, we will do the Lord's work," the Reverend incited.

"Yes!!!" The zealous crowd concurred.

"The birth of the New Jerusalem, the birth of a state of God's beloved people, is to guarantee the second coming is at hand. Let us not tarry!"

Part of the council's creed stated that the "Council of Truth" of the world in need chose to have no specified burial site. Furthermore, their bodies would be remembered as nothing more than mere vessels for the Great Commission. Whether given to fowls of the air, or laid waste by some native malady, or devoured during the process by violence, it was all for the cause to counsel the world in need of a savior—a reason for which to live and die. The flesh was weak, and needed Christ for redemption. Men before and after them were but vapor in this grand design of God, who, in His sight, a thousand years is like a day and a day is like thousands of years. So, their existence, past, present or future would be just a fragment lived to entertain the self through fleshly desires that ceased abruptly. The councilmen were nothing more than what they were; or, what they would become wherever they lay in the end. After all, God could cause even the stones to worship him. Fearfully enough the Reverend had this dark belief that his life and the lives of those on board with him were already preserved for salvation, but not the Zong. And, all who had chosen to come on this journey, had vowed to the Council Creed; and therefore, living and dying depended on the order of salvation. At all cost the Zong stood greater judgment; thus, their lives were more precious than the councilmen, who believed in the resurrection of Jesus Christ and therefore, their mansions was already glowing in the celestial clouds of heaven. In order for the Zong to have their mansion also glowing in the celestial clouds of heaven, there have to be some greater sacrifices including the spilling of blood from even those on board of the ship.

These statements, which they boldly pledged at their initiation had never been tested this deep. For many it was an engagement of passion for the Lord and a moody endeavor never considering the gravity of such undertaking until now. Especially now that they were confronted by violence and the journey back to Bentuh had no guarantee that the ocean would permit their safe return. Even worse, the Reverend was expecting them to consider this suffering as nothing of a surprise; but a cause well anticipated and one they must not fear but endure for it was stipulated in the duty. Moreover, the taste of freedom, from the rugged rood, which was on board in their hearts, was too immense for the councilmen alone. It needed sharing. And the Zong must have a taste of it regardless of their arrogance and ignorance.

Now, here they stood at the verge of the land that needed to hear the Good News. Traveling for over two months had finally brought them to their destiny, though it was becoming a harbor for disaster. Slowly they were beginning to realize that the Zong were really savages, and Basin was the sample of their deeds. Slowly they were realizing their leader had no valid plan for the mission and their sense of superiority to the Zong was dwindling. Furthermore, with the amount of men on board even more unprepared now since the battle, which left them with less ammunition and fewer men, they wished for some intervention or hope. Reverend Kline had been less of a soldier or an encourager. He was more of a man of words—platitudes to be exact, and the men now looked to Reverend John Buchanan, who seemed to isolate his ship almost ready to return to Bentuh and save the remaining flesh on board.

It was as if the first attack had fueled the Zong with more appetite for blood. The shore intensified with multitudes of giant men in formations, shaking with rage. And the Reverend had not come up with a plan on how to reach these men parading the shore day and night, with aggression vibrating under their armors. Furthermore, the Zong were not only waiting on shore but had also extended their defense at night, streaming over the water to the ship that sat idle in the middle of the sea. Even though the Zong returned to the shore with more casualties after each attack, if they continued their constant nightly invasions, the men on board would become more exhausted and yield to the might of the Zong.

The last attack was deadly. Though many survived, the next promised more casualties and there was no guarantee for the morrow. Reverend Kline had declined the order from Rev. Buchanan to attack in full speed. This, also, gave his men more reasons to dismiss his leadership and consider him unfit. His men felt he honored the lives of the Zong more than theirs; and some were planning to take over. "Either we kill him or take over." Some had whispered.

In all this, the Reverend desired the trust of his men so that he could keep his focus. Yet, the slowly erupting clamor among them so loud that even the Zong on shore tilted their heads to listen, made him realize his leadership was in shambles. Some men gathered on board of Rev. Buchanan's ship a few hours later and plotted their next moves, without consulting the Reverend who, by then, had cleaved to his Bible in supplication below the deck. Furious that his good friend's inability to plan and execute their defense would cause detrimental consequences, the young councilman, Reverend John Buchanan, ordered an attack by nightfall. They were unsure if the morning would find them alive. Furthermore, they realized that the energy spent to arrive here left them weary to sail again so soon. Something must be done now for the violent oceans and seas may engulf them or they may run out of nourishment before reaching home. Therefore the best solution after the discussion was, "Gather up all men and ammunitions. We attack by nightfall!" Reverend John Buchanan had ordered as he rose from his seat to inspect his weapon.

When the men returned to their home ship all motivated, Reverend Kline realized his power was under siege. No man regarded him as the leader afterward. They even refused to answer his questions. In their war mode they went about the ship retrieving every arm and ammunition available. Though it was a quiet talk, men loyal to Reverend Kline were quick to inform him of the decision.

First he had attempted to take a canoe, sail over to Reverend Buchanan and rebuke him for ordering the attack. Then he pondered the thought a bit more and eventually settled at the back of the ship away from his men, looking toward the dark side of the sky. A little light peered through the dense dark cloud. He then realized whatever his men would do by nightfall was justified. He was also convinced that the grace of God was blind to justice. If it were not so a man like him must receive a bolt of lightning strong enough to torch a thousand horses into particles of charcoal.

His brief moment in the extermination camp at Treblinka had been the delicate subject he had suppressed since the World War; but it energized him still. In those days he had sat in darkness and allowed his voice of justice to falter in his throat. Then later, it surfaced like a vapor of bile, which turned into bitterness and sat in the linings of his young eyes that now were growing old and dim with distress. Many times he had refused to honor this voice out of fear. Many times he had gone against his will; and instead of saying "no" he said "yes." Instead of pointing the rifle at his commander who ordered him to kill those Jews, he had pointed it at the Jews and fired. When the time came and he was drawn in his guilty conscience, he took Fredrick up over the avalanche of snow and bashed his head in.

Fredrick had been similar to Pilate in the days of Jesus. Like Pilate, Fredrick was either desensitized or ignorant to the magnitude of the event before him. Pilate happened to be in charge when Jesus was arrested. Knowing that Jesus was innocent Pilate hoped that his order that Jesus be flogged would calm the crowd. But after this act his hands were unclean. He was not innocent of what happened to Jesus thereafter. Pilate was considered by history to have partaken in the killing of Jesus.

Fredrick happened to be born in a time where the only position safe for him was that, which he had. His father was a commander and in order to keep his son from being vaporized by heavy artilleries coming in the name of the allies, it was safe to turn him into a soldier and a personal bodyguard. Even so, there was no record that Fredrick pulled the trigger on a Jew or on people protesting the atrocities.

"Have you killed a Jew lately, Fredrick?" The Reverend asked the young man that cold night as they ran up the hills veins soaked in alcohol. Fredrick laughed and steam evaporated from his mouth as he gave a reluctant response.

"Heimer, the Jews are rats and need a lot of poisons. But I don't have to do it. That's is why you are employed."

Anger ran through the young Isaac Kline that night and he clenched his fist behind Fredrick. He was convinced that he was to murder him in that cold brisk wintery night. Not only his conviction to kill Fredrick came from his lack of sense of right and wrong, but also Fredrick had called him the name imprinted on his birth certificate.

"My name is Alfred Heimer." He waved the birth certificate that afternoon, as he stood in line along with many other young men ready to be called to duty by the recruiting Nazi general. As he stood over Fredrick now, he wished he told the recruiting general his real name that afternoon. The name of his father—the man he knew and loved. He tilted his head downward "Isaac Kline is my name!" He shouted over Fredrick's bashed-in head. He then looked at the bottom of the hill where Nora was waiting his return in the car. He dropped the bloody stone by Fredrick and walked away.

Now, once again, he was faced with something he had no control over. There was a pending war and more souls would perish to hell tonight. His eyes stiffened at the thought and he slipped slowly to his usual spot below his deck. A few men discussing the plan paused as he passed. The Reverend ignored their presence and shut the door behind him. There, he wept for what he was about to do.

He thanked God for salvation and the destiny that lay before him. He then questioned God why his destiny was thwarted to this point. No answer came. Then he wept some more and stared in the mirror, marked with rust and a little fog. The figure in the mirror was not him he felt. That little boy who was well raised, well educated and sheltered in loved and care was now a thirty-five-year old man confused and dejected and at the verge to relive once more what he ultimately feared. He had come here to save lives and not to take any. Yet there were some decisions made again that he was to sit a watch helplessly.

The dreams he had come here for, unaccomplished, flashed before his eyes and he wept bitterly. To his unborn children, how he would have protected them from the evils of this world. How he had loved Nora and shielded her from assails of this world, but something menacing had crept in and took her away. That little boy, who was loved by his mother in that gray-painted house overlooking the road where, when he walked to school he could see her watching eyes guarding him from the window, was now below the deck of a wooden ship lost and alone in the midst of what he thought would be a redemptive adventure from his cruel past.

Sounds above the deck pulled him to reality. Reverend Kline, then, made the only decision he thought would set an example for the coming hours. He grabbed a rifle and a few cotton clothes and walked toward the canoes at the back of the deck. His next move shocked his crew. He was over the sea in a canoe heading to meet the Zong. He must be the sacrificial lamb, as he had said, for his people on board and avoid more Zong from plundering to hell. It was not about him or the people on board. It was about salvation for the Zong. He would go with peaceful intension. He left a note.

"No man on this ship should suffer again; nor, should the Zong pay for something any man who feels threatened will do. I am going to see to it that they stop their violence. I feel strongly about this; but, if I should perish, I perished trying to be a wedge between my past and my present.

Know that I was a good man who suffered greatly for the right cause. Let no man forget that, so that I should not be another history fallen through the funnels of time and forgotten. As of now, that I write this note, I have no one to survive me. May you all forgive me if this is a poor choice on my part. I will see you all faithful men, again, here or in heaven. Amen,"

In the canoe, he stared back and saw his men looking distastefully at him. Some called his name. Some prayed for him. The Reverend turned his head slowly for the shore.

Chapter six

Mebzongbre

*T*he sun sat in the distant sky and was now dimming for the night. The heavens were blue and white but dense with plain fogs. The ocean lay calmly and trees wavered slowly. In the canoe Reverend Kline prayed. It was a simple payer. Unlike the prayer at Nora' grave before his departure, this prayer was with a burdensome heart.

"Dear God,

Here I am, your child, lost and in oblivion. My love for you has not died even though the man that I am is empty, searching for you. I am your son and I have obeyed your words since I left the war. I am still searching for my way yet tonight, I am lost even as I head into a world that my death is even promised more than my survival. Let your will be done."

The Reverend turned his head and looked to the shore. It was packed with men in great zeal and they moved about making the noises of terror, readying to attack the Reverend. Some began aiming their arrows. The first few arrows missed and struck into the sea. The Reverend closed his eyes and continued paddling the canoe. The noise even intensified and more arrows came towards the Reverend and struck into the sea. Then a giant Zong cried out to his men and they halted. He pushed the crowd and gave a surprised look over the sea at the approaching Whiteman. For a while, he stared at the Reverend until his foot touched the sand. It was as if the giant Zong was paralyzed and was unable to strike the coming white man. As if there was power in his presence, and for a moment, they stared in disbelief, watching the white man descend from his canoe.

By now the Reverend expected a blow or a violent force against his body but none came. Then suddenly a Zong screamed from the crew impatiently and ran toward the Reverend brandishing his blade. The Reverend lifted his arms with the rifle in it, turned his back towards the coming man and shut his eyes. For a while his eyes remained shut, body stiffened, but he felt no pain. He opened one eye, then the other. His eyes caught the ship over the sea, his men on board spying through binoculars. They that were on board expected a wave of men devouring the Reverend to pieces. Yet strangely, the shore was quiet.

The Reverend looked at his feet. He took in a deep breath, "I am alive," he exhaled.

He turned around and saw the Zong, who had come at him with

sudden force. The Zong was awakening from the sand, bleeding from the mouth. Over him stood the same giant Zong, who had halted the assault earlier, breathing with a tightened fist. The blade, the fallen man had dangled, was struck to the sand.

The breathing giant turned to the Reverend and their eyes met. It was a pure stare devoid of harm and hatred. Silence ran through the entire Zong warriors staring at their leader in confusion. It was a dense shore with all kinds of men and animals but even the horses shut their mouths. Strange. Without moving his eyes from the giant, the Reverend reached into his pocket and took out a bullet and put it into the rifle. He called out to the giant, but the man stood idle for a while and then yelled out another name. Then another huge Zong came forth. The giant then lifted his heavy arms and pointed a finger towards the Reverend. The Reverend shook his head.

"No I want to talk to you! Please, please!" The Reverend's screams were to no avail.

The giant Zong walked away and left the huge Zong to face the Reverend. This huge Zong reached for the blade stuck to the sand and approached the Reverend breathing with tightened lips. Confused, the Reverend stared at the Zong who was hovering over him and mumbling a few incoherent words, strongly swallowing his saliva.

"Me, uh, Isaac—uh..." the Reverend pointed his finger to the man, "You?"

The man looked back at his staring men, thinking that the Reverend was pointing at them instead.

"Me, Isaac Kline. You?"

The man stood still confused.

"Me Reverend Isaac Kline, I want to be...your... name huh? I want to be your friend. My name is Isaac Kline."

The Zong looked back and realized the Reverend was speaking to him. Suddenly the Zong yelled, dismissed the Reverend's words and approached him with an arrogant force. The Reverend lifted his gun in a peaceful fashion. Then the bundle of the linen cloth dropped and the man stopped and picked it up. Those on board the ship spied more attentively through the binoculars.

"Get the guns and pack up the ammunitions!" They screamed.

By then the Reverend was numb, an out of body experience it was, for the giant Zong held onto the large blade in a fashion that signified to the Reverend that his life was over. By now, it seemed, he had lost the meaning of why he come to the shore. Reality had sunk in and he stared back at his ship and hoped they could come and torch the entire shore with fire. His neck stiffened sadly as faint echoes of angry voices exhaled from the ships vaguely.

The sunset over the horizon made life even sweeter. The Reverend held on tight to the rifle for a miracle and turned his head toward the Zong staring back with the most terrifying look that could have only come from a devil out of hell. He shot the rifle into the air, hoping to frighten the Zong, but it fueled him. And with a violent run and powerful screams from his fellow warriors that shook the heavens, "Mebzongbre!!!! Against the Zong— Offender!!!" The giant bit his lips and approached for the kill.

Suddenly the Reverend felt emptiness within his stomach and vomited a bit unto his tongue. It was the bitter taste of death the little puke that lay upon his tongue. His legs felt weak and clapped together. Without warning, he dropped to his knees and spread his arms apart. The Zong stopped over him with the blade to his neck. Then he turned to his men as they all stared sternly at the knelt down Reverend.

"Mebzongbre!!!" They screamed again.

The Zong struck the blade to the sand and grabbed the Reverend by the head and slammed him against the mouth of the sea and rocks. He pulled the blade from the wet sand and commanded the Reverend to his feet. He, then, challenged the Reverend to a fight. Intensely breathing, fear filled the Reverend's eyes and he yelled, searching for the attention of the giant Zong who had saved him earlier.

"No I am not a fighter but a lover! I come in love, please. I gravely prefer us as friends," The Reverend pled in shaky yet stern tones. The giant Zong stumped over and swung his blade with force. The Reverend ducked and crawled away.

"No, stop! I am not here to fight you. I want to be your friend!"

The man continued to swing his arms aggressively towards the Reverend. He, then, kicked the sand into the Reverend's face. The Reverend crouched to the ground, but he heard a heavy pounding sound against his chain followed by an intense headache and pain. He dropped to his back. The Zong rushed over and began choking him firmly. He placed his stiffened clasped arms about the Reverend's neck and he pressed harder almost to the point of asphyxiation.

The Reverend being trained in physical combat used his military skills and with a sudden reflex, he pulled a rock from the water and gave the

Zong a heavy blow to the head. It was a violent hit, a fight for life, which dazed the Zong instantly and blood leaked from the head.

Then the Reverend pulled one leg from beneath the Zong and pushed his heel into the Zong's face and cut his nose. The man got up with blood draining from his nostrils and head. Dizzily hanging his head, stumbling away, the Zong fell to his face onto a rock. His head was buried in the sand when he fell, and his arms stretched apart as he pushed his hands into the sand trying to recover his balance.

The Reverend spat blood and stared at the terrifying faces staring back at him intensely. All were appalled at the fight. Amazingly the Reverend was still to his feet and the Zong moaned to the sand from pain. A Zong in the crowd cried out, as would a boy, and removed his helmet made out of stone. His mouth was foaming as he stared at the almost lifeless giant lying on the sand. He was about to attack the Reverend again, but a shrieking sound from the leader, who had saved the Reverend earlier, made the young Zong stop and shake with rage.

The Zong lying upon the sand stood up weakly, wobbly legs, and searched for his balance. The leader screamed at him and demanded that he kill the Reverend. But wounded, the Zong was already being over-powered and was dazed from his head injuries when he collided with the stones. He walked with lightheadedness.

Then the Reverend used the bottom of the rifle and slammed it against the wounded Zong's head. He dropped and passed out, gulping for breath. The Reverend stared at the group of Zong now attentive with bafflement. They all were breathing intensely.

Impulsively, the Reverend dropped his rifle and ran to his canoe breathing and screaming for his life. Looking behind him, he realized the Zong were truly merciless. If only he knew—or get to his ship now! But it was too late. A crew of angry Zong were already chasing after him.

"Mebzongbre!!" They captured the escaping Reverend and knocked him down from his canoe and dragged him in the salty water attempting to drown him. The leader began to yell and rushed among his men slamming a few heads out of the way. There lay the Reverend hopeless into the saltwater spitting out slime and water, eyes red from the hands that pulled him from the canoe. The crowd slowly gave way to the master, who stood firmly over him. After a thorough inspection of the Reverend lying in the water eyes piteously upon him, the leader raised his head, looked at the defeated Zong lying on the sand, then at his men.

"Coward is not permitted here!" He said in his language and looked upon the Reverend again. "He came from his big boat over there and fought fair. We want a fair fight," The leader looked at his men again. "Fair fight he shall have. Tonight the fight is to the end!" He paused. "Let him go!"

For a while they stood over him, breathing heavily and holding onto their blades. The leader screamed again. They put the exhausted Reverend into his canoe and set him on his way. Before the Reverend anxiously departed, the leader grabbed his canoe and stared into his eyes angrily, and pointed his finger to himself.

"Uda." He said, and he pushed the canoe away into the sea. Eyes still fixed upon the Reverend Uda made a fist and lifted it to the air. His men zealously screamed as the canoe sailed away with the vomiting Reverend in it. They watched him until he climbed aboard his ship.

The Reverend was angry, disappointed and once more defeated. He pulled away from his men who were trying to take him for treatment. He stood on the deck for a while and watched the shore still filled with screaming Zong. Then he stormed below the deck and baffled everyone. A few minutes later Reverend John Buchanan knocked on his door.

"Yes?" He answered, sitting by his bed with back towards the door, no thought but pure frustration. This room had been a place of solace for the past months for this now defeated Reverend. It was right below the open deck of the ship covered with just nailed planks and dust. The inside was somehow dark but the beaming light from outside usually peering through the cracks gave it stripy linings of lights. The spiral stairs from above the deck descended right at the door, which revealed a small wooden bed at the inner upper left corner from the door. The foot of the bed was faced downward to the right and came in view once the door was opened. Above the head of the bed, a long tall wooden cross was hanging. The bed had a frame with pocket where the Reverend kept his little black leather-skinned pocket bible. Downward in the room a few planks were nailed to the wall for storage of bigger bibles, books, dishes and little wooden statues of Jesus and other religious figures. At the left side of these storage bins was his rusted mirror. It was not a large room but good enough to tuck him in with whatever else was lurking in his mind.

Reverend Buchanan entered and without saying a word, sat beside him quietly facing toward the half opened door. For a moment, all was silent and they stared in opposite directions. At some point the Reverend looked at the cross above his bed and then at his little leathered bible. The bible, he had taken with him when he left the ship to meet the Zong. Now it was put to its usual spot. Reverend Buchanan then took in a deep breath and asked.

"What must we do now?" Eyes still fixed away from Reverend Kline, who was purely embarrassed. "I suppose you are against the attack."

"Attack!" He responded without taking his eyes away from the wooden cross.

His friend turned to him to be sure. He stared in Reverend Kline's eyes searching for a true confirmation, but, after some duration of continuous silence, Reverend Buchanan left the room. He confirmed the pending attack to the men waiting for him to surface above the deck.

"I will be back with more men and ammunition from my ship." Reverend Buchanan climbed into his canoe and sailing away to his assigned ship.

The two ships had gathered their plans to attack for the night but such idea was a bit late. The Zong had other plans. By sundown, when the sky was colored red by the sleepy sun and the stars turned their sweet and shining eyes away from the restless sea, the Zong crept for the final attack. Well armed in armors and shields, they were like torrents against the ship. They covered the entire body of water from all sides of the first ship. The number was so vast that the first man who saw the approaching army stood in shock with an opened mouth.

The sea was covered with large canoes of men in armor, covered with dark mud, and carrying an abundant number of deadly and sharp tools for their flesh. They approached the sleeping ships fearlessly. The councilman saw them from the beam of his lantern and the light of the moon against their shining armor over the sea. He dropped his lamp and ran below the deck trembling and sweating but without saying a word to anyone. They were like wild sharks swimming toward them. The other guard saw the fearful escape of his man, who had dropped the lamp, and he abandoned his little harp playing and stood up firmly. Eyes stiffened, he screamed.

"The Zong are coming!!! Defend yourself!!!" Those in slumber arose suddenly, some in underwear holding on to their rifles. All men assumed their positions. It was as if this was the final test, determined, they began to load for defense.

However, these groups of Zong were unlike the previous attackers. True warriors they were called, and were mostly men not less than six feet.

Their arms were as large as the thighs of some soldiers on board the ship.

"Zee!!! Haa!!!!" They screamed in terrifying unison. Their waves were so vast that the entire sea was flooded with their canoes to a point that men on the canons were confused of the main target. With every fire from rifles and canons the noise from the Zong became louder and louder. It was like a fuel. The Reverend heard the name of Uda made in heavy unison. The pattern was repeated with another names.

"Uda balaheawah!! Uda, the master of death! Gomsug balaheawah!!! Lemong balaheawah!!! Nufonmog balaheawah!!! The names continued according to the troops and leaders bringing the attack against the ship. There were countless names and countless screams fiercely proclaiming the names. Some of the names within the screams were familiar with the converts on board. They recognized them as legends told by bonfires about the scary days of terror, when the Zong sailed the sea searching for slaves. But now it was a reality and it shivered them to the core.

No man should have been in the presence of such forces, for death itself at times, had pity on its victims and made less violent noises when it came for them. But the shrieking cries, from all corners of the sea, made the existence of defense for the men on board somewhat useless. It was sudden. It was immense. It was with force that was perhaps more than the atomic bomb.

The name Gomsug was the most recognized. It was said that he was the walking terror who was the arms and legs breaker, who ate from skulls, and that pity for men was washed from his eyes by his upbringing. It was said that he was filled with unknown anguishes, which made his eyes red in the day and silver-like at night. The legend of Gomsug was as ancient as the existence of the Zong's terrors on other shores. When his name was mentioned, those who were familiar with the legend fought bitterly, unwilling to let such screams or name climb on board and terrorize their lives as he, Gomsug, and his crew did in the past to their forefathers.

Suddenly a giant in armor appeared to two converts. His eyes were as bright as the moon. Underneath the mask he uttered sounds, like hungry snakes over their prey. His mouth stretched to the fullest, he yelled with thunder. By then it was late. He had a wooden mace dressed with heavy gears and plucked with sharp bony objects at the ends. He landed it swiftly before the converts were able to turn their rifles toward him. It was Gomsug. He let out a terrifying scream and shook like a dog ridden with rabies.

On the other end came Uda and his men. He had no mask but his face was engraved with black muddy earth. He was muscular, strong and well built. Every violent strike he landed shook his thick breasts.

From the ship of Rev. Buchanan, which was late again to offer any reinforcement, they could hear voices and cries only uttered on battlefields. The sounds of canons, rifles, blades and steels echoed beyond the now darkening heavens. The ship was filled with smoke, cries and strange songs from the Zong. Some fireballs let out from the cannons could be seen far against their oncoming canoes, which shattered some before they climbed the ship. Some canons where ripped from their positions and rolled about the ship, hunting down the Zong. Watching helplessly from Reverend Buchanan's ship these canons were turned on some men and they were ejected from the ship with fire and blood, and they were dashed into the sea shattering everything in the way. Without hindrance, even though many floated at sea already from the shooting men on board, the Zong climbed upon the ships like armies of wild ants against their prey, swinging blades, spearing and bashing the sailors on board. Flesh and body parts began to fall on the decks and the air was thick with the smell of blood. Painful cries became louder than the fiercely blowing wind. Teeth began to grind and jump from pounded mouths. Dead men moistened in blood and saltwater lay close to their violently removed limbs.

Uda laid his eyes on the Reverend, angrily firing his short pistol in one hand, sword in the other. His back was turned to Uda but then he turned and their eyes met. Reverend Kline saw the most violent stare any living man had ever given him since his encounter with the "Hammer D" in the concentration camp.

In those days, only the dead or those close to death filled with bitterness and anger looked in this fashion or gave such look now on Uda's face. Among the Jews he watched die by his hand or another, there was a lawyer who had just gotten married three months before, and was expecting a child when he was shipped to the concentration camp. Everyone knew him for he was a fine lawyer they said. In times of peace, he made himself wealthy from his profession. This man, by the name of "The Hammer D," was dragged into the square for some unknown reasons and was about to be executed. He was pleading for his life, asking that he be allowed to see his pregnant wife one more time. But, in the midst of his pleading a bullet caught him in the forehead. He dropped to his back and slumped down.

The Reverend, being present for the execution and unaware of the sudden shot, panicked and held his breath.

"The Hammer D," who was called so for he landed big cases, had a real name called David. Lying on the floor with blood draining out of his head, it was as if "The Hammer D" had refused to 'die. He suddenly sat up and stared about blankly. The blood, now streaming from his head drained into his white eyes that were filled with terror and becoming red from the blood, he gasped for breath with nails plunged into the sand as if it fed him life. His face suddenly swirled and was distorted and filled with the unknown.

The guard walked over and stepped on "The Hammer D's" chest. Standing above him, he shot him twice. But "The Hammer D" grabbed the guard by the legs and sunk his nails into him grouching loudly, as if he would arise again, although the guard still had his foot in his chest. Then, the Reverend, being so disgusted with anger, rushed over with his automatic rifle, shooting "The Hammer D" and almost killed the guard. It was an odd moment.

Breathing intensely, he laughed sourly as the guard squinted with surprise. It was almost like he began his assault on "The Hammer D" with a cry, as his voice trembled when he screamed and let loose a few rounds into the dying man, then his heavy tone became lighter like a real laughter. The soldier standing by, after a long pause, they all laughed with him as "The Hammer D" lay, his body mashed.

As they departed from the scene, the Reverend turned his head and looked at the body of "The Hammer D". The stare he saw from that dirt in that dead pale eyes haunted him for years until now. It was transformed into the face of the Zong staring for a kill.

Uda lifted his mace and ran to the Reverend. The Reverend turned and fired the last shot. Uda staggered backward. He then stood his ground and yelled, face tightened and shoulders pumped. Before the Reverend could bring forth his sword for an attack, it was too late. Uda was quick to bash him to the head. The Reverend slumped to the deck helplessly. Uda threw him on his shoulder and called out to his men.

"Back to shore, we have the prize!"

Suddenly the Zong began departing the ship. The ship of John Buchanan stood idle in the distance. They had watched as their brothers succumbed to the fury of the Zong. The attack was so rapid that those who were passionate enough to throw some canoes into the sea to assist their brothers were a bit late.

"We have to help them," a native councilman spoke paddling the canoe swiftly.

Some were quick enough and arrived. They intensified the fight. However, the gunfire, bows and arrows, the sounds of spears and blades rubbing against one another in an unceasing manner, were so overwhelming that Reverend Buchanan realized sending more men out to the battle that was already lost was a detrimental call. He ordered his remaining men to return to the ship and create a better defense, if the Zong came. For their brother ship, it was too late. The Zong were deadly and vigilant in their attacks. A swift blow from Gomsug cut a man into two. With the amount of ammunition on board, the councilmen were not ready for the wave of the Zong and lost the fight. The ship was on fire and the Zong disembarked. The surviving missionaries and soldiers who escaped the burning furnace began to jump into the sea and swam for their lives towards the other ship.

Their brothers coming to their aid rescued them and looked from afar as the ship split at the middle and burst into flame. It was a sad sight. All was in shambles and Reverend Kline was gone, taken away on the shoulder of Uda. From on board the other ship they watched slowly, as the ship sank with its casualties—the wounded, unable to swim and the dead; Zong, councilmen, and native convert included.

"We shall travel back. And we shall be back with a real army to demolish this savage shore." Rev Buchanan said regretfully as their ship sailed away from the harbor leaving the dead and Reverend Kline behind. From their shore, the Zong stood with pride and jubilation as they watched the councilmen vanish in the distance before the glimmering moonlight and bright stars illuminating the sea.

Chapter Seven

The Preacher's God

Vanity, vanity, says the preacher, all is vanity—even my flesh; vanity is my heart, vanity is my life, vanity is my...soul? Hah—what is vanity now that my soul has pleaded to God for forgiveness; I have given myself to the wild, yet heaven shuts its ears from my cries. Have I come to the point where my iniquities have flooded my life? Was it my fault that I was ordered to commit unimaginable transgressions against my people? But were they my people?

No! I have no people for as long as I can remember, I was told I was an orphan—a poor German orphan—a child of a German maid in a Jewish home—abomination? They took me in and they said I was a Jew. This too is vanity; for in the heap of my love for them I was told my name was Heimer. Alfred Heimer. The blood of the Arian race ran through me. For my own protection I had to leave home—the home that I knew, the home that I loved, the people I called mother and father. I am split! I am rent! I am a victim of the war!

I partook in the killing of my people. I am haunted by woes! I belong to no race! Which one am I? Which one am I? —What I am—this too is vanity for I will never know the answer. Who will tell me? Who will show me mercy when I am alone and ready to be a meal for the Zong? Bless my soul O my Lord, bless my soul. If they were to protect me, by disowning me, then shame on them for I should have died with them. They loved me—no Hitler, no Christian, no you devil! You were the one who should, and have suffered in my place. You were the one who shot them. Told me you loved her long time ago in college, but she was engaged to a Jew, so you asked me to kill him and you raped and gassed her. Dear Lord when? Why can I run from them? I should have told him what you did was wrong and I hope you are dead? No, I should have fought you in that cold, thrown you my fist like the Zong I fought today. In that avalanche of bloody snow, where Fredrick lay, that soiled dirt where David lay, his eyes turned to the north, lost to his pregnant wife forever. And the screaming girl you defiled, these soldiers laughing outside. You were all cowards to smoke in the cold by that bloody fence and pretended that her cry was a silent whisper of pleasure. Couldn't you have smelled the reeking smell of their oily leaking corpses that extended for miles? You must receive your punishment in hell! Tonight mine is up to my neck—if I ever did wrong. O Jews, my people—

but I have confessed and I am ready to die. I am a sinner Lord, I am a killer. Will my selfish soul yield? I have witnessed atrocities and I am ready. I am ready to see my Nora. I am ready to see mother and father again and tell them how I paraded the world preaching the good news but found no remedies for my sins. I am ready to die Lord, and all those I could not save, let the Zong spear me.

He lay there, awake after regaining consciousness. Staring at the roof made out of barks of trees, his eyes glared slowly at his surroundings. He could hear the voices of men singing and shouting. He thought he was in hell and was hearing voices of the devil's angels calling out for him. The call was familiar. It sounded the same as those terrifying Zong boarding his ship. Yes, he was in hell! Good God! He had heard those voices over the last few weeks. There was no way that those men they murdered, those men he laid the bullets in, were here now with him in hell! His sins had taken him here!

It was dark and his cold blood had dried to his head. Hell must have turned cold? Why? Has the devil cheated judgment and turned hell to a suitable habitat? Nonsense! Maybe he was somewhere different. His sins must have been forgiven and he was in paradise. But, if so, then paradise was a gruesome and cold place for he could taste and smell his blood. Paradise was supposed to be clean and sublime. Furthermore, if this was paradise, then his spent energies were all in vain, for the Zong were violent, unrepentant and were also in paradise.

No, wait. This was hypocrisy—a lie. For, if they repented, it was not in the name of Christ, for Christ is the only source for salvation. Therefore, what is this place? Though he, Isaac Kline, had come to save their souls from eternal damnation, they pummeled his head with a giant stake and might even slay him in the end. With all their violence against his innocent soul, did God still let their filthy souls into a place reserved for saints? What is this place? Where am I!?

Was he, Isaac Kline, a saint? No, he killed Jews! Old ones and young ones. And he killed Germans too. Fredrick. The guard who killed "The Hammer D" and his family.

That night after Fredrick lay bleeding on that hill, stiff and cold as ice, he said to Nora, "We must take a last drive."

Then at the guard's house, he called him out and gruesomely stabbed him as Nora watched from the driver's seat. It was intended to end there, but he heard the laughter of the wife and children from the house. It irritated him. He was not contented. Over the bleeding guard he stood and spoke Hebrew, informing him he was a Jew. And as he jabbed him with the bayonet, his sweaty face tightened and he told the guard that he would erase his entire generation because he, the guard, killed "The Hammer D."

The night was velvet dark and silent. A few little stars glimmered visibly in the night sky and crickets talked. The Reverend used his handkerchief and cleaned his knife. Below him, by his foot the guard lay dying and, a few of his fingers were into the punctured wounds as if to stop the blood. The Reverend peered through from a distance and he saw the wife and her two children; a boy and a girl shadows moving about the house.

The mother sat by the table waiting for her husband to return for dinner. Instead the Reverend entered, ignoring the signal of Nora's desperate call that they must depart immediately. With the gun silencer he entered, face drenched with cold sweat. He was beginning to weep slowly and his body trembled beneath the military fatigue. Breathing slowly he stared with sorrow. Perhaps he wished he did nothing then but the Reverend was filled with anger after he had watched so many massacres.

The wife of the guard somehow knew his intensions. She also knew her husband was dead. Her eyes stiffened in her head and without removing her sight from the dish she ordered her older son to the barn and feed the sheep.

"Gehen Sie und geben Sie den Schafen etwas Wasser bevor wir beginnen Abendessen." She said and was quiet. The son remained seated. She was trying to save him. But the children were the first to see the Reverend, breathing and sobbing, fingers upon the shorthandled pistol attached to the silencer. She lifted her head slowly wet with tears as well and she looked into his eyes, then at the pistol. Her face was suddenly occupied with terror. She looked at her children sadly and then she looked back into the Reverend's eyes, beckoning for mercy. All the while the Reverend sobbed slowly and his face was also covered in tears. He lifted the gun and pointed it at the boy. The mother's voice then trembled and she asked the Reverend for her husband.

"Wo ist mein Mann?" Smoke and flash with fire flared from the gun and the boy dropped to the ground instantly. The mother screamed and came to put herself in the way of the next shot so that her daughter could run. But before she could get in the way the Reverend shot her in the head and then turned the gun on the girl. The mother fell to her back into the food she had set on the other table behind her. The girl fell outside at the back door with a bullet in her back. All was silent. The Reverend sat and sobbed a bit before returning to Nora. With the house filled with innocent blood, in the food and on the floor, he came out and knew that Nora was not happy. He sat quietly without looking into her eyes. She drove to the border that night and they escaped for northern Africa.

They must have hunted him if they found out what he did, but he was gone. Gone from his failure. Gone from the endless anguish of watching daily as people he knew and hoped to save were shot and killed. He had hoped his nightmare ended then once he and Nora purchased that desert camel in Gambia. But that was just the closing of the old chapter, his experience in Europe. A new one was beginning. A new chapter, layered, dark, mysterious. It was the unknown—.

Now, where was he? He wondered. The Zong were singing outside. Maybe they were rejoicing for their saved lives. However, they were singing the same violent song! This was not what he expected. Paradise should not hold the same terror he felt before Uda came against him with a swift blow.

The Reverend tossed and turned to make sense of his surroundings. He tried to feel his body, but it felt paralyzed. His spine was somewhat numbed, but his eyes made rapid movements about the room. He strained his legs and felt a sudden blood rush.

"I am alive and well! Well, damn me, I am their prisoner." He breathed out in anxiety. The voices were not peaceful, but he lay there still. He was tied with rope and stripped to the pole of the hut. Alongside him a fireplace was blazing bright illuminating the dark room. Over the fire a clay pot was boiling, almost spilling into the fire. The Reverend looked through the crack of the house and saw the men playing with more fire. He pulled closer to see. The sound of the sea and the echo of the breeze were close. He was aware that he was not far away from the shores.

Looking through the cracks he saw giant men all moving stiffly in a cyclical motion around a blazing flame. Gomsug, their leader, screamed with a thundering voice; then it was followed by a resounding tone that shook the earth. In unison, the Zong war dance sent certain numbness down the Reverend's spine, reviving his terror. It was a resurrection of the incident on the ship when Uda came to him with the mace and slumped him to the deck. The voices were heavy and reached the heavens. It was powerful, commanding and violent in sound that even the beasts of the forest complained once more of the disturbance.

"Zong shake with zeal! Yabbakana!!

"Uhlloh!!" They screamed.

 "Yabbakana!!"

"Uhlloh!!!!"

"Hayiiyah!!

"Uhlloh!!!"

"Hayiiyah!!

"Uhlloh!!!"

"Hayiiyah!!"

"Uhlloh, uhlloh, uhlloh!!!!!!!!"

"Zong are the mightiest of all," they responded.

"We are known throughout the lands for our greatness!"

"Uhlloh!!"

"The Zong are the mightiest of all."

"May he who comes against us suffer and perish like the Izeonah caught in Monshung's snare.

"The Zong are the mightiest of all!"

"Remember your ancestors, O Zong, of the iniquities of the white man. Not too long ago you witnessed their rivalry that continues into our time," The leader stretched his arm toward the hut where the Reverend lay. "He is our slave. What has given them courage to raise arms against us?"

"The Zong are the mightiest of all men!!"

"The white man, like always the white man, is known as the divider of our people. We defeated him this night, just like old times!"

"The Zong are the mightiest of all!!"

Gomsug continued his speech.   "I assure you—those ones looming our forest, if you establish me as the *Gamrah*—their heads will hang about town as proofs for being the Mebzongbre to our land."

"The Zong are the mightiest of all!"

"No man comes against the god of the Zong! I am Gomsug!" He pounded his chest.

"Gomsug, the mightiest! Gomsug the Gomrah! Gomsug the *Gamrah* to be! Fear him greatly. Fear him for his fist is made out of lightning! His voice is the breath of the gods. We salute him!" The crowd lifted their hands and made cyclical motions, screaming and dancing.

Gomsug walked toward the hut and called out, "Gomrah Uda!"

Uda approached with forceful energy and stood before Gomsug. He gave him the short leadership staff made out of crystal. It was rounded on one end with the head of a snake and sharp at the other. The middle part was long and made for grabbing.

"It is time to prove yourself otherwise. Zong huh kah, Izeonah yah huh kah...you are a Zong and not an Izeonah. Prove it brother!" Gomsug yelled out to his men and they disappeared into the forest.

Uda stood still and stared at the hut where the Reverend was lying. This crowd now present had certain uncomfortable expressions on their faces. Their zeal was a bit dented as they squinted upon their leader now carrying the staff. Uda was aware of their stares and shouted.

"I am not weak!" He released his arms in anger and struck one of his men to the sand. "Bring the white man." He said bluntly directed his men to the hut where the Reverend lay.

At first, the men were a bit reluctant to enter the hut; then when they saw their master Uda's disquieting, yet angry look, they quickly entered and stood above the Reverend with sharp axes, looking down on him. The Reverend looked up at them out of confusion, fear and curiosity. He screamed.

"Who are you people?" The Reverend's voice came out bold to a point that even he was surprised. The men looked at one another and laughed.

"Even in chains the white man still talks like he has something menacing under his sleeves." The guard said and struck his axe to the dirt by the fire and grabbed the Reverend by the arm.

"Ha, he thinks his God will save him," another guard, who went down to help, added. "Get up, since you are still bold to speak even in agony."

"Should we break his legs?" The guard standing asked while readying his mace.

"Get the white man on the horse!" Uda's voice intruded and shivered his men.

They hurriedly pulled the Reverend out of the hut and threw him over a gray horse. The men began their journey back to town.

The war on the beach was surely over and their seas were quiet once more. The remaining white men were gone with the wind.

Uda and his men, along with the Reverend, entered into a strange forest. It was a quiet and dense savannah plain. Tall trees protruded into the sky with wild ropes linking trees to trees. Wild grasses and ferns lay about the sandy trail and they walked from a sandy land into the muddy plains. They walked for many more miles and found themselves in grassy mountainous regions and back into the forest.

Sweat rolled down the Reverend's face. For some unknown reasons, as he watched about with dismay, his fear was transformed into a strange numbness that caused him not to feel his heartbeat. All was subtle, painless and surreal. He just stared about on the galloping horse with Uda and his men alongside him speaking Dahnkka, the most popular of the upper echelon part of the Zong's language.

"I bet by the breast of my wife, this white man will be hung in public tomorrow."

"Are you prophesying—or your neck?"

"I said I bet on the breast of my wife."

"It is flaccid—six children suckled it all away, there's nothing left for even you." A man said calmly spitting out some seeds.

" You should bet on fresh palm trees, not the one without the wine leaking from the core." Another Zong, who seemed interested in the conversation added.

"Always thinks his wife has an unmatched beauty." Added another.

"Hey, ah, that does not do me justice speaking of my wife in that fashion!"

"No, I am afraid of nightmares. You are a false teller. This white man will be spared. The prophet said so. His foot touched the sand of our land."

"For what? Master Uda, will you intervene? What do you think?"

"I think you must all shut up and ride. You can bet on the vagina of your wife, or your fresh young virgin. Prophecy makes no difference to me. The priests have the final saying. But I say the white man is like a weed. You cut a bunch from your land and five more bunches, more powerful, more vigilant spring up in their place and spread even more to your land, consuming your crops and even turning it into poisonous feeds for other crops. I detest the white man. They turn brothers against brothers. Who would have thought the white man would come again. As did our brothers in the hills, escaping our hand every time we attack, they are the cause, keeping the white man spirits alive. But that will not do. This white man, I want to kill him myself. When that time comes, I will beat him with my fist until his face is mud. For Nicaso, for my family and for his greed to want another man's land and ravishing our gods."

Uda's speech silenced the men instantly. There was a certain mood that came over him suddenly and they knew what would come next. Being stirred up, they knew it was risky to provoke their leader. The Reverend felt the tension in the speech, as Uda was dramatic, raising his fists, and staring directly at him with eye full of furry and bushy brows clenched together.

"How do they know where we are, anyhow?" A Zong carefully broke the silence. "I thought N'Daygmong cry made our land invisible. How do they still see us?"

"The white man knows everything." Another said and gave his master a cautious look, as if expecting to be clobbered on the head.

"Shut up your foolishness already!" Uda interrupted with a fierce voice. "The white man knows nothing but deceit and greed. This is what drove him to our land. Nothing else!" With such a tone, even an ignorant man would know it came from a man with dark intentions. The Reverend knew that and gave a quick stare at Uda.

Alterations came suddenly into Uda's life since Basin escaped. When Basin escaped from the Sacred Forest where he was to be fed to the snake god, Monshung, it changed the movement of the land, mostly for the leaders striving to attain the *Gamrahood*, the highest power of the land. There was an internal war happening in Meheyassahapunawa.

A special group of Zong called *Ixeonah*, who were the minority, hiding in caves and burrows, were in strife against the Zong population as a whole. The *Ixeonah* were Zong who were converted to Christianity centuries ago when the first white man landed on these shores. But now the white man was blotted out from the land by violence, and the rest of the converts or *Ixeonah* dispersed into exile. They became the minority and were under intolerable persecutions. If a man was considered an *Ixeonah*, this meant sudden death no exception.

It was thought that Basin belonged to this group. Basin being a common man, a bit insane but greedy went down to the Spirit River and caught a few fishes for himself. When the rumor spread that this was Basin's habit, it grieved the Spirit greatly and the only explanation was that the *Ixeonah* had converted him.

The truth about Basin remained shrouded in confusion. Since he was considered savage and an *Ixeonah* and had eaten of the Spirit River, he was quickly apprehended. Fishing in the Spirit River was the most abominable act according to the Zong's tradition, for in the Spirit River swam the sons and daughters of the land. Basin pulled them out before the mothers of the land could conceive them. Only the *Ixeonah* fished in the Spirit River, for they where known for defiling the traditions of the Zong. And when Basin was labeled as such, death by sacrifice to the snake god, Monshung, was the final punishment.

Fortunately for Basin, the *Ixeonah* were convinced that he was converted. By night and by surprise, as always, they surfaced from their burrows and attacked overpowering the guardians of the Sacred Forest. When they arrived to liberate Basin, he was already gone. He had vanished from the torture rope he was bound to with one arm dislocated from the socket. To this date no man had fathomed how Basin escaped. Some said he was accused on false account and the gods released him to punish his accusers.

Many of these interpretations and rumors circulated for a while until the Prophet, Nephrotone, ordered the leaders to bash any man or woman vainly prophesying the outcome of Basin's escape. Basin's escape set in motion one of the greatest generational fears of the Zong. It was never understood how Basin escaped and where he went—a primary source for Uda's indignation against the Reverend.

Indirectly, Uda linked the Reverend to the *Ixeonah* hiding in caves and most often surfacing to their own demises. The *Ixeonah* were growing in large numbers and it was predicted that their growth would soon revive terror for the Zong and their leaders. The Zong were once more at war within themselves. It was a centuries old war. When many of these *Ixeonah* were captured and killed, the war subsided but now it was about fifty years since the last rage against them and once more the *Ixeonah* have grown in their burrows and was now surfacing again to cause terrors with their old-fashioned rifles.

But Basin escaping without a trace meant the blood of the sons of the land was about to be poured to the lands and forests in a larger amount. The skies and seas would be stained once more, and mothers would weep for their dying sons. For the Zong had no patience for the *Ixeonah* and would go to the extreme to make sure their venom of converting the Zong to the foreign white man's God never saw the light.

When Basin disappeared, the Prophet Nephrotone prophesied that the worst of this war was to begin from the sea. His prophesy was that since the leaders were careless to see to it that Basin was fed to the snake god Monshung, the cry of N'Daygmong, the head god, centuries ago, which shut all other eyes from coming to the land was lifted. Therefore, without the curse of N'Daygmong to shut eyes away from the land, the people were to expect turmoil from their fiercest enemy, the White man, who would be coming to their shores in no time. Nephrotone was stern in his prediction and expressed with great sadness knowing that this time the coming white man would also revive the spirit of the *Ixeonah* and their unity would be stronger than ever before.

Nephrotone therefore ordered the Zong to take full precautions in the coming months, for they would be the darkest of all in their existence. Moreover, it was clear in his vision what must be done to prevent the second coming of the white man.

"No white man's foot must touch the sands of Meheyassahapunawa! No white man's foot must touch land." Nephrotone was passionate about his vision and described in detail what he saw. "Where he stepped," Shouted Nephrotone, "Blood spilled out like the ocean. Blood of our gods and of our land and the sons and daughters of Meheyassahapunawa became the red ocean. We must fight for our survival Zong, for there is no mercy in the white man's speech, his arrogance we are accustomed to for we have *Ixeonah* in our hills since the Whiteman first put his foot to this soil."

Nephrotone walked about face moistened with sweat and terror. His eyes became red as fire and almost entered the back of his head. It was as if he had already lived the demise of his people if ever the white man's foot touched the land. "His foot unto the land is a bad omen. It would ignite a series of unpredictable outcomes that will begin the fall of the Zong." The Prophet Nephrotone stopped his speech and paused suddenly. As if it was over, life as he knew it for the Zong slowly vanished before his eyes. He was at the end of his prophecy. He was seeing the last days of the Zong when the white man's foot touched the land. The land was divided in his eyes. It was desolate, plain and devoid of the gods and the voice of the people. The white man roamed the streets, carrying his precious book speaking of his blasphemy against the gods. He chastised the Zong who disobeyed and shot many in the mud. The white man's merciless hand was against his people. Nephrotone shouted in terror as he slowly revived from the spell of his prophesy. He then shook the Zong army before him and was swift in his order. He demanded camping on the beach forever, if possible for this was the last act of defense against the coming white man.

Sacrifices were made to Yore, the water goddess that she would swallow up the white man before he sailed in view. But, almost a year later, the Reverend and his men appeared in view. The worst of the entire occurrence was that the Reverend's foot touched the land. This was the original source for Uda's anger. Until the Reverend made that detrimental foot landing, the Zong had kept their ground. But the white man landed his foot and caused a cloud of complete doubt to hang over the Zong. Furthermore, all this was done because Uda was incompetent and weak to strike the white man and he landed his foot on the sand. Now the future was bleak. Even bleaker for Uda, for he knew what awaited him as he headed back to meet the Prophets and the priests in the coming days. The land of the Zong was in demise because he refused to complete his duties as a leader.

For some unknown reason, which other leaders were still confused about, Uda allowed such a predicament to befall his people. This made many question his leadership and his eligibility as one of the men to stand on the pedestal, as the highest leader of the land. However, even in this regretful state, Uda had a vision on the beach that afternoon that made him forget his usual violent tendency and allow the Reverend to set his foot on the land. Basin's escape, which made all leaders vigilant to have the most powerful position of the land, led to many nightly discussions. Thereafter, Uda had a recurrent dream that he could not grasp until the day the Reverend landed his foot on the shore.

On the day the Reverend landed his foot on the sand, Gomsug, who was to be leading the army for the day, decided to remain in town with a local harlot. Perhaps he was in love? But this caused him more regrets then the mood of love often created in men. He left his best friend Uda in charge. And then, Uda saw his recurrent dream manifesting itself in reality. Just as it happened in the dream, the sea was filled with men in white garments walking across the water towards the shore of Meheyassahapunawa. In the most sublime state, the dark cloud with light protruding through roared and followed the men. In their midst, Uda saw a sad boy with his face drenched in tears. It was as if the boy was lost and had nowhere to turn. He began to call Uda by his name as if he knew Uda. Though Uda knew not the boy's name, yet for some unknown reasons the boy seemed familiar—perhaps because it was such a frequent occurrence. In this recurrent dream, Uda always did the same thing. Surrounded by men walking over the sea, bright light beaming from the sky, Uda had to move backward to see. Several times he had this dream, and all those times he walked boldly and struck the boy with his blade before the boy landed on the shore. In his dream he stood by the sea staring at his bloody blade regretfully and the little boy being washed away by the sea. Sometimes in the dream he wished to ask the boy why him, but the boy usually lay lifeless in his own blood. By then Nephrotone had not dreamed of the coming days of the white man.

When Uda awake from his dream it always haunted him for days. Though it was an extremely dangerous preposition for a leader like him to show weakness, the innocent boy lying to the seashore was a gruesome memory that stayed with him for a prolonged period of time. Uda had a ten-year-old son and seeing the boy's blood drain out by the sea in his dream was a painful scar daily. When the memory of his dream dominated his days, Uda would promise to save the boy the next time in his dream. But then in the dream, Uda struck the boy again. It was a routine that Uda was familiar with. Yet in reality, he failed to even use his blade against the Reverend's flesh. Standing at the shore that afternoon, he saw the Reverend coming in the same manner as the dream and Uda froze. He kept his promise and made sure no man laid a hand on this innocent boy. However, by the time he realized what he had done, the Reverend had escaped from being drowned by his men and was sailing away back to his ship. The dream and the event could not be torn apart. He had broken the prophecy, but kept his promise to the dream. It was all a deception now he realized however, for that boy he saw was the white man, an *Izeonah*, now tied to the horse. He was sure the future promised no smile any time soon, so he frowned strongly knowing that he could not strike the Reverend, now that the priests had ordered that he be captured alive. With hope still a looming possibility, the captured Reverend would be used to fix the problem either by sacrifice or another means ordained by the priests. The cloud ahead was surely dense. Uda and his men made their way to the town.

Chapter Eight

The Irrevocable God

*I*n the Zong language Dahnkka, *Izeonah* meant the white man and his descendants. *Ixeonah* meant the converts or any Zong who was converted to the white man's religion. The entire cluster of *Izeonah* and *Ixeonah* was referred to as *Mebzongbre*, which also meant offenders. In some context *Mebzongbre* also referred to enemies or those who came against the Zong.

The land of the Zong was not virgin to the white man. The white man once lived here. The story began on May 9th, 1722 when the ship leaving the shore of South Africa to either tame the revolution in Virginia or carry a message to the Queen, disappeared from the sea. It landed in Meheyassahapunawa wretched and demolished from the bashing of the sea waves. The Zong were innocent then and thought of the white man as their friend. This was such a curiosity that people travelled from inland to see the Izeonah, men with "new complexion." But soon the Zong would give this expedition a new name: Yiti or the dark era.

The Zong had civilization long before the white man arrived on their shores. And being so, they sent a special group of messengers also sorcerers named the Sadomrah to investigate the Izeonah. The Sadomrah were filled with wit and prophecies, knowing the future and the past intertwined. Two weeks later the Sadomrah returned wailing to the priests and cried of the Yiti.

"The white man is a destroyer! We must kill them!" They clamorously exclaimed before the priests. "Yiti! Kill them all and burn the vessels they travelled in. They must not return to their homeland for more will come after them."

The discussion was filled with so many fears that the priests ordered that no man visit the white man thereafter. However, this order was to no avail. Soon the white man had lands and farms.

The white man's first attempt was to repair their vessels and leave the land and return with more guns and men to tame the Zong. At the present moment it was filled with violence. Furthermore, the manner in which they arrived, and the equipment they had was not enough to overpower the Zong in the way they intended. They came here unplanned. Travelling towards the Americas, a violent storm in the Bermuda triangle swiftly brought them to the land of the Zong. The white man first thought the Zong were Indians but soon realized they where unique in the strange land. It was an unknown destination and it frightened them. The land itself was a peculiar place. The people were savages and very intolerable. Even though it was so, the Zong, still filled with curiosity, were quick to surface and gave the white man a warm welcome. Nevertheless, soon all changed when they discovered the white man's potential.

Since there were missionaries on board the ship, the Lord's work must go on. Furthermore, their shipmen were encountering obstacles as they tried to rebuild the carrier. It was demolished every time they made progress.

The Zong considered the presence of the white man on their land as the greatest threat. They watched. Every now and then, as the white man tried to put the ship together, at nightfall, a group of Zong led by their leaders, went in and either set the ship on fire or dismantled it. When the white men called for a meeting and expressed their concern, the Zong listened. But then they sabotaged the next vessel that stood the chance of leaving the harbor. They swam beneath the ship and made holes in it. The white men became desperate and worked night and day and left guards to watch the ship at night. However, by the morning the guards were gone and the ship was destroyed.

Meheyassahapunawa was a strange island. It behaved incoherently with what one would expect Mother Nature to do. Most of all, the unpredictable behavior of the ocean and sea surrounding the land were turbulent at times. For decades the sea remained unreceptive to the people and refused to allow any sailing over its beauty. It became violent and raged against any floating object until it was found at the bottom. After these perilous periods ended some other misfortunes always followed. They were soon replaced with great epidemics, droughts or something unexpected that caused the Zong to pray even harder to their gods.

The gods were the source of their beliefs, the emblem of relief from the suffering land. Therefore, the gods played an essential role in their daily lives. Hence, violating the gods was a direct desecration of their culture and their way of life. It alluded to catastrophes. The coming of the white man seemed to have increased the anger of the gods.

After several years of unsuccessful attempts to leave, the white men accepted their fates that they might never leave the island. And they began to make some claims to the land and crafted new tactics on how to make friends with the Zong. The white man began to weave himself within the society of the Zong, beginning with those who accepted their faith. This was no harm, the priests and prophet thought at first. Soon the white man would die off from the deadly maladies and floods, or perish with age. But they must not depart from the island alive. However, this was a mistake by the Zong. After the Sadomrah returned, their concepts of the white man changed. But it was too late. The Izeonah had already sunk some roots in the land teaching the Ixeonah to embrace the western tradition and influencing them to question the existing one.

It was a Yiti for the Zong. One they wished never to be repeated again. The mouthy and boisterous Izeonah thought to preach the gospel until old age or some form of malady would end their lives. It was a race against time because they realized there was no way they could leave the land. They held their Bibles and began the conversion of the people against their law, promising eternity and freedom from the gods who punished them with floods and other deadly maladies regardless of their spiritual rituals. The white men talked about the man who died on the cross and saved them from the devil.

"One sacrifice is all you need. His name is Jesus!" Screamed these arrogant, yet, powerful missionaries.

The white men made a life out of what they could find. With the help of the Ixeonah, they confronted the inhabitants every day. They moved to the town of Sacamontey, which they later called *Sacremount*. There, in Sacremount the Izeonah formed the first church. Soon a Zong girl was given into marriage with a white man and had a boy. Then three hundred believed in the white man's God—and fifteen women were pregnant again. And then two churches were built.

During that time, the Zong were not as united as they were now, and it cost them greatly. At first the white men tried to make peace with the Zong, but the Zong, rowdy with indignation, wanted the white men dead. The rules by which they required the white men to abide were against the white man's belief, and this was unacceptable. In the last meeting a leading Zong impatiently yelled and rushed with his blade in frustration. A few shots rang out and a few blades landed and they went their separate ways, still living as mortal enemies.

Soon the land was divided. The Izeonah and the Ixeonah became the Mebzongbre, going against the Zong. The Mebzongbre owned lands and houses and built big white walls around them. Inevitably, an upheaval was imminent. The Mebzongbre, in their frustration, soon levied their destruction against the Zong. In the coming war, no side was promised a clear victory.

The white men however, promised the converts a better life once they sailed the sea and returned. To do so they must stay alive by setting up defenses in their compounds. With the rifle in their hands, the White man was ready to shoot. The Zong feared them greatly for they knew the bullet reached a Zong quicker then he could pull and release a bow and arrow or a spear. The white men even became inventive by creating more bullets out of stones, minerals and substances buried in the soil.

In the market ground one day a rifle sounded out of a common dispute when a Zong called a teenager a disgrace, because the youth was a descendant of the Ixeonah, and was a duplicate Zong.

"Mebzongbre!" The teenager screamed and was shot and left to die in the hot sun, face turned to the sky bleeding and weeping.

A rifle resounded again another day. At the washing creek a Zong was dragged out bleeding from the stomach. Zeblah, the polio stricken knave with a dead eye, intentionally jumped over the white wall at night and defecated into the drinking well adjacent to the church. Before he could wipe and run to boast about his evil in town, he was found with legs swinging above the brick stool and trouser around the ankles. The guard, who lighted the torch that shone on Zeblah's face, took him to the center of the compound naked and with some manure painted to his rear. They whipped him severely. Thereafter, Zeblah slept for days eating only soft food, for his wounds were great and painful that even his mouth caused him distress when open. He became a symbol proving to the Zong that the white man was a force to reckon with.

It was thirteen years later that the white men took their first trip to the sea excitedly. They were mostly middle aged or old men. Along with them, they took some converts and their children. However, ten years later, there was no sign of their return, and no rescue came. A legend was told that Yore, the water goddess, knowing what would happen if the white men left the shores unharmed, caused the sea to close its mouth and foamed violently, gnashing its jaws against the intruders. The ships along with the content within were spat out into pieces of wood and so were the white man and his people.

There were two more attempts, which yielded the same results. Thereafter, the remaining white man learned that Meheyassahapunawa was their home—a place where they must now live and die. Eventually the

Izeonah perished completely from the land, leaving only the faith and the crafts for the succeeding generations, who were the Ixeonah and the remnant of their children, those who had half the Whitman's blood streaming through their veins. With their lite complexion resembling their forefathers, they were the new and mixed generation to lead the Ixeonah and the *Ixeonah*.

For decades thereafter, the Zong watched and waited for an opportunity to strike and exterminate the Mebzongbre. Little strife led to a Zong's death and the people crying. Shooting a Zong happened every so often especially when the Zong interfered with the Mebzongbre and his belief. Even the priest, named Seeney, was amputated, loosing his legs up to the knees. There was no immunity from the power of the white men's guns and the domination of their God. The Zong cursed and threw stones, but the retaliation from the white man was so deadly that almost every week a Zong was buried from the hot steaming copper of the white men's guns.

On the other hand, according to the Mebzongbre, the best way to tame a Zong was with violence. The Zong tendencies called for no leniency. It was weakness to show kindness toward a defying enemy. Violence was necessary to control the Zong, or the remaining white men would have perished out of history, and the masses of those who were converted would have been disposed of at the blades and axes of the angry Zong standing outside the white walls quivering with thirst for blood.

An army was built to defend the Mebzongbre. Back and forth, the urge to dominate the land became a quest that the white man and the Zong struggled to attain. The white men stood their ground, built more homes and reproduced. For nearly a century it was the case on the shores of the Zong. The Mebzongbre knew no place else but the land of Meheyassahapunawa and their God. The western world was the origin of their forefathers but the new land was their home—the place they knew and loved and had no intention of abandoning.

However, on one Tuesday morning something happened and the Zong reclaimed their land and grew stronger and united thereafter.

When the sun made its way, removing itself from behind these thick sheets of cloud, it had been a gloomy day in the white walls of the white man's compound. The first cry echoed through the soft sunlight during the morning hours. It began as a quiet day over the town while dew, from the previous night still clung onto the freshly green ferns, sparkled brilliantly from the sunlight. The herds and their shepherds were in the field searching for fresh grass. The mountains were still covered with fog, and the gnarled trees had begun to give their fresh leaves to the frigid hands of Mother Nature. The clouds were gray and still, and the solemn and cold winter wind echoed between the houses. Men, women and children were clothed in warm vestures and shivered to the whistling wind. The church bell rang in the Mebzongbre compound intermittently calling for the morning devotion. It was just another day the Zong expected to watch the Izeonah dominate. Then, suddenly, things changed in the Zong's favor.

It was the death of the leader. He was pale and dehydrated by the malady. His face shrunk, and his ribcage stuck out piteously. He was buried and his soul was committed to the lord. The leader was a man known for his diligence and taught his people the way of their faith, the true and holy God, who they must obey and follow even unto death. It was said that when a Zong believed, he believed. This known belief was on the verge of being tested for the Mebzongbre, but they knew it not. At first, after the leader was buried, the Mebzongbre speculated that it was an act by the Zong. An assumption that either the well was poisoned or the Zong has forgotten their lessons when Zeblah was scarred as an inscription for all to see.

"Have you forgotten the example we set with Zeblah?" They pronounced with intimidation.

However, all this was to no avail. The malady had already sat decadently in the veins of the people, and was about to surface from their skins and any other opening on their bodies. It would have been easier to abandon the white man's faith by then and return to the traditional way of life. For, the sorrow, which blew thereafter, lasted for months. It became the darkest in their days of worshiping the white man's Jehovah. Not only were they ravished by the malady, which struck throughout the land of Meheyassahapunawa, but also the vigilant and united Zong pursued them into the hills and exiled them in the end. When the sickness had subsided, the camp of the white man was weak and had diminished. There was no hope and no remedy in sight. Death was so present that it took a believer while he had his dinner in his mouth. Children died while breast-feeding from their mothers. It was a nightmare that could not be contained, senselessly wiping out the camp, then the Zong alas.

Many became weak in the compound and died. The following weeks after that many more died. It spread throughout the land like a wild fire pursuing dried foliage on a windy day. A whole family in a house slept forever and, as their dead bodies were being buried, more collapsed and died as well. The gravediggers soon collapsed and were covered up with the earth they dug for the dead. The disease was so pervasive that at night, beneath the full moon, the land stood idle of voices of joy.

The next harvest season brought drought and more disasters. The land had starved so greatly that even livestock suffered to the grave. In the compounds of the Mebzongbre, this disease ravished even more people so that their dwelling places were called the compounds of the walking dead. Many searched for answers during this time and prayed to their God or gods for answers, but the heavens remained quiet and the land remained sick. The sun came and went and the moon came and went. The forest blew red and dusty winds and wild beasts and locusts ate up farms.

When the malady subsided, the Zong concluded that their gods were furious because their sons and daughters had abandoned them for a foreign God, and since it was so the gods sent the malady to punish them. Nephrotone, the prophet and foreseer, had lamented with a deadly scream, "Mebzongbre—gah! —Kill the Mebzongbre."

And so it was that they attacked the camp, which had been greatly reduced in size. They were too weak to defend themselves fully. It was a sad, bloody and merciless day. After many years, this event became a legend. The Zong harrowed through the white fence and massacred anything that breathed within the compounds of the Mebzongbre, and they burned them to the ground. Neighboring towns that had been converted hopelessly dispersed into the woods for safety. The preacher and his followers dwelling in Sacremount were hung to trees with stakes through their rectums and the church was reduced to ashes. During and after this massacre many Zong witnessing this change, for or against it, wrote a series of scrolls described below. These were a few selected scrolls of the Zong, recounting the series of events that transpired:

The last Nightmare: The man circumcised against his will by the white man, is gladly recounting, with a smile, his experience as the Mebzongbre blood was spilled as well.

"I am Jimbty, a victim of the white man's folly. It was the white man's turn to suffer as my people did. The cause for our desolation has arisen. For many years we have embraced him, ignoring the warning of our prophecy. Any foreign god eventually yields to the cold grim hand of N'Daygmong. The white man came proudly raising his chin, and talked about a strange god. They performed sorceries in distinct fashions and lifted the cripples and the lame from their mires. Even those who were blinded by N'Daygmong could see when the white man placed his hand upon them. These acts were abominations to our god!

Concerning even me, my greatest mistake was when the foreskin of my penis was cut involuntarily. I was convinced it was the will of the white man's God that I remove the foreskin as a covenant to him. But yet I waited for weeks, sore and in distress. My wife became a harlot while my penis remained in napkins, rubbing painfully against my thighs. This happening even depresses me now as I recollect this incident.

The white man's new movement was intense, as our daughters and sons believed and left N'Daygmong for the dark. However, it was soon they realized the white man's god was a folly, weak, and deceptive. He lured many to his "cross" and nailed them alone. Thus, N'Daygmong abandoned his people and left them alone with the white man's god.

We became vulnerable to the Yellow Ghost. He struck us with the yellow fluid that even the white man suffered and died and could not be buried with our ancestors. Their bones, which are evidence of their blemishes left by the Yellow Ghost, lay in the Forbidden Land. Their tools, most powerful than spears and arrows, the books from which they chanted and performed great lies and supernatural deliverance with vanity, lay along with their bones.

Hail to N'Daygmong, and woe are we who left him to follow Jehovah. He could not save the white man, and by the precedence of the yellow ghost, an order was given. The rest of those who followed the new god were murdered and slaughtered by the masses, in their own wet yellow stools. Their skins became as pale as pigs, their bodies became thin, fragile and wrinkled, their faces sunk so deep, their eyes lay out of their skulls, blinking slowly like lizards'. Even the remnants of the white men were victims in their manures.

"Knives were sharpened, blades were readied. Knives and blades were used. Even spears were plunged. All this was to alleviate the yellow death from our land and those who brought it with them. From east to west the land lay reeking of blood and manures. When many warriors went by the creek and washed their blades, they made the river red. The wheelbarrows were full with cadavers of the white men, their converts and offspring. Anyhow, it made no difference because they were carried away to the Forbidden Land along with all they brought when they sailed the sea."

Hail, N'Daygmong! Farewell, white men. To those who genuinely believed, you are constant weeds we will seek to root out of our land. The hunt is on. Those who escaped into the woods are being pursued like a wild hunter against his prey. They must be gone! Hail N'Daygmong, farewell white men and those who followed them.

The fifth Scroll:
"The Gina of the Yellow disease"

Men reached for hills in far places,
Seeking help and life.
Even the rooster grew weary of announcing
The morning, for it was hungry,
And the ground was occupied with human manures:
It was yellow; it was fluid.
It tormented our stomach,
And sends us strictly to the grave.
If you can't kiss your wife in three days
Farewell, kiss her in the after life.
O sorrowful Zuxbaha!
How much did you eat
Of that which your ancestors forbid you?
How much did you drink of that which comes out
With your life in three days?
How much curse did you find when you
Provoked the gods to great anger?
Tarry not this night to sacrifice your
Dearest valuables to beg for release from this
Yellow spirit swimming out of your rears.
O fathers, O sons of this great land see you not
Your duty? This is not a prophecy; only the
Prophet makes such claim, and I wipe my lips clean of
Folly talks but eyi, I don't want to die leaking
Like a dipper at the well.

O neighbor, I wave my arms to you with respect and disease.
Don't fight. Don't panic about the yellow fluid.
It wrestles your stomach like it owns it,
And fires your excrete hole with fury and bring inside out—red.
Your colorful rear surfaces every time,

—

I will be very weary if I become sick.
I know this is a silly wish but *eyi,*
I don't want to die like a broken alabaster.

"Weeping Zuxbaha"

"Whether it be fishing from the forbidden river, or the swallowing of the yellow nuts, or the throwing of manures into the Forbidden Land, or degrading the oracles—what brings this on us? I have no insights. I may not tell a prophecy and deliver my neck for slaughter. But this I know. Death occupied their faces, and they lay paled and drained, wet with disturbing smells from their intestinal wrath.

The land is loud with cries and the graves refused to accept the dead. There were many lying with yellow galls and the humming of flies. Zuxbaha was hollowed and bewailed with her daughters and sons. The white sandy land grew idle overnight; with fear and the sweet noise of little ones disappeared from the moony night. No one danced to Monshung under the stars, and every heart beat with worries and complaints for their lives. Huts stood under the clear and quiet sky at nights without a sound.

"Some men, women and children ran for the hills, but decayed there as well. Hut by huts, mouths remained open with grief and lamentation until the morning. Mothers laid their babies heads upon their lonely laps, shaking and weeping and wailing with sorrow.

The diggers have yielded to their exhaustions, and the yellow viper still roamed, leaking fluids from corpses that expired where life abandoned them. Generation before me until now, I found life so sweet, I hold mine close to my breasts and wept Darcyu, who lay on our built bed in her own stool."

After this event, the Zong promised to honor their gods and protect their generations, even unto death. It was a stern call, which came from the prophet Nephrotone. The first of this was a successful chase of the Mebzongbre from the inner land. It was a bitter and long fight, which was fully recorded in the Sacred Shrines of the gods, from whence the above scrolls were taken. In the end when the Zong lifted their blades, elated, the remnant of the white man's descendants and converts were on the run and dispersed into the woods, hills and exiled. They had remained in hiding forever. The white painted compounds were set on fire and the Zong armies remained vigilant ever since, searching from town to town for any trace of the Izeonah and Ixeonah—the Mebzongbre.

When Basin disappeared from the land and onto the land of Bentuh, and made Reverend Kline and his men sail the seas and oceans once more, this time safely to their harbor, the Zong were taking no chances to rekindle the past. It was time to defend.

Chapter Nine

The Zong That I am

"Oh to the palm trees or the bamboos that lie in the swamps, here I am: a man and a Zong. I have come to choose my destiny. Let me be free as a youth, full of energy for this life. I remain unsure of that which may entice me to live as I wish. My dreams now, may not be what they may be for tomorrow. I know not what adventure may befall me when I acquire a wife, a son and some tragedies—a witch! Ha, I cry to N'Daygmong, the father god and the godhead of the land, and I look to the east—the shrine of Monshung—he who mercilessly judges the living and the Mebzongbre, as well.

I plead with Usula the mother of all mothers this hour, please be patient with me, for my ancestors had taught me many things, lest I default into a common man and you give me a child unworthy to bear my name. To all you neighboring tribes: brothers and sisters, those who have diverged from the ways of N'Daygmong to form a new god—away from your core, from this land, the Izeonah's God—the Zong are coming for you.

I want sons; many sons to defend the heritage that I shall bequeath to them as a gift, a burden, a curse and a status. However, most of all let him have the responsibilities, which will not be calamitous; but a privilege of being a Zong, the mightiest of all men. It is nothing more than to preserve the dignity of our gods, our culture and our lives from maladies, disasters and most often, the threat of sinister Mebzongbre creeping from wherever they hid.

Time has changed, so does this privilege. But he who stands fearlessly with a brandishing sword, and bloodthirsty eyes in defense against our foes, I salute you. Yalashimba, if the gods will not guide you, the mystery we are—Effina, will lead you. We are told of our ancestors. This journey in life now leads us there. However, I quicken my step with a close watch for you don't know when you might fall. Yalashimba, may the gods guide you, the mystery we are—Effina."

By the time the Reverend learned the peculiarity of the people who had held him captive, it became clear to him that he was in it for a long haul. Many months passed however, before he came to grip with the reality. The land was filled with great orators, skilled men with passion about their beliefs, arts and great intimate affairs between lovers.

Like all creatures of the earth, bound by a certain tradition, some of the Zong's traditions were sacred; especially the class order. This was imprinted into every child from birth, and they were taught to strive and live by it.

The land of the Zong was divided into many clans, towns and villages far and near. Some were separated by rivers or mountains and some were spread out between pastures of plains, swamps, prairies and savannas. According to the history and particularities of a town or village, it was honored in that regard and the same language made their bond unbreakable.

The law of the land was the same for all Zong. Warriors, common men and women were expected to live by the rules and code of ethics, or offer their necks for slaughter or pay a costly price of some sort. Offenders or Mebzongbre were punished absolutely.

However, within this mixture and complexity, there were three main gods of the land: N'Daygmong, the father, Monshung, the punisher, and Usula the mother. Next, there were five priests: Seeynie, Magello, Zongdah, Yore and J'rum. Nephrotone was the last of the priests and also the only prophet. Any other prophecy was met with death.

The Zong also had several guardians or messengers, who interacted with the people, the gods and the priests. These guardians or messengers were referred to as the Sadomrah. The Sadomrah were creatures that that either lived with the people in town or with the priests in the mountains, each serving a specific purpose. A typical Sadomrah was a beast, a woman or a man, and they ranged from the most violent to the most adorable and the passive. The nature of their deeds depended upon the purpose for which they were ordained. Some Sadomrah could be seen typically walking about town harmlessly mingling with the people, but then, again, other Sadomrah came at night and took an offender away into oblivion. Some gifted Zong had their own Sadomrah as a protector that interceded for them between the spirit world and the living. However, The most violent ones were kept in the forests to protect the shrines of the gods.

All requests were made through N'Daygmong, the Father god. The legend of N'Daygmong was as old as the land itself. He was the provider of everything the Zong needed and the defender of all who believed in him. The spirit of N'Daygmong lived in a boy, who resided in the mountain surrounded by the Spirit River and the Shrine of Usula. The boy was filled with power once the spirit streamed through his core.

The power of N'Daygmong had remained among the people since then, and had been transforming from one boy to the next in each succeeding generation. Such magnitude of power was taken with great awe and supreme readiness. It was a gift from the Spirit River for the chosen boy. There were fishes in the Spirit River that carried this quality and mothers had mixed feelings about accepting this precious responsibility, for once a pregnant mother ate such fish, the forming embryo within her womb became possessed with the qualities that were suitable for N'Daygmong's spirit. No one knew however, which fish it was in the river that they could eat or avoid, and the birth of the new N'Daygmong was always unpredictable.

These fishes were very rare and only three existed at a time. Once the mother ate the fish, she would dream about the future. In her dream the priests chose her boy. Later on in the boy's life when the time was appropriate, a Sadomrah came to the mother in the dream and informed her. The Sadomrah would direct her to a path in the forest where the boy was abandoned so that the Sadomrah took him into the mountains and he became the next N'Daygmong.

It was said that the power of N'Daygmong was bound to deform him who possessed it. As the spirit entered the body, it contorted; and according to the strength of the bone, heart and spirit of the body, which housed the spirit, so was the magnitude of the transformation. Sometimes it was an appalling transformation, which began from the head even down to the toes. One feature of the current boy housing the spirit of N'Daygmong was that he was part snake, and part a lizard. His head had continued to grow and was extremely large and, at times his body was unable to hold up the weight. It was said that his spit was an acid that burned through the skin even down to the bone.

Usually if a mother disobeyed and refused to submit to the request of the priests, the land suffered maladies and drought, and even death on the rampage. But when a mother willingly gave the child, she and her family suddenly got a pot of wealth and their lineage remained blessed forever. No family was allowed however to have more than one N'Daygmong from their lineage.

Ultimately, this boy, who was now N'Daygmong would come of age and become the father to the five priests through the mother god, Usula. The ordination of Usula was never a willing process for a virgin was taken from the comfort of her parents because of her parent's iniquities against the land. When a Zong offended the land greatly, if the punishment did not warrant death, this Zong was to give up a virgin daughter for sexual intercourse with N'Daygmong. The virgin was to remain celibate until a designated age before she was given to N'Daygmong. According to the Zong, at that unspecified age, the age when N'Daygmong's appetite for her had grown, this virgin was also at the pinnacle of her sexual starvation, and therefore she was receptive to bearing the Priests and prophet. When the time was at hand, the virgin was taken into the mountains in N'Daygmong's Shrine against her will and she remained until she was impregnated by N'Daygmong to bear sons and daughters, to succeed the current Priest and prophet.

The priests and the prophet in combination were also called the Fathers of the Land. Their tasks were vast and their duties were many. Mainly however, they were the mediators and judges of the people. They stood as the portal to the spirit world and as the voices of the ancestors to the people. Only the Fathers of the Land and their Sadomrah visited the shrine of the gods.

Amongst the five priests there was always a priestess and her name was Yore. She had direct link to the seas and oceans of Meheyassahapunawa and was therefore referred to as the Water Goddess. Yore controlled the tides of every liquid streaming from and to the land.

The mother of the Fathers of the Land, who was the virgin taken from her parents was also called the Black Lady. She was called so for many reasons. She was never to taste the follies of this world again. She became sacred even though she lived among men, but she was avoided and reverend with great awe. Her children were to become the Fathers of the Land and she was to sleep with N'Daygmong the father god, the boy turned into a beast.

The act of choosing the Fathers of the Land through the virgins was one of the most brutal processes of the Zong ritual. After every childbirth, the baby was determined if fit to be the Father of the Land. If not, the baby was thrown into the Spirit River, perhaps to be reborn with perfection and become either one of the Fathers of the Land or a common child through a natural woman. At the end of the process only five babies would be saved: a girl and four boys.

Usually the virgin mother, the Black Lady died before her duty was completed with N'Daygmong for her tasks were tedious, as she had to produce five perfect children at any cost. There were many virgins about the land waiting to take her place because they too were selected because of their parents' offenses. It was just a matter of time and perhaps appetite, for the father god to call upon them for duty. Sometimes it took more than two Black Ladies to birth the Fathers of the Land.

As the Black Lady walked about the land, still with the family, they were a constant reminder of their parents' iniquities. Though it was painful to see an innocent child forfeit the beauty of life and live with a beast until death, this virgin was also a blessing to the succeeding generation of her family. The Zong believed in order to please the gods and wipe the slate clean from generational misfortunes, an innocent virgin was the price for the gods to pardon the family's offenses. Sometimes it was a lad, but this too was gruesome for his arms and legs were broken and he was fed to the snake god, unless he miraculously had the qualities needed to become a Sadomrah to the Fathers.

If the Black Lady survived the Shrine of N'Daygmong, she would be moved into the Shrine of Usula, as the gateway to the Spirit World. Once she was taken unto the shrine of Usula, she would meet many other Black Ladies who had served their parents' offenses and survived N'Daygmong's Shrine as well.

The Black Ladies were also known to the Zong, as the Sadomrah Usula, for they were waiting for the spirit of Usula to come upon them.

Furthermore the accomplishment of their duties as mothers to the Fathers of the Land made them supernatural. A Priest's Sadomrah came into N'Daygmong's Shrine and erased their minds in a fashion that granted them a new life, making them a pure Sadomrah to their people. The Black Ladies dwelled to the east of N'Daygmong and were not permitted to live with man again. They had contact with the spirit and they were, therefore, of a higher standard than man. They remained in the hills until death; unless the spirit left them suddenly, which meant they must come and live among men again. In this case they were the rejects of the society for even the spirit rejected their body after suffering for the land and bearing sons and daughters to become Fathers of the Land.

Legend had it that a woman who was rejected by the spirits and left Usula shrine was a disastrous omen and was to be surely avoided at all cost. Upon her death, her spirit dissolved into thin air and entered into any woman that she laid a finger on, defiling and possessing them with unwanted spirits, wantonness, prostitution, miscarriages, and other filths that lure their lives and damage them in the end.

"Fear her greatly, if she was rejected by Usula's spirit! Both men and women, hide from such a beast; for she has a dark taste for your specimens, unless impotent, then become her friend."

When the spirit rejected the Black Lady, she was found at the entrance of the town, brain washed, crazy, innocent, useless and most often cold. This was a rare occasion however, for no woman who had endured the sight of N'Daygmong would give up the privilege of reaping the grand reward of becoming the next Usula. There were many Black Ladies in Usula's shrine but only one had the main spirit of Usula. Every other Black Lady was a pure Sadomrah and servant to the one with Usula's spirit. They would have their terms when the current Usula expired to the grave. The spirit would then choose the next Black Lady to serve as Usula.

Becoming Usula's Sadomrah however, was a suitable niche. It gave the Black Ladies complete powers and multiple tasks among the people. The Sadomrah of Usula cleansed the land of impurities and assisted mothers in need. It was said, with such status they travelled on winds at night and no man looked into their red fiery eyes. In this state of their lives they were extremely valuable to the people. They were set on pedestals and revered with awe.

The Sadomrah of Usula could also interact with the people on complex and simple levels and performed countless tasks. They were the most merciful of the divine spirits, giving children to mothers and fathers, establishing orders and settling domestic disputes among troubled families.

A wife who was found to be disobedient by her husband and close to punishment could call upon one of Usula's Sadomrah who would plead her case and save her life. Suddenly a Black Lady would appear with glowing red eyes, in the night, in a form of a ghost floating in the air like water vapor, smoke blowing through her nose. She would call out to the disputer, mainly the man, and warn him to desist from beating his wife or the punishment he had planned to give her. And then, the Black Lady would disappear into the woods to her natural dwelling.

It was said that every woman had a Sadomrah from Usula protecting her virtue until separated by the grave. It was a misfortune when a girl's Sadomrah died. It meant that she was vulnerable and alone in the harsh world of the Zong. There would be no one to plead her case and save her from the harsh hands of her aggressors. It was said that when many misfortunes befell a girl at once, it was a sign that her Sadomrah was dead, for it was never known when a woman would lose her Sadomrah to the grave. Thus, she was told to tread lightly and not offend.

The Sadomrah of Usula also took care of the sick, the possessed, and the needy. She was what the tender hearted Zong needed. It was said that her spirit came and slept with the sick at night and made them well by the morning. It was also said that she came and took the possessed away to flush out the bad demons from within. At the middle of the night she also came in to town and blessed the inhabitants, nourished the crops and fattened the herds. In the end she was the mother goddess.

The last of the three gods was Monshung, the snake god and the collector of the waste of the lands. He was the hated god and the most violent of all. Even his Sadomrah were violent to the point that they ate each other out of anger. For this reason only one Sadomrah existed at the gate of his creek. This Sadomrah was the strongest of all and had eaten the rest of the pack. It was said that this Sadomrah was tied to the Priest Zongdah and was therefore called Zongdah of Monshung's Creek. Zongdah of Monshung's Creek was frighteningly ugly and deformed unnaturally. He suffered greatly from scoliosis and his left leg was as large as a lymph edema patient. Legend recounted that this left leg was filled with boiling bile of anger, which boiled up to his head and caused sudden, unpredictable outbursts of anger that had lasting effects on his victims. This Sadomrah was always restless and committed violent acts for odd reasons. He was called the extreme assailant, for he broke limbs of offenders and fed them to his master, who also existed for only one purpose; and that was to sink his teeth into that which the society had rejected, condemned and prohibited. Every offender, anything vile, Mebzongbre, impure entities, people that have diverged from their duties of worship, men, women and children with abominable infirmities, every diabolical beast were given to Monshung as food. He was the final punishment, which one feared and would go to extreme lengths to avoid. Monshung was both a male and a female in one body.

When a man or woman was given to Monshung, such death was a disgrace. Monshung's Creek was the nastiest place on earth due to the nature of its duty. The site reeked with odor that could kill a flying insect, for it contained specimens ranging from spilled out guts of both beasts and men, and slag and mire of centuries of feeding on bloody creatures. There were sometimes rotten cadavers of mammals lying by the wayside and the foul smell could shrink and crumple the hair lining in the nose. It was said that the Sadomrah guiding the creek enjoyed these smells and sometimes partook in the eating of the creatures given to his master by the people.

Regardless of their extreme theology and beliefs, the Zong were a contented group of people in their own fashion. All men, most often, respected and honored the gods and the rules of the land. Chastisement was reserved mainly for harsher crimes like being a Mebzongbre, who were treated with the "left hand" as a Zong would say. Those who also committed unpardonable offenses that had lasting consequences for the land and could not be alleviated under any condition were also given to Monshung as food. However, the Fathers went to great lengths to avoid feeding their sons and daughters to Monshung and usually fed him other roaming mammals of the forest and offenders like Mebzongbre caught in the act of worshiping another god

A local Zong was however, as free as a free flowing river and was expected to perform only two rituals each year. One was for his crops for the farming season and the other was to protect his family from maladies that came too easily to the land. There were other rituals for mothers needing a Sadomrah to guide their unborn children. They made other sacrifices while pregnant and asked that a Sadomrah left Usula's shrine to visit her at the day of her labor to take possession of the child and guide that child throughout the life journey.

Furthermore, if a parent wished to find the right destiny for the life of their newly born baby boy, the parents took their children to the motherland called Zuxbaha for the blessing and ordination by the Priest Zongdah, the only Priest a common man or woman was permitted to see.

In the natural world away from the shores of the Zong, for other cultures to understand the origin and the existence of the Zong could be a source of contention because of their rigorous and strange rituals and beliefs. But a subjective understanding across the universe of our existence, the reality of life is always expressed suddenly. The common truth is that a child is born and life begins. Faith and beliefs are the products of the aftermath. Even the strongest of faith has doubts sometimes, and no man or woman has the slightest idea about his or her origins. Faiths and beliefs may suggest some reliable and comforting perception of our existence and perhaps our origin. But in the end, the search for meaning, origin and a purpose of existence remains a debatable reality varying from one culture to the next.

For the Christian man, like Reverend Isaac Kline or any other councilman, the search was over. The empty sepulcher was evidence that the resurrecting Christ defined the origin and destination of man on planet earth. However, this narrative was just for him who believed in the resurrection and the hope of the returning Christ. But in this great and mysterious universe, the Zong and the councilmen were still separated by these differences in beliefs and, now, they were clashing furiously against each other. In the end, one must dominate.

If the God of Reverend Isaac Kline existed, he must prepare his hand for the god of the Zong; because, the Zong were sure that N'Daygmong was the creator. When the first Izeonah came to their land and attempted to stop them from following their rituals, the Zong believed N'Daygmong was the reason they reclaimed their land. The gods were their guidance to the other world and a gateway to their ancestors and peace—a rule they religiously followed in order to live a life bound with privileges.

The Zong knew well what they needed to survive their foe the Whiteman. As in the past, when they returned to a true worship of N'Daygmong, the God of the Whiteman could not stop them and N'Daygmong brought great Maladies that purified the land. Although the remnant of the Whiteman dwelled in the hills in hiding, their elimination was just a matter of time. The Zong will find them and clean the land forever!

Now that Reverend Kline was on their land, they became vigilant to follow their tradition and pray that the gods help them overcome again. From the inner to the outer lands of the towns and villages, the word of the gods echoed even more. All rituals must be followed.

And so the Zong stood religiously, enforcing their hierarchical order, even down to the least of them. Excluding the three gods and the companions they kept, there was a simple, yet very important order of leadership within the Zong society. Every Zong was born as a common or local individual who chose a destiny after being born. Yet, it was clear no one knew what the gods had instilled into one's bosom as a burden for his people.

As a child, a Zong began laying his own foundation from which his prowess, his weakness or fame derived. The greatest achievement of a boy in the Zong society by age fourteen was to be selected by a leader of the Zong elite warriors called the Zongah. A group of Zongah is referred to as Zongy. If he failed by that age to show his competence so that a leader saw him and took him, he was to accept a trade or become a farmer. A girl had to be a good housewife and master the duties of motherhood. Her mother was expected to have spent time and energy trying to teach her.

Though girls were expected to bear these tasks, they were also called "the foundation of life" because a girl chose her husband and the men begged for their wives. It was a ritual known as the *Mensochsue* and it happened every harvest season. A girl's first *Mensochsue* began at age twelve. However, it depended upon her willingness to participate. Furthermore, she was under no pressure by anyone and could choose to remain celibate until age thirty. At this age however, she would be forced to choose her husband or she was sent to Usula's shrine and she became a special Sadomrah to the people.

The art of war was in the veins of a Zong. Their fierceness, since the Izeonah was removed from the land centuries ago, had kept them restless until now. Many more Mebzongbre remained in unknown burrows, but the Zong had not given up on the fact that one day their land would see no more of the Izeonah or Ixeonah. They were determined to see the end of this fight. In this regard, the Zong had an army trained only to attack their enemy with the most violent force known to man. A Zong was trained to eradicate his enemy by any means, even if that meant he and the enemy were to see their end in an instant. This training was perhaps unique to the land of Meheyassahapunawa.

The hierarchy of the Zong warriors began with the Zongah. He was the young warrior or the true disciple chosen by a leader. He had shown his competence and was therefore worthy to be called a Zongah. The Zongah was then to follow his leader, who was called the Gomrah or elder. A group of Gomrah was called Gomry. The Gomrah had troops of Zongy who went to battle with him. A Zongah that had shown his worth took training with his Gomrah, and sat outside the walls as the Priests and prophet discussed important matters with many Gomry who came from all parts of the land. When the Zongah's deeds were known and he was ready to become a Gomrah he begin to gather his own group of Zongy. The Priests sent him on a quest to search for his army. The Zongah would begin the most arduous of his journeys to travel to the lands of Meheyassahapunawa, searching for Zongy to call his own.

Before he departed for the journey however, he was carved with the seal of the Zong, a mark from the gods. It was engraved with the heads of a snake and a man joined to the body of a woman. To engrave the marks on his body, the steel brand was heated in the fire and struck to his upper back. And then he was taken into the Damned Forest, by his Gomrah, and left alone with a goblet.

This initiation was at the will of the Zongah wiling to take this step. And only a Zongah worthy to bear the name Gomrah could survive the Damned Forest. To do so, the Zongah was to first please the gods, and have the love of the land imprinted on his heart, for the Damned Forest was the last place for a man. There were beastly Sadomrah residing within this forest that ate the testicles and eyes of men and left their bodies to decay in the soil. These Sadomrah were said to reside at the borderline between the world of the living and the dead. The Damned Forest itself was the border between the world of the dead and the living. Anything that existed there was an abomination and a terror for the living. At time when a Sadomrah living in the Damned Forest lost his way, it was said that he came to the living and spread terror and killed like a plague. The Zongah willing to become a Gomrah was sent to this borderline world with his goblet, and was expected to survive and return to the living to lead his group of Zongy.

When the day of his departure to the Damned Forest drew nigh, his life up to this point was celebrated. A feast of nourishment was set before him and he was given a few harlots to ease his manly nerve. A death dance was performed, for it was never certain if he would return to the living once more. So then they cried for him, and he cried for himself. It was a weeping event that lasted for three days. The next morning, the Zongah arose early while all remained asleep and he embarked into the bush, heading for the Damned Forest. He would meet his Gomrah along the way and he was given the goblet to take.

The goblet contained a special juice called "the goblet of death," for, the Zongah was to drink it when alone, and survive the wrath within. It was said, after drinking of the goblet, the Zongah died for three days and lay in the open. His mouth remained open to flies, insects and all other creeping things. First he must survive the drinking of the goblet, then the crawling insects; and then, if he had not been eaten by walking beasts, a starving Sadomrah, or bitten by venomous reptiles; and nothing had laid a deadly egg in his stomach, he arose and ran into the world of the living. He was then ready to become a Gomrah.

When he arrived at his house, it was said that he wept first, for half of his darkest days were behind him, and he must now enjoy and dominate the remaining. Then another feast was held and he ate and was merry. His first meeting after his arrival was before the Priest. A specially made ring, from the hand of N'Daygmong, was given to him. At this point he was treated like a prince and was sent on his journey to build his army of Zongy. He was now a travelling Zongah.

At every town he entered, he was welcomed by the Gomrah and was treated with great regard. It took years for the travelling Zongah to return to his homeland for he had to take the best of men. At each village he resided in, the Gomrah took him about the town showing him capable men he would chose to follow him. It was a privilege to be called by a "travelling Zongah." This meant there was potential to be a Gomrah some day. When the Zongah had gathered up a sizeable army pleasing to him, he brought the troop to his homeland and they were given a spot in which to build and settle. They were then trained and tested by the travelling Zongah's Gomrah; and when they passed, each became the Zongah to the travelling Zongah. The last ceremony was an initiation of the travelling Zongah into the realm of Gomrahood. The feast lasted for several days. From then on he could speak his mind and sit with the Priests, the prophet and other Gomry like him forever.

Most Gomry were leaders and elders of a town. However, there was no limitation regarding the number of Gomrah within a town. They had power to rule their Zongy, sentence and override laws—even punishments of death at times. Once a Zongah became a Gomrah, it was irreversible until death. It also came with indispensable status that had great weight, respect, and power. He could only be uplifted from there forward. And if he became so powerful that his stature grew beyond the expectation of a typical Gomrah, he was to bear the last and highest rank of the land, which was the *Gamrah* (not to be confused with Gomrah).

In the outside world, a king is great, but not greater than a *Gamrah* in the world of the Zong. A president can veto but could never have as much influence as a *Gamrah*. Not every generation saw a *Gamrah*. It was a rare selection by the Fathers of the Land, for the *Gamrah* was god in a human form. Every now and then a god came and lived among the people and he was the *Gamrah*. The Fathers of the Land dreaded this, for once a man was named a *Gamrah*, all power was given to him. He was more powerful than the Fathers, and no man talked to the gods but him. He became the first and then, the Fathers were second. They consulted him first, then the gods, for he was god, now, among men.

The power of the *Gamrah* could only be spoken of as absolute. It was the power every child dreamed of having, an envied position that was only given to a Gomrah who had grown powerful in leading his Zongy and had proven his strength to bear the burden of Meheyassahapunawa as the *Gamrah* to the people.

There was always a group of Gomry who, the Priest often predicted, would achieve this mighty status. However, many a time, before they matured enough to show their prowess, they were either overtaken by death, or by some unfortunate circumstances that arose and robbed them of the chance. For such a potential Gomrah to reach this standard, he must have surpassed all spaces between man and the divinity, and shown immortality warranting the position. When this power was given to a Gomrah, he took a drink from the Spirit River and from the breast of Usula, making him immortal, divine and a god.

When the *Gamrah* was old, he was taken to the hills of N'Daygmong where he grew wings and became as white as snow and he flew away, rejoining the gods once more.

A generation who had a *Gamrah* was a blessed one, for when the *Gamrah* was old, people came from far and near to see him and give him messages to take to their dearly departed loved ones. He sat, helplessly drained with age, excessive violence, and apathy and was too old to move. Gomry, who wished to one day become like him, carried him about and they sought to gain his blessing. Usually these Gomry had abandoned their Zongy or given them to a travelling Zongah. As the *Gamrah* began to be carried about by the Gomry, many would come and sit at his feet lamenting and reminiscing about those days when so and so was alive, and how life was now different in their absence.

Great singers played and sang, with tear-stained visages, telling the *Gamrah* about their cries when they buried so and so, what song they sang at the grave, and who the children had become. Then, as these people traveled from far and near to give news, suddenly the *Gamrah* would go to the hills of N'Daygmong, waiting there to be transformed and taken back to the ancestors and maybe to deliver the news of the wellbeing of the Zong. It was now the end. The circle and search began again.

Part II

Chapter Ten

The Son Of Zion

*T*he suffering for the Gospel came to the Reverend, unexpectedly, in the land of the Zong. The hour he must take his last breath seemed to have come faster than expected. Uda and his men were taking him to the motherland, Zuxbaha and there, his fate would be decided. Yonder, the clouds cluttered the heavens and the horizon showed the beauteous landscape covered by projecting mountains. The fog sat above the beautiful clips and mountains of volcanoes seeped heat and smoke to the surface. Visible sights still held the stains of winter's melting snow and draining valleys of water and mud. Erosions on stones made way for the remnants of that which the sun had found to melt.

Another area held the sparse green grasses, wet dying ferns and less ripened budding plants slowly wilting in the passing autumn heat. The shadow of Spring was settling in on the not-so-green leaves which sat below the fading trees shooting above the men who, by then, had galloped for hours and were approaching the town.

The night had already fallen and the echoes of life and lamps and fires beamed from the town and reached them below the valley. Crickets sang serenading songs and fireflies lightened their way with their flickering taillights. The dry warm wind blew a dejecting feeling of loss for the men approaching the town with the Izeonah, for they knew their master was in trouble with the land. Above the hills, the sounds were made greater with jubilant and anxious noises of both young and old. Some were in forms of songs, and others were just babies needing care. But all were extremely loud, and the Reverend knew the songs were for him.

The news was already the talk of the town. Once more the Zong were the mightiest of all men. The Izeonah were defeated. The last of them sailed away from the shore with shame and sorrow. More importantly, there was one being held captive in the hand of the Gomrah Uda, another mighty man of their race, who fame echoed far and beyond the borders of the land. Led by a lady Sadomrah of the town, they celebrated the return of their sons and the defeat of the Izeonah. Uda and his Zongy rode into town reluctantly passing the energized crowd in silence. In their midst, the Reverend seemed calm and composed. He was afraid though, very afraid, for the masks of the celebrators were not only frightening, but also they came close and some pulled at him in an odd ways. Some even spat fire into the air and blessed N'Daygmong for his success at protecting his children.

Bound in chains now the Reverend was forced to retrieve his mental bible attempting to disappear from the carousing crowds of Zong. He tried to quote a Psalm but it was useless then. The voices were loud, violent, and distracting. He breathed louder and louder hoping for some form of release, then suddenly something came over him, and he remembered the conversation he had with Nora's grave before embarking for this journey. 'Yes it is time Nora', he said to himself, 'I am coming home. Really, to be absent from the body is to be present with God.' The tugs and pulls now were only an echo in the background as the world he imaginarily slipped into came to life.

It was 1930 and he was home for vacation. That night he stayed up late with his father and they talked about matters of the heart. It was a curiously deep topic for the father to share with him, because for the first time his son was brave enough to talk about other manly things. In time past, their discussion was often about solving empirical problems, talking about the constellation of the far, far away galaxies and discussing the political upheaval of the time. His father was growing old and from his standpoint as a philosopher he knew it was time to teach his son a few things about love.

"Love is an intricate subject, that is incomprehensible for him who never felt it, but real and strong for him who is living it, my child," he said, glancing at his son from behind the heavy lenses that put a dent over his nose. He made this statement to invite his son to join in the conversation. The young Isaac was always a serious boy and this had not changed since he became a man. However, for the first time his father saw a different side of him, glowing with happiness as he talked about Nora, the blond girl who made him happy. This gave his father joy and encouraged him to continue the conversation.

Only two days earlier the young Isaac Kline, Jr. had returned from college with a smile for that blonde girl, who always asked him strange questions at the cafeteria. She was not a shy girl, and because he was a quiet man, he was intimidated at first by Nora's questions. She smelled very sweet then, even in the midst of sweet smelling rolls and melting jellies. And day-by-day, her voice grew sweeter with every question. Nora's favorite questions, which she asked him almost everyday were, "Why are you so quiet? Are you afraid that I'm going to eat you up?" The quiet and shy Reverend became uncomfortable with her sometimes, for she was loud and drew attention to him as he stood in line with others to get their morning meal. He began to notice that she was always his server in the cafeteria, and oddly, it pleased him every time to see her lovely smile behind the counter. He was aware that Nora was the only girl who really cared about what he said, and though she was loud at times, but she was lovely and he would later smile alone in bed when he reminisced about the experience. He began to look forward to breakfast, lunch and dinner in the cafeteria, for it was the only setting where he received any attention if even he felt it was negative at first. Unlike Nora, most women thought he was strange and never engaged in much talk with him. His conversations usually pertained only to chemical reactions or the galaxies far away, and these subjects were foreign to most of the girls.

He liked a girl once, but then she became engaged to his roommate. Once in their dorm she managed to sneak in unannounced when the roommate was not present. They talked a bit that afternoon and then strangely, he confessed his love for her. She laughed at first, almost mockingly, and then kissed him calmly on the cheek and told him he was dreaming. A few weeks later she snuck in again with his roommate and they made arousing noises on the other bed above him. It was becoming a bit regular for the Reverend and his roommate. In a week he brought the same girl twice, standing at the door with an almost burned out cigarette, the girl cuddled in one arm. He asked the Reverend for some privacy. So, the second time around, as he stood at the door the Reverend knew he was about to make the same request, he voluntarily decided to give him the privacy. However, the Reverend was not completely out yet and their voices had begun to fill the room. Oddly, from the Reverend's perspective, they were loud and strangely menacing, along with the squeaking bed. The Reverend had to leave the room in a hurry for the cafeteria. There he saw Nora, for the first time not behind the counter.

He and Nora had been having some lovely eye interactions, brief conversations, and strong smiles during suppertime, but they never spent alone time together prior to this day. The companionship that afternoon was like a match made in heaven. She was not loud then, and she confessed to him her true feelings. Yes, she was in love—but with another man. Nora told him about a student whose attention she sought by being loud. For some reason he was always in line with the Reverend at mealtime. He was Nora's neighbor and she liked him then. On one drunken night at a local festival she met this student. He was charming to a point that he managed to lure her in for a kiss. Later on in the week he invited Nora to his room and wanted intercourse. But Nora refused because of her Christian faith. Though she liked the young man, she was not rushing into life at such a drunken pace.

She wanted to get to know him more, and she was up early every morning to walk with him at the train station. Nora had hoped that the young man would see her inner beauty first before he engaged in pressing on her breasts and moving his fingers about her thighs. But the young man wanted nothing to do with her after her refusal to give in on the first attempt and he sent her home. Later in the night, she saw him outside with another girl and he made sure she knew his intensions. The next morning he walked with the same girl to the train station and pretended that Nora never existed.

Nora was furious and used the Reverend then to get the student's attention, but it had not worked. Furthermore, this particular night, as she sat with the Reverend, tears welling up in her eyes, she asked him some more odd but concrete questions this time. Perhaps it was from the frustration of what this young man had done to her. Suddenly the Reverend was a shoulder for comfort and she talked and he listened. She wanted a man who would become a friend first. As she was taught by her mother and had seen in her house, good friends were great lovers. These needs, or wants, came out in a form of a question as she stared innocently into the Reverend's eyes and asked.

"Do you read the Bible?"

"The Torah sometimes. I am a Jew."

"Of course." Then she stared toward her feet and what was inside her longed to come out. She had to look again into his lonely eyes and asked. "A soul mate, does the Bible mentions the idea of soul mate a lot?"

"I read the Torah sometimes." He pronounced, again, calmly. Then Nora looked toward the door and before she wept, he resumed his speech, "My father told me that a soul mate is not biblical and it's not found in the Torah." He paused and looked at Nora. Suddenly her face became sad and she took his statement for discouragement. This made him sad also, and he suddenly became brave. It was as if every fear or nervousness was lifted. His voice became clear and he comforted her.

"My father also said, I must believe in soul mates and I believe. To me it simply means two lives made by God to live together forever. As much as I don't see it in the Torah, I'm sure it's not biblical too Nora, but we must believe in soul mates. It can be real to us if we want it to be. It can set us free." Nora turned her teary eyes to him with surprise, wanting to hear more. The Reverend then bowed his head. Though all he had said to Nora was true to him, it still had made no difference in his life. So he cleared his throat making sure as much as he attempted to comfort her, he would also show that he was vulnerable. "I am just as confused as you are when this subject is brought up, but I don't talk about it because I am always alone and I sincerely believe in soul mates."

"How so? Have you ever been in love?" That was a strong and poignant question. He made up answers in his troubling mind before saying yes. However, the fact was, he had loved different women several times before, but they did not return his love. He was either made a fool of, like this night he sat with her now feeling rejected, or by every squeaky sound of his roommate's bed. Sometimes girls liked him, but they quickly became tired of his uninteresting companionship, which involved nothing but total quietness and boring conversations. He was not a virgin though, because on some nights that he was drunk, he would stumble into a local brothel, waving his cash, and he left with empty pockets and a heart filled with regret. At other times, the girls made him feel the way she, Nora was feeling now. It was a mutual experience and he had probably given up on love then also. These were some of the reasons he talked less to girls, especially the ones he admired. And even now, as he felt hurt, knowing Nora's true intention for her talks in the cafeteria, he continued to console her until she smiled and the tears went away. In those innocent moments that he spent with her sitting and counting their heartbreaks, love and marriage was his last expectation. However, their bond grew stronger in time and yes love and marriage became their reality. But now all that time was past, he was alone and Nora was gone.

Thinking about Nora's tears that night was painful now, even as the angry Zong put him down from the horse. He was sure he was alone and if he cried, he felt God had left him as well. There would be no counsel and comfort to push his tears back into his head. He toughened up as the Zong pushed him toward his designated demise. The angry shouts and mockeries suddenly appeared as if he was Jesus and the unknown language about him was the chief priests crying, "Crucify him!"

He bowed his head. Death alas. Then, quickly he lifted his head before the thought of death left his shivering nerves. He looked ahead at the house he was pushed toward. It was dark and two giants stood with pieces of wood and heavy chains in their hands. Their faces were covered with masks, and the crowd continuously screamed, "Crucify him! Crucify him!"

The angry mob's voices echoed behind him still. Then within the midst of their voices, a lone voice echoed from the crowd. This time it was plain, simple and astonishingly, he understood what it said. He was sure they were not angels but real Zong speaking. Still, the voice was distinguishable and it resonated in English. The Reverend was in such a strong grip that he could not turn his head, yet the strange voice sounded from the crowds.

"Blessed are the feet of him who brings the Good News of the Gospel to the Zong. His feet are beautiful for they carry life eternal. And even unto death, may the Lord stand by his side, for in the land of the Zong he might need all there is to endure their wrath."

"I must take a glimpse!" The Reverend thought while he fought to look behind. Yet, all he saw were the disappointing faces of angry Zong shrieking their profanities in the tone he could not understand.

When the mob dispersed, the feet of the man who brought the Good News were not left empty. There were two pieces of wood held by the two giants, and chains extended from the wood were tied to the Reverend. One chain extended to his neck, one around his waist, and one to each end of his extremities. The blocks of wood were enormously heavy that the men had to tow them in order for him to walk. They threw him into a muddy pit where another chain was tied to him and extended to the top of the pit, and hocked to another piece of wood that lay across the pit. The Reverend could hear their voices above the pit as they laughed and spoke in their language, Dahnkka.

A few hours later, a few more men came and they yelled some more and then they pulled the Reverend out aggressively and took him to Uda. A crowd of energized Zong stood in the night, their blades glimmering in the moonlight, their faces stern and sweaty. It appeared, so far, that it had been a tense night of discussion between the many Gomry present and the Reverend could feel it from their demeanor.

The Reverend was cold, from the wet drying mud that was now painted on his skin, and he trembled before the giants. But the rage in Uda's face was swift to wipe the shivers away. There stood Uda authoritatively. He yelled and his men shoved the Reverend over the horse. It was a rough handling and the Reverend said his last prayer as they drove him away, speeding through the cold night

They brought him to the center of the town where more Zongy and their Gomry gathered. On the other end, there was a podium made out of wood and stones, which was raised higher almost overlooking the town. A crowd of people with lights, lamps and glimmering firewood gathered and whispered staring curiously at the intense Gomry and their Zongy encircling the Izeonah. At another end more Gomry entered into what would be a hill but with dark mouth. It was as if they vanished, instantly, upon poking their heads into the mouth of the hill. Then Uda got down and spoke some more, still stern, poked his head into the hill, and vanished as well.

It was late by then, but no one slept and the crowd was filling the square. Many came from their houses with lanterns and blankets and found seats waiting for the Gomry to finish their discussion. Then one by one the Gomry came out and rode away with their Zongy until Uda resurfaced at last and gave a disquieting stare at both the Reverend and his Zongy. He inspected the Reverend quietly and then walked away toward the now greatly increased crowd. He climbed the podium and looked over the attentive groups, which became silent as he stood above them, staring firmly below.

His men brought the Reverend up. And then the crowd was stirred up and murmured again. Uda yelled again and silenced them. The refreshing oceanic breeze lightened the air between the houses and above the white sandy land as all eyes stared straight at the sparsely dressed Izeonah who was frightened, tired, and by then hungry.

Uda spoke with conviction. With a thundering voice he announced, "The Izeonah is not our friend but a pet waiting to be slaughtered! I am sure by now you are aware. You would not treat your goat like a friend. I warn you, there will be serious consequences against him who defies these orders; for the Priests proposed this order."

The people murmured and babbled to themselves. It was out of curiosity though, for the Izeonah was viewed with the same repugnancy as the Ixeonah.

Another dilemma was in the air. They were aware of the recent attacks and the escape of Basin. Furthermore, in the east they heard sounds of the Mebzongbre tool, the gun, which was faster than their spears and arrows. Some Zongy were taken on a speeding horse into the healing house the other day. Then the horse came out, its coat stained with blood, and it was taken to the creek for washing. It was important that they listen to their

Gomrah who was indignant that he had missed the first chance to strike the Izeonah. He was now aware that this had pushed his name down in priority for becoming the next *Gamrah* of the land. An Izeonah on the land meant a coming upheaval, either from those Ixeonah in the forest or the Izeonah themselves, who might return in numbers detrimental to the Zong.

The crowd, however, set aside their curiosities and listened to the Gomrah on stage. The Reverend stood amid them confused. He knew that this night was just the beginning, and his days were numbered. Once again, Uda made it clear through his demeanor, his glare and his dramatic performance, that the abstract reality of death knew the white's man existence and the blade he Uda, now swung from his shoulders would make it a reality. When he had compelled the group to keep away, they watched him and his men carried the Reverend away into the dark night until the sounds of horses and their silhouettes melted into obscurity. The Reverend was taken back to Uda's house and thrown into a dark room.

Chapter Eleven

The Not So Enchanted Path

*I*t was the month of December and the harvest season had just begun. It was the time of feasting, finding a mate and small celebrations that lasted for several nights. Everybody was so full with harvested crops that some could hardly sleep, for they suffered from over-stuffed bellies. They had eaten more than the stomach could hold, and they sat in groups with bloated bellies burping or farting uncontrollably and playing games of chance at the moonlight. The sky was clear and peaceful and the moon sat at a distance above and became the light for the night, shinning its beauty for the men to toss their dice and take their chances.

The time of harvest also brought in good fortunes as mothers ate together from earthenware pots and stayed up late drying the meats from the traps over a crackling wood fire. The pounding of mortars with pestles could be heard from between houses, while children held hands and sang to Usula for her kindness of the good harvest. The children were also full of new rice mixed in palm oil and hot peppers. And this took them to the center of town, first, to burn off the peppers and then to celebrate life.

It was a busy night for Uda at his house after putting the Reverend away for the night. Even his house was vibrant with noises and people eating their fill. Those who missed the gathering came over to stare at the Gomrah who had apprehended the Izeonah and to see the Izeonah as well. When they annoyed Uda he screamed with rage and, the crowd dispersed.

Uda lodged himself in his room. It was a place of memories of battles won and glories attained. It was a large room with a fireplace at the center. At one end hung the skulls of valuable enemies killed, ornaments and tools he had used to bring his enemies down. A large stool two feet long built out of mud almost like a master bed was planted at the right side of the door. In it, a bed made out of bird feathers and hay compressed into a bag made out of cotton and shaped like a bed. It felt soft when rested upon. The other end had a mat made out of ropes and was spread across the floor until it reached the fireplace at the middle. A small opening, called the prayer room was behind the mat close to the trophies hanging against the wall.

The door to this room was covered with a dull mirror, and a three-foot clay pot filled with water was adjacent to the left of the mirror. A table was next to the water and had three small pots for washing. Two feet towards the left, there was a wide opening hole that had its drainage outside. This hole was plastered with aluminum made by a local blacksmith, who was called the "melting man," for he used special tools and intense fire to melt the aluminum to the desired condition and shape. These were one of the skills the Zong acquired from the Izeonah before the days of "Yiti." At night, these shaped aluminums would shine bright from the firelight. Uda did his sacrifices and washing into this hole which was cleaned every morning by a Zongah, who hoped one day to follow Uda's footsteps and become a Gomrah.

When Uda entered the room, he stared at his defeat-stricken face in the dull mirror and then at the ornaments. There was a bag hanging on the wall and he brought forth some sweet smelling incense and candles. He lighted them, chanting a few prayers. Later, he went to the water pot. He washed at the hole and took a seat. It was a few minutes later that his daughter, Nicaso, brought his meal. He sat by the fireplace with its orange light glimmering in his face and projecting his large wavering shadow against the wall. He washed his hands again and plunged them into the food. The meal was a purplish starch ground from eddoes and a Zong-like herb. The soup had the leg of some meat sticking out of the serving pan. The aroma was delicately sweet and Uda salivated.

Standing over her father, Nicaso asked with caution, "Mother wants me to ask, must we make a meal for the Izeonah?"

"He is none of your concern or your mother's. Take that news to her and stay away from the Izeonah!" Uda responded, a bit harshly and continued to indulge himself with his meal. "You must be preparing for your Mensochsue and not be occupied with the Izeonah. Make sure you choose right this time, for I will not be a father of the bride to a lazy fist man who can't plough my land. Leave my sight." She exited quietly, perhaps regretting ever mentioning the Izeonah.

Uda was a huge, strong and large man with a giant-like figure. His palms were large and his chest was well built. He had large ears and he was bald with some hairs lining the sides of his head and heavy dark eyebrows. His large nose was shaped like the beak of a cockatoo, but with wide openings. His roaring voice was sometimes thunderous. He walked as if his heels would never touch the ground. He walked on his toes severely, and this became more extreme when he was angry. Though he was well respected and honored in the town because of his status, he was a man of quick temper. His family feared him greatly, and so did the people of the town.

Tonight, there was a lot on his mind to be bothered with and he perhaps regretted being so harsh to his innocent daughter. She was his only girl. Uda had a wife Sophon, and three children: Dio, Nicaso and Niejon. They were a very honorable family in the clan of Yasulah. Many far and near knew his fame and prowess. Unlike many Zong, especially his good friend Gomsug who had over ten wives and counting, Uda was much closer to his family. Regardless of his temperament, he had time to entertain his family at the fireplace, and told stories that made them laugh. But he knew that his behavior this afternoon, which allowed the Izeonah to deceive him with what he now considered sorcery that allowed his foot to touch the land, made the Priests very furious at him. The consequence, which he expected soon, made the food taste like gall, and was hard to swallow. His forefathers were now disappointed in him, knowing that his action broke the spell of the protection they had placed over the land for centuries. And now the land remained open to the Izeonah invasion.

As one of the Gomry, Uda's duties came with many territories. He was also a man of principles and values. His commitment to the Zong was a matter of passion and of the heart; and he was ready to pull his eyes out for the Zong, if it was required for their survival. Even though the coming morning held serious consequences for his actions, Uda had not lost his faith in the gods of his people. He was one of the Gomry chosen to one day attain the status as the *Gamrah*. But with such demonstration of his incompetency, which had threatened the future of the Zong, there was doubt in the air. However, unless the Priests had other plans to take his life instead of allowing him the chance to set things in order, Uda struck his mouth with the purple starch, and looked at his statues of victories and glories hanging on the walls. Redemption was surely ahead.

He had power, influence and could set things right before the day came if he were ever to be punished at Monshung's Creek for his iniquities. As a leader of approximately three hundred Zongy, he had his way of convincing the Priests. However for now, he must draw on his time of invincible adventures, where he and his Zongy had led massive attacks against the Mebzongbre. He must call the Priests' attention to his prowess in time of war and show his capability, to the Gomrah, that he was ready again to rectify his mistakes. The hour was coming soon to meet the Priests for his sentence.

Uda shivered and smiled simultaneously. "I am Uda the son of a great Gomrah. It must go easy. I will escape a harsher punishment." The end, he now perceived, was: he, Uda, as the great *Gamrah* standing on the hills of the Zong, face and hair as white as snow, beard dazzling from the chin, all this blowing in the wind as he held the beacon to the land which he overcame by his manly persuasions, strength and love for the land. "Come quick, dear morning, for I must see my Fathers of the Land." He licked his fingers and bit some more on the dry meat. It was good nourishment; and he ate to his fill for he was a large man with vast appetite.

When his fingers reached the bottom of the bowl, the town crier was announcing the most anticipated event of the night. Whatever worries a man had, it was to be postponed for another tragic day. But for now they all were focused on the activities ahead, which was to commence in a few hours.

The existence of the Izeonah was only a dimple into the grand plan that was set up for the night. And when the Gomrah had made clear to them what they must do, in regard to the Izeonah, all dispersed and the plan for the night was resumed. The event of this night, which happened every year at the time of harvest, was one of the greatest events in the life of a young Zong. It was time of the *Men-soch-sue*—the time when the youths of the land pulled in from all corners to the motherland Zuxbaha, to civilly battle for love. Like no other event of the Zong, this event was considered the blessed gift from the gods; and those who attended the occasion realized their importance in the society.

Nicaso, Uda's daughter, was among this unique crowd and when the town crier's voice resounded in a distance, it sent excitement down her young spine. Nicaso was excited not only for the event, but also because a tall young fellow named Jebu, who was one of the most famous bachelors from the town of Bethelot, was in town.

Jebu came from a famous and wealthy family. He had a drink with Nicaso two days earlier and was smitten by her charm. Nicaso was in for the kill and Jebu was already wounded with love for her. Other girls envied her, but it was too late. Jebu's demeanor had changed since he met Nicaso and he was therefore repulsed now by any attention from any other girl. He wanted to show Nicaso his commitment so that she chose him. It was said that Jebu descended from the line of the Izeonah, for his skin was lighter than many. His generation had long left the God of the Izeonah and they were now devoted followers of N'Daygmong.

After that second evening with Jebu, Nicaso fell into her mother's arms softly thanking her for raising her well. Now, it was the climax of what she had been feeling. Finally, she could release herself into Jebu's arms and be taken away into the land of peace, tranquility, happiness and ultimately love. It was sealed. No other girl could be as charming as she was. Even Jebu had sealed himself behind closed doors to avoid temptations.

The stars were up and the moon was icy. The soft wind from the north was allowing its light and windy texture to seep through the center stage, which had taken a few months to prepare for this occasion. When the voice of the town crier came through echoing to the youths of the land it was time to fall in love and perhaps play the games of love.

At age twenty, Nicaso was more than ready for love. Her mother warned her, seriously, that she should take more than one suitor instead of settling for Jebu. Though he was the ideal man, the mystery of the Zong still existed and the unpredictability of events proceeding thereafter might be uncontrollable. However, without anticipating a negative outcome, her mother felt that love should take its course and control in the end. And Nicaso should give in to the man who made her spine shiver softly at every glance.

Like many beautiful girls readying for this wondrous event, she had reached the age of maturity and such advice from her mother was only a suggestion. Nicaso knew and was aware that it was her Zong right to choose one or as many as she wanted and allowed them to battle for her love. Though, only one was expected to win in the end. This was the normal tradition that every man anticipated and lived by.

This ceremony was reserved for special girls who were considered the work of the goddess Usula, to have kept them this long from falling into the distasteful lavishing pleasures of men. They now had the chance to be the only wife to a man. It was in this fashion that Nicaso's mother, Sophon, had married Uda and had trained her daughter to do the same.

Besides the spectacles of the goddess' handiwork to preserve these girls, this ritual also brought great satisfaction to the proud parents of the girls who attended, for, life had not cheated them of some of their hard labors and it was good that their daughters, who were now women, would choose their husbands. A girl could not leave her husband once she took him at the Mensochsue, for the decision was final, but a girl who reached this ceremony had the eyes of the goddess; and she had the wit and character to see through the heart of the man she must ultimately bear children for and grow old in his bosom.

Choosing a man was the only time a woman of the land was free. There was no question from anyone in her family or the land, for it made the gods angry to deter their servants from their destiny, and there must be no interruptions in the process. He who did was worthy of being stripped with arms locked in the back, leg lashed with strong cords and the neck tied to a stone and cast into the Spirit River. He must drown head first, and perhaps next time he was reborn, he would think twice before deterring a girl from living out her only dream given to her by the gods.

Many parents preparing for this event were aware, that if their child made the wrong choice, only the afterlife could free her. However, fortunately for the girls choosing tonight, the ceremony had another intricacy before the man took his wife. The more choices the better, and therefore, most girls took more that one man. This meant more works but with important rewards. The few men chosen had to perform additional duties for the girl; and the best man won the bride in the end.

When all was settled and done, all of the men chosen by a girl were to perform the last tasks before taking her to their fathers' homes. This practice was not polyandry but a unique form of courtship within the tradition of the Zong. The man had no sexual intercourse with the girl during his stay. The multiple men chosen by a girl were simply "working their way to the girls heart." Each man made arrangements and scheduled a time—a year or more, one at a time, depending on the wishes of the girl, and he left his father's house and lived with his potential bride to be. The transparency began thereafter, for the man would work to please her. His love and commitment then was to be tested by the fathers and family as a whole. He who was not wealthy performed hard labor. And he who was wealthy lived comfortably with her, enticing her with servants and other necessities until his term was over. After the term of each man was concluded, if the bride was not pleased, the man was sent away. The next man was called for his chance. In some cases the first man, being pleasing to the bride, would win her over and cut short the chances of the remaining men. At the end, the girl eventually acquired one of the men as her husband.

Zuxbaha, the motherland experienced a temporary influx of people this time of year, for people came from far and near for trades and to experience the reason the Town Crier's voice echoed through the dark night between the houses. The Crier's sensual voice called on all bachelors to arise from their weariness and slumbers and meet the women at the center of the town for the dance, laughter and joy. The Town Crier was a young female Sadomrah, with beautifully meandering curves like a wavering snake. She was a special Sadomrah that dwelled in the hills with the gods but had vowed to only charm men with her voice. She was once a part of the living and attended these ceremonies as a young and vibrant girl. However, she returned to the world of the gods and made it her home. In her cries, though she called on all to assemble, there were other stories she revealed, including her own. One could hear her mourning about the one thing she had never enjoyed. Love.

Long ago she had fallen in love with a man and had her heart broken thereafter. However, this broken heart of hers was not caused by her lover but by the mysteries of the gods. Her lover died early on, either by a violent malady or a sudden circumstance, which left the crier alone; and now, she narrated their tragic story and grieved him through her sensual but gloomy voice echoing over the town. She was almost blind for she had asked the gods to blot out her sight so that she remained pure until she met her lover again in the afterlife. In exchange for her sight, the gods gave her the power that he who laid his hand on her sexually would reach a merciless and fatal end.

It was said that her breasts were as strong as a grapefruit and her lips were as tender as the wind from Usula's Mountains. It was also said that the same breasts and lips were poisonous. However, some lucky man was allowed to once in a while coercively touch or suckle her nipples, but then his glands swelled and he died. A tourniquet, they called it, for him who chose to touch death wrapped in beauty.

The crier was free and roamed about and sometimes tempted men to touch her breasts. But only a fool did so if he had not recited the famous poem of the Olds, which was associated with the Sadomrah, the Town Crier of love.

"Bound and Desired"

These dark nipples of poison and passion,
I taste of you and die!
Your warm breasts, cold at times
Such a grip I am held in,
Must I leave? Must I stay?
I'm helpless even now!
The springbuck jumps higher at danger,
But here I lie, at your mercy,
Strike me! Wound me! Chastise me!
But do not turn from me,
Or hide your chest lest I die!

When the Crier's voice faded in the distance, the girls' mothers met and chose the colors and flowers each daughter would wear to distinguish her from the others. Sophon had chosen a flower colored white and pink as the color of clothing for Nicaso, and she made her a short cotton robe with little balls at the bottom. The dress stopped just above Nicaso's knees. Her long, dark and silky hair was braided and tucked with the wild flowers unique to her identity. Her dress also carried the flower, which was designed perfectly with spots. The flower derived from the riddle of abstinence suddenly coming to bliss. It represented mystery and was called Effina, for it was said a woman who wore Effina was a woman sent from the gods to ease the burden of her husband. He who wished to marry such a woman must be multi-talented, for the woman of Effina always posed challenges for men presenting their talents, but the reward, if accomplished properly, was that for which every man was willing to sacrifice all that he had. This made Jebu nervous at times. Though he had no talent and stuttered a bit, he was sure his wealth was enough to get him through any heart. And Nicaso, by far, was one of the most beautiful girls of her age.

There was also a girl named Felomine, who was to wear the Crown of Beauty, for she surpassed the beauty of human imagination. She wore the flower Effinata—called so for it was a flower of the Olds—bound and desired from the gods, but allowable. Far from death, Effinata had given the ecstasy that jittered the being of a man to the core but caused no death, as would the breast of the Town Crying of love. The rumor filling the moonlight then was that Felomine would be a source of great distress for him whom she found distasteful and reject in the end.

It was also a custom that men plotted from the time they arrived, hoping to intimidate one another to give up on fighting for the prettiest of the girls. Although it was pleasing to find love, it was said that at this Mensochsue, many men returned to their fathers' houses more brokenhearted than when they arrived. They were to present their talents for the women they loved, yet, there was no guarantee that the women would do the same for them, since the women held the final word. Many men, capable suitors for the evening, were ready to perform the most outrageous and extreme tricks for love.

With warm air, the beaming moonlight and stars and white sand through the town, mixed with the voice of the sensual Crier, the atmosphere awakened the most charming bachelors of Meheyassahapunawa. It was said that unless impotent and a heart filled with bile of impure pleasure, all men of the land arose from far and near. They left the comfort of their homes, the sweetness of bachelor-hood, the lust of chasing other girls (who could not wait to choose, or widowed because of some circumstances ranging from their husbands being sacrificed for offending the land, killed in battle, or of natural occurrences), and strode, some for terribly long miles, to be present for the night.

Some worried that the same incident, three years ago, with Uda and his daughter might happen again. In that ceremony, when Nicaso was seventeen, she took four men as her possible suitors, but they all returned to their homeland unsuccessful. She was a young girl who had allowed the men to work for her. However, she never got around to choosing any as her husband. And leaving the father's house without the bride was a shame. One of the men was a fine artist and he had drawn the first portrait of Uda and his family. Then, by the third day, Nicaso's interest in him had diminished and her father sent the artist on his way to his hometown. That morning many gossiped and watched as the frustrated artist left the house bewildered.

Though a woman was allowed to take as many suitors as she desired, if there were more than one girl for a man, then the tides were reversed. The man became boisterous and arrogant as he wished.

Jebu and Nicaso had promised each other a few hours before the Izeonah had arrived in town that there was no need for games and that their love had erased the taste for another man or woman.

At age twenty, Nicaso was a girl with tender grace, bright smiles and a strong spirit. She had the sharp cheekbone of a goddess, firm breasts and long dark hair. She had light and tender skin, which were marks of the descendants of the first missionaries. She resembled her mother in her young years with curves, possibly to induce strong and adoring stares. Her long fingers and toes were even adorable; and her soft voice, which also came in her nature, was guaranteed to set any man at ease. She was tall with heavy eyebrows that made her eyes like a bouquet of flowers, or the budding of young dandelions. Her stares were sometimes considered a stab, for they could make an angry man smile, raunchy men beg for mercy, and a sensitive spirit wish to behold.

A man once gave Nicaso a strange compliment and his friends ridiculed him. The man had considered Nicaso's feet as something he could fit into his mouth. She was flattered, blushed a bit but moved on without giving any importance to the comment.

From all corners, the zeal of searching for love had intensified the youth of the land. It was, by then, midnight and the moon was at its peak, glassy and bright. The young bachelor men were the first present. Dressed in their own fashions and according to the manner in which they preferred, they were ready for the girls.

The second group to assemble was the fathers of the girls, followed by the mothers and then the spectators. Niejon, the youngest son of Uda, brought a stool for his father and a pot of fermented wine. The young and excited bachelors assembled on the other end somewhat nervous for the occasion. Among them was Uda's eldest son Dio, staring about nervously. He was like his mother in complexion, but had the visage of his father. He was tall, slanted a bit, with soft hair and wide eyes. His forehead had a strong presence of diabolical influences, for it was thick and thought to have strange force; and many feared that one day he might use it to kill a man. Although many regarded Dio that way, tonight he only had one focus, which was to find a wife. The young lad felt a trembling within when he saw his mother wave to him, along with the strong but encouraging stare from his father. He then turned to his friends and they made exceedingly great noises. "Let the beauty out! Bring the beauty to us!"

The last group to assemble was men who wished to have a second wife. The girls, in a certain way, chose these men for unknown reasons. They must have been very enticing to get a woman free of care to fall for them. Usually a Gomrah, a famous Zongah or a travelling Zongah, was fortunate at times for this aspect of the game. Gomsug, the Gomrah of the fiercest Zongy, a friend of Uda, sat amongst this group. He had gained four brides in this fashion.

Gomsug was a man of sarcasm. He was a slightly fat man with wide mouth encaging his large teeth and chubby cheeks. He was losing his already thin hair, which he fixed in a fashion he hoped would cover the baldness in the middle of his skull.

Gomsug was one of the tallest giants of the land with an intimidating appearance that brought his enemies to their knees. The night on the ship of the Izeonah, his name was the most pronounced and feared. He descended from the line of giants that the Zong and other foreign lands honored. Even in Bentuh, one of the gods the natives spoke about had the name Gomsug. This Gomrah now finding his way in the crowd came from such a distinguished lineage. As Gomsug made his way in the crowd he was aware of Uda's pending sentencing. Though, there was still some unsettling contention that he had put Uda in command that day and Uda had failed him by allowing the Izeonah to step foot on the sand, he was sure to use this to his advantage. Gomsug's nose was like that of a violent bull breathing tensely and loudly, while his large vibrating ears sat on each side of his head like a donkey's. He had strong and powerful hands that grabbed like forklifts clasping together with immense force; and he was a man bound by no morals. His strength was said to be that of many bulls rushing in disarray, and his battle cry was that of many gushing waters. He was a giant unmatched, and he was bold and supercilious in dealing with others.

This night Gomsug had come mainly to torture Uda; better yet, have the chance to take Nicaso as a bride. He always traveled with a gang of Zongy; and this night, they crowded the ceremony with an overshadowing power. He soon walked over to Uda, authoritatively, and smiled.

"My friend of the olds!"

"My friend of the olds." Uda responded.

"This is a great night to reminisce on our days of youth, huh?"

"A great night to celebrate." Uda tensed up and looked away. Gomsug smiled and raised his voice. This time he spoke louder for the young men were now in full speed with their noises calling for the beauties to come out.

"Nicaso may choose tonight, I suppose." Gomsug muttered with a huge smirk.

"Life is still good in my house," Uda replied with hope.

"We must all hope for such a life forever."

The crescendo of the drums began to get louder and louder, and the anticipation for the girls grew more and more.

Uda smiled, sarcastically, aware that Gomsug had an ulterior motive. Then he said, "She is bound by no pressure tonight."

"That is good, old friend, that is good." Gomsug said.

"She is twenty now and still has ten years to decide her fate."

"I am not sure, old friend, that I will be bold to say such a thing; but, perhaps after your sentencing?"

"I am a man who has served my people diligently. My mistakes are my own to endure."

"Were they mistakes?"

"I have called them what they were. I wait to face the Priests."

Gomsug smiled with an exhilarating pleasure and stared at the girls coming to the dance, "Nicaso is a beauty. Set your house in order; and may I warn you to prepare for the worst. I have heard the Fathers will be in swell moods, and N'Daygmong's penis has grown as large as three donkeys combined. A large specimen reaching up to his knees, bad for the Black Ladies."

Uda gave Gomsug a shocking look and Gomsug knew his words reached Uda's core. He continued his condescending rhetoric. "I am the future *Gamrah*, we all can agree."

"If you will be, then life is still good. But, O friend of the old, I look tonight for the bright smile from my daughter and her dance. May we expect a good night and leave the future as it is."

"You speak with wisdom, old friend, but remember amongst the Gomry of Meheyassahapunawa, only my hands have found favor with the Priests. I stand a better chance." Gomsug gave another blunt and filth-ridden smirk. Looking into space, as if to pull down a cloud of imagination upon Uda, Gomsug pronounced wryly, "I am sure no father wants to imagine his daughter between the cold and dusty legs of N'Daygmong." Then, with another glaring stare, he concluded, "Only me, my friend, only me. I might save her then. But we can always discuss this later." He tapped Uda on the shoulder and walked away.

Uda looked with disdain, but was soon distracted from his anger when he saw his daughter appear under the moonlight in her white cotton robe. Her happy face, a jive-like dance, made him proud to be a father and he watched with joy.

The girls were in line dancing and jumping and the suitors stood on the opposite side watching. A multitude of men, women and children stood as spectators and made a big circle where the dancers gathered. It was a rowdy crowd, but with the awareness of not disrupting the order of the night, for this dance was the most provocative event anticipated each December. No man would like to be thrown out before it began. Furthermore, it was an entertainment worth the insomnia; for the beauty of the bouncing girls called for all respects. The singers and drummers played relentlessly with melodies of love songs.

A fat lady with hanging chin, but with elaborated vocal cord, opened her mouth and sang beautifully. Her voice was soft and melodious, which silenced and lulled the crowd to their greatest state of calmness and serenity and they dreamed and wished for love from the cores of their hearts. The fat lady smiled and began with ridicule.

"This is the saddest day for the impotent man; for what is the use of living when he has no strength in his veins to indulge in the orgasmic pleasures of life? He may eat the entire forest of wild plants' roots to reduce his sad state, but there is nothing compare to this night of men ready for what the daughters of the land brought to the dance. For the impotent man however, there is no pleasure to gain by it. Between his legs there it lay, cold and lifeless!" The crowd roared with laugher.

She began to make hand gestures and moved about. The fat lady was dressed in pantaloons but half naked. Her sunk-in navel and belly hung over the stripes of napkins and rags bound together by a string and wrapped around her waist in which the string sunk. Her face was tender and her eyes were bold. She had white teeth and lusty smile, which was illuminated by the shining moonlight; and she was lovely even in her state of corpulence. Her name was Majoree or Melody, for she was known as the lady who brought life into young hearts. Melody had many lovers; and she was known for her wantonness and lovely persuasions. She never had a home for, wherever she went, there were men desperate to become her suitors. She never attended the Mensochsue, for it was useless for a lady like her. She was also called the expensive whore; and she sang her lovely songs in this fashion. In her serene tone her corpulent state never appalled the rowdy men, for her voice was the best in the land surpassing all. She moved with grace and her eyes glared with complete confidence. Her smile, which showed her white teeth, was calming and lively. With these combinations, and her voice, Majoree was a beauty worthy of exploration.

Behind her stood a choir with alto, soprano, tenor, and bass voices. Alas, it was time for passion! Her mouth opened to the sky, her vocal cords vibrated the loudest soothing sounds. The drummers threw their muscular arms against the drums and blam-blam-blam.

At first, it was the dance to entice the men. Each girl intended to know her man by giving him the strong glance as she danced. It was a silent language of its own, and the men had to answer it in their dances as well.

"Do you want me?" They asked with their eyes, their feet, their fingers, their waists and hips, their chests and every part of their bodies that moved. "I am precious—I am tender—I want to be happy—children, I want children—I am to hold you if you cry—When you bleed--am what to hold! —Here I am—do I charm you? —Will you love me forever—I can be yours…" So on and so on.

Depending on the girl's need she communicated through her eyes to her lover and he in turn, used his eyes to see and not blink at the crucial moments while the girl danced. All his nerves were then ratcheted up with pressure for it was then that a man proved his potential with a stern eye interaction called " The Lover's Silent Eyes."

For the Zong, love was an intense matter and whosoever sought after it must have diligence and remain intense until love found him or her. Each girl approached the man she admired and took him to the dance ring. The dance was evocative and entertaining. The elbows were tucked back, arms and hands forward weakly, and legs thrusting rapidly forward with strength in an angle, as would one dancing a jive. They jived away jumping here and there, arms and legs thrusting in all directions, flirting with the eyes, smiling and making impressive moves. It was life at their feet. It was life in their eyes, and the crowd roared when a girl showed her move of the Old, which was a dance that derived from the gods.

When it was Nicaso's turn in the ring, the noise grew louder. She became very evocative in her jives. Among the men lined up for Nicaso stood Jebu, poignantly. He was a bit nervous but ready to hold Nicaso in his arms. Her smile was soft and stabbed through his heart. She was happy and her eyes were filled with unexpressed feeling that when she took Jebu by the hands, he melted in her eyes and he tried his best to stay on course and remain on his feet. He was a proud man, though, as envious eyes stared back at him from the crowd of men hoping for a chance with Nicaso, it was clear love was present. Eventually all applauded for the lovely couple; for, even in their eyes, the language of love was expressed. When they left the dance ring, Nicaso's mother, Sophon, wiped tears away from her face and thanked Usula for the blessing.

Another beautiful girl appeared in the ring and subdued her lover with the loveliest smile. More beautiful girls one after the other came into the ring and transformed their lovers to their desired states.

Then it was Felomine's turn. The drum stopped as she made her grand entry. All men held their breaths, for it was her first appearance. Because she was chosen to wear the flower of Effinata, which was death but gave life, she had not mingled with them; and then, there she was, tamed in beauty. She removed her veil and all gasped for air, for her face shone under the moonlight like a lone star resting on a dark velvet cloud. With authority, she called in the first suitor and the drums resumed. He nervously walked toward her and was unable to maintain his movements. Soon he was sent to his seat and then Jebu was called.

Jebu looked away, respectfully, declining Felomine's request. Once again the crown gasped. The next man fainted before he was called. Felomine took her seat, waiting for the man to be revived. A group of Zongy made a hot stone and laid it to his neck. He jumped and trembled. His eyes met Felomine's again, and he fainted. The crowd roared with laughter and they dragged in away. Felomine called upon the next man. She danced with them all, and took her seat along with the girls.

When the dance was over, and the lovers took their seats for a rest, the orator of love appeared to teach the lovers a lesson about life. He was an old man with wrinkled face. He had a hat made of wild ropes that carried fresh flowers, which contained each type of flower held in each girl's hair. He was bear footed and dusty. He was a shirtless man with cotton shorts. His wrinkled nipples stood sternly in his chest and his belly was flaccid. His mouth was almost devoid of teeth and he chewed and spat needlessly. He had a certain melancholy attachment to his visage, which had a natural softness yet, with a pitiful appearance. There was no ease to his movement; for he was old yet he strolled to the center ring ready to perform his duty.

The water drummers took their positions to accommodate the orator. The drums were alabaster turned upside-down into canoe-like woods filled with water and slapped with stakes. The orator erected his back and stood up with dignity, looking about the audience with pleasurable eyes. He opened his empty mouth and smiled.

"Ah....Love!" The orator uttered breathily. "What can I say about love? We are creatures bound by it—though those of you warriors here, you may wish for the vow of celibacy to live in the woods. You may deny my claim, but I have seen you in the whore house." The crowd roared with laughter, the water drum sounded, flowing with the beats of the old man's words. The orator pushed his forefinger under his lower lips, searching for words. "I was there and I was out." tom-tom-tom, "but I knew what love was." Tom-tom-tom, "The whore house is not the place." Tom-tom-tom.

"The whore house is only a place for release not a sanctuary for love you old bum!" A young lover screamed from the crowd.

"Yes," tom-tom-tom, the orator responded, removing his finger from beneath his lip quickly, as if he remembered something important, "I can guarantee you that after a while, without love, your empty heart leads you to places." tom-tom-tom, "Darkness places," tom-tom-tom. "Love must save you." Tom-tom-tom.

The orator floated his hand through mid air, as would an ocean wave, and stopped suddenly, as if he touched a sharp edge. He paused and made a strong face. "Slowly you slip to the deep oblivion," his voice grew louder and stern; and what he said he also felt. "Slowly and slowly you are lost; then you vanish, in thin air, in despair and from the lack of touch of tenderness," tom-tom-tom.

The old man pointed his hand at the crowd, turning in a circle. The depth and density in his voice almost like a cry caused great silence.

Then he smiled lightly as if what he said was to tantalize the stern and attentive crowd. "Ah, such ridiculous expressions I make claim to, why take heed? I am not here to make you weep, but to celebrate," tom-tom-tom. "As I have lived, I have seen the face of love," tom-tom-tom. "And it is beautiful," tom-tom-tom. "It is very cold." Tom-tom-tom. "It is hot." Tom-tom-tom. "Love is disheartening," tom-tom-tom. "But I can tell you, young men and women foolish with love tonight, you need love to survive this cruel world," tom-tom-tom. "You need it to find your way in this lost world," tom-tom-tom. "You need it to suffer in this desolate world," tom-tom-tom.

"It found me from right where you lucky youth sit tonight." Tom-tom-tom. "You are in the stream of life to experience love, you lucky fools," tom-tom-tom. "But, do not complain of your lovers yet, care," tom-tom-tom. The old man clenched his fist as though he grabbed the abstract essence of love in his palm. "Take gain of it!" Tom-tom-tom. "Use it." Tom-tom-tom. "Take pleasure in it." Tom-tom-tom, he smiled in reminiscing thoughts.

He reached into his bag and pulled out a fistful of white powder and blew it into the air. Some powders remained on his nose and made his face white and ridiculous. Little laughter came from the crowd, but mostly all were attentive. The orator looked about and spread his frail arms. "Don't be foolish to desecrate love, as life would do unto you like this vaporous powder," tom-tom-tom. "Tonight I stand before you, a widower and alone; groaning for my youth," tom-tom-tom. The orator paused, took in a deep breath and tears set in his eyes. He looked to the moony sky and saw the stars beaming their lights from the heavens. His lips began to tremble, and then he stopped suddenly and turned to the lovers.

"I'm longing for my wife," tom-tom-tom. "I'm longing for a new life!" Tom-tom-tom. "I say to you now, take not this moment for granted," tom-tom-tom; "for love will lead you as high as N'Daygmong's mountain, and as low as Monshung's creek." Tom-tom-tom.

"A man with a sweet wife is like a saccharine fruit tree between the gnarled vine tree crowded by thorns." Tom-tom-tom. "In her core there is life and care blossoming for his use, which gives him grand approval for life," tom-tom-tom. "A man who loves his wife is more than Gomsug or Uda in their fiercest hour of battle," tom-tom-tom. "Their arms are fixed with love, and the power is a blow to annihilate the earth," tom-tom-tom. "Love's pain can soften a stony heart," tom-tom-tom. "They say, even the after life envies life because of love, which is felt both in the flesh and the spirit—the after life is a spirit world." Tom-tom-tom.

"Speak a clear tale, you raunchy old man!" Another lover interrupted loudly. "If love is two times sweeter in this life, I don't want to die; and if it is painful too, I won't want it. So tell me, you old ragged bum, what shall I do to have it all?"

"Love." Tom-tom-tom.

"I am bleeding already." The lover looked at the girl of his attraction and smiled. Others laughed along with him.

"Love can heal you," tom-tom-tom. The old man took some white powder from his bag again, and sprinkled a bit in the air. He took more and blew it out.

Tom-tom-tom-tom-tom-tom-tom-tom-tom, the drummers resumed the play and a few more men got up to dance with their lovers. The old man took his seat and the grand event, most anticipated was about to unravel. It was time to select a mate. The men were about to show to their potential wives what they had in terms of sustainability for the family.

A young fellow, not more than twenty-five, arose from his seat suddenly, and requested the hand of Felomine. Going to his knees he called out to her, "My Felomine, take me as your man and let me live this life spoken about tonight through those who once lived it. I have money, wealth and most of all my heart is filled with love for you."

He was in ecstasy of expressing his great art and his voice echoed in the thin dark air like an unknown melody ringing from some unknown destination. The moon was fading away by then and the clouds were returning. The wind of the soft December morning was fleeting through quietly. The moment was right. And while the young fellow stood awaiting Felomine, she smiled and asked him to sit and wait.

Then, a sudden disappointment rushed to his face. But two girls quickly battling for his attention soon distracted him. The younger girl came up and exposed the tip of her breast in an evocative manner and gave the young fellow a soft and daring smile. Her eyes were innocent and glowed under the shining moonlight. The young fellow was smitten and followed her without giving a second thought to Felomine. It was the end— the young woman had won him over.

Her friend cried out, to no avail. But the two lovers took their seats hand in hand while the older girl stood in the ring confused; until the other fellow, who had fainted so many times throughout the night, came and swept her from the ring with a stern cry of rescue, "Take me now!"

It was the end. She rested her eyes on his childish face and gave in. Thereafter, many more came and talked, showing their wealth, tricks and talents. Great poets appeared and emphasized on love and life with eloquence.

Then Jebu rose from his seat quickly. A man from the neighboring town with immense zeal and wealth was present. Rumors had it that he came to lay claims on Nicaso and she was a bit curious. Jebu bowed before Nicaso, and his servants brought a mini-house built with gold. Such a magnitude of mineral wealth appeared so vibrant and evocative in the dark that Nicaso's heart leaped in her chest.

Jebu caressed the house with ease and sighed, slowly lifting his eyes to meet Nicaso's. "This is Nicaso's house." He said and looked about the crowd and then back into Nicaso's face. Her tense nerves felt at ease. With a strong look he spoke like a true Zong. He then turned to Uda, and Uda stood upright, showing his authority mixed with respect for his future son-in-law.

Suddenly the stuttering man was fluent and spoke his deeds with ease. "I am a man bound in wealth. But, Nicaso, you are the wealth I wish to keep forever. Take me now and let me have the dream I have had since my eyes rested on yours. I breathe calmness at the thought of your beauty by my side. You are the only gift I have asked from the gods. If life promises any gift, I want it to be you Nicaso. Here I am standing wealthy, yet poor until you become my wife."

Nicaso suddenly jumped from her seat, in the loveliest yet innocent manner, and rushed into his arms. The crowd was quietly watching with pleasure, for Jebu was a quiet man who had spilled out all that was within him. It was a magical moment and Sophon, who could not reach her husband, gave the loveliest look Uda had not seen in a long time. It was a flashback to their youthful days.

But, before savoring their merriment the rich fellow, who Nicaso was curious about, posed the challenge. Rising form his seat he yelled out tensely, "Fathers of the land stories of the Old, it is my duty and my Zong right to protest this union for Nicaso. I also expect to receive affection and love from her!"

Nicaso became a bit frightened and appalled for this fellow suddenly appeared bold, authoritative and a bit arrogant. Nevertheless Jebu, who was also short tempered, rushed for a fight. His wondrous moment was ruined so soon, which devalued his words. As a customary display at the Mensochsue, men were allowed sudden bursts of emotion since it was an affair of love, and Jebu was about to exhibit his emotions. However, as he moved violently through the night to assault the boldly standing gentleman, Gomsug yelled from within the crowd.

"Halt!!!" The voice had such power that Jebu suddenly paused, trembling from the echo. Looking about with arrogance and almost in a spiteful mood, Gomsug called out to the young fellow who had posed the challenge. "Come over and state your claim. This is about love." He pointed his fist at Jebu. "The woman chooses, not you. Shut up and let him speak."

Both men were powerless to protest, for they knew the reputation of Gomsug. His presence had even stolen the attention from the young lovers who were mingling into the corner after they had chosen their lovers.

"I chose Jebu!" Nicaso screamed with teary eyes.

Uda was about to rise to his feet and end the matter when the young fellow called out and took a piece of goatskin scroll from his pocket.

"I understand. But, before you are satisfied with your choice, the floor is still open and I must speak." He walked calmly toward the center stage and waved the scroll, showing it to the crowds. "I travelled the distant of lands to be here tonight. I had insomnia last night composing my words for you Nicaso. Even if you have chosen a man, it is only fair I gave you what is yours. It is my Zong right." He cleared his throat and made a strong face. "My name is Lomeh, the one and only true love of Nicaso. I am not here to cause strife, but to find love." He looked about him, making sure his previous statements had landed on keen ears. "If I must read now," he continued, "I am late but will still take my chances." He soon read out the long lists of prizes for Nicaso:

"Ten horses and five slave girls; a house with underground rooms and white aromatic candles; two golden spoons and a box of jewelry made from stones, rubies, gold and diamonds..."

Sophon's eyes lighted up and she was almost tempted to scream for Nicaso, "Yes, yes, yes." However, she mumbled from the crowd, but could not utter a word; for it was the time in the Zong tradition, that the mother had no utterance on her child's destiny. Nicaso glanced at her mother and saw her hands folded over her breasts, her eyes were beckoningly, projected forward. Nicaso turned to her father and he stood up firmly. The answer was in his eyes—the Zong way. Lomeh had listed countless numbers of things and he still continued on.

"Acres of land stretching beyond the great swamp of enrichment, where crops grow fat and brown, donkeys with legs made for strenuous works..." Lomeh squinted at the crowds; and there were mouths of astonishment glaring at him in dismay.

No girl in her right mind would decline such offers for any other particles of riches. Rarely did men like Lomeh come for this ceremony. Women cried for his love and lavished themselves at his pleasure, but Lomeh was a man who believed in love and the path to earn it. Until now, what he felt was an illusion. Suddenly he had found himself in bed with a woman who had betrayed him, hoping her goods would lead him to a soft heart. But it was later that Lomeh realized there was no love involved; and he sent the girl away in tears, and shattered heart.

And then, it happened again. Until now, he had concluded, love must have a dark and tedious road. The gods were obliging him to take the path of the Zong hence, the *Mensochsue's*.

Lomeh was not a shallow man, but, he was a bit desperate for love and as he called out to Nicaso while reading from his scrolls of riches, she cried out in tears.

"Stop!!" She screamed, "I want none of it!" She walked over angrily, and pulled the scroll away from his hands and tore it into pieces. Breathing vehemently, as would a weary mule, she looked into Jebu's eyes, piercing his soul to his core. Her luscious eyelashes were moving swiftly and with such ease that Jebu's heart rose up and he fixed his legs beneath him, standing like a man so that he did not fall from the pounding of his heart. "I love Jebu," she said calmly and ran to him. Turning to Lomeh, who was by then confused of the path of love, she sighed softly, "Sorry."

And with such utterances, a burst of clapping erupted. It was a magical display of affection for such an occasion. These were the moments that kept the huge crowd awake, unwilling to cleave to their beds in slumber. Such a celebration consisted of moody men, sorrowful women, charms and affections, great displays of love and great narrators of love stories.

Nicaso and Jebu left the stage filled with unspeakable happiness. Lomeh was allowed to say no more and he turned away leaving the crowd a bit angry and defeated. A few girls chased after him and their voices were heard in a distance within the dark night, as they tried persuading him to stay.

Suddenly he screamed, "Yi men lockah, Loc-men-la-sue!! Love is all I wanted! I want love," a few more echoing voices resounded in the distance and then there was silence. Lomeh was gone.

Soon the girls returned, nervously staring at the next men ready to display their hearts for love. There were a few more men who did not possess much wealth. Dio, Uda's son, was one of them.

Uda, being a Gomrah, had not brought his son riches as it had been expected. Though he was violent and well respected, misfortune had always followed him. The drought, a few years back, left his riches in a pile of dry despair and rubble. He was just recovering. Although he had a few substances he called wealth, which he was about to show, men before Dio, had expressed their loves multiple times and he knew his wealth was not enough to win a girl's heart. Thus, instead of wealth, Dio wrote a poem for the girl he loved.

Nervously, he arose with his passion filled eyes, and the warmth within fell over the crowd. Dio approached the girl of his dreams. He noticed a sullen disgust in her eyes and she twisted her lips in a condescending manner because Dio had chosen her. However, Dio, being so aroused with love and filled with passion for the girl, ignored the signs and recited his poem with eloquence and reverence.

> "The Lady With Long Legs"
> I speak for myself,
> For I am a man without much wealth;
> But, O, the lady with the long legs,
> How gay are her thighs;
> Their spreads are as delicate as liquid eggs.
> I am filled with awe, lust and love in her stares—
> So blissful I stand with mired thighs.
> In slumber or blunder, I am forever her fool;
> Though not that she cares,
> To take a second glance at my manly tools.
> But, O, lady with the long legs,
> Take my hands; here I stand.
> I am here to be your man.

The crowd applauded with laughter; for Dio's intensions were made clear in the poem. Suddenly, all eyes steered toward the girl expecting a reaction. She sat baffled and confused. Somehow, she enjoyed Dio's manly display where every word he expressed from his poems was followed by a physical gesture. At times, even though the girl seemed a bit embarrassed or disgusted by it, she continuously squinted at him blushing. Overall, Dio's performances and gestures were interesting combinations. The girl rose to her feet; perhaps angry or teasing the young fellow standing, aroused, eyes reddening and fixated on her tensely. Suddenly, she ran from the crowd and into the darkness, which was now dissolving from the coming morning light.

Dio chased after her, and they disappeared behind a compound and left the crowd amused, astonished and excited. This too, was an innocent demonstration on the part of Dio who, being a few years older than Nicaso was in the terms of the Zong, a young seed. Perhaps still, he was a virgin in that light. A woman grew up sooner than a man in the Zong's culture, and she would marry often earlier. However, Dio's infantile attitude, filled with childish moods, was not a shock to his family. Nevertheless, the girl he had chased after was no different from him for this was her first Mensochsue as well.

The town was almost visible through the morning fog. The cold wind was becoming chillier and the ceremony was beyond its climax. The spectators knew the drama was coming to a closure and most lovers had done their deeds of love. The rich men were most often arrogant, and the girls were in no regard giving up on an opportunity for wealth. This year the Effinata, Felomine took a boy from her town. He was the richest of all men attending the ceremony, and it was clear he was reserved for Felomine. He said a few words when it was his turn. Being fearless, he stood up and Felomine almost bowed to him. It was the end of the ceremony and those who had not gotten the love they deserved would wait for another December.

Melody appeared in view, well entertained by the young lovers. Her expressions and gay laughter filled her distinct visage and she sang the last melody, "The Farewell Treat." It was a song, which spoke of a father leaving his children and wives for the journey into the Damned Forest, hoping that he would return as a Traveling Zongah. But the violent Sadomrah within the forest ate his penis and heart and his carcass was left to the soil and worms. Then the mother looked to the east towards the gods and wept, for her lover was now in the afterlife and she was left alone.

Then she spoke of the cold wind of disaster, which blew on the family thereafter, for many men came and the mother was so filled with grief and without nourishment, that she gave herself over and over to every man, so that she might have food for her young sons and daughters. Sometimes she was tempted to give her young daughters, but then, she gave herself instead. And when a profane man asked her why, she cried, the Mensochsue!

In Melody's voice, it sounded as though she cried when she sang, and then she burst into laughter and ridiculed the lovers then parading with big smirks. She then gave the stage to The Orator, who came up again, already to express the harm of gloom.

"There is a mischief and an unknown future awaiting you outside of your happy days…" he then became passionate and spoke of senescence.

One by one the crowd thinned out in little disbursements, for all hearts were weary of the old man's gloomy narratives, and when he was at the end of his tale, those who were left were only his admirers. A few lovers who sat deeply enmeshed into each other had forgotten that the wind was colder and the morning sun was coming to town.

The night was over. The crowds dispersed, returning to their places of comfort. But as for Reverend Kline, there was no comfort in sight. In fact, he was not promised the coming morning; for the Zong, as he would later write in his diary:

"They are the most violent people, such creatures of God. How distinct they are, one must see to comprehend. Yet, in their unique quality, they find time for domestic matters. They have a language of their own; and there seems to be a fascinating prospect to their daily living. There is something peculiar about their habitat that one from another land familiar with the western culture, might suggest that once upon a time, there dwelled some westerners on this land. However, if so, it is a wonder; for there is not a trace of them, only the remnants of their way of life and technologies—well, of course, except if one looks at the mixture of complexions, where they range from light complexion to the darkest man who; a man in slumber may mistake him for a chimpanzee. These people, who refer to themselves as the Zong, are workers, farmers and fathers—one man possesses all these titles at once. Lord, I am amazed! Come and save me!"

Chapter Twelve

The Human Child

ear Isaac Kline, child of incident, here comes your full destiny at a blast. Shamed and unprepared, there you are, faltering and faltering into oblivion; and your eyes are cast against the sea. This insurrection you are unfit to withstand and the sorrow echoing now, must shrilly drill through you a hole, in this land, even with tenacious ego, the water is not yet tested; and the incident has arrived. Oh well, I wish you well.

His eyes were now that of a lost man, who the cause of his journey to the land of the Zong was beginning to escape his captured soul. Was it for the sake of the Gospel that he travelled to the land of the Zong, or, was it a quest for redemption from the lives he ended in Treblinka's extermination camp? The regretful journey he took to the northern part of Africa and ended the life of his dear, beloved Norah? Perhaps he should have given up a long time ago and turned his back away from his miseries, or God, mainly, when Nora yielded up the ghost. Perhaps he should have left the Jews to fight their own battles. Ah, these contemplations. Useless!

Uncertainty still filled the air; and if he surrendered these memories now and relinquished the hope for redemption, all that would be left would be vanity, and vanity, he could not have. Vanity was painful and dark. Bewildered, he would have run until these haunting thoughts turned to sweat. But he was in heavy chains cleaved to his limbs. Everything was heavy: the past, the present, the future, the chains and the guards standing outside the barn.

Two weeks after The Hammer D was smashed with bullets in the square, he managed to see his frail wife full of grief, bereft and on the other side of the ghetto. The man she loved was already covered in the gutter, body decomposing in mud and water. Reverend Kline stood afar and watched her with the most pitying eyes; and then he took his leave. That night he went up into the mountain at the summit and had pity on himself. Sitting in the barn in the land of the Zong, now with the horses, these memories were vanishing and new, but not so different ones were beginning to take shape. And while the night transformed into a different reality, it was no different from those nights as a soldier up in the hills where the soiled body of Frederick lay covered in ice.

Although there were no chains on his limbs then, but he was a prisoner to his actions. And if there were ever redemption or retribution from his past, he was becoming sure the land of the Zong promised little of that. The language was strange, and the people stared upon him with disgust.

He was cold and hungry. He was alone, a prisoner, a man and a Reverend? With the agony, growing with the chains, Rev Kline remembered the words of his good friend and leader, Rev. Elton Goodspeid, "The emptied sepulcher gives new meaning to life and revives hopes that even he, who is suffering to carry out the Great Commission, is pleased to endure; for, in the end, there is a promise greater than the endured pain. Who knows the day or hour when the rapture shall come and take the righteous along?

"None! Through the faith to endure to the end, the malice inflicted by the world, when the last day is at hand those who have chosen to follow the truth, will have saved the souls who will rise from the old moldy graves as the earth shall be separated by the glorious light beaming from heaven. When they crawl from their graves to meet the Lord in heaven, those who have suffered for their sakes will smile and say, 'my struggles came with a price. But it sets you free unto eternity. I am grateful.'"

These words, at the time spoken, were convicting. However, by the time the Reverend was held as prisoner, they harrowed through him like an open sepulcher peeling away at his condensed heart, unveiling that darkness he could not locate. He had not come to the land of the Zong to redeem any soul but his own. And he was not sure if he would ever reach that mark, which would give him the same contentment he felt long ago in his father's house as a boy. His hope stood ready to wither as the guards intentionally sharpened his ax all night, indignantly staring at him.

"Come and ax me, you savage!" He yelled, and rattled his chain about restlessly. The guards stared at each other oddly, and burst into laughter and ridiculed. They were aware that he was a rowdy lost Izeonah incapable of keeping his mouth shut. All he did was bring woes upon his own flesh. Laughing, the Guard with an eye draining of fluid, almost to a point of blindness, resumed the whetstone upon his ax.

The Reverend pulled away into the corner and turned his face toward heaven and prayed. "Lord, let them spear me, as I am sinful. I am filled with sin; it reeks. Come spear me! The bodies in the gutters and the stench of the dead—Please, don't throw my body in the gutter. Don't break my arms like Basin. Just spear! Just stab me with your long steel! Don't let me suffer long. I have had enough! Enough!! Yeah Lord, I cry for my soul and not my flesh. In this flesh of mine, I have seen atrocities that I cannot peel away. Therefore, please let the Zong do it quickly—are you pleased with my soul? How will they kill me? Will it be as fast as those innocent men slaughtered on the ship? Regardless, grace lord...grace. Let my soul be in your hands. The Reverend sighed and wiggled the chains again.

His melancholy stares seemed to hope for a voice, yet none came. Through his distress and groaning in chains, the guards thought the Izeonah had some spell; and they moved out into the darkness fearfully hoping the morning came soon; and that they were found alive. This Izeonah was evil and the prophet must find his fate or deliver him for slaughter by dawn.

All by himself in the barn, he passed the next few hours slowly and painfully with no relief in sight. But the thin air blowing softly, which he suddenly felt, called for life and whistled hope for another day. It came as a relief for the Reverend to look through an opening in the ceiling and see a bright star right above him. It was shining as if to communicate with him. He paused for a moment and realized he was carried away in thoughts.

His flesh had taken over and he had not stood firm in the face of his adversities and become the sacrificial lamb he had promised his fellow councilmen. The devil had intruded into his emotions to drift him in the place of doubt. He must get back up. "Get back up!" He whispered encouragement to himself. He wanted to rise with the Zong from the grave on the day of the rapture. It was his chance to set things right. He was not perfect, and he was a murderer of his own people. In that sense the Zong were not perfect either, and therefore, they deserved heaven as well. As a Reverend and an evangelist, it was his duty to accomplish that. "Take them from hell!" He said again quietly.

Soon his eyes shrunk and his face spread as if he would spit. "Vacate from me, Devil!" He shouted violently rattling the chains as if to pull himself away from the spot.

He looked at the star and smiled bravely raising his chest. "You are here with me! You are here with me like you've always been. I am not dying. I must live! I must live to see the Zong come to repentance. The devil is a liar!" He looked to the star again, and whispered heavily, "I must live!"

He smiled and looked into the air, and took in a deep breath of comfort. Soon his spirit was renewed and he jubilated in his chains. The star above his head continued to shine, brightly, alone in the clear moony heavens. The cloud passed slowly, giving the wind a wing to blow the Reverend with comfort and hope for life instead of death. Sleep was coming to him and his energy was gone. His body burned from exhaustion and vain contemplation. He lay back slowly, and closed his eyes.

Chapter Thirteen

The Visitation

When the Reverend's foot touched the sand, it sent a wave of panic across the land and made him an even greater foe. It had affirmed the prophecy gravely spoken about by the Zong prophet. Shaking in his shrine, with eyes almost drawn back into his cranium, the prophet spoke of great darkness ending the fusion of the culture forever, if the foot of any Izeonah from the approaching ship were ever to touch the land.

"They are demons in different complexion," quivered the prophet. "And to avoid such a destiny, kill them all before they kill and exterminate us all."

Sadly enough, with their struggles at the beach where many brothers met their demise and became food for the fish, a leader, Uda, allowed the consummation of the act. Disoriented by the revelation of his recurrent nightmarish dreams, Uda allowed the damnation to befall his people when he bashed his man to the side instead of the Reverend. When Uda was awakened from the mire of his dream, the Izeonah was safe below the deck of his ship floating ahead.

Those violent screams he made later on board the Izeonah's ship, with his blade quivering between his clenched fists, must have been too late, for the spell was lifted and the potential assailant was in their land. When he emerged from the ocean later with the nearly lifeless Izeonah swinging about his shoulder, the seawater escaping both bodies like a drainage, as shouts and praises of victories were elevated high into the night bound with cries of drowning men echoing from the burning ship yonder, the dark shadow of his deed was the stain in every Zong returning from the shore. Uda would have given up when he realized his deeds. However, a violent Sadomrah appeared in their midst and gave a strong command. If ever there was hope for the Zong again, this same Izeonah must be captured alive at all cost.

The Sadomrah had appeared suddenly within their midst, and was quickly followed by a Zongah from Uda's crew lying with missing limbs. The Sadomrah had eaten a part of him out of anger. Like a beast out of a terrible flame, steam leaked from the Sadomrah as it approached menacingly toward Uda, grinding its bloody mouth filled with the Zongah's flesh. It crawled on four legs, with its head in a form of a bat covered in very white hairs now bloody from the Zongah's flesh. The eyes were intensely white as if blind.

The Sadomrah's body was shaped like a leopard with shoulder blades pushing forward. The limbs, which stood about five feet from the sand were extremely large and made great disturbing commotions on the very ground it walked upon. From the neck down, the Sadomrah was naked. It had no fur or hair to cover its private parts. Its dark skin glowed brightly with oil, and strong billows of steam leaked out from it. A part of it had fresh burn marks, like a fire victim; and it shivered intensely. Growling, it breathed into Uda's face. Its obscured inner mouth filled with slimes and its teeth opened slowly before the Gomrah.

With a gurgling throaty voice, the Sadomrah cried out, "When the Izeonah landed his foot on our grounds, a stream of lighting struck my master and me. Gomrah, I am here to eat your genitals and convert you into a woman, for the Zong you are, you are weak! But I will not, just yet. I'll wait for another day."

The beast stood on its feet and every man within its range suddenly dropped to his knees and stared at the sand. It cried out, so menacingly that its voice, which was said to have been the cause of miscarriages in women, dominated the night even beyond the Izeonah's ship. Bring me this Izeonah, before this nightfall, or bring me your body for my nourishment! I want the Izeonah alive! Grab your blades and lead these men out to the sea. Massacre or perish at sea." Breathing intensely the beast got to his four legs again and sighed softly. "This is a shameful day for us all. I am saddened to put my sons and daughters in such a predicament, where I now expose myself. Now I must go and disintegrate into the earth."

Suddenly a strange and cold feeling ran through the crowd. The

Sadomrah had vanished.

This episode was then many days old. And though prominent in the mouth of the town, and many looked towards Uda's household wearily, it had not removed the confidence Uda had as a Gomrah. The future was not without hope. There were still those who felt that the destiny of the Zong was on Uda's shoulder when he came from the sea drenched with saltwater.

Many were tempted to strike the Izeonah out of rage when he was brought from the sea, as his unconscious body rested on the dirt. However, Uda knew such an act would only cause more damage to his already coming sentence, particularly when the Sadomrah from the prophet had ordered him to bring the Izeonah alive, if there were ever hope to undo what he had done. Thus, he protected the Izeonah, even though he, Uda, bounded in his Zong way, was not without the thought of severing the Izeonah with his axe.

Strangely, these moments counted greatly to Reverend Kline, for he perceived them as Uda being his protector, and he continuously stared into his eyes softly. However, for Uda, the Izeonah's stares offered not only what the prophecy predicted, but also within those illusive eyes there were confusions and mystery.

The morning sun was peering through and the day for his sentence sat at the mercy of this passing sun. The coming night must pass to be assured of the future. The Gomrah watched the lurid sun make its way over the soft sky. Morning turned into noon and the then sundown. When the sun disappeared, Uda became entirely a different man. It was time to be vigilant. When the night drew nigh, Uda, a bit jittery, made a sacrificial offering and prayers to his forefathers. As he retuned from the forest, his eyes grew red and his face appeared strong and serenely altered by the sacrifice. There was no telling what he did in his sacred shrine, but he looked in no man's eyes, not even his wife's. He stared downward and his body shook violently. His entire household was aghast and left him alone. Only to Nicaso he offered a few kind words, which he gave without even looking into her eyes. Those words, which perhaps frightened her, for the manner and tone he used, were also unexpected. Out of the ordinary, he told her that the beauty she carried was an emblem of eternity. Uda then bolted into his private chamber and from there he ordered her to summon her brother Dio.

Dio entered the room filled with ornaments and a bowl of blood. Uda was standing at a dark opening in his room with blood sprinkled upon his head. A few drips of blood flowed from the sides of his face. The opening was a portal into an alternate world facing the forest of Usula. The entire room was filled with smoke and lights, but the portal remained dark and mysterious. Before the portal Uda stood chanting sorrowfully and violently. His son, knowing the man his father was and hearing his tone almost screamed out of fear.

Dio leaned against the wall, for he became weak instantly and could not support his legs. "Father, I have come!" He said with a trembling voice.

"I am aware." His father said without removing his eyes from the dark opening in the wall. Uda walked slowly toward the blood, washed his hands in it and sprinkled a bit into the dark portal. Voices of whispers, like beasts feasting on fat nourishment, slowly came through the portal. "The gods have turned their backs against your father, dear Dio," Uda uttered slowly flashing his bloody fingers into the portal. The voices continued to whisper. Uda turned his red eyes towards his son and called. "Come, they must see you now."

Dio was appalled and unprepared. He stood frightened and paused. Being confused by his father's utterances he almost refused the call of his father. His father demanded again.

"Fear not, dear child. To you they mean no harm, for where I am going tonight, it is wise that they see you before I depart."

Dio's feet suddenly felt several pounds heavier, and he dragged his legs until he reached a distance from where his father could lay hands upon him. Uda grabbed the frightened boy and placed him before the portal and slowly whispered in his ears.

"The mantle of this generation is being placed upon you this night my child." Then Uda lifted his head and screamed into the portal, "Here is my child, my firstborn. He whom you must come to in the hour when you visit and find me not." Uda paused and took in a deep breath as if he were to sell his son. "...Dio is his name. Dio...the household that yet waits to see its final cause." The name echoed into the portal and resonated beyond. It was followed by multiple whispers, which frightened his son so much that the boy fainted and collapsed in his father's arms.

The next thing Dio remembered was being awakened suddenly from a dream. He sat on the edge of his bed and stared at his surroundings. He was hot and sweating profusely. Dio arose from his bed and walked into the night, going towards his father's house to meet him. Outside was silent.

There was no voice heard in any house. The hills were even darker and the town had a certain creepy feeling that Dio tried to understand. All lamps were out and the moon shined quietly on the white sand between the houses.

The crickets' songs sounded louder than they ever were, and domestic mammals seemed to have found hiding places. The soft wind was felt meandering between the dying winter trees, whispering a call to the wild.

When he arrived at his father's house the lights were dimmed. Nicaso responded to the door with a mask on her face. This night was known to the Zong as the "Night of Visitation," for the Fathers of the Land had come to town. All Zong must remain behind closed doors until the fathers departed. If they laid their bare eyes upon the Priests, they would suffer a destiny filled with calamity until death. Unless a Gomrah, those who dared to venture out were in grave danger. It was an abomination to see the fathers, as the screeching village crier announced, even for lads or virgins. Unless they preferred growing abnormally and barren in adulthood, they must avoid seeing the fathers. The locals found themselves locked inside their homes, for venturing into such a night brought misfortune to their crops. As the screeching cry resonated through the dark air over the town, those who remained out ran for their houses.

Dio had walked through this night unharmed. Nicaso was on her knees, head bowed, showing only the mask when she slid the door open slightly and uttered the usual words any Zong would utter in such a time. "Come in, whoever you are, and spare us any grief, for I am with mask in this hour of visitation."

Dio rushed in and shut the door behind him quickly, breathing intensely after having travelled through the night safely. His mother screamed and pulled him closer beside her.

Chapter Fourteen

The Mark of X

*T*he sanctum for the meeting lay at the verge of the Damned Forest, the forest which housed the most violent Sadomrah. The sanctum was in a mountain, which reached as high as one could see, with an opened entrance at its base facing toward the motherland Zuxbaha. This mountain divided the living from the dead, for beyond its boundary lay the unknown, and the unpredictable. The Sadomrah dwelling within ate on flesh and drank blood. They were beasts from the other world and only the gods and Priests controlled them.

Once in a while a powerful *Gamrah* came along and was given the key to venture beyond those borders; even beyond where a traveling Zongah ended his endeavor. However, the last *Gamrah* met his end behind the mountains. Therefore, the mountain was put out of the reach of men and considered taboo until a suitable *Gamrah* was found to once more venture into the miry terrain and return to his people. Furthermore, ever since the demise of the last *Gamrah*, a very long time ago, only the Priests visited the mountains.

Over the mountains grew forests of unimaginable size. The protruding trees were said to come alive at night to cover the land with dew, which blessed the crops and healed the people.

At the back of the mountain where the meeting was to begin, flowed two sacred rivers of the land: the pure and crystal-like Spirit River leading to the Shrine of Usula and the dark Creek of Monshung, the snake god. These rivers represented life and death. The Spirit River in Usula's Shrine gave life and the Creek of Monshung took life. The rivers were also named mercy and judgment. Usula was merciful and Monshung was the judge responsible for disposing the condemned and those beyond the saving hand of N'Daygmong. Legend taught that N'Daygmong designed the mountain in this fashion for the protection of the people so that they would never lay their eyes on him. If a man laid his eyes on N'Daygmong, it was the end—he would be found dead. He either died instantly or rotted away over time, with his flesh decaying until it fell from the bones.

That ominous night the entrance of this sacred mountain was filled with Gomry entering to discuss the fate of Uda and the curse of the Izeonah lying in his barn helplessly. Each Gomrah represented a clan and had his seat already assigned. The last to enter were the Priests who, according to legend, had their unique ways of showing the people their personalities. Suddenly the cave was lighted up with yellowish incandescent lights, allowing the Priests to move into the mountainous cave.

However, they had to be careful as they moved about in the night because, it was also forbidden for any ordinary man, woman, or child to see them. If they desired to maintain their powers, they had to prevent all locals from seeing their entry into the cave. If they were ever spotted entering the mountain, some of their power left them and entered the person who saw them. Though it was never guaranteed if the newfound power of the viewer would be a vital source, there was potential in the power for the new owner, but usually it drove him or her to insanity, or he or she died soon after that, for the power was an energy that dominated the possessor's body with extreme control. Therefore all commoners refrained from ever trying to possess such power, and the Priests made it possible by being cautious. It was a mutual understanding and a gravely reverenced aspect of the ritual.

The first to enter the cave was the water Priestess, Yore. On this occasion many saw the might of the Priestess with her legs made out of a fish tail. She moved fiercely through the night. It was the dry season so the dusts were lifted up.

Yore had a beauty unmatched. Her face ignited any man's phallic imagination, but her presence drove the same man to fear and reverence. She was what every Zong craved for in a wife. Her body was said to be as smooth as the waters of the land and her hair as long as the spring brook of the Spirit River. Yore's beauty was not to be tempered with, for she was fierce and would lash out if a man even thought of her as an object of desire for his bed. There was a saying that compared Yore to the young Sadomrah crier, who announced the Mensochsue. Men touched the crier and died thereafter, but it was a more daunting task to approach the Priestess Yore. Such a man with a wondrous death wish enjoyed the moment with the town crier and died later. However, with Yore, no such pleasures would be enjoyed. Her body was in a form of a mermaid. It was not made for pleasure. And all a man achieved was working for days on her body, and in the end, ejaculated on his knees and died in vain. For this reason, Yore was only an object of imagination. At her sudden entry among the Gomry, many had fantasies of being with her, but they quickly returned to the reality of the night.

The next to enter was the priest Seeney who had a debilitating deformity in the form of leprosy, which had devoured his legs up to his knees. He was large and shaped like a gorilla, with big muscles and powerful arms, which were longer than his entire body and assisted his movement. It was said that his anger gave him legs and he moved viciously upon his short legs that were now covered in hard tissue like cysts. Seeney's anger had caused many to tremble in his presence, for when he stood upon his scar-filled thighs in anger, along with his wide and larger palms, he could split open a man or a tree with one stroke, and with the same stroke he set lands on fire. The Zong chattered about a deserted land that lay waste to the north. They said it was burned when Seeney was driven to anger once, and his friction caused lightning and fire.

His face was that of a spectacle resembling a buffalo, upon which sat his big and wet nose, almost covering his entire face. It was covered in brown hair with his mouth unimaginably large, nearly reaching his tiny ears glued to each side of his head. He was an herbivore, and his favorite nourishment was the delicacy of watermelon, that he consumed until his belly became a round bloated pouch and moistened his already greasy face with the juices. When hungry, Seeney could shove half of a fully ripened melon down his throat.

Seeney's head was like the back of a ladybug—round, large and smooth as though it was infected with cancer. His eyes were like an owl's, each wider apart from the other. He was mainly nocturnal and spent less time with men. His big, wet nose made him a hideous and fearful creature. His moods were often filled with displeasure and he growled constantly with discontentment whenever he was found among a large crowd. However, seldom did Seeney grow angry, and he seemed mainly a shy beast finding his way only in the darkness. From the corner of the dark wall he appeared springing forth his large arms, with slime-ridden visage glowing beneath the illumination of the fire burning in the middle of the meeting. He took his seat.

Soon a white shadow flashed swiftly through the night, then a roar shook the village like an earthquake. The flying Priest Magello had entered.

The story of Magello goes beyond the mind of a natural man not accustomed to the way of the Zong. Magello was the strongest and fastest of all, and he had lived as long as the land. It was said only one Black Lady at a time could rebirth the spirit of Magello into a boy, and died thereafter. Magello was a descendant of the gods themselves, and a special guardian to the *Gamrah*. With his ten-foot height, and twenty-foot wings, he was swift in the air and quick on the land. He was a passive Priest by nature, who only showed violence when the *Gamrah* was in danger.

Another duty of Magello was to help the Prophet perceive the future in reality. As he inhabited the skies, lands and ocean, trailing for any danger, he brought news from far and near. It was the sight of Magello that made the Zong take guard against the coming Izeonah.

Naturally, Magello resembled a reptile from the Jurassic period, but he carried a sublime appearance, most stunning, yet beautiful. His feathers were of mixed colors: white, black and brown. His legs were fashioned like all men's, but his toes were shaped like frogs' and were joined by layers of skin. His face was also that of a man, with brown complexion, but blue eyes, pink lips and pale appearance. His entire body was covered in feathers except the face, and his eyebrows and head had strings of bushy long and silky white hair projecting downward. He had more than five normal fingers. His dark palms, covered in white feathers, were like a newly budding flower that slowly opened or closed to the changing weather. The white-feathered features illuminated beautifully in his dark palms. And below the bushy debris of the feather-entangled hand he grappled to his seat.

Magello had never acted on his own accord, but by the order of the Gamrah who, there had never been one in a very long time because the last one had gone to be in the afterlife, for he travelled to the unknown unprepared and perhaps was eaten by the violent Sadomrah or taken away suddenly. But Magello was the special guardian to the *Gamrah*, and could be called upon by the *Gamrah* from anywhere in the land as needed, since he flew with might. Many believed he was neither a priest nor a prophet, but a beast from the underworld of the dead—an ancestor sent back in time to guard the most sacred man of their society, the *Gamrah*. Magello was more active when the *Gamrah* was old. For this meeting, he was more of a spectator than a partaker.

A fire bolt ran through the sky like a lightning bolt, followed by a thunderous roar. The priest of fiery head, J'rum had entered. At the center of his skull lay a soft opening tissue, as would be a newly born baby, emitting hot steams like boiling volcanic lava when he spoke. Around his ears there grew long thin filets-like hair resting upon his shoulders. He drank fresh blood for every sacrifice and needed two white cows at the end of every year. His eyes were red and smoke emitted constantly from his dark and empty mouth whenever he spoke.

J'rum had a nose like that of a swine, but with tenderness of a newly born baby's face. He had four teeth, which were long and sharp fangs in his mouth full of slimy saliva. His feet were those of a swine, and his body seemed to be made of the contents similar to rocks after a volcanic eruption. J'rum was very tall and strong with a frame of a man. He took his seat.

The next entry was the priest of the land Zongdah. He was a gaunt beast about four feet tall with undeveloped arms, but powerful and large legs. He was the tiniest Priest, shaped like a T-Rex dinosaur with body contorted—a man suffering from extreme scoliosis. Zongdah also ate while crouching on his knees like a dog, for his arms were unable to feed him. His head was shaped like a snake, but all other parts of him resembled a normal human being.

Zongdah was vicious at times, especially when treating a Mebzongbre or offenders of the land. The offenders were what Monshung, his master, devoured to renew his life cycle. Zongdah was responsible for breaking the offenders' limbs before they were prepared as meal for his master. He used his giant legs and stepped on their limbs, with force and crushed the bones within. But, most often, his Sadomrah passed the arms through a special tree and bent the arms the opposite direction of their normal flexibility until the arms were completely detached from the joint and hung loose. Zongdah had no signature entrance, but a feeling, which ran through all, and they were aware that he was present.

The last to enter was the one and only Prophet Nephrotone. He was a possessed man and the only mouth allowed to speak of things to come. Anyone caught in the act of prophesying was fed to Monshung, for prophesying was a blasphemy against the Zong unless carried out by Nephrotone. Nephrotone quivered violently for he was always filled with prophecy, which always kept him rambling and dazzling himself to the ground. His eyes were as white as chalk.

As the main speaker of the Priests, and the judge, his voice was always what was heard when he entered. Along his side came two beautiful but crazed virgins, Sadomrah who always carried two bowls made of clay. One contained smoke, which he sniffed on and predicted the future, and the other a black powder, which was sprinkled over him from time to time by his Sadomrah. His entry, which was considered the most boring of all, began with the clinging sounds of bells attached to his legs.

These entries, over time, were stories told to the young. The villages and towns knew which entry was associated with whom, and it became a matter relayed in the morning as the night resonated with sounds and noises echoing from the mountains.

The Priests and Gomry made their entries and took their seats. Then a few travelling Zongah, who had finished the initiation of becoming a Gomrah, entered and knelt, and held their heads down behind their masters. They were only spectators learning from their Gomry and waiting to take over when the Gomrah was disposed of by nature. Amongst the Gomry, began little talks about which entry was most impressive. This was the tradition before the urgent concessions. The Gomry held little conversations, mumbled until all was settled and sat in their respective destinations. Then a scream, "Silence!" roared Nephrotone. And the entire group became silent.

Uda made his way to the center of the group, with head bowed as a sign of respect. "Fathers of the land your names are well known here and beyond the swirling ocean. You are mighty, I salute you."

"Uhlloh!!!" The Priests cried together.

"We have gathered here for a great discussion. I salute you."

"Uhlloh!!"

"Our greatest fear may be on our shores. But I, mighty Uda, can deal with it as my great fathers have done in the past. Give me your blessing to kill the Izeonah!"

"Abomination!" The prophet Nephrotone spoke impulsively. He took the center stage and began shaking vehemently. "The only fear that lurks our shores is that you hold the staff of our great ancestors in your hands! The gods have refused your plea!"

"Haaaa!" Seeney ran to the back of the cave and struck it. The ground shook. He shifted back and forth, and made a hole where he had struck. "Uda had served us well! Even the prophet spits lies sometimes!! Indispensible lies! Hush your speech of purity. The Izeonah will be a food for Monshung in the morning!"

"It will change nothing of our fate." The Priestess, Yore spoke. "More Izeonah are still coming to our land with the intent to ravish us. We must send him back to where he came from."

"Not yet," interrupted Nephrotone. He slowly opened his arms as if peering into something mysterious, and he looked toward a dark corner of the cave. He made a quivering fist and stared about him strongly. "I have seen great distress, my brothers of old," He raised his voice, "Caused by this

particular Izeonah. It was an abomination when my order was defiled."
With a furious stump he quivered and spoke. "His foot touched the land!"

"Haarrr," the crowd mumbled amongst themselves.

"Do something!" Screamed Yore.

"Violent things, name it and it shall be blotted out of our land with
my fist," Screamed Seeney as he struck the ground multiple times.

Murmurs amongst the *Gamrah* filled the room. It was certain now
that the land of the Zong was surely in great danger.

"Preposterous!" Cried J'rum, the priest of fiery head, breathing
heavily, "We are Zong! No man shall be the lord of our land but us! The
Izeonah is as fragile as any man even compared to our slaves we took from
the lands beyond the swirling ocean. Do not drive me to anger with your
rhetoric. On my land I am invincible. All the follies of the Izeonah are
done somewhere else, not on my shore! Tomorrow the Izeonah will be led
into the jaw of my master!" He walked and faced the prophet, "What is in
your word that guarantees that?"

"The Izeonah has power. Great inventions, sorceries and mighty
arms to roast us from our cave," Nephrotone spoke from the floor as he was
filled with a spell.

"Haaarrr!!" Roared the group. Then a scream stopped them all.

"We've seen that before! Our sons sunk their ship the other day.
It is not as mighty and fast as my elevated fist!!" Seeney roared loudly,
brandishing his fists in the air.

"Not as mighty and swift as my soaring wings!!!" Magello spoke
standing with a pumped up chest, with his wings waving on his back.

"Hohohohohoo!!!! My fire shall scorch and consume them with
the fury of my mouth!!!" J'rum stretched his mouth apart, his throat
vibrated wildly.

"Men of great valor, we must desist from this clamor. The time
has not yet come. We have not a *Gamrah*. The shore was moistened with
the blood of our sons and we showed no face because of this reason.
Nothing has changed since. We will all perish if we do without a *Gamrah* to
protects us." Yore spoke, waving her stench-occupied hairs. "We must
return to the pressing matter at hand. What say you, Nephrotone?"

"We cannot kill this Izeonah," The Prophet spoke as if to have
dipped into wisdom.

"Why," Screamed Seeney, "It was your idea to attack. Why would
our sons waste their blood in vain? This Izeonah must die!"

"I am the Prophet! I know my reasons," The Prophet took a bold stance, staring at the group of men and beasts gathered. "I must speak now. We are Zong and we are violent, but we have wisdom."

"Wisdom is only for the prophets. I am just violent! I have no need for wisdom," J'rum spoke with contempt.

"Yes, I understand your claim. Be it so, heed to my call for I have a plan. We are in mire that I am intending to release us from. I must re-express, we are Zong and we are violent. This time we must add wisdom to our nature. It is good for survival. This is what the Izeonah uses." The Prophet took in a deep breath and suddenly stopped quivering.

His young Sadomrah with a clay pot of smoke brought the smoke to the Prophet and he inhaled it with great pleasure and smiled. The other Sadomrah brought the powder and sprinkled a bit upon the Prophet's head. The Prophet dropped to the floor suddenly, and contorted like a snake. He made violent noises as his mouth opened so appallingly into the dark that even his esophagus became visible as he wailed in agony.

The people of the land heard his cry and shut their ears, for they knew what it was and the danger it brought to those who listened longer. It was a long and strenuous cry, which suddenly stopped and Nephrotone lay on the floor with purely glaring white eyes, almost backing into his head. Then, he slowly arose while speaking. His speech was weak and slimes leaked from his nostrils and mouth.

"Never before in our history have I seen such great divisions among our people as I am seeing now. This comes from our own sons, the Mebzongbre, whom we have not found and flushed out of their dwellings. Their prayers to this Izeonah's god are being answered once more. Do not take the Izeonah's god lightly. He has power." Hummm mumbled the Gomry sitting inquisitively watching the Priests manage the situation.

"Nephrotone," Called Seeney, who seemed to have pondered his question for the prophet. "I have watched my sons die in these few days. What is the guarantee of our survival? From your utterance, a *Gamrah* will lead us out of this mire. Well, be quick and choose. We have a Gomrah ready to enter the unknown."

"Ha, my brother, haven't you gained some wisdom yet, to understand the task of the *Gamrah*?" The prophet was a bit annoyed and he shook. "You remembered what happened to our last *Gamrah*. Let us not be foolish again." The Prophet pointed his finger at the priests, one at a time, then to himself. "For this, we have been punished with these hideous deformities. You, Seeney, with such a loud mouth, you are a beast still. Your face is of a gorilla's and your arms are your only sustenance." The Prophet turned to another priest, "Zongdah, your legs are filled with dirty bile," The Prophet's expression became a gruesome reminder of the event, which led to their deformities.

They sent a premature *Gamrah* into the world of the ancestors but he never returned. It was a disobedience to the rules of selecting a *Gamrah*, for he must be fully ready and equipped before venturing into the world of the ancestors, which was the land beyond the Damned Forest. In consequence of their disobedience, the spirit of the *Gamrah* returned from the dark world and entered the priests causing their deformities.

Suddenly, as Zongdah lay by his master's creek, a dark spirit with gray cloudy eyes streamed through the air with a rattling cry and entered his body. Zongdah's body became a thick rubber and contorted in all dimensions, his eyes pulling out of the sockets, arms and legs shaping painfully. When the spirit left his body to attack the next priest, whichever way he was contorted became the form he was left with until now. Though the spirit did not deprive them of their powers, it left the priests completely deformed and there was no promise that they would return to their original forms, even if they went through the proper ritual of selecting the *Gamrah*.

"Enough," Interrupted Yore, after she was reminded of the day the spirit entered her beautiful body and turned her into the mermaid she had become now, "I've seen my beauty turn to shambles. We must not offend the Spirits again. I want my form restored when the next *Gamrah* returns from the unknown. We must be selective."

"I agree," Spoke Magello. More head nodding in agreement followed until it was becoming disorganized, then Nephrotone screamed.

"Silence! Now you understand we must return to the pressing matter at hand." Nephrotone walked toward Uda who, within this commotion, had been attentive but most importantly, he was hesitant to receive his punishment. The Prophet once more dropped to the floor and spoke from there. "I stared into the Izeonah soul last night when I called it out of him." All leaned in to hear more, astonished and gasping for air. "Vanity!" Screamed the prophet again. "It was surrounded by strong fire yet, he stood amid of it untouched. This Izeonah has his god protecting him!"

Murmurs and astonishment were on their faces and in their mouths. The prophet appeared very frustrated and gashed his body until his raw flesh remained in his nails and blood showed on his skin. He fell to his knees angrily and steam evaporated from his body. Yore arose and twitched until a load of water ejected from her and cooled the body of the prophet lying to the floor now in mud.

"A great sorcerer," Screamed a Priest. "Such agony I find my brother in. I am indeed in haste to strike this Izeonah."

"Yes indeed, a great sorcerer is this Izeonah, he was surrounded by a great fire and was not burned," Said Nephrotone, regaining consciousness from the wet earth. "Yet it rained all about greatly and the fire was unquenchable and he stood amid it in repose. I will fight him still!" The prophet stood on his feet, exhausted and dazed. "Uda," he called out, "We must put out that fire. I am confused, even as a great prophet, a foreseer of the future, this still baffles me. But I have a solution."

The group was afraid, silent and attentive. Uda stood upright, frightened and unsettled. The tired prophet managed to grab Uda. "Blood," he said, "Blood sacrifice may be the solution. We need to put out the fire with blood and stop the pouring rain. I am exhausted even now and need time to fight him again. The blood of your daughter will be the ultimate solution. She is pure, a virgin and has the heart of the gods. Her blood will relieve us of our impending misery from the tongue and fire of this Izeonah."

Uda's eyes stiffened in his head and a stream of tears spilled from his red eye. He was weak and almost vomited, for the liquid spilled from Yore reeked.

"Great misfortune," screamed a traveling Zongah from behind the group out of distress.

"A Zongah spoke instead of letting his master. Who is such a man to interrupt the father's word?" J'rum yelled from his seat. "Bring him and let us spill his blood into the earth for the pain my brother felt last night in combating this Izeonah."

The group of traveling Zongy, fearing that if such a man was not surrendered more might suffer punishment; they tossed the Zongah to the stage before the distraught Uda and the prophet. Seeney rushed to strike, but the prophet yelled out and saved the man.

"Enough! Enough of this bloodshed! I am in agony now. Can't you see that this may be the outcome to get rid of this Izeonah and his spirit? Enough blood of our sons has been spilled in the past weeks. The neck of the sea is clogged with their bodies. Enough, I say, of this violence for a while. Leave my sight and take your seat at your master's feet. Let him deal with you after this night. There are more pressing matters to discuss. We are aware the morning cannot find us here."

The prophet turned to Uda and looked into his saddened eyes. "Blood is not all if you are strong to do this next proposition I will ask of you. Let not your weakness fail you this time. Not only will I drain your daughter and feed her corpse to my master but, O Uda, even your head will not come out of it attached to your shoulders."

The prophet turned to the priests and breathed deeply. "I am the prophet and I see the future. Great men will fall and great cries will annoy the ears of our gods. This land will crumble and the sea will open its jaws to the Izeonah and his gods. A new river will form." The Prophet paused. "It will be our blood, or the incoming foe—the Izeonah. This land will see its greatest division yet, if I fail to defeat the Izeonah. I am not alone in this fight am I?" asked Nephrotone.

"When the time comes, the blood of the Izeonah will wash our land pure again!" screamed Seeney, and he struck the ground with such a force that the earth fell from the top of the mountain.

"Well, heed to my proposal therefore, and join me. We have no *Gamrah* to usher us the freedom to join our sons in defense of this land and the war that is drawing nigh."

"An abomination! It cannot be so!" Whispered Yore.

"We are with you, brother," screamed the Priests, and then followed by the Gomry and their traveling Zongy. The Prophet slowly turned to Uda.

"This may be your only hope yet to save your daughter's neck for now at least. I am at no leisure to foretell the outcome but the wall of fire surrounding this Izeonah must come down. I gave him unto you. Teach him our ways. Show him our language. Nourish him and set his heart at ease. Whatever measure it may require of you, make him throw down this wall and let me in. When a man is in the most profound state of peace with his enemy, he may forget his distress and become less defensive. We must fool his gods to think we are his friends! In this light his wall might diminish, and I will get in and draw out his soul for our gods to save our land. You must not fail us Uda, but redeem our land and the life of your daughter. Until then, she must not be touched by any man, and she must remain pure until our fight with the Izeonah is resolved. For now she is the Black Lady, no more belonging to the affection of men."

Silence filled the room. Uda's lips trembled and he stood with weak knees. The prophet shook some more and turned to the crowd, showing his proficiency in foretelling the future.

"I have seen five years of this Izeonah's life on our shores and this is the farthest I can foresee. After his these five years, what I see is darkness. A time that I fear, only blood will redeem us if we fail to shatter his wall of fire and pull him out as a token that we can save our land from this curse. It will be your daughter's blood that we must spill Uda. Unless we crown a *Gamrah* to visit the unknown beyond the mountains and open the portal to the gods, perhaps, then, it will please the gods for such a man to lead us out of the coming danger this Izeonah will make us suffer. With a *Gamrah* present the gods may teach him wisdom, which he must apply to lead his people out of this fury brought upon us by you Uda." The Prophet stretched his finger forth towards Uda and gave him an angry look. He stared about him at the completely attentive crowd and he breathed in deep. In the prophets eyes the crowd saw the disappointment and fear as he explained the dark future that lied ahead.

"Yet," the Prophet continued, "here we stand with no roof to cover our heads because a *Gamrah* is not available to save us at this crucial time. We, as priests, we are limited in his absence, for through him we gain greater power and perceptions into the unknown. And since we are yet forbidden to see into the unknown, a worthy flesh, which must be that of your daughter must represent the sacrifice that will protect us until a *Gamrah* is found and crowned."

The Prophet looked toward a crowd of Gomry and he strolled along with his vibrating chains attached to his limbs. "I have records of your deeds that resonate over and beyond the land. Alas, there you stand as a defeated man in the land. Your weakness disgusts me, and you must pay for your iniquities. No harm must come to the Izeonah, for we are unsure of the outcome." The Prophet bowed slowly as if with shame. "My foreseeing limited me in this aspect and I am afraid I am clumsy in the dark. For now, we must have no more bloodshed. Five years!" He pointed his fingers at Uda again, "If you succeed to break through the Izeonah's walls of fire you might save your daughter's neck for the moment, but she remains a property to the land forever. If a *Gamrah* is found, he shall decide her fate or she will die without an offspring from her virgin womb, for she must remain celibate until this curse is lifted. And then her fate shall be decided."

"You are truly a foreseer, my brother Nephrotone, I am

convinced," Seeney finally admitted, pulling his half limbs closer together.

The crowd talked among themselves. For the many Gomry present, it was a relief knowing their friend Uda had a chance to redeem his life and the life of his girl if he broke the Izeonah's walls of fire. However, to Uda, this being so, it left him with doubts and unanswered questions. He wanted the Reverend's head on a platter on the town's execution stool. Furthermore, the least of his expectations was to safeguard his enemy, the Izeonah. Such a command revived old spells and unpredictable outcomes, for the Izeonah could be killed in his absence by his rivals and such an act would bring down not just the life of him and his daughter, but his entire generation.

The race to the *Gamrahood* was fierce, and many Gomry did unimaginable things to eliminate the competition. "One less was always good," they would say. Uda stood amid of the commotion and would have refused the command for he knew the dark cloud of despair was only extended to another future date. Yet, as he pondered the idea, he realized it gave him a chance not only to redeem his house, but also to once again elevate his status that was now dissipating with degrading rumors and a shameful house.

"Silence," Screamed Zongdah, "Daylight is coming and this matter is still unresolved." In his eyes there was quest for knowledge as he approached the Prophet, "What else must we do, dear Nephrotone?" Nephrotone, being in control of the crowd, smiled with pride.

"There is one more demand I must make of you, Uda. I call upon all Gomry of this land here present to heed and be vigilant. Watch your land and your people for Ixeonah, and no man shall stand in the way of progress." Nephrotone turned to Uda and gave him a disgusting smile. "Uda, your Gomrahood is reduced to an extent that you must move with your family into the motherland. There, we are sure your task shall be less burdensome and safe. And you shall govern correctly."

At the back corner, Gomsug's eyes lightened sullenly, "I must speak..." his voice was impulsive and stern. "Give me the floor, fathers of our ancestors, for I have an opinion in the matter."

"Approach us and express yourself!" cried the Prophet.

Gomsug cleared his throat and walked to the center. He looked around, then cleared his throat again. "Fathers of the land I salute you."

"Uhlloh!"

"My life is the Zong and my death is the Zong. I salute you."

"Uhlloh!"

"My mighty arms, as well as my wisdom, are given into your care. I obey you."

"Uhlloh!"

"I recollect, my father lies with our ancestors—the destination we all seek loyally in the end—I am Gomsug, I take the stand. May I speak and let the fathers, both dead and alive, hear what I say to the living tonight?"

"Speak on," The Prophet waved his hand over the floor.

Gomsug looked at Uda and at his fellow Gomry. He stood up straight like a man in command. "It has been a long battle," he said, clenching his fist. "It seems to me the prophecy is on the verge of fulfillment. An Izeonah lives with us now as we speak."

The Prophet roared with agreement.

"What do you propose," Cried Yore.

"I am just a man. I follow the voices of my ancestors echoing through the might of my Priests but I rule Zuxbaha, my master!"

"Haaarrr," Roared the crowd, for he had caused offense by speaking in such a fashion, and they watched the Prophet's next gesture. Gomsug's voice was with such thunder and power that even the Priests heeded instantly. There stood Gomsug breathing as if fumes would evaporate from his nostrils out of anger and his arrogant stare. His chest shook and his left arm gripped his blade.

The Prophet sighed slowly. "I know my son, I know," he said. "Zuxbaha must shield us now from our plight. Uda must cater to the Izeonah, but you rule Zuxbaha still. Your greatness shines even in your voice. That is why you must be the first ruler and Uda the second. You now rule Zuxbaha and his land. Be his helper and a friend. Rule the outer land and that which extends unto Yasulah, the land of Uda. He, Uda, must take the middle and rule with his Zongy."

The Prophet then stumbled toward Gomsug and grabbed him by the head and stared into his eyes. Suddenly he removed his hands and looked to the ground. He turned toward his two Sadomrah, sniffed into his clay pot and had some powder sprinkled. It was with joy that he lifted his head this time, and gave Gomsug a firm look. "You are one of the few men ordained that Meheyassahapunawa must fall into your great hands my child. May you not let simple matters of men deter you. You have the favor of the gods, maintain it," He said and pointed his finger towards Gomsug's seat.

Gomsug returned to his seat displaying the recognition that he had received upon his glimmering, boisterous and arrogant body, while staring at all Gomry present. To him it was confirmed. The mantle to the *Gamrahood* was almost at his door.

The story of Uda and Gomsug was a story that many knew and talked about. Uda and Gomsug, according to legend, were once two best friends. They grew up together and fought many battles side by side. Their names, which were generational names, were among the names of men worshiped in lands beyond the sea as gods. Gomsug was however, was the best in many things, and he had always strived to maintain his status. People talked about him in parables and always compared his strength to that of N'Daygmong's, but without the supernatural power.

Gomsug was known for his violent rage against his own people. Many knew his unkindly manner for burying some of his men in quicksand. He was a man known for his quick anger and impulsiveness with his blade. Even though killing of a Zong by another Zong without a genuine cause was a serious crime, Gomsug had done it several times in the past even before he became and a Gomrah and continued to do so as a Gomrah in the name of N'Daygmong.

His fame was large and grew laterally throughout Meheyassahapunawa and many feared his presence. His friend, Uda, had been one of few Gomry to withstand the rage that poured out of him. The complexity of the Zong tradition and demand to be the best for the *Gamrahood*, drove a wedge between the two. However, ancient stories of the two men would not be complete without the mention of the main reason Gomsug always sought Uda's demise.

It had to do with Gomsug's lost love, Uda's wife, Sophon. It was said that in the culture of the Zong, a man was made with multiple penises where his lust was only quenched by mold in the grave, and that his appetites were an abyss of endless search for the woman's inner thighs. One woman was never enough for a Zong. However, once in a while a woman came along and caused heartaches, pain and division for many, and this same woman would also quench the man's endless search for the woman's inner thighs. Sophon was one of these women.

The most unforgotten pain for Gomsug came when Sophon took Uda as her husband. She was the love Gomsug quested for but never attained. He was disgraced in the end and Uda took his bride. These events had added constraints on their friendship for years. Within the reality of this night at this meeting, many knew it had festered a ground for disaster.

Though these two men had shared some quality moments where their friendship grew stronger, the decision by the Fathers that Gomsug must now share his land with his rival friend Uda was a painful reminder to Gomsug.

Tension was increasing amongst the Gomry, knowing that the future was promising more upheavals between the two rivalries as Gomry of the same land. None could utter a word as they all watched with dismay, and Gomsug breathing intensely looking about the room. Though Gomsug, being the man he was, had more fame, power and was the most feared and respected Gomrah, yet, for the second time in his life, in public, he faltered again to this wimpy Gomrah Uda. Gomsug relaxed his shoulders and pulled in his seat.

The Prophet sighed, took out a staff and pointed it toward Uda. "Come to the center Gomrah, and take your final sentence."

Uda approached, a bit reluctant but not without a violent stare, for he knew what was next and he dreaded it. Though losing the freedom of his daughter to the land was painful, it had not disgraced him more than the next word readying on the slimy tongue of the Prophet.

"Any word for Uda before I curse him forever?" The prophet screamed, looking about the room.

Seeney cleared his throat and used his big arms to compose his stance. He lifted his eyes to the crowd and tears sat at the lining of his lashes. "It is a pity that you have caused us this great distress, and history will never mention your name forever in the line of *Gamrah*. For this, I weep; for I know your deeds and have seen your love for your people. Yet, what you have done erases your name and the name of your generation forever, from the rite of *Gamrahood*. The path to redemption is almost non-existent. Nephrotone," Seeney said before releasing the floor to Nephrotone who walked to the bewildered Uda.

"It has been a long struggle." Nephrotone began when Yore suddenly interrupted. Her eyes were also soaked with tears when she dragged herself to the center. Her entire body came with darkness so that her fishtail remained hidden, and her soft and beautiful face shone into the light beaming from the firewood. It was as if she floated when she raised her hand and touched Uda softly on the face, and gave him a motherly stare. "We all know this is not the end of the Izeonah intruding upon our shores. We have seen the disaster they caused to our brothers who embraced them. I have no more to say but let the penalty for Uda come with some leniency."

"Ulloh!!!" The Priests cried together and gave the floor to the

Prophet.

"Take the next harvest seasons to console your family and set your house in order," the Prophet ordered, paused and breathed deeply. "I must echo again that the land, both of the living and the dead will not refuse my chastisement if you fail me again. Your Daughter belongs to the land for a blood sacrifice if you fail on your first obligation. Her life and death lie in your hands now brave Gomrah. Carry on your duties accordingly for the burdens you brought upon yourself. Run down to the river of Usula hereafter, and express your grief in a manly fashion for that is not all of your sentence. When the dark dust of the Izeonah returns to the ashes from our land, I am taking you away into the hills of exile in the land of Bethelot—a place of which I heard many dark things. The attack from the Mebzongbre remains a foe that we must vanquish. The people of Bethelot are in need of a Gomrah and they shall benefit from a leader like you. There you might regain your status as a worthy Gomrah again. By now it is clear your generation is lost forever until then and there will be no more *Gamrah* born from your bloodline. This decision is set." The prophet turned to the congregation as a whole and waved his hand. "We are dismissed."

Each Gomrah got up and bowed as the priests and Prophet disappeared into the darkness. Meeting with the Fathers was a rare occasion. This happened only for judging the Gomrah. Everything else was left to the Sadomrah who interacted with the people daily, and settled disputes and domestic matters among them. However, the Sadomrah's final judgment was brought to the Gomrah who were the absolute power within the clan they governed. The Gomrah then would carry out any necessary punishment and if need be, they would involve the Fathers. Now that the sentencing was done, the Fathers departed to their dwellings.

Throughout the night, the town was shut away when the Fathers came, but their presence was felt. The blunt slams of Seeney, the heavy stumping of Zongdah, the fierce movement of J'rum, the shrieking cries of Nephrotone were the commotions that vibrated the people from their beds. Many dreaded such a night and as it was over, life once again resumed within the mountains and valleys of the land.

The orange morning sunlight was peering through the fog and beaming over the town. Crows of roosters announcing the morning were heard in the far away distance. Early birds' songs sounded melodiously in distant trees and nanny goats calls for their young reached the hills. Being the victim of the night, Uda's fellow Gomry gave him a warrior hand shake and they all dispersed into the morning, each to his destination.

Walking toward home alone, Uda began pondering the night more vividly. He prayed to the gods, rehearsed his defense and planned his escape from the curse the Fathers had placed on his generation, yet, it all came to nothing in the end. He was unsure how his family would react to this news. Moreover, what would become of the young Nicaso, who was now in love with Jebu.

The night after the Mensochsue, he noticed how she ran into his arms with a smile. Never before had he seen her so joyous and talkative. Jebu, the shy man, was also vocal that morning and it was an event that made him as a father, very proud. When Jebu left with his servant, he kissed Nicaso passionately and paid his respect to Uda. He promised his return to claim his bride in the coming month. But with such news Uda knew in the coming days he would prepare a Zongah and send him on a horse to inform Jebu of this misfortune. It was a sudden disappointment for them all that even he, Uda, was unsure of how to sustain himself from the emotions rushing through his core knowing that the fate of his daughter was sealed in misfortune.

Uda looked to the hills and called upon his ancestors. His daughter was innocent and vibrant with life. Such a burden was immense for her. It left the purpose of attending the Mensochsue empty and vain. She had danced that night for Jebu and amused many, yet she must now refrain from such emotions and await for the Fathers to pull out the Izeonah's soul or worse, gave her life as a blood sacrifice. Uda sighed with distress, unsure of what to do next. For the first time, his vulnerability as a Gomrah was before his eyes. He quickened his steps to once more lay eyes on this Izeonah who came and changed the pace of his world.

Chapter Fifteen

House of Exile

The journey to the motherland was immediate. Why wait for another day when what was already his, has been given to Gomsug? Uda's power or existence in the land of Yasulah was suddenly obsolete for Gomsug was quick and demanded that Uda leave the land at once. Uda gathered his family that morning, with his eyes still plunged in despair they embarked for the motherland Zuxbaha, a three days journey.

The morning he descended from the hills, Uda composed his thoughts concerning how to approach his family in disclosing the nature of their new existence. Not once did he stare into their eyes as he explained the night's experience with the Fathers. His words were direct and without hesitation.

"I no longer own this house, this land or Yasulah," Uda said with a bit of sadness but never looked up. "We leave for the motherland soon."

When he had finished his talk, he knew from the silent reaction in the room that his family's relationship with him was altered. Dio's response was immediate, then, followed by Niejon. Though the boys' lives were not threatened, the curse was daunting as well to the two brothers. It was every young Zong's dream to one day become a *Gamrah*. Furthermore, it was every Zong's greatest accomplishment to serve as a Zongah, face fear in the unknown and spend his days of solitude in the dark fight his enemies. There he was tested, and when he passed, he became a Gomrah then a *Gamrah*. This quest, which distinguished a true Zong from the common men, dissipated into thin air right before Dio's eyes—his dreams were no more. He was to live as a common man and farm and therefore become one of the least of the men in the land.

Dio was already a carpenter by trade. This was now his only means to live. And if ever there was to be fame ahead, carpentry would be his only hope. In anger, he grabbed his tools and departed their home. Later, he found temporary relief by smoking some wild roots in the lap of a local prostitute.

For Niejon, the magnitude of the situation was not felt yet. He was a nine-year old lad still questing only after pleasurable things that little boys at his age sought.

For Nicaso and her mother, this shook their world beyond pain and despair. They sat in silence and despair, paled for some moments, staring about the room, each enduring the pain according to her own fashion.

Uda made no apologies. Furthermore, as he noticed their moods, he got up and exited the room. It was no time for weakness or embracing fully what he had done. If he became like his sons, wife or daughter, he might not survive the rush of emotions combating him within. The fact that not even the sons of his sons would ever be allowed to serve as a Zongah was unbearable. He grabbed his machete and went to meet his Zongy to discuss the migration.

Nicaso turned slowly and looked into her mother's eyes. Her mother stretched her arms apart and Nicaso crawled in and they sobbed.

"Mama!"

"My child!"

"Mama!"

"My Nicaso!"

"My young life."

"Your young life."

"My Jebu?"

"Forgotten!"

"Doomed!"

"Life?"

"Doomed"

"Love."

"Love...?"

"Buried."

Shopon's teary eyes dragged across the ceiling of the room and then, she pulled her daughter's head away from her and stared into her eyes. Slowly she moved her trembling lips and began singing a lullaby. It was a traditional song, sang whenever a family came to such a brutal outcome. The mother often made gestures, which were usually a narrative of some form. Sophon chose the poem called, "A Child of Sorrow." Looking down at Nicaso, with both faces drenched in tears, she spoke of the Child of Sorrow.

"Farewell this beauty; that it was with sorrow,
You gifted me.
Long across that filthy land walks this child,
Without a name, fame or dream.
Meme, there is an ax in her hand that she drags,

163

Across her life carrying the stain of her father's curse.
I have heard her cries all night,
In that dark room drained of mercy;
And she takes it to the streets now weeping;
Through the lashing rains and frail winds.
Her wailing echoes beyond the mountains,
And gnarled trees of the hills.
She limps wounded from her father's house,
And mobs of mockeries left with her name in their mouths.
Her eyes had a certain melancholy
Stared now that she is the victim.
Naked, without defense or love—
That poor child who parades the wet mud,
Cussing out the thunder was with misfortunes.
Misunderstood from birth, strange deformities of her existence,
There, her defiled beauty is out for all to see.
Her ax is with blood,
Yet, there's no body in sight.
Her agony is now like N'Daygmong's mountains and
The blood on the ax is hers..."

Uda was within range to hear his wife's song, and somehow it shook him to the core. Not with sadness or anger, rather, it was confusion with a disturbing sense of abandonment. What he had done was by no means of his own accord. If he had known better, the Izeonah would have been killed on the shore. But, the same misfortune from the shore had come to haunt him in his house and he had no hand to alter the consequences.

"There will be no sad tales in my house," Uda said within his burdened heart, and with such uncontrollable feeling rushing through his nerves, he interrupted the mother and daughter bonding by calling out to Nicaso with a stern voice. "Come out and get the Izeonah some pottage!" He turned his back and began walking away. "Take Niejon along," He added.

Nicaso wiped her tears away and made peace with herself. And like a little girl seeking solace from her father after a tragic incident, she came out of the house hoping her father was still present to console her. Uda was gone. Those who passed by saw the bewildered Nicaso and they picked up their pace away from her, for the news of their curse had already polluted the air of her father's clan. Thereafter, she was avoided and many young men who never hesitated to compliment her now looked away or avoided the path she walked on.

She went to the water well alone. None of her friends came by to travel along with her. After she called Niejon, whom she could not find, she went to the creek along with her donkey. She shed a little tear on her way and perhaps her donkey was surprised, for Nicaso was a happy girl until now. The woman she had become overnight was to unwillingly become the sacrificial lamb that would keep her house from the debris of the Fathers wrath. She might have said a few words to the donkey then but it was just an ass incapable of hearing the mourning of a cursed girl. It just came along to perhaps have a drink and fetch the water for the Izeonah, whom against every unwilling vessel in her body she must care for and hope that his life would end so that hers might begin.

On the other side of town where the Reverend, who had accepted his fate in redeeming the Zong on the day of rapture, was imprisoned, it was nearly a week before he had a real human contact. The guards had always tossed in his food and shut the door immediately. However, on the morning of the migration, he had been moved to a new location giving him the opportunity to have a genuine visit.

Suddenly the sounds of wagons approached and then, the door opened. Standing at the doorway were two giants whose shadows nearly covered the protruding light, which irritated his eyes. The Reverend was still blinded from the light half covered by the shadows to the door when he was abruptly pulled outdoors. He was in the hands of Gomsug who chewed on a root with rage.

On the other end Uda stood along with his Zongy. All were tense, almost in the state of violence. As the chains jingled and clanged, the Reverend was thrown over a horse and they sped with him from the back of Uda's house. He was shoved into his new home and the door was shut again.

The group advanced to the center of the town where Uda relinquished all responsibilities to the new Gomrah. It was done with less surprise, for the rumors had already spread like the daylight they sat in while listening to their Gomrah. The town was however displeased with their new Gomrah. They knew his violent ways, though none could protest because Gomsug was present and cast his intimidating eyes over the crowd. Uda then moved to the courthouse where he debriefed his Zong on the nature of the departure.

The room where the Reverend was now residing was slightly more livable. And the chains were removed from him. There was a bed in the corner and an empty bucket sitting over a pile of gravel at the other entry, which looked like a bathroom. While he tossed and turned, figuring out his new surroundings, in poked the youngest son of Uda, Niejon, to his surprise. Since the back house was unguarded, the boy snuck in, knowing fully well who was within. This was a curiosity to the lad, for he was not old enough to understand the magnitude of the curse. When he knew the guards were all summoned to his father's calling, he rushed to see this Izeonah more closely.

At first he played a little game with the Reverend. When he noticed that the Reverend was aware of his presence, he quickly ran behind a wall that hid him from the Reverend's eyesight. The Reverend, at first thought he saw a shadow. He then intently watched the area until he thought the shadow might have been in his imagination, and then he pulled his head away. Niejon suddenly appeared. After he calculated the Reverend's head was turning toward him, he quickly ran behind the wall again. They repeated the process again and again. Then the boy snuck and spied through the crack, and when the Reverend noticed his presence where the crack was, he ran again.

After the constant occurrence it became a game to the lad, and the Reverend made him believe it was. Eventually the boy's fear of the Izeonah was dissolved and he came in. He sat in the corner and watched the Reverend with extreme curiosity. There was a peaceful silence for a while, then the Reverend made funny gestures and the boy laughed. Somehow they formed an instant friendship and the boy came close to the Izeonah and poked him with his fingers. They continued the play until Nicaso arrived with the potage and a bucket of water. She was appalled yet glad to find her brother not crushed by the Izeonah's sorcery, as everyone had said he would be in such situations. With obvious dismay on her visage, she avoided speaking to or staring at the Reverend, and she called to the lad.

"Niejon! Thank Usula you are alive. Come home with me now. Your mother is almost to her grave from fear of your disappearance. Come to Nicaso."

Niejon arose with a smile and stood by her, still staring at the Reverend. Nicaso placed the food by the bed, set the water on the gravel and grabbed Niejon. Niejon gave the Reverend a friendly smile before leaving with his sister. A moment later Nicaso came in and collected the other empty bucket. She was careful as she exited. Though obeying her father's wishes, she had no intension of ever befriending the Reverend.

The Reverend sat quietly looking into her eyes as if he begged to gain some favors, but he received none. Nicaso was not really a shy girl, but she was cautious. Before leaving for the second time, she gestured to him the sign of bathing and mumbled something with the name of Uda's oldest son Dio in it. The Reverend looked confused, but knew her message was related to bathing. He nodded and thanked her by placing his hands together and bowed. She gave him a strong glare and shut the door.

On their way back to the house she screamed at Niejon, "You are a fool! Never see the Izeonah again, do you hear me!" The boy agreed by nodding his head.

When the door closed, the Reverend picked up his attire, preparing for the bucket bath, a booklet wrapped in plastic dropped from his pocket. It was a Bible, his personal devotional Bible he had taken with him the first time he landed on the shores of the Zong. He grabbed it from the floor, removed the plastic and stared upon it with intensity.

He felt as if the Bible was to bring him sustenance beyond measure, for it was a special Bible to him. It felt like a friend that he had once again encountered in the time of need, and must pull solace out of it. This Bible, which consisted of both the New and Old Testaments, had taken him through his darkest days, especially when he grieved for Nora. It was the first Bible he ever owned, given to him by Nora when she converted him to the faith. In his eyes tears swelled up, settled and dropped. The Bible was his only friend in the land where he was now lost and perhaps forgotten and alone.

He began imagining many things. He began reminiscing how the first time they came from church that afternoon, they were so filled with joy, and she kissed him on the lips. How his heart almost fell into his abdomen from uncontrollable poundings! Suddenly he began imagining how the war had ruined all of it, and the overwhelming atrocities that followed thereafter.

The Reverend then imagined hopeful things—dreams of the coming days and the power he held in his hand. Somehow holding on to the Bible tightly, it refreshed his mind and he recollected how it came to be with him through the commotion and violence he experienced on the ship at the hand of Uda and his men. It was a little damp from the swim. He remembered how he squeezed his fist while holding on to the Bible as his head was slammed, knocking him to the deck. Flashes of painful memories washed over him. He touched his head and felt the wound, which was by then dried.

The Reverend moved toward the bed and sat down. Like a wave of calmness, as he opened the bible, even his heart sang deep in a state of peace. Though he was physically hungry, now he was full. Though he was dirty, now he was cleaned. Forgetting the hearty meal steaming on the table and the warm bucket of water over the gravel, the world around him disappeared and the page he opened took him away from his pains. He delicately read from the book of Hebrews 12:2—"*for looking unto Jesus the author and finisher of our faith; who for the joy that was set before him endured the cross, despising the shame, and is set down at the right hand of the throne of God. 3For consider him that endured such contradiction of sinners against himself, lest ye be wearied and faint in your minds. 4Ye have not yet resisted unto blood, striving against sin. 5And ye have forgotten the exhortation which speaketh unto you as unto children, My son, despise not thou the chastening of the Lord, nor faint when thou art rebuked of him...10For they verily for a few days chastened us after their own pleasure; but he for our profit, that we might be partakers of his holiness...*" The Reverend breathed deeply into his lungs as if sniffing the entire room. He closed his eyes, opened it and continued his reading.

Through the readings his memories moved him back in time to some joyous days he experienced with Nora. By then the friendship had turned into isolated kisses and long friendly visits. He remembered how she was a soft devout Christian and had vowed to abstain from intercourse until marriage, although at times the temptation was so charged that even the Reverend was left exhausted.

One of the nights, which he remembered vividly, was the night he made love to her. This memory softened his heart and he closed the pages of the Bible and laid it on the bed, allowing his mind to take him to that time of ecstasy. Though it was an unofficial marriage, that night, but even heaven and earth must have approved, for the intensity within the room, as the thunder blared through the dark cloud outside; the restraint that had kept them from intercourse in the past was dead, weakened or defeated. Their young nerves, streaming with hormones and estrogens, could no longer be denied.

For the Reverend, the night had started with a bit of despair. He burst into his room to find his roommate in bed with the same girl, who had ridiculed him in the past. Her slanted naked body was uncovered over the Reverend's roommate who lay beneath her with an opened mouth, nerves sharp and stern with pleasure. She turned her slowly moving eyes toward the Reverend and exposed her breasts and smiled. This startled the Reverend and he quickly shut the door.

For a moment he tried to rid the disturbing image from his mind but it was impossible. He then sped down the hallway attempting to recompose his mind. She was not as beautiful as Nora, he convinced himself. Nora was beautiful within her heart and in character. Her blue eyes and blonde hair, sharp cheekbone and red lips, always put him to ease. She was of a perfect height with heavy bones but athletic. He must see her now, for his current state of mind left him defenseless.

When he knocked on her door there was no response. A moment later, as he gave up on knocking, his mind had settled and the image of his roommate's girlfriend was gone from his mind. But still, Nora had not returned. He walked out into the dark and sat in the courtyard, their usual meeting place. Suddenly, the rain began to fall. When the Reverend made his way into the cafeteria to escape the rain, he saw Nora and her friends leaving for their respective destinations.

At first he attempted to hide, for he had just seen her not too long ago and informed her that he was heading for bed. The Reverend's attempt to conceal his presence made him salient, for he stumbled over a stool and was noticed by all. When Nora saw him, she knew he was troubled, for he looked pale and vulnerable. Observing her eyes, he knew she was glad to see him again, and she left her friends to put her hands out into his and kissed him softly. Nora was not curious to know why he was out. Moreover, the Reverend's state of mind, at that moment, had been a displaced sense of composure and she reassured him that she was his comfort with another kiss and called his name softly.

"Isaac." She said while looking closely into his eyes as if the beam from her eyes would restore him.

The Reverend reached for a kiss again, and tensely sucked on her soft lips. With her soft yet firm breasts pressing against him, she pulled his hands around her waist. By then, the feeling was assured, and nature gave way to the rushing emotions. When the lightning flashed out under the cold rain as they stood in her room, he asked for her hand in marriage. Nora smiled and agreed.

169

"I mean right now," He said with a manly stare and then they laughed.

"Yes," Nora said, almost in a whisper.

"Should we pray first?"

"There is no harm in prayers."

"Well, let me." They held hands and knelt by the bed and the Reverend prayed. His prayer was genuine and was with power. He mentioned his love for Nora and asked God for his blessing. When they opened their eyes, Nora was streaming tears and then she smiled. To her, he had already become a preacher and this softened her heart so that she surrendered completely.

"Oh Isaac, I love you!" She whispered softly and kissed him. When they rose to their feet with both their eyes set, unable to leave each other's face, the bonding was at its climax and both hands trembled in each other's. The touches were electrifying and sublime, and they felt as if they floated in a serene world of eternal bliss. When Nora went to her knees before him, he emerged from his imagination.

Lying now on the bed in the hut surrounded by the two giant guards, he noticed he had been crying. Each side of his eyes had drained tears, which were then, rolling past his ears and onto the bed. He pulled the Bible close to him and sat on the bed. The day Nora gave him this Bible she was at her happiest. The manner he held onto her that evening was as real as the present moment. The texture of the Bible was still good.

The Reverend was not an old man. He was, at the present, thirty-four years old. So far he considered his life to be of mixed experiences. Yes, at some point like now, he was a man of devout belief and dedication. His conviction of the cross and his past, which haunted him, were matters sending him deep into contemplation at times. However, so far, they never drove him to utter darkness where doubt was victorious. At every junction where he had turned his sad face, a hinge of hope always surfaced. Nevertheless, he was drenched with emotions and regrets still, but these mixtures of feelings were the motivations that kept his past and present intertwined. And they drove him forward.

Being a Reverend had not exempted him from the nature of men, but with the help of his convictions in the cross and the belief in the man he was, he was still in the world. Acknowledging that he was not a part of it, gave him courage to withstand the temptations of his flesh. After Nora's death he had cast his eyes on Calvary and there he was staring at the beacon of salvation—the treasures of the world disguised with illusions and vain pleasures, lusts and deceits, greed and antagonistic attitudes rolling on in vanity—vanity, vanity!

The Reverend was not impressed with life's vain pleasures. His body trembled on the bed, as these thoughts possessed his mind. The salvation of the souls of men was what led him to the land of the Zong. It was that which made him a Reverend, and that which his wife had died for in the end. He was not giving up now, for they were the matters of his heart as well—they were quests he had to pursue by crying out to the world, expressing their need for a savior, and to make them hunger for redemption and the hope of life after death. Cleaving to these beliefs surpassed all other dilemmas.

The Reverend was exhausted then, for his thoughts were intense and they ran through his nerves robbing him of his last energy. He lay on the bed staring at the ceiling for a while. Sleep did not come. He then arose, for he must shower and put on a fresh face. He had been a prisoner for a week now, and so far, there had been no brutality, as he had expected.

The Lord must be working. "God is working!" He said with smile, and he removed the crisp cloth and folded the Bible within. His naked body moved toward the bathroom.

As he tossed the water above his shoulders, the other part of the room where the bed was located was visible. He was reminded that the door could be opened at any time yet, he stood boldly in his nudity perhaps, overjoyed of the word he spoke internally to himself a few minutes ago. He was not afraid of who walked in, even if it were Nicaso.

She had struck him in an odd way. Though she gave him threatening looks, he understood her position. Moreover, her most ferocious stares were somehow tender to him even when she attempted to conceal it behind anger and discontentment; it never broke his spirit. If anything, it showed the uniqueness of the creature she was, needing salvation. He must give her a cross to bear so that she could stare at the beacon of salvation like him.

Chapter Sixteen

Sudden Intrusion

he journey began early the following morning. It rained heavily the
T previous night and the road was wet and muddy. The mountains sat
with fog and the clouds were still heavy. The dense rain forest of tall
trees and open plains soaked with puddles of un-drained rainfall were rooted
in their saturation. The galloping horses separated gutters of tadpole larvae
and threw the earth vehemently behind them.

The lines of Zongy extended beyond the horizon. Close to a five
hundred men, along with their families, came along with their master and
his family on this three-day horse ride. More were to join later, when the
land was finally rebuilt to accommodate the entire Uda-commanded Zongy.
In the new land there were only a few houses on mostly vacant land, where
the Zongy were to work diligently to erect the houses they needed to live in.
As the leader, Uda was to occupy a compound already prepared for him. It
would be a long struggle before all the houses were completed, but the plan
was to serve Uda, although his Zongy suffered the curse that they must
follow their leader into exile. Suddenly, the land and the people they once
knew where now the things of the past. They were moving on, leaving the
land of Yasulah and heading for Zuxbaha because of their leader's offense.
The transition was not so easy because it meant rearranging their lives once
more to fit the new land and perhaps new rules.

The Reverend was given a horse and he rode along. Uda had a
strange interaction with the Reverend before the departure. Somehow, it
was friendly but odd. Uda smiled and gave him the rope to the horse.
Sophon had made him fresh cotton clothes, which soothed his body well
and made him comfortable with the ride.

Sophon was in the wagon, her face covered in a black shroud. She
was timid and cold. Dio, on the other hand was with the group of Zongy
ahead discussing matters of men. Though no one said a word to the
Reverend, at times Niejon smiled at him and then stared at his sister; all
seemed in perfect order. When Nicaso noticed her brother's actions, she
stopped the wagon where her mother rode and put the lad in.

Once more the Reverend observed her firm look. He would have
smiled, as a sign of respect, but Nicaso departed quickly. She gave him a
certain warm and unexplained feeling, he thought. This made him even
more determined to convert her family to salvation.

As a widower, the Reverend was strongly convinced that he was uninterested in the hope of fleshly love and affection. He had overcome the grieving for his wife and five years later he was in the land of the Zong. It would be a distraction from what he really thought of Nora. Those times with her, the manner in which he grieved for her, it was as if Nora was a part of him now. There had been no woman lovely enough to give him such a rush of emotions as Nora did and he was not ready yet to move on. Furthermore, he was in a mysterious land of the Zong and nothing deterred him, not even the rush of ease and warmth he found in the presence of Nicaso's discontented stare. However, with her soft lips, eyes budding beautifully, full breasts, long dark hair and curvy body, there was something about her that made him feel as if he already knew her. Perhaps Nicaso had the same feelings, but the Reverend was not certain.

Moreover, his emotions and feelings where not fully understood yet to be considered as love, affection or even infatuation. But from the few interactions with Nicaso, he knew it a pure mutual and unexplained feeling, which had a potential to become anything but hate. These feelings were the main reasons Nicaso became uncomfortable with the Izeonah.

For the first time there was no certainty as to why she trembled with such warmth for the man, who because of his presence she may never taste love or feel the strong hands of Jebu upon her soft skin. She was confused and was not fully in control of herself around the Reverend. Though her father persuaded her that befriending the Izeonah might give them hope again, she continued her arrogant stares as a restraint to the mutually flowing feeling. She made a vow to herself that if there were any hope of loving and being loved, it would only come when the Izeonah was gone. But she also knew it was only a fantasy for she was now a Black Lady. Befriending him or not made no difference even if she was told that it was to her advantage to make the Izeonah feel at home.

These unmanaged emotions not only left Nicaso enraged about the Izeonah's presence, but there was something about her tradition that she also wished she understood. Though she heard the stories of the Izeonah and how centuries ago they once lived in Meheyassahapunawa and almost destroyed the land, Nicaso could still not understand the entire story from looking at the Reverend. After all he really posed no threat to her physical being. If anything, he appeared to be the victim.

'Hush now Nicaso,' she whispered to herself, 'this ground you walk on now is dangerous. The gods do sometimes read minds; especially when it is a mind in doubt.' She turned with her thoughts in her head, glanced at the Reverend and galloped away, joining the group of women, the wives of her father's Zongy.

On the day of Nicaso's birth a Sadomrah of Usula who became Nicaso's Sadomrah left her shrine to visit Uda and his malady-stricken wife. According to her, the visit was because of the dream, which startled her greatly and she had to become the guardian of Nicaso. Two angry bulls fought against each other with fury in her dream, across the plains of the land. Eventually, one bull became victorious by thrusting its powerful horns into the neck of the other. Once victorious, the bull then devoured its victim like a malnourished tiger staggering upon a meal in its greatest hour of hunger.

The reason for the dream, the Sadomrah explained, was what happened after the carnivorous bull lifted its head and bloody mouthful of the carcass. The bull turned into a large vulture and flew away. The Sadomrah, being a spectator with special powers, turned also into a vulture and also flew after the beast. She descended along with the transformed bull at Uda's house where there were many more vultures watching the birth of Nicaso.

Since this visit, every year the Sadomrah came to see Nicaso, hoping the dream would be realized. She was not completely certain of the outcome of such a dream. However, she knew it would come as a revelation either at some gain for the family or a misfortune.

The Sadomrah anticipated that in one season of Nicaso's birth, the bull which turned into a vulture would return in a human form. When the Izeonah came, it vivified that which the Sadomrah had longed for. In the end it was a misfortune for the family.

Now, knowing that Nicaso was set apart, though it concluded the long mystery, it also opened a new door. The Sadomrah, as the guardian of Nicaso, became so burdened with the news that she entered the dark World of the Old—the ancestors' world—beyond the mountains of N'Daygmong, hoping to capture enough power to save Nicaso from the curse.

It was a dangerous undertaking for rarely did any Sadomrah of her kind enter such worlds and return. The Sadomrah was determined to enter the World of the Old, hoping to win redemption for Nicaso or die trying. The bond she had with Nicaso was so powerful that it compelled her to make the sacrifice. It was always a worthy gesture for a Sadomrah to die trying to save the individuals it guarded, and such Sadomrah became famous and revered in the afterlife. Furthermore, if she succeeded, there would be an even greater reward. For her fame as a Sadomrah would resonate with the living and the dead, giving her greater access to both worlds.

The Zong believed that every dream had two interpretations, like the paths that lay before all Zong. There was a belief that nothing was permanent except death. Even the greatest woe could be transformed to a great fortune, if it was manipulated with charm to please the gods. However, these adventures were in a sense, an assumption and the choice each Sadomrah made was dependent upon the relationship it had with the Zong it guarded. Such a choice took many days of contemplation and most Sadomrah never attempted the worthless adventures for no man had returned from the World of the Old, as some believed, to describe its structure in detail. But the ancient tales of the Zong were filled with adventures of great Sadomrah who had given their lives for the person they guarded. Moreover, it was written in the Zong tale that this process could be accomplished if the person the Sadomrah guarded was special enough. However, the same writing also stated that the curse was never removed and if the same person guarded by the Sadomrah was defiled by dark forces of another world, then any attempt from the Sadomrah was a worthless plight.

Nicaso was a special girl to her Sadomrah and the relationship was more than a guardian and the guided. She was once taken into the shrine of Usula as a child by her Sadomrah, and she returned undisturbed. This had been a story that circulated within the clan's circle of Yasulah, for, whoever entered that shrine was destined to either serve as a Sadomrah or accomplish great things. The Sadomrah of Usula were the most beautiful and adorable among the endless lists of gods and their Sadomrah; and they were women who involuntarily entered the world of mysteries, but in the end they accepted their fates and were never willing to return to the world of men. Yet, shocking enough, Nicaso, in relation to her Sadomrah saw the darkest place of the Zong and returned home safely. By the time of the migration, many thought that it was her destiny to be that which the land must feed on to survive in the face of adversity.

These contradictory interpretations had not deterred her Sadomrah, who was willing to make the great sacrifice by entering the unknown, hoping to save Nicaso.

It was this same Sadomrah, who came to her at the creek when she was alone with her donkey that afternoon; knowing that her friends had abandoned her after the news that made her a spectacle of eerie stares and sullen restraints. Nicaso was comforted in a special way that afternoon, but she told only her mother about the experience. It was a curse, and perhaps detriment to both Nicaso and her Sadomrah, if the plan was revealed. For who knew what or who was watching and might attack such a kind Sadomrah while on this adventure? Nicaso cried, knowing that while away she would be left alone to her own devices. Therefore, if any misfortune came in the absence of her Sadomrah, she would be at the mercy of her aggressor, for her Sadomrah was not present to protect her.

"No," Nicaso insisted at first, "My father will make the Izeonah the sacrifice instead. Don't leave me, for I am worthless in your absence!!"

"The future is bleak Nicaso," The Sadomrah said, looking into the wind and caressing the frightened donkey. "You must let me go; for I intend to return and grow old with you."

"To the unknown? Very few return from such a place!"

"Well then, I must be one of those who return."

"How so? Without you I must walk lightly with my words and deeds, I am afraid I will not survive to see another farming season!"

"You must be vigilant, my child, and take caution with your life, but for now I must bid you farewell. It is the wisest thing I must do for us."

"No, I forbid you to go. I have asked for none of this. It was not me that invited the Izeonah. I hate the Izeonah and my father now. Why should I suffer? Why must I give up love and happiness and live like a knave?" Nicaso wept into her Sadomrah's arms.

The Sadomrah grabbed her by the hand and screamed, "Shut up and be brave! You are stronger than you think. You were made for something greater than this and as long as I live as your Sadomrah, I will pull you away from your father's curse." The Sadomrah then took a deep breath and bowed a bit, seeing that Nicaso was frightened. "You live in the world of men. Our sadness and pain does not always quicken them to our rescue. Sometimes we have to stand firm and alone to surpass our misfortunes. Wipe your tears." Nicaso wiped her tears. There was silence. The Sadomrah rubbed her frail hand across Nicaso's face. She was an old Sadomrah covered in black cloak and only her face was seen. She was fully human and smelled sweet from the herb she rubbed on. Her hair was gray and her face was wrinkled. Her eyes were dead and white in her head, yet she saw the world with supernatural power. After a sad observance of her guided being she breathed.

"I will not stand here and watch you began to break down when my adventure has not yet begun!" Nicaso looked into her Sadomrah's eyes firmly and she became strong, showing the strength on her face. The Sadomrah gave her a waist ring, which was made of beads. "This should never leave your waist until I return. When you are tempted, touch it. It is a reminder that I will return for you and save you from the curse."

Nicaso hugged the Sadomrah and held on tight. "Promise me we shall see each other again," she said, staring in the direction of the hills steaming with volcanic particles and smoke.

"You are what I live for. There is danger out there, but I shall not die. My love for you will keep me alive. I must return to you my darling, now let me go."

They slipped out of each other's arms and the Sadomrah turned her back, walking away and melted into the forest. That night in her room Nicaso performed a ritual that had given her some personal peace as she hoped the Sadomrah return from the woods with favors from the gods.

It was a clear moony night and the town was vibrant with life and amusement. Nicaso ignored all the luxurious sounds of water drums and air blowing pipes, with euphonious tones of children between the houses and the laughter of youngsters in the square and she entered her room as a way of accepting her consecration.

Her father was out to consult his friend Mileseh about the journey, her mother told her in an ill tone, and entered her bedroom. Nicaso stared about her and noticed that all was silent. Niejon was not even around to keep her company. She felt tempted at first to go out and join the amusement, for it was time for feasting and merriment at this time of year. But how would they perceive her? she realized as she stood before her door. Did this mean I must be alone forever? Forever! She cringed at the thought and stared about.

Her memories of Jebu, how he was subdued by her look that afternoon in the little gathering at the wine spot. How she pretended to be drunk to test him and he kept his hand about her so that she would not fall. And as they walked back to her house, she noticed how he became serious suddenly and wanted to express how he felt and she let him. It was a magical night. She let him kiss her once or twice and then she noticed he was nervous and the brisk wind came from his mouth when he laughed after confessing that wealth was only a foundation, and happiness was exclusively a different matter, which he believed she, Nicaso, would bring him. Then they walked below a almond tree and sat. The owl sang to the night and the moon and stars sat in the black sky and the wind blew. There they talked about their lives as a couple, and they planned. But now all had slipped away suddenly before her eyes, like water seeping through a sieve.

She imagined her house, which would have been built on the land Jebu had taken her to. It was lavished with tall palm trees, an endless view of ferns and other dying grasses, six water wells and waterways, many slaves to cater to her, coupled with nights of unimaginable pleasure in Jebu's arms. She envisioned her herds of cattle, loud bulls roaming her land and the voices of her children running about with joy. Those imaginings, which had been as vivid as her room, began to fade away. In the end she stood alone, in this isolated and desolate place, and the drought of her heart extended beyond the darkness even into the unknown future. Tears streamed down her face. She touched her face as if to feel her diminished existence and called her name softly, "Nicaso, daughter of Uda Daha, how pitiful you are!"

Sophon heard the soft sigh and leaned against her doorway, unwilling to disturb her daughter entrapped in her moment of grief. Nicaso removed her hands from her face and entered the room. She then grabbed the waist ring given to her earlier by her Sadomrah. There, she shut her mind from the world echoing outside with joy, and stood before her custom-made mirror. It was silver with special coating, which gave it a glowing reflection. Nicaso then stared at herself with great sadness. She reached over her shoulders and loosened the knobs of her dress, exposing her unclothed body. She walked closer to the mirror and touched her chest and stared down at her body. With her reflection in the mirror detailing her firm and sensual body and her long dark hair falling down her back, she grabbed the ring and placed it about her waist.

The ring suddenly changed and it captured her attention. The mirror became gray and faded into a portal where Nicaso saw a mountain. On each sides of the mountain grew tall trees that extended even up to the mirror in such a manner that a path was formed and went up high into the sky. The leaves on the trees were red, black and green with some fallen leaves sprinkled on the path that led to the mountain far yonder. It was a bright and beautiful sight.

Above the trees the mountain was covered with gray clouds and the sky slowly faded to a rainbow that blended into the horizon. As these changes miraculously reflected before her eyes, she touched the mirror and her hand entered. She immediately pulled it back out of fear and fell to the floor. Still in shock, she removed the waist ring and sat back. The images in the mirror slowly disappeared as they had appeared.

Nicaso shook her head as if to have been awakened from a nightmare. She grabbed the ring again and attached it to her waist. With precaution, she arose and stood before the mirror again. It changed to the same image as before but was now windy. The path, which was covered in leaves became a crystal river, flowing from the root of the mountain. It was an appealing sight that invited her in and she stared in awe. With caution, she touched the mirror again. This time it resisted her. As her hands bounced against the mirror, she heard a knock.

"Who is it?" She asked.

"Your mother. Are you well my child?" Her mother asked with urgency in her voice.

"Yes, mother. Why ask such a question when you know my current state?"

"There was commotion from your room that led me to believe you were not alone, and that you sounded cheerful. I wish to join you in your jubilation."

There was silence and then Nicaso staggered around, a bit confused and she tried to conceal what had happened. The image had disappeared and she was still naked standing in the middle of her room. She put on her dress and paused, still looking about. "This is my mother," she reminded herself and opened the door.

"A visitation," she said to her mother.

"Pure?"

"Crystal pure."

"Usula's river!" The mother smiled and rushed in. "Show me."

Nicaso pointed at the mirror. "It changed from my Sadomrah's gift."

"A Sadomrah gift!?" Her mother asked with urgency. Nicaso pulled her dress upward and showed her mother that which was around her waist.

Sophon eyes opened in astonishment. "Blessed child," she said and touched her waist slowly, her now baffled face stared into her daughter's eyes.

Nicaso understood little of her mother's expression for what she had seen was something out of her imagination. Such a place, if it existed, made her fear death and embrace life. It was desolate, cold, lonesome and without contentment. Was such a place her dwelling after she was taken from this world against her will? Was this place a terrain for the gods, where her Sadomrah had now gone risking her life to save hers? Confused at her thoughts, as her mother investigated the ring, she felt her mother pull her into her arms.

"You blessed child, you are favored! Come let's celebrate. I must find your father and brother. We must celebrate!" Sophon walked away with a smile. Nicaso walked back and faced the mirror.

"My Sadomrah," she said with a contented face, "Whatever is good, let it remain that way in my life. Whatever is bad let it remain that way. I accept my destiny." Nicaso dropped to her knees and a warm feeling flowed over her. "Father, I pardon you. Father, I pardon you. Uda, I pardon you," She crawled to her bed and pulled up the cover.

The motherland where they headed for was now within sight. The entrance was a busy market. Butchers standing beside their skinned hanging meats, vegetable sellers, herbalists, medicine men, clothes made from variety of materials local to the Zong, fresh fruits, cassava, fresh palm oil, eddoes and lush nourishment lined the busy streets. Wagons and horses added to the noise of sellers announcing the prices and virtues of their products.

The harvest season in Zuxbaha brought unrest for men and women as they filled the streets for transactions. There were projecting trees slowly reflecting the yellow sunlight and sounds coming from nearby animals, both domestic and wild. There were also refreshing sites difficult to ignore. The beautiful and splendid overlooks of the motherland was alive. Her large pastures of grassy plains stretching as far as one could see, the ornamented autumn morning was usually soft and brilliant. Yonder, mountains covered with green grasses and gnarled tall trees exposed her to all the incoming strangers and visitors. Zuxbaha sat in a valley of sand and red earth and her visitors were always in awe watching her beautiful scenery from the mountains, which had roads leading to town. The sounds of mortar and pestles pounded together by mothers in the process of breakfast making, the smell of boiled cassava and eddoes, the sound of axed wood cracked by men working made Zuxbaha a place for life and security.

When Uda and his men entered the town, it was filled with spectators waiting to meet the new Gomrah. Though the rumor of his migration had reached them, they also heard of his good deeds, and many came to express their condolences and welcome him to his new home.

Going through the market, the noisy streets did not go unnoticed. The people were well organized and adept at their crafts. All sellers had regular selling spots and stood above what they sold, talking to customers until they were distracted by the large line of Zongy and the Gomrah walking through. The people were in straight lines extending left and right. There were also spaces in between where people walked through to go to the other sides where more sellers interacted with customers. Men on their horses galloped about and wagons wallowed around—a busy site of people transacting.

Though the Zong eventually drove the Mebzongbre from their land, it was evident that such a place as Zuxbaha was a reminder to some that the residue of the Izeonah still remained. It was the assurance that they resided here once, displaying the origin of the now flourishing culture—at least for the Reverend. These were the things he observed as he galloped through. He was amazed at the sight and watched in total disbelief. He had been hesitant to inquire more about the Zong. Now, what he saw in Zuxbaha changed his perspective. The houses were built with mud and some with roofs made from flattened sheets of aluminum. Some houses even had a design of bricks, and the roads were ploughed well to accommodate the horses and wagons. Though it was made of sand and red earth, these roads also had constant travelers going to and fro from the land.

As the Reverend's eyes wandered about in a strange way, many disregarded his presence as they saluted Uda and continued with their transactions. He expected a wave of Zong coming up to him or pulling at him, but contrary to his expectation, those who came to see the Izeonah were all strangers who were later threatened with beating, for they made a spectacle of him. They were those who came from the outer lands and were in town for business. Their frightened faces watched and believed more in N'Daygmong for delivering them, once more, from the evil of the Mebzongbre. Surely he was of a strange demeanor that even he caused fear among his spectators. Such a fear was not of him, however, but of the stories told beside fireplaces about the Mebzongbre's arrogance and violence. And how when the Izeonah came to Meheyassahapunawa they suddenly attempted to claim the land and reduced the people to slaves. They talked about how the Izeonah had powerful weapons that they used mercilessly against the Zong and its people, and how they had lured many to his cult, caused divisions, war and terror. The Izeonah were terrible people, they were told. So they watched the Reverend imagining all they had been taught of his degrading activities toward N'Daygmong.

The area of the town where Uda was to be lodged was fenced in.

Around that vicinity were opened fields of vacant lots where his Zongy were to rebuild houses to accommodate the entire clan migrating with the Gomrah. Many Zongy returned to the land of Yasulah, for the motherland had few spaces to lodge them all at the moment. Those who remained had relatives with whom they made arrangements to reside while they rebuilt their lives in the new land. Soon many volunteers came and assisted in the building process. Six months later Uda had become an established Gomrah of the inland part of Zuxbaha.

Somehow, this new home changed the mood of Uda and his family. Not many knew their deeds. Furthermore, those who knew their deeds also heard how unfair the Fathers had been in judging the Gomrah and they took his side. Most young men came about hoping that one day when the Izeonah had paid for his offenses and become the ultimate sacrifice, that Nicaso would once more be released and that they would have the chance to charm her. With this prospect Nicaso was happy again, and the family saw the future with strong hope. The people made friends with Uda and his family and gave Nicaso and Dio each a selling spot at the market ground.

Nicaso and her brother went to their spots and set up their tents. She displayed dried meats for sale and her brother resumed the carving and selling of his canoes. Many came by, either for business or to greet the beautiful Nicaso. Some girls, who adored Dio, also came by and paid their respects. They were aware that Dio was at the first Mensochsue and was unsuccessful in the end.

Life in Uda's house was once again steering towards redemption. With constant good deeds to the Izeonah, they remained confident that the near future brought the relief they hoped for, and that the Izeonah would be taken for slaughter, as predicted by the priests.

A one-bedroom living space was built adjacent to Uda's for the Reverend. The entrance of the house was an L-shaped corridor that led to the living room. After entering, one moved left then right, and then straight into the living room. Such a corridor was larger in order to contain water pots and drinking utensils.

The bedroom had two doors; one was before entering the L-formed corridor to the right, and the other was also at the right hand side of the corridor just before the entrance of the living room, which was down at the bottom. The house was painted with red earth, and it had a large yard that sat below the open road. One had to cross the road into a bushy brook before entering the Reverend's compound, which stood open and visible from all sides. It was below the hilly road, which was less of a hill and more of a plain, there were tall grasses with seeds covered in dust. It was only so because the Reverend's house seemed to be built lower than the road. It was difficult to recognize the passers on the road over the plain because only the legs or the legs of the horses where visible from the Reverend's window. The doors to the house opened directly into the living room where the dining table sat in the middle with four chairs made out of rope and wood. The L-formed part of the corridor had a bench close to the water pots, and above this bench the window opened overlooking the road. One could walk into the living room and pass the tables and chairs and walk into the bedroom door to the right, or turn left, passing the water pots, window, and bench in the corner, then turn right into the corridor that led to the back. Before entering the back, the second bedroom door was at the right as well. From outside of the Reverend's yard, one could see both the living room and the chairs, and the first bedroom doors. Uda was making sure the Izeonah was comfortable and forget his suffering. In that way, as the prophet had asked, he might break down his firewall that guarded him in the spirit and the fathers will see the future then they would deliver him to his demise.

When all this was done and everything was in place, Uda, along with Gomsug and their Zongy, went to meet the Reverend for a certain ritual. Since there was a language barrier between the two, a Sadomrah by the name of Maïrah, was requested to help with interpretation.

Maïrah was a midget with large personality. She was also elegant in some ways, yet obnoxious and extremely hideous. Her visage was compressed in a manner that made her skin folded like a mat, her eyes were almost yellowish and her nose seemed pushed into her head, like an ape. She had long gray hair and tiny little ears hidden behind her gray hair and round face. All her features seemed to have been pushed into her head, which was round with a sharp chin. Maïrah also suffered extreme scoliosis, even though she was a midget, and this made her appalling to many who stood in her presence.

It was said that given a sample of a foreigner's blood, Maïrah suddenly possessed the ability to speak fluently in the foreigner's language. According to the legend of the Zong, this trait was passed on from one Sadomrah of this sort to the next. From her native land, which was said to be the shrine of Monshung the snake god, Maïrah watched the land seeking the next child capable of receiving such gift. When a child was found, it was said that she called the child as an infant. The infant or toddler would arise in the midst of the parents' slumber and crawl into the forest to be with the Sadomrah forever. This was the only time a being was safe to travel through the Creek of Monshung.

It was said that many mothers awoke to the vacant cribs and wailed for days, to no avail, for there was never a warning or sign to predict the personality of the infant. Suddenly the child was taken, and the mother was left with motherly sorrow and breasts filled with milk, that would be drained now by other means. Such a cry was often because of the nature of the surrounding forests and mountains, which were unpredictable to the people.

A child was never secured or called a child or a human being in the land of the Zong until the age of ten. At that age the child was then secure and could begin choosing his or her destiny without the interference of the gods. Until then, the child's fate was as uncertain as the winds blowing from all corners of the land. It was more likely that a child experienced premature death, sudden disappearance, requests by the Fathers to serve as a Sadomrah or give other services, a cruel pull from bed before the mother's eyes by a violent entity from the forest, or for Monshung's special nourishment.

Monshung had a ritual that it demanded three living innocent children every year, taken by violent means. Without warning to the mothers, the child, who was usually a toddler, was taken away. All of these mishaps led to much insecurity in families, and mothers held on dearly to their children until the age of ten.

Such was the case of Maïrah that now came to teach the Izeonah the way of Zong. Until the day she arrived, where a few words were spoken between Uda and the Reverend, the Izeonah was treated with special care. After her arrival, the attention to the Izeonah increased. At first it was a brutal encounter when the Reverend saw her. Riding through town on a white horse and accompanied by Gomsug and his Zongy from the outer town, she arrived to Uda's compound and demanded blood from the Izeonah.

It was a clear sunny day, and Uda's compound was quiet. The palm trees outside the town were soaked in sunlight and the dusty ground above the Reverend's quarters sat decadently beneath the wavering dust and sunbaked grasses when the crowd of men, beasts and the two Gomry arrived before his door. It was a planned occasion, for they anticipated that the Izeonah would cause some commotion and possibly perform some sorcery and the Gomry feared that many might get hurt. The Reverend was in bed napping after a long walk in the market, accompanied by Dio and four guards. Lying in his bed he heard the footsteps and he awoke to see his room full of men in armor and carrying sharpened blades.

"Uda!" The Reverend pleaded at first and cowered in the corner of his bed. He stared below them and saw Maïrah the most hideous of them all. She was calm and held onto her dagger as if the incident unfolding was normal.

Gomsug, without hesitation, was about to pull the Reverend from his sheet for the ritual when Uda screamed, "Halt, my brother of great prowess! It is indeed true that this Izeonah must bleed, but I must maintain his calmness for I intend to save my family in the end."

"To what end?" Gomsug screamed. "He needs no composure. We must apprehend him violently so that he has no time to perform his sorcery. Bring him down from the bed so that the Sadomrah may cut into his pale flesh!" Gomsug pointed to the group of Zongy.

"My brother I protest against this act," Uda screamed again in agony.

"Gomrah, you were weak when you allowed this Izeonah on our land, will you falter again? What must this land do to get rid of this Izeonah that you are protecting with all your might? Must you now give him Nicaso to fuck?"

"Slanderer! I am still the Gomrah of Zuxbaha and I hold my power." Uda turned to the stern crowd of Zongy and screamed, "Maintain a calm composure, for I must not make this Izeonah slip into his state of defense!" He turned to Maïrah who stood idle, as if all that was happening had no effect on her.

"I have worked hard," Uda said. "I have sacrificed my sense of right to laugh with the monster." He pointed his finger at the Reverend. "I have no tolerance for his life but only to restore my family. Once I have succeeded, I pray the fathers give me the right to strangle him with my bare hands. For all he has caused me, by dishonoring the house of Uda, I, Uda, will be obliged to kill him."

Uda turned sternly toward Gomsug, in his eyes there were signs of respect, and he bowed. "My brother Gomsug—unless it is your plan to see my demise—hear me now and let this ritual only stand for what it is."

All the while the Reverend was pressed into the corner out of fear, as the men moved about him. He did not understand the reason why they were in his room but he knew Uda had once again stood in his defense. This made the process a bit calmer.

Uda called to Maïrah and asked that he be cut first to the same spot that blood was to be drained from the Reverend. Maïrah, without hesitation, and with calmness, grabbed Uda's arms and moved the blade across and blood surfaced. Uda turned to the Reverend and showed the blood as he wrapped his hand. He pointed to the Reverend and called him to the front of the bed. Like a child or a slave coming to his master, the Reverend came obediently to the edge of the bed, and his hand was sliced. The drip of blood was put into an alabaster jar and the crowd departed. Uda remained. He sat on an edge of the bed and wrapped the Reverend's hand.

While in the process the Reverend asked, "Why," with a gesture that Uda understood. There was no response, as Uda stared at the door. Then he stood up, put his hands on his heart and bowed, as if to thank the Reverend. Uda left the room.

It was a few days later that Maïrah, along with Uda, burst into the Reverend's house. Excitedly but clearly, Maïrah began speaking in nearly perfect English. Shocked, the Reverend watched as she expressed her first few words.

"White man," she said, "I, Maïrah, here to teach you Zong and then you learn to be good man in the people's town. Listen to my voice. Zong good people, but Uda, you master, not happy. But he here to help give you everything you need."

The Reverend raised his hand to speak. "Speak," Maïrah ordered.

"What are you doing with me? And how did you suddenly know my language?" His face still showed his bafflement.

"I answer all questions one by one. First, I tell you, the world you came to is different from Zong. Only door open sometimes we know not why."

"I am confused. You mean to tell me you live on a different planet?"

"I answer one by one."

"Well then my main concern is I want to go home."

"No home. Impossible!" Maïrah was insolent and looked away from the Reverend.

"Why no home?" The Reverend asked.

"I can't help you. You find your way. We Zong and your world never friend."

"I can see that," The Reverend paused, took in a deep breath and looked at Uda then at Maïrah. "Well, what do you intend to do with me?"

"Well, offend nobody and live long. Here, no marriage for you, no child friend for you. Obey and live long. Your Master, Uda," she pointed at Uda, "and me teach you everything you may know about Zong speaking."

"If I understand, I live here never to return home?"

"No." Maïrah responded.

"No to what?"

"If you want woman, Uda bring woman for you next day, she go, never to see you again. Uda feed you, care for you all but, you don't offend and live long here with Zong."

"It seems like I am a prisoner, then. What are the offenses I must avoid?"

"Do no sorceries, take no woman Uda don't give you, make no child friend, no leave Zuxbaha. You die if you do one."

"I am no sorcerer! There is no sorcery bone within me, I tell you now," the Reverend exclaimed.

"Yes you...," Maïrah stopped short and gave Uda a glance. Uda shook his head as if he was saying no. "Speak only of things of the Zong." She said in a stern tone. "We Zong don't care about your world and will be sorcery if you teach us your world."

"I am a prisoner, then." The Reverend was angry.

"No." Maïrah said, shaking her head.

"Do not tell me no, for I am not stupid. I can't go home but I have limited rights. That, in itself, is a prison."

"White man, you are stubborn. I tire with questions already. I come here to teach you Zong. I not understand things of the gods." She looked to the roads. "If you go home or no go home, the gods and you decide. Learn Zong first, then ask questions later. You no listen you die sooner!" Maïrah turned to Uda, exhausted, and spoke in Zong. "Dreanapie," She walked out.

"What!" The Reverend screamed and stared at Uda, who also followed the Sadomrah.

Outside he could hear Maïrah's voice, "I tire, Izeonah, I tire. Tomorrow I come, no question. You learn Zong. Tomorrow you learn Zong."

Six months later the Reverend was well adjusted, and he became very acquainted with Maïrah. She was no more the hideous beast he once perceived. She was kind and took him to the market grounds and taught him things of the Zong. During her six-month stay he had little interaction with Uda and his family. Though they provided for his needs, he was mainly with Maïrah who, in a strange way, had left with "a beauty scar" as she told the Reverend.

"I go but my spirit left well with a man like you kind. I have a beauty scar from you."

The Reverend gave her a huge smile and shed some tears. Maïrah climbed up on her horse, with her bent back turned toward the Reverend, as if she would cry if she looked. She waved her hand. "So long Izeonah." She galloped away, leaving the Reverend to the care of Uda and his Zongy standing in the quarter.

The Reverend watched until she was no longer in view, and then he entered his house and shut the door behind him, leaving the Zongy and the Gomrah outdoors. A strange feeling came over him as he sat on his bed. For a while, in the presence of Maïrah, he was not alone. She had become almost like his mother or a dear friend. Yet, once again, he was alone and was greatly grieved.

Maïrah left without warning. When she knew the Reverend was fluent in Zong, she announced her sudden departure to Uda and then she was gone. Reverend Kline could now communicate with the locals due to her kind teaching and friendly presence. Day and night they had studied together and even travelled to distant lands under the supervision of Uda's Zongy, the Reverend learning along the way. Now that she was gone, only angry faces were left once again, staring at him with disgust and disdain. This sort of treatment made him suddenly cold and he withdrew into this house to be alone.

Maïrah's sudden departure also recalled old things he had experienced in his days in Europe. In 1938 he met a Zionist named Phanuel. Phanuel was such a good man that it left a scar when he learned about his death. Sitting in his dark living room that night, his sorrow-stricken face lighted only by the burning candle. Nora was out for groceries and fell into his arms when she returned, and they wept over the death of Phanuel. On the table beside him lay the letter from his father, which explained Phanuel's death.

"Phanuel was shot by an unknown gunman," the letter reported. "It is a tragedy that we all must suffer." His father added, "Phanuel was a man of wisdom and I enjoyed our political discourse and his intricate ways of seeing the world."

Phanuel taught the Reverend the things of Zion and the cause. He taught the Reverend about the God of Israel, which was later, reinforced by Nora's claim that the God of Israel was embodied in Jesus, and therefore serving Jesus was serving the God of Israel. The Reverend may not have understood all he learned at that time; however, the friendship was strong and Phanuel was a good man by nature. His death, therefore, came as a shock.

The day Phanuel departed to enter Pakistan illegally and join the alliance against the English and other foes, he exclaimed with a sad smile, "You Isaac, live for us. Love for us. Learn for us. Go to school and have a voice and knowledge. I know in my soul that the nation of Israel will one day exist again and that it will be because of people like you." Phanuel pointed his fingers and raised his fist. "The people of Zion will rise again from wherever they are. One nation powerful and strong will rise. Believe it Isaac. No matter what, we are God's chosen people. No hatred, no animosity against us, will stop Hosanna's love."

Into that dark night Phanuel, with some shallowness in his eyes, but also with a sense of existence and vision, hopped into a black sedan along with others passionate for the cause of Zion. They left the Reverend and his new bride waving after him.

Now, once more, he had become attached to someone special, and again, she had abandoned him without warning. At least in his mind Maïrah's departure was no different from Phanuel's death. These feelings were so overwhelming, that his demeanor changed and even Uda became aware it was time that the Izeonah was left alone for a while.

That afternoon of Maïrah's departure, there was no guard left at the Reverend's door. For the first time the Reverend slept without a guard snoring in his living room. The following morning, still bereft, Uda brought him a slave girl. The Reverend became enraged and cried out, considering the gesture a disgusting disrespect.

"I am a Christian! A Reverend of the Council! I don't fornicate! As long as I live in this god-forsaken place, there's nothing pleasurable for me. Especially a woman, that's the last thing on my mind!" He went to his room and shut the door.

Uda was confused, as the Reverend spoke fluently in his language. He placed the girl on a horse and departed with her. Many days passed before he was visited again. Uda came with a beautiful horse and it lifted the Reverend's spirit. He named the horse Mercy, for it had kind eyes and rich brown coat. It was a zealous horse and full of life. Mercy began galloping about his quarter like it had always been there. Such behavior made her his new friend. He began to talk to Mercy as though she heard and understood him.

Chapter Seventeen

Eden's Own Shadow

Life was good for the Reverend in the land of the Zong. He roamed about the land freely and became acquainted with the people. His daily activities seemed to have pleased Uda so much that he removed the guard completely. Although no one in Zuxbaha was aware of what the Fathers had decided as his fate except Uda and perhaps his family, the Reverend was regarded as an avoidable trouble. That was the belief of many, except Niejon. His interest in the white man continued to grow. He became very persistent in visiting the Reverend. He snuck up at night to see the Reverend and they talked for hours.

Nicaso was aware of Niejon's inability to resist the Izeonah. She tried to get her brother Dio involved, but as a carpenter, Dio was always busy. Furthermore, as he was cast out of the line to compete for the *Gamrahood,* Dio's interest in the rituals of his people had diminished. And when Nicaso mentioned Niejon's habit of seeing the Izeonah, he thought Nicaso was looking for sympathy.

Dio now resembled his father at twenty-six years of age, large limbs with wide open nostrils, his head shaped in a square pattern with a heavy voice. He had grown to be a man; tall and well built. Unlike his father in other ways, Dio was a man with strong control over his emotions. He often found life to be more than what his tradition had taught him, and he was not as religious as the rest of his family. He had already established his own career and spent most of his time at work. Besides the interference of the farming season, where he paused in working at his shop and helped his father, he was an isolated man since his family was ostracized by authority from the greatest power of the land. Before then, he cared little about being a Zongah and was not interested in what the Izeonah had to offer. Fully committed to making his own name in the end, Dio would rather to be left alone.

In contrast, Nicaso, regardless of the persuasion from their father, had not developed a single nerve in her body that would make her grow fond of the Reverend. And as the woman of the family, as her mother began to grow older due to grief and the changing tide of her the family position in the society, many duties of the house rested on Nicaso's shoulder. She was unwillingly bound to cross paths with the Izeonah frequently. The Izeonah was happy and she was sad. She endeavored to reverse this. Furthermore, Niejon, who took a strong liking for the Izeonah, was becoming a problem she must address. Friendship with the boy was fatal for the Izeonah, and this could also cause unwanted consequences for her brother if the relationship was not aborted. However, the bonding was so strong that there was no way to defuse it.

At a point when it was becoming obvious, the Reverend attempted to push the boy away for his own safety. But Niejon then was saddened greatly and showed unhappiness. This, conversely, saddened the Reverend also and he found ways to sustain the friendship without raising concerns. Nicaso was aware of all this and she blamed the Izeonah. If he had not left his homeland to be on their shores, life would have been still joyous and the boy would not have been tempted. Nicaso's fear, which arose from her realization that if any calamity befell her family again she would be the ultimate victim, made her determined to put an end to the relationship.

Her first attempt was to tell her father in private. She suggested to her father that the guards should be with the Izeonah again. Her father refused. Instead, he told her that the coming days of the Izeonah in Zuxbaha were numbered, for he saw that the Izeonah was happy. And he knew that the Izeonah would soon be slain and the family would be restored. Lately, Uda had regained some confidence. He had an encounter with Nephrotone who praised him for his fine manipulation of the Izeonah.

Nephrotone said that the rain surrounding the spirit of the Izeonah had stopped and they awaited the slowly dying flames. Nephrotone also suggested to Uda that the sooner the curse was lifted, the sooner he would determine what was next, if ever there were a chance of restoration. And, although he was never to be a *Gamrah,* the current improvements of his work had shown that in the future his sons could be restored to his missed glory of the *Gamrahood.*

Excited about such news, Uda began to inquire about the situation of the Izeonah. He heard many stories that the Izeonah had become lighthearted in his dealings with the Zong and appeared content with his current state. Uda, also was aware of the burden that was placed upon his daughter and how it had deprived her of joy. However, he believed that this was temporary. He lifted his balding pate, hoping to rekindle her smile, when she shocked him with the news of Niejon and the Izeonah.

Nicaso thought about what she would say, fearing that her father's reaction might be severe. She had a special bond with her little brother, which she did not wish to destroy. Nevertheless, the pressure of him going to see the Izeonah every night while the two—boy and man—studied each other's language, was becoming very uncomfortable for Nicaso. Even with such pressure, she had conflicts within. She might leave the situation alone, but this meant Uda would find out eventually, and would grow angrier that she had not stopped her brother. Furthermore, it would be detrimental if anyone but her family discovered this broiling tragedy. Unable to fathom her next move, Nicaso was at her breaking point.

"The Izeonah now speaks Zong," she said sternly, as if desiring to cause her father to rise in rage against the Reverend. But he laughed instead.

"Nicaso," He said lightly, "The Izeonah has been here for a long time now and Maïrah thought him Dahnkka. It is natural. There are some smart Izeonah. Bring my food and sit by me. When I am done eating, Dio should be here. I have a new story to tell you all."

Nicaso, realizing that she had no effect on her father, blurted out news that drove him mad.

"Niejon speaks the Izeonah's language," Nicaso said, drawing back as if to avoid an impulsive slap.

Uda had just washed his hands and was about to eat. When he heard the news, he took his hand from the food slowly, and stared at Nicaso with terror.

"The Izeonah's language?" He asked demandingly.

Nicaso began hyperventilating in confusion. Perhaps she had broken her brother's trust or maybe she had saved him from a more menacing wrath of her father. She was not sure what would happen. She stood still, petrified.

Uda saw in Nicaso's eyes that her story was true and that the Izeonah had been in the company of his young son many times now. What had the Izeonah taught him, Uda wondered. This was unacceptable and something must be done. But as he stood up, his posture changed to a more relaxed state and he seemed to have solved the problem in his mind before even saying a word. "Who else have you told?" he asked with a less harsh voice.

"Mama and Dio,"

"Mama and Dio, the two only?"

"Yes, father."

"How long?"

"From the first week the Izeonah came."

Uda's rage seemed to increase again but he concealed it from his daughter. His son had betrayed and disobeyed him. Boys like that are sometimes the children from the foreign world reincarnated into a Zong. They were filled with torture and death for their fathers. It couldn't be true! His son was adorable. A fine Lad! What misfortune is this? Uda began pulsating for if it was so, then, the Fathers also knew; since they also had been watching the Izeonah. They know! They know! I must see for myself.

"Get me Niejon!" He screamed impulsively and startled Nicaso. Her face, which now showed fear of the repercussions of her action, shone in the night. She was covered with a dark veil. Her long and elegant toes were laced to a leather sandal. Her black dress that clung to her ankles and her light cream colored blouse exposed her in the dark. She ran out of his room feeling even more uncertain about what she planned than when she went in.

Uda left the food and ran to the door as if to reinforce his words. "Nicaso," He called out into the darkness. Nicaso turned. Her father's voice came rushing at her. "Tell no one else," he said and walked over to her. The rage still filled his firm chest. "You are a foolish girl. You waited long before you voiced this venom to me. Leave my sight now!" Nicaso departed feeling ashamed. Not only had she betrayed her brother, but also her father had lost confidence in her.

It was about nine at night when Nicaso left the scene of disgrace. She returned and sent Niejon to meet his father. She cried with Niejon for giving away his secret to her father and she asked him to pardon her. Niejon had learned a lot from the Reverend, including forgiveness. The boy was calm and accepted her apologies. He went to meet his father.

That night, Nicaso had her first close encounter with the man she hated. She called Dio to accompany her to the Reverend's house. At first Dio protested and suggested that it was a dangerous idea. Then, Nicaso shed some tears and Dio firmly held on to his machete and followed her.

Dio was very protective of his family. He had given a concussion to a suitor who tried to rob Nicaso of her virginity. He dragged the man away from over Nicaso and nearly spilled his brains with a rock he repeatedly slammed against the man's skull. Nicaso remembered this and she hoped that this night Dio would feel the same way about the Izeonah as he had against the suitor then.

However, for Dio this was more of an adventure than a clearly planned act of revenge. He was aware of the consequences of harming the Izeonah, and he was ready to allow the Izeonah to be free so that the spiritual wall that had prevented the fathers from capturing his soul be removed. As he followed Nicaso into the night, he was more interested in her safe return than harming the Izeonah. Nicaso sobbed continuously until she burst into the Reverend's house without knocking. They found him perched peacefully reading his pocket Bible. Behind him a fireplace burned with a pot of herbal tea, and a steaming mug of tea was on the table.

The Reverend was calm and composed. He listened carefully as Nicaso expressed her grievances with Dio holding the machete behind her. She explained to the Izeonah that he had brought shame and disgrace to her family and her virginity. That he had made her father a bitter man, and he had caused her father and her brothers to be in grave danger.

Nicaso continued to express her hatred for the Reverend, and when she was done she breathed deeply. It was a long and windy explanation. After she rambled in her native language, even Dio was confused. He thought the Reverend did not understood what Nicaso had said because Nicaso was rapidly and constantly looking at the Izeonah with vindictive eyes while giving him, her brother, empathetic and sympathetic stares, as if to make him, her brother, ready to strike the calmly sitting Izeonah. But Dio had no intention of hurting the white man. While waiting for Dio's response, she heard the Reverend speak.

"Mehlasue," he said, "I am sorry. I have tried to keep your little brother away."

Nicaso suddenly interrupted, pointing her little finger out of anger, "You tell Niejon you are not to see him again. Leave my people alone!" Tears rolled down her face, putting Dio in the mood to threaten the Reverend.

Waving his machete fiercely, he added, "She makes sense, Izeonah. If I have to come again, I will leave with your blood on my blade."

Nicaso continued to stare at Dio as if she needed more from him. Confused at her daring observation, Dio lifted his voice higher, "Oh I will kill you next time, Izeonah. Stay away from him!"

He walked over and spilled the Reverend's drink and stared at Nicaso, as if to gain her approval. She rolled her eyes and they left the house.

The Reverend was calmed somehow as he watched their drama unfold, and when they left, he went to refill his drink and continued reading his scripture. A feeling crept into his veins and he knew the hour of darkness had arrived. Maïrah warned him about this outcome and that it would cost him his life. Until this point, the Reverend had gotten no concrete answers why he was kept in the land of the Zong. He knew how merciless they were on the shores upon their first encounter. He witnessed their brutality against his friends that night and how they boarded the ship and sank it with fire. With these daunting images in his mind, which were never explained, he became aware the hours ahead would be more brutal than ever. This relationship with Niejon had cost him his life. And before this night ended, as Nicaso had said, he was sure the Zong would come for him and lead him to slaughter. This troubled him greatly and his body trembled. He crashed to his knees and prayed violently.

"Lord, have mercy on me," he screamed, "I am not ready yet. I am not ready for this. I have suffered and wish for redemption now. Help me Lord!" His voice vibrated with crying as he held onto the chair tightly, as if it were a person ready to console him. Every sound of people crossing the road made his nerves jerk, and he screamed even more with his prayer. Hours later, his door, which was left open remained open when he opened his eyes, one at a time and sat in his chair. Outside was still dark and silent. He pulled his Bible and opened it to the book of Ezekiel 37. There he read with great conviction;

"The hand of the LORD was upon me, and carried me out in the spirit of the LORD, and set me down in the midst of the valley which was full of bones…and lo, they were very dry. And the LORD said unto me, Son of man, can these bones live? And I answered, O Lord GOD, thou knowest. Again he said unto me, Prophesy upon these bones, and say unto them, O ye dry bones, hear the word of the LORD. Thus saith the Lord GOD unto these bones; Behold, I will cause breath to enter into you, and ye shall live: And I will lay sinews upon you, and will bring up flesh upon you, and cover you with skin, and put breath in you, and ye shall live; and ye shall know that I am the LORD. So I prophesied as I was commanded: and as I prophesied, there was a noise, and behold a shaking, and the bones came together, bone to his bone. And when I beheld, lo, the sinews and the flesh came up upon them, and the skin covered them above: but there was no breath in them…"

Suddenly the Reverend's broken heart softened, and he paused from his reading and lay back in his seat, relieved, smiling at what the scripture had revealed to him. He was the son of man, and the Zong were the valley of dry bones. He had to raise them unto salvation, beginning with the house of Uda. He had to give them flesh and sinews, and he had to speak into their empty bodies so that the Holy Spirit would dwell within. It was his destiny, which must be accomplished.

From the concentration camp in Treblinka, to the mold stricken grave of Nora in Bentuh, this was his moment. This was why he was created—to be a witness in the land of the Zong, the most savage people he had ever seen. This was why the Lord made no provision for him to leave this land, which he now realized was stricken with the dark calamity of the devil's deceit and falsehood. Bentuh must wait. The Zong needed him! All that Maïrah taught him was a lie.

The war and the people he killed were all tests. He was made to redeem the Zong! Without those tests, there would be no testimonies!

"Ha, this life of mine, why twist and turn on me? Why confuse me as if the LORD was not in control? Haven't you heard that I was made to accomplish greatness and walk with the Zong into the New Jerusalem? I am not afraid. I am not afraid. I reclaim my tests as testimonies. And this time hear me, devil, I am not afraid. I will defeat you!"

The Reverend was zealous afterward and he began to overheat from the encouragement he felt in his heart, mind and soul. He stared about and looked to the window where he heard noises of people laughing across the road.

A confirmation! This laughter must continue in heaven. It was time for redemption. He got to his feet, walked to the door, took a glance outside and saw a few people with lamps crossing the street. He looked to the heavens and it was dark.

"The devils world," he mumbled and shut the door. "I know you listened to my plight this night, devil," he exclaimed and began rebuking violently. "Your plot against me shall not work. No accidental death shall come my way, as you retain your stronghold in this land. I am a child of God. Soon your darkness shall be blotted out from this land!"

The Reverend clenched his fists and raised his hands to the ceiling. "No more shall they be hell bound, for I have come to make them heaven bound...!" The Reverend sat in his chair again, truly convinced. "The Lord is with me, for He knows I need Him to demolish the strongholds that have entrapped the people of this land. The seed of salvation shall be planted!"

Slowly the Reverend glared about again, and he imagined and envisioned his present surroundings with smiles, the land of Meheyassahapunawa being transformed into the glorious name of the Lord, who put him there against his will; but for a greater endeavor and redemption from his past. The grip of sadness and the pain of solitude suddenly dissipated from him. He reflected on what had happened with Nicaso and her brother and he laughed. He finished his reading and closed his Bible. He prayed that God would keep the revelation in sight. He concluded in his prayers, that God grant him endurance and bravery. The night was over. He needed to sleep. Under the sheets the Reverend found rest and slept light-mindedly for the first time in the land of the Zong.

Chapter Eighteen

The Sage and the Savage

he after-farming season between planting and harvest was the most
T savage of all. Many approached it with a mixture of excitement and fear.
It was the most dreaded time and perhaps that which mothers feared
and took precautions to prevent unfortunate incidents. It was the time
when men became drunkards and caused desolation and unnecessary brawls.
It was a time known for neighboring strifes and deaths. The métier of
thieves became popular, and at times bodies were discovered in gutters and
alleyways at dawn. This season was also considered a dark time for the
crops because they were at their most vulnerable to either blossom into
edible vegetation or be ruined by the brutal pace of nature. Everyone
prayed to his or her Sadomrah and offered sacrifices for a good harvest.
Some went to the extreme by stealing property and children, and babies
were missing from their cribs if infant sacrifices for the crops were required.

The after-farming time brought in weary men with less to do,
sitting around in groups and discussing love affairs with history rolling over
their tongues to either aggravate a neighbor or bring laughter to their
audiences. Pots of fermented wines created sensual arenas for lust,
infatuations and orgies that only those with clean hearts cared to avoid.
Even Uda was involved in some incidents where his guards removed his
daughter, Nicaso, from a neighbor's house. She entered there and threatened
to bring the house down with fire the next time the lady entertained her
father and caused distress for her ailing mother.

"Harlot," she screamed as she was pulled away, "Close your filthy
legs the next time you hear his name."

The streets were packed with people moving about either on
horseback, in wagons or by foot searching for whatever the night could
bring to their pleasure-seeking hearts. At times, when the brawling was
spilling out to the morning hours, the Gomrah organized a game where
angry men fought in a circle of crowds until victims were dragged away
breathing at the brink of death.

Many Zong settled their disputes in this fashion. It was said that a
Zong kept his anger for the after-farming season, because there, he could
express it to the fullest.

"My first energy is for my crops," they professed if offended during
the farming season. "I will train and flex my muscles when I farm. After my

crops sink their roots into the soil sucking on the sweet breasts of Usula, come and provoke me and you shall see my anger explode like the violent wind that will rage against your malnourished crops. Let him who was weak and lazy and had no skills of defense keep his tongue behind his teeth. Let him who had experienced pain and had suffered the last farming season at the hand of his neighbor, break bread now while the weather favored him. He must befriend the neighbor who almost took his life last year, for there was no guarantee that this year would change his circumstances."

This time was also the season to travel. It was time for visiting relatives and rekindling lost friendships. It was time that the people learned and experienced the full beauty of the land. The trees were blossoming and the forests were producing vegetation of green luscious plants that beasts, both wild, tame, and savage fed on and became fat, so that even the carnivores enjoyed preying on them.

The land of the Zong far and near enjoyed and suffered in the same manner, for where there was pleasure, also lay unimaginable violence. Though Uda was also involved in this time of enjoyment, he was occupied as well with many activities. He was the Gomrah of what was then the most populous clan. He served as the judge who traveled to many small villages settling disputes. Most of these disputes were simple but sometimes they were daunting. At times he was exhausted and he found time in the arms of the local women who were happy to share their beds with the Gomrah.

Sometimes the Reverend came along. Most times he was just a spectator who offered his opinion after Uda had already made his decision. Uda rarely considered his voice to be valid. However, the Reverend was happy too, for the people were accustomed to him and left him to his own devices.

However, through all these commotions, where people were living and behaving naturally according to their Zong traditions, there was one incident, which scared the Reverend and many others who attended. It was the harshest reality the Reverend had experienced yet; and perhaps it caused a part of him to rethink his position as a stranger in the land of the Zong attempting to convert the inhabitants. The incident took place in the town of Bloe, at a funeral of a famous Traveling Zongah named Nufommog, who, as the rumor went, suddenly died from a venomous snakebite. Many said however, that he died as a result of another cause, and that it was not an ordinary snakebite.

The rumor was that Nufommog survived his journey of initiation into the Damned Forest because of his secret activities, which were also the same that led to his demise. Nufommog was a man who would transform himself into a wild bull at night, and appear to local hunters in their dreams and challenge them to a game. However, his last challenge was detrimental and Nufommog wished he had not done so. One night the bull appeared in a dream of a famous hunter by the name of Leblah, and challenged him.

Leblah was a famous vender of animal skins and other useful tools, which the Zong used for writing and communicating information. The Reverend was a customer of Leblah. Very experienced in his art, it was said that Leblah had his barn full of bodies and the remains of individuals who had challenged him throughout his career. His skills were enhanced by his strong dogs, which were said were part dog and part leopard.

Anyhow, the story of Leblah, Nufommog and the nature of their households became the talk of town by the time the season was over. After Nufommog's brutal experiences of suffering some cold nights fighting the elusive spirits and other unknown creatures from the dark world of the Damned Forest, he returned and challenged Leblah for a final brawl. Leblah had a dream in which Nufommog challenged him to meet in the jungle. It was a life or death challenge. In this case, Nufommog, had to prove his prowess by transforming into a wild bull and allowing Leblah to hunt him. This had been a famous game of hunters and their rival preys in the tradition of the Zong. The point of the challenge was that Leblah had to aim his arrow for a kill or Nufommog would penetrate vital parts of his body with his horn and kill him. The winner of the game would become famous and achieve an elevated rank and power among the men of his world. And as he walked about town proclaiming his deeds, other men who transformed as well would submit to him if they had never attempted such a challenge. So it was that Nufommog appeared to Leblah in a dream and proposed the challenge.

Upon awaking from his dream, Leblah went into the forest that was rich with poisonous plants. Leblah then made some rubber trees bleed out their latex. He boiled the poison and the latex together and poured it into a narrow mold to make a poisonous arrow. Leblah knew it was a fight to the death and he prepared well. He then took his arrows and dogs into the forest. Many hours later he and his dogs returned with a wagon soaked with blood and the carcass of a dead bull. He called the people of the town and shared the kill. However, Nufommog would have survived his brutal defeat, if he had received the heart of the bull and buried it in a cold place until it naturally decayed by time. If it had been so, his life would have been spared, and he would have had the chance to transform into the beast from the wild again. But Leblah, aware that he had won the challenge and not knowing who had challenged him, fed the heart to his dogs in the presence of his audience. Then they applauded and said farewell to whomever it was that had challenged him.

"I Leblah," he said boldly, " I am a great and violent hunter. Let no man challenge me to a game he will not win. Here lies a vital kill. This is a transformed body of a man amongst us. He challenged me, Leblah, the greatest hunter of Bloe, and now he has lost the battle. His heart my dogs shall eat. I say he is dead!" The crowd roared agreeing. "I say his life now decays in the rotten, slime-enriched belly of this terrifying hunter here." He touched the dog that had eaten the heart.

"He came at me writhing like I must release into my trousers what I ate for breakfast!" The crowd laughed. In Leblah's eyes though he spoke jokingly, the idea of releasing into his trouser what he ate for breakfast revived a bit of the fear he had felt facing the now dead beast. He paused briefly and then as if he was returning from his vision, he burst into laughter.

"But no, it was a mistake on his part, for I can duck and roll and still release my venomous arrows. And my dogs can chew on his manly tools. A beast like this was no match for us. Jellom," Leblah pointed at his dog chewing on a bone, "He sprang to the neck and I released my arrow like Yore's waves rushing against the shore. Wherever the beast's head turned my arrow was there. Vicious and painful, even in his nose so that it dashed to the earth and trembled. My dogs remained attached to his neck and testicles. It thought it could swing them out by jumping and kicking. Yeah a fool it was to think of such a trick. My dogs were vicious with agonizing teeth and they only tore deep into his flesh when he swung and kicked." Leblah beat against his chest and stood up pompously showing what he did next with a stance. "I Leblah with confidence stood over him and thrust my knife. Now he must go to the creek and die—hahahaha!!!!"

The crowd roared with excitement and took their share. Everyone ate the meat, for it was said to be a great source of life and even increased the fruitfulness in a family and made a man's ejaculate ten times thicker. And so all men feasted with pleasure, and their wives adored watching them. Though in the dream Leblah only saw a talking bull challenging him to meet at a specific location it chose, he was glad to have won.

Many famous hunters have met their ends in this fashion. But, once again, Leblah won, and was glad. But he was not aware that this bull he had killed was Nufommog, his brother. Nufommog could have asked boldly for the heart and saved his life, but that action would have revealed his identity. For the Zong, this was a total abomination against the origin of the gift of transformation. It meant that the spirit would have come for him and caused him to suffer and wish for death many days before it came to him. In such a predicament, either way, death was inevitable. And the disgrace would have killed him if he had begged his brother for the heart unless, Nufommog, had killed Leblah after receiving the heart of the beast. It was a serious decision and in the end dying in such a way, without begging for the heart, was the proper way in accordance with the gift of transformation. It was a glorious death meriting recognition in the world of transformation.

The gift of transformation was one of the most respected aspects of the Zong tradition, and many wished for it. It meant they lived in two worlds and could escape to any at their own leisure. It brought power regardless of the animal they transformed into.

Many loved the hog transformation, for it meant they were skilled farmers who had large lands and planted faster. The skill of the hog, using the nose to dig into the earth for food, made it very skillful in planting seeds faster. Another gift mainly cherished was the gift of the eagle. He who transformed into such a bird was the predator and established dominance over other animals.

A story of the great eagle that ravished the land in ancient time was always told with great respect. It was said that the eagle was a menace to the people. Being from the damned forest and trapped in the world of the living, it came in daylight and took its price. People were taken from their meals into the air and became dinner for the large eagles. Disappearance was a common thing then, and when men sat in groups, they tied ropes to their waists and tied them to large trees so that when the violent eagle came it was difficult to pull them away. At times the ropes were not strong enough, or the eagle was in such great turmoil from hunger that it took the man along with the tree he was attached to.

It was said that voices of those taken echoed from the ground and into the air. At times, roofs were ripped away at midnight while people slept so that the eagle could eat a man from within. There was a story about a man in the middle of intercourse taken from on top of his wife and his ejaculate stained the wall of his house. His wife filled with sorrow never cleaned the spot, as it was a reminder and a memory to her sweet days with her lover. Also, two forbidden lovers, who met in secret in the forest, experienced tragedy of the violent eagle, which took the girl and left the man throwing stones and weeping as his bride called his name with sorrow from the claws of the eagle. Many lamentations of great sadness were associated with that time. Once a bride, on her way to her husband was taken away at midday and the husband grieved without consolation.

Such a beast, which roamed the land suddenly vanished and had never returned to torment the people again. Some said it became Magello the priest. Some said it went into the underworld to return one great day. Some also said, it was hunted and killed by a great hunter who was in the descent of Gomsug's family line. Whatever it was, at a ceremony like Leblah's, the people were always reminded of the old legend. However terrifying the story, many still considered the gift of transformation a blessing and hoped for it someday. This was a gift, which was acquired at birth or received from a dying parent on a deathbed.

Nufommog was unsuccessful in his final test. Testing a famous hunter and becoming victorious was the last test. Nufommog failed.

"Let us eat and celebrate my victory!" Leblah said and put his arms on Nufommog's shoulder. Together they watched the dogs devour the heart of the bull. Then three days later Nufommog was found dead, with yeast eyes, swollen jaws, bloated body and mouth filled with flies and larva. His body decomposed just as fast as the town devoured the bull. The faster the people defecated the eaten bull, the faster it was with Nufommog's physical decomposition.

It was uncertain whether Nufommog was actually the bull, though many signs pointed toward it. The known fact that he died three days later became the greatest confirmation.

Nufommog's death revived old scars and created new ones for his family. When Leblah found out that he had killed his brother, he wished that Nufommog had come to him in private and confessed the ordeal. However, it was an unfortunate predicament. The animal component of Nufommog was completely controlled by the nature of the beast. His initiation to Gomrahood could have raised the family to a new status. And since he had a premature end, it caused the greatest divisions that made many wish that such a curse was not upon them. Nufommog's family was destined for failure. The people laughed and gossiped about the family.

Nufommog's death was a relief for Uda, for Nufommog was being prepared to take over his clan since Uda was growing old, and his family had been banned from achieving the status of Gomrahood.

When a man reached the status of Nufommog, he was regarded as a man who was at the verge of the highest pinnacle in the Zong tradition. Therefore, upon his death, which happened so suddenly, an important ceremony was held for him. Since destiny acted cruelly against Nufommog, he was sent back once more to the living to tell the people about the transcending moments of his life. In so doing, he was allowed to borrow the skin of a Sadomrah. It was an involuntary visit, they said, for it rarely happened. In a lifetime of a man, if he saw such an event once, he was said to have had a good life. For Nufommog, the people knew it was to happen.

"He was special and showed great potential," his family wept. He died so young and suddenly, it made the grief more shocking and overwhelming. There was so much promise in his life that the gods had to send him back to tell the reason for his sudden departure. The news travelled so fast that many gathered three days after his burial at the entrance of the gravesite awaiting the Sadomrah through which Nufommog was to come.

The midday sun sat over the middle of the Bloe, and beamed with intensity upon the people. The Sadomrah started with a screeching sound of an animal unknown to the living, followed by the flock of flies. Slowly, from the narrow road, which led to the graveyard an entity with body entirely covered in black raiment approached. The shape of the Sadomrah was gaunt and dislocated. The torso was disjointed and sat almost apart from the lower limbs like a stick bent in a sixty-degree angle.

As it appeared in view, its demeanor showed that the day was about to turn into calamity. At first it stood afar, afraid, and watched the group that suddenly became silent when the first signal of fleeing flies greeted them by pounding upon their faces and in their mouths. Suddenly the people covered their noses, for the Sadomrah was close and had a reeking stench of wet mold and death.

The Sadomrah was somewhat afraid of the living. His demeanor seemed as one who would have returned to the grave and never confronted the people. However, it was up to the ancestors to decide and they wanted to expose what transpired when Nufommog was alive.

With little joy, in a gloomy and sorrowful tone, the Sadomrah spoke, addressing the deeds of Nufommog's two wives: Sola, the younger and Moleymuh, the elder. Tarnishing secrets they were that needed the light, and Nufommog, sent in a form of a Sadomrah, grievously told the living and their Gomrah. It was with justice though, that Uda investigated the matter and rendered his most brutal judgment the Reverend had ever witnessed. It was not only the Reverend who left the scene with the feeling of sadness, but many of those who where at the ceremony wished they never attended.

The Sadomrah's voice echoed and recounted all that had happened. It was sentimental, sad, and astonishing. Nufommog's household was filled with so much animosity caused by the elder wife, that she was roasted alive the same day after the Sadomrah revealed her deeds. Her violent deeds were so insidious that even Monshung was not allowed to taste her flesh. With the most vicious screams ever, the Sadomrah was filled with sorrow to reveal such evil activities.

"Sola," screamed the Sadomrah, "How pitiful are you to have borne me five children and never seen any live to see another week?" One could feel the Sadomrah's agony, standing at a distance to avoid human contact, as it dropped to its knees and wept loudly. "I am in agony to live," screamed the Sadomrah. "Me, Nufommog, my spirit is restless until I see justice for even you, Moleymuh. What a terrible bride you are! Get out of my sight, you miserable woman!"

The crowd began to murmur, and in Moleymuh's eyes, knowing what was to come as the matter unfolded, tears of sadness settled upon her breasts. Sola, who was the younger wife against whom the evil was committed, stood on her feet attentively. In her eyes there were also tears of indignation that settled as she gazed at Moleymuh.

The Reverend was confused and curious. Never in his life had he seen such a creature. Furthermore, it was surprising to him that such a creature could exist. In his mind, he screamed blasphemy! Another trick of the devil, he confessed to himself, for only Christ came from the dead. Now, whatever creature was pretending to be Nufommog from the dead was a complete deception. He wished he had stood up and asked the beast to reveal its true identity. However, he knew if he screamed loudly with what was beating upon his heart, he would have sold his own body to suffer pain at the hands of the angry mobs of Zong. It was a death sentence. He was out-numbered. He watched with the most puzzling eyes as the Sadomrah spoke, rising to its feet, almost incapable of gaining its balance, for regret was great in Nufommog, and the Sadomrah rolled to the earth in distress.

"Evil," the Sadomrah pointed its finger at Moleymuh and it fell to the knees and wept some more. Beneath the raiment, the eyes became as red as fire. The crowd was astonished and gasped.

"Tell us in full, brother," screamed Leblah from the audience, in tears.

"Indeed," responded the vile beast, lifting his head, and the eyes glowed deeper red as it cried. "Brother, we are blind to the devices of women, a curse we refused to accept. She is a child killer!" The crowd screamed in astonishment. "How evil you were to me, Moleymuh! I am going to explain in full so that you pay severely for all you have done. My ejaculations were in vain that they produced offspring you murdered mercilessly."

Moleymuh rose to her feet wailing, then she ran in the opposite direction towards the town in utter confusion and remorse.

"Grab her!" Uda ordered, and the Zongah on horses chased after her. The crowd was now turned to the running Moleymuh, who was by then pleading for her life. Her anguished face became simple, destitute and blank. Her hair was in disarray from the rough handling by the Zongah who apprehended her. Dragging her across the dust, they began to pound on her, making demands.

"Talk! Confess," the crowds demanded. "What evil have you done?"

While all attention was focused on Moleymuh, the Sadomrah turned and began walking toward the grave. The Reverend cared less about the deeds of Moleymuh. A certain fearless feeling crept through his mind and made him walk toward the Sadomrah who was returning from the dead. He would have reached the grave, except that Uda yelled, in the most vicious voice, and called him to his senses.

"Izeonah, we move to town!" Uda gave him a hellish look, which he grasped immediately, and watched as the Sadomrah disappeared into the woods.

In town, Moleymuh was already covered in her own blood and excrement as she confessed to killing Sola's five innocent children. One by one she said as she bathed them, she took a sharp pin, which was as small as a needle, and pierced the pin into each infant's softest spot on the top of the head—the pate, which moved or quivered near the frontal lobe. The infants panicked and jittered in a horrible fashion before giving the most excruciating screams for survival, as the embedded pin reached the brain and caused internal bleeding until the brain was drowned in blood. Eventually, even the infant's eyes were stained with stripes of blood and the body became as hot as fire with fever.

Then, each time a Sadomrah was invited to investigate the horrible deed, it found no cause. Eventually the Sadomrah would conclude that the child had come to torture Sola, the mother, for her wrongs in the past. A few days later, each child died and was taken to the grave; its brain soaked in blood. The family and neighbors had no understanding of what had happened,

It was a repetitious process that followed days of weeping by Sola, Nufommog and Moleymuh. Sola remembered how she, along with Moleymuh, wept together, and that Moleymuh showed great distress to a point that many feared she would have died from her grief. It was a piteous moment that drew Sola even closer to Moleymuh, and they shared the strongest bond through the grief. However, learning that the crying from Moleymuh was an act to conceal her true intensions, Sola was astonished and bitter. She suffocated while hearing Moleymuh's confession.

Sola dropped to the ground and fainted, after hearing the stories. She was revived with a cold bucket of water poured over her. Moleymuh began to weep sorrowfully. She asked that she be burned immediately, for in her own eyes the evil she had done was great. Moleymuh began to curse her barren womb and blamed it for her actions. She cursed the earth she had walked upon, and she cursed even the crops now blooming on her farm. When Sola was revived, she ran to Moleymuh and dropped in her arms and they wept again together.

"Mother," Sola cried. "Mother, my sorrow is too great. I am afraid I should die also."

"No, my child," Exclaimed Moleymuh, "I have done you great evil. Even death is more welcoming than life to me." She pushed Sola away, "Depart from me! Haven't you seen how cursed I am?"

Sola tried to crawl back into her arms but Moleymuh looked away into the blazing sun, cursing her life and calling on death.

"Mother," screamed Sola, as she was pulled away. "Mother, how shall I live my life a widow and without a mother! You have killed me, mother!"

"Yes, my dear, and I killed your children. I am not your mother!" Moleymuh screamed and took her ears away from Sola's voice.

Sola was taken from the scene, for fear that she would not live to witness what was to happen to Moleymuh. A group of women went into her house to comfort her, allowing the Gomrah to finish his judgment.

"Strike her indeed!" Uda ordered his Zongah.

A Zong threw the most vicious blow into Moleymuh's left eyes so that he drew blood. She dropped to the floor with open mouth gulping for breath. Her fingers trembled slowly, as they tore away her clothes until she was naked.

Suddenly Sola returned to the crowd with a burning piece of firewood and struck Moleymuh repeatedly, causing blisters.

"Remove her," Uda yelled, and they took Sola away.

A group of women followed again. Her voice, so piteous, resounded as she was permanently removed from the scene. Her grief was becoming great and overwhelming.

"Mother, you have done me a disservice that I cannot recover from in this lifetime. Mother!" Sola's voice echoed and faded away.

Uda rose to his feet after he watched Moleymuh lying to the floor almost at the point of death. He ordered that she be dragged to the center of the town so that she could be set on fire alive.

The Reverend wished he had the courage to beg and preach for forgiveness. But the rage in the people's eyes would have made his pleas to no effect, and perhaps endangered his own life. His skin became numb as he watched Uda take out a blade and shave Moleymuh's hair until some flesh was taken along with the hair.

Moleymuh was without strength then and her face was drenched in blood. Naked, she defecated on the earth in plain sight. Sitting under Uda's blade, she grabbed him and pleaded that her life be taken quickly for the pain was now great. "Gomrah," she said with a sorrowful voice, "Let it be over now, please."

Uda struck her so violently that the blade sliced her against the cheek and she mourned helplessly. "Your shit smells like death!" He said angrily and called the angry mob of Zong to take her to the center of town.

The next man, who came close to cause her harm, complaining about the smell of her excrement, was met with an unexpected mauling. Moleymuh, wishing for death urgently, wished to cause such a great disturbance that they would kill her instantly. She was like a savage dog infected with rabies. She grabbed the man's legs and began eating his flesh like a cannibal. At first the man attempted to use his last strength to give her a strong blow. It was to no avail. Moleymuh was almost numb and would have eaten the man's fingers that he used to pull her mouth away from his bleeding leg. When he knew that Moleymuh had completely turned into a menacing beast on his legs, he turned his head in pain and cried for help.

"I am being eaten! I am being eaten by the witch!" He screamed.

Many came to his aid. But Moleymuh refused to let go until a Zongah slammed a steel bar into the back of her head and she released her teeth from the man's flesh.

The man left the scene limping with a dent in his right leg. He was heard later cursing Moleymuh, who stared at him with great satisfaction. The man tended to his wound with his eyes watering and a face filled with pain and perhaps some regrets of ever coming so close to Moleymuh.

A strong rope was thrown around her neck and she was dragged to the center of the town to be burned. She was placed upon some wood in the middle of the town and set on fire. It was a scene of an angry mob cursing, spitting and denouncing every association with her.

Moleymuh's ashes were not to be buried in the fertile soil. The Gomrah and his Zongy took them into the forbidden land and sprinkled them upon the earth, which was also filled with filth of other evildoers.

When the men returned to town Sola was no more in sight. They later found her over her husband's grave bereft. She was helpless and had to be attended to. Sola's life was altered thereafter, and she was found dead in her bedchamber a few weeks later. By the time Moleymuh was being consumed by the fire, the Reverend had had enough and galloped away on Mercy.

That night the Reverend questioned many things. He even had a bit of doubt, for not only did he witness violence once again, but the memories of the Hammer D and other victims of the war came to him and he cried like a boy, so that those who passed his house talked about it the next morning.

"He wailed all night," They told Uda.

The memories on the beach the night when the Reverend was captured had become dull. So far things was not as gruesome as he expected until he witnessed the burning of Moleymuh. Furthermore what transpired on the beach was justified, the Reverend concluded. But also he was now convinced that nowhere was safe after all, and the memories of the war were refreshed. Even more daunting, the Reverend thought he knew the man Uda was. However, after he saw him perform such acts the day before that he began detesting the Gomrah once more.

When the sun came up Uda, along with Dio, went to the Reverend for a visit. Then Uda, being a man without remorse, demanded that the Reverend leave his house and head to the forest to hunt. The Reverend was quiet, and although he did not refuse the demand he became exhausted just being in the company of Uda.

"Why change moods on me, Izeonah," Uda asked sarcastically, "I have not caused you harm yet."

"I am not afraid of you causing me harm," the Reverend protested and looked away.

"Well then, be of good spirits, for we will go for a hunting experience. One I reckon you shall enjoy."

"Blood is all you seek," the Reverend said with a stern face.

"Izeonah, one day I am sure."

"Are you threatening me now too? Why not kill me in public like you have done to Moleymuh. Have you ever heard of forgiveness?"

"Oh, shut up your nonsense talk already, Izeonah," Dio said with laughter. "I understand you are virgin to blood. But we are Zong. Blood runs from our veins to the earth."

"I am not a virgin to blood," the Reverend added. "As a matter of fact, I have seen blood and have cause some to drain from people."

"You man of tender nerves, who was the coward you killed?" Dio added lightly.

"Ask your father," the Reverend said and stared at Uda. It was as if he was depressed and wished for death also. But Uda defused the tension by shooting an arrow.

"Look," Uda said, "There is a gazelle. Let us leave tension for later." He and his son began after the gazelle.

The Reverend was still burning within and searched for confrontation. He chased them and screamed. "Uda I forbid you to cut off this conversation," he exclaimed. "Why do you treat me like I am a prisoner? Kill me or let me live like you all."

Uda stopped and turned to him with a smile; then he gave him a menacing look. "You Izeonah," he said, "You are on my land. I slammed your head to the deck that day on the ship and took you like a boy. You are a slave. To me you are nothing but a hindrance, and one day I pray soon that you find your demise." He turned his back and galloped away.

The Reverend stood for a while and then screamed again. "You are weak! Strike me right this moment and I will see how strong you are."

"A time for that has passed," Uda said. "It may come again but not today. With your fire spitting devices you called guns that day, I am sure you remember, we used our axes against your mighty men successfully and left your ship aflame. The belly of the sea is still digesting their remnants."

Dio was already after the gazelle and was not in sight when they continued this riveting conversation. It was as if he refused to listen to the tension. He was now returning with the dead gazelle.

"Look, why talk vainly? We are here to hunt. My son has a kill, now it is time for harmony. Come Izeonah." Uda galloped away.

The Reverend breathed in deeply, realizing there was no need to continue on, for whatever he had done, Uda continued deflecting the conflict.

Later that night, while they sat by the fireplace plucking at the savory viand, the Reverend initiated a new kind of conversation. "I am sorry," he confessed at first, and then he stared at the stars above. It was a clear night and the crickets made very loud noises. Silence ran through the men while they plucked the meat and then the Reverend asked Uda, "Why are you still good to me after all I have done to you?"

"Izeonah," Uda said, "You are filled with sorrow all the time. Look to the sky, it is bright with stars and life. We are eating meat soaked in sweet herbs. It is juicy. Keep your mouth full and you shall forget your sorrows."

The Reverend grimly smiled and cut away at the meat. Serious conversation with Uda was always pushed to a later date, sometimes deflected or ignored. However, after this night, he had a chance to talk. It all began because Niejon's persistent visits were becoming a hindrance, and the boy was removed to another town.

Chapter Nineteen

Tempered and Temperament

*T*hat child of unforeseen promises was taken away into another town where the Izeonah would have no more authority over him. When Uda became aware that his boy was able to visit the Izeonah without restraint, he took the lad away early one morning. Uda had a sister who was married to a Gomrah and lived miles from Zuxbaha in Sayapoe. Uda's sister was a Sadomrah who revealed the fate of the Zong society in particular ways that was not considered prophecy.

The Reverend was present that morning when Dio and his father took Niejon to meet his aunt. A sad departure it was, and many wondered secretly about the fate of the lad. Furthermore, it was not disclosed why he was taken with such intensity early in the morning. His mother watched with a face of sullen despair and his sister, Nicaso, left the scene sooner to reduce the grief she would have felt watching her brother leave the house under such circumstances. Though it was Nicaso's fault that he was being taken, she also knew it was necessary.

Nephrotone and the other priests had watched from the dark and planned a more ominous intervention, if she had not told her father, who in his silent rage was taking a precautionary reaction to save his boy. The Izeonah was a weed in his family with roots deeply planted in every sensitive part of his life. Into that early morning fog, the two horses disappeared.

In his leather sandals and cotton gown the Reverend stood by sadly that morning, knowing once more that he was the cause of the incident. He grieved alone. During the two days journey that Uda and his sons were away, the Reverend refused to eat. It was a fast he deliberately took on as he prayed that the Lord would deliver Uda's family and that the travelers would return home safely.

Nicaso brought the Izeonah's meals the following day, but she was unable to get into his house. At first she thought the Izeonah had escaped. Then later she saw Mercy tied in the barn and the doors were locked. She ran into the square and returned with two guards who shattered the door with axes. They found the Izeonah before his fireplace writing on some goatskin he had gathered. The guards did not care about what he wrote, and when they saw his face filled with sorrow they laughed and ridiculed the Izeonah, saying that he had foreseen his soon-approaching death.

Nicaso set the food on the table after she gave him a look of disdain, and she left along with the guards. A few hours later he opened the door and fed a malnourished dog, which came by every so often scavenging through his backyard. By the time Uda returned, the dog had befriended the Reverend and was with him in the house.

The curious neighbors revealed that Uda had returned. They ran to see if the lad was with him. Their commotions and gossips were loud enough that the Reverend knew Uda had returned. After he was done fasting for the day, he bathed and went to meet Uda. Along with him came the malnourished dog, which he had named Murphy. It was an obedient friend that stared constantly at the Reverend, seeking his attention. Murphy was a dog of black coat and sunken in stomach—telltale signs of hunger. It was part Malinois and part Border collie that loved the Izeonah so much that it slept by his bed. So they left and found Uda smiling peacefully. It scared the Reverend even more and he felt a coldness running through his veins. He paused for a bit and would have returned, but when Uda noticed the Izeonah, he called.

"Ah, the man of sorrow, come and keep me company." Nicaso gave him a grim smile and dismissed herself. It was now the Reverend and Uda once more sitting outside. By him lay Murphy. "The wind tonight is fine," Uda said lightly.

"How much damage have I caused this time?" The Reverend asked forcefully, looking into the dark night as if rescuers from his world would come for him.

Uda was about to be stern, but then he thought it over and lightened his mood. "He was a lad blinded by your charm. He is safe now."

"When will you talk to me like a man?" The Reverend asked with a trembling voice. "I know I am not your friend, but at least I deserve some understanding."

Uda was silent. The Reverend touched Murphy and caressed it a bit. It caught Uda's attention and he glanced and took his eyes away quickly. Murphy enjoyed the Reverend's caress and licked his hand.

"His name is Murphy," the Reverend said. "He is my only friend right now." He looked at Mercy. "At least for her," he said, "she sleeps outside so she barely gets to see my tears at night. I am teaching Murphy English, you know." He gave Uda a glance. Uda was silent still. The Reverend then smiled in a grim fashion. "You know, when I am alone at night, I talk to Murphy. And then I ask him, 'what are they to do with me?' You see, everything is vanity here. It is like I am already dead. Even though my heart beats, I feel nothing lively. I tell him, 'I was once a violent man who killed my own people and lost a beautiful wife.' I sought redemption beyond the swirling sea, hoping and willing to make new friends to forget my sorrows. I was wrong. So wrong that I wish I would return back in time, to the child I once was, who had everything."

The Reverend paused and there was silence still. He caressed Murphy some more and gave Uda a look of wonderment. Murphy licked his hand.

Uda pushed his chin into the air, avoiding looking into the Reverend's face. There he left his face and asked, "Izeonah, are you in need of a woman now?"

The Reverend smiled without taking offense. "No," he replied. "I need a friend, Uda." He looked into Uda's eyes but they were still not ready to look upon him. The Reverend shook his head with disappointment and said, "You know my country was already filled with unrest, with people fighting and killing one another before I became a soldier. I thought I could save lives, you know. Instead, I took many." The Reverend shrunk his face imagining things.

"It was never safe, anyhow." He gave Uda a glance. But Uda remained silent. "I didn't start the war you know. All those killings, people being burned in the oven and mothers losing their loved ones and children being killed for no particular reason, were all overwhelming." He gave Uda another glance and remained silent. The Reverend smiled grimly. "You know, come to think of it, nowhere is safe. Man is always violent. I ran from violence and found it here. I killed people too, you know. Sometimes I see their faces. I killed a boy in the snow. Well, he was not really a boy. He was a useless soldier come to think of it." The Reverend gestured in the fashion that demonstrated what he did to Frederick. "I bashed his head. He was my enemy and a friend you know. I don't regret killing him though, for he was neither a killer nor a savior. He killed no Jews, yet he did not protest either. Not hot nor cold." The Reverend smiled again. "Not hot nor cold," He repeated. "You know, in my belief, when my God talks about His second coming, He said he would spit out those who are neither hot nor cold..."

"Izeonah," Uda finally interrupted. The Reverend lifted his head as if he had a breakthrough to the Gomrah. But Uda yawned, "I had a long day on my return. I must lie down." He arose and took his leave.

In the dark the Reverend sat alone and tears rolled from his eyes. The despair was immeasurable. He walked to Mercy, and rode home with

Murphy trailing behind them. He went to bed.

Chapter Twenty

A Certain Calamity

*I*t had been almost five years and no one came from Bentuh to rescue the Reverend from the Zong. His hope to become the redeemer for the people was fading. It was dangerous to mention anything concerning his belief. The test he was now facing was greater than expected and so he was refusing to bear the burden any longer. Sometimes he wished that it was all over so that he could return to Bentuh, but he did not know what to expect because the Zong were impulsive and violent. And the sea was calm without any sign of a rescue party.

He also heard many rumors concerning the behavior of the sea and Yore. It was said that when Yore was pregnant with deeds, which she most often was, she caused the sea to swallow up those who dared venture out on it. Maïrah informed him that the sea sometimes stayed violent for decades. There were bones of the sons of Meheyassahapunawa beneath its embellishing roars and dark depths because they dared venture at the time when Yore was pregnant. Though he laughed when she informed him, her statement seemed to bear some truth now that no rescue came to him five years later.

Will Reverend Goodspeid and the councilmen ever send help? If he were ever to get out of Meheyassahapunawa alive, the help would have to come from beyond his means. He was a man without hope and all that streamed through him was vanity. His moods began to fluctuate because he was in a place of confusion. Redemption had not been reached and he was five years older with no goals achieved. By now he was sure that he was forgotten by his fellow councilmen, and that his legend was to remain behind the closed sea of Meheyassahapunawa.

He hoped Nora was remembered in a special way, as a faithful woman who converted a stubborn Jew to Christianity. Phanuel's words to him that night, as he embarked the Sudan was that he, Isaac Kline should live and help form the New Jerusalem by becoming an educated man with power and knowledge to cause enough upheaval so the world could see the true existence of Zion and his people. But all of that was now left to the Zong to one day reach their tempers and strike his life out of him and kill that dream he had promised Phanuel. The Reverend was convinced that this was the only land in modern times in which a man like him was treated in such a fashion. He came to realize that the people were not primitive enough to be converted easily by his proselyte preaching, or the way he tried to console those he referred to as desolate, downtrodden and defeated.

In fact, they were very defensive against any of his utterances, especially when he spoke of N'Daygmong in ways that were critical and degrading in comparison to his own God. The Zong usually ran away from him and avoided him thereafter. Over these few years, with his graceful nature and soft laughter, some Zong even found him appealing and came for visit or brought him some gifts including cotton cloth when the winter came and Sophon's poor health kept her from meeting his need to cover his frail body. But one by one these same friends began to disappear as his conversation continued to be not to their liking. Over time, he came to rely more on Murphy and Mercy for comfort. The people defended themselves well against his God, and it was a challenge to convert them.

At times, the challenge to convert the Zong came with doubt, and he questioned the integrity of his faith. How did he become a Christian to have invested his life in Nora's God? Reminiscing, he remembered, a member of Nora's family named John of Cantony introduced him to the group in South Africa.

One cold winter night he came back from the Nazi concentration camp and he smelled like burned bodies and was covered in ashes. His eyes, and every aspect of his body projected defeat. He had failed to save any Jew, and in his hand was the letter confirming his deployment soon to the front. The momentum of the Allies was beginning to get the world's attention and Germany had to crush this force before it became a problem. To do so, more soldiers were needed at the front. He was among the group to be deployed next.

After a warm shower and dinner he went to bed in a foul mood, but Nora was not letting her husband remain in that state for another day. She awoke in the middle of the night and spoke of her distant cousin, John of Cantony in a missionary group called The Council of Truth. It was a long discussion, thinking about ways to escape his deployment to the front, and, even more, a way to escape from all he had seen and done since he became a soldier. A few days later, Nora had procured a way for their departure out of the country. With that, she also received mail from her cousin, who spoke highly of the Council of Truth and their deeds beyond the blue ocean. According to John of Cantony's letter, the Council of Truth was a group dedicated to the purpose of the Great Commission. Even more so, they were to preach with blood, sweat and tears where necessary.

They were to counsel the world in need of Christ, and were willing to die as Christ died on the cross. It was a righteous cause, a righteous life, and a righteous fight. It was a duty that only death would separate them from. As long as they lived, the proclamation of the Gospel was to continue resonating through their lips. In normal days before the war, he and Nora had talked about one day traveling to unfortunate places around the world to help the needy. It was Nora's passion before they were married. With their world shaken by the news of his deployment to the front, this opportunity was in accordance with Nora's dream and a relief to the Reverend. The way to escape had been provided in a detailed plan in the letter. A Nazi officer, who secretly hated the uniform he wore, was to use his power and influence to get them away.

These incidents were decades ago. Nora was dead and he was with the Zong, oceans away from the Councilmen and everything else he knew or understood. And, though these retrospective thoughts pervaded his mind at the moment, they did not remove his belief of the God he had vowed to serve until death. If anything they confirmed it looking at the nature of the Zong. For all he had done; killing his own people and watching with eyes of cowardice as many innocent body fell to the earth by his bullet or another Nazi screaming profanity, God had been merciful. Furthermore, he was convinced that the Zong were possessed by the devil. However, the manner to bring redemption to the land was the challenge he constantly faced as he lived among them. It had been five years and the sign of change was no longer in sight. All he had was this bible, a dog and the horse. Somehow they were not even his. Murphy suddenly appeared and became his friend. Mercy on the other hand, was a gift from Uda. He was surely alone in a sense and should he give up now, the answer was darkness. Moreover, he had a feeling that this darkness would create a space that he was not ready travel through. He envisioned the space as an endless dark space of time, taking him through events in his past as fast as the speed of light. Along the way, as he moved with such speed, he saw flashes of light that were filled with memories of his life torturing him forever. This vision of such darkness created limited choices. If he gave up now he was still alone. Therefore pressing on, believing that one day redemption would come, was the only hope he cleaved to.

Pressing on meant, however, that he was no longer subject to the councilmen, but to his heart and the quest that brought him to the land of the Zong. This quest, somehow, had become obscure. Was it redemption for the Zong or a subconscious reality to save his remorseful heart from his past? The Reverend was desperate for an answer but he knew sitting under the strong hand of Uda would bring no outcome. The house he sat in was a prison. The people he considered friends were all part of Uda's world in some way, and were temporary. So, therefore, if the conviction that brought him to this land had substance, he needed no reinforcement from Bentuh to cause the Zong to bow and worship the living God.

Furthermore, the choice he made to accept Christ as his Lord and Savior meant that his belief was true, and that if God was true and with him, then he had an army that was mightier than a thousand ships swimming across the ocean to rescue him. It was time to move on past the drags of fears and waiting upon Reverend Goodspeid to send his vessels full of men and arms.

If the God he served were truly the creator of the universe, including the universe or world of the Zong, then He would save him. But if the gods of the Zong were truly alive and had powers to overpower his God, then the Zong would win. The Reverend would wait no longer. H was subject to no internal voice but the one that spoke, "Change has finally come!" He said boldly to himself out loud, "I will be that change. I am moving on."

He was not looking back any longer, or counting on the Councilmen to rescue him. He was surrendering to faith and ending all his quests and all his fears. It was not just for the God he so desperately searched for ways to please, but it was also a faith that would either cause him to lose his life or redeem him in the end. This faith was to create a new man within himself—a new man bound by no boundary of the war or the rules of the Zong. It was to create a new man bound by no painful memories of Nora's death, and a new man free of the weight of the world, even the world of the Zong. He was accepting his faith for the first time, wholeheartedly without emotions, Nora's voice, or any sermon he had heard over his lifetime. This was for him, Isaac Kline. The Reverend suddenly paused and looked about his surroundings. Yes he believed!

Realizing all this, the Reverend got down on his knees and prayed the simple Lord's Prayer and ended with, "Jesus, I believe." He put in a bag his bibles and some clothes, including everything else he had since his captivity and rolled them. It was morning outside but the sun was still waking from its slumber. The sky was gray and still. Many had arisen and were going about their routines, but the entire town was not yet up. Over his head a few flocks of birds headed for the east. By the wall of his house the pigs were mating and fighting.

The lives of the Zong were already in motion. Yonder, a boy with a bucket of water returned to help his little sister who had fallen and spilled her bucket of water. A man whistled and passed on the road just above his compound. Life in Zuxbaha was beginning to resume for the day. The Reverend felt that he must now put his plans into action and begin right away.

By him Murphy stood beckoning for attention. The Reverend knelt and touched the dog. "I didn't know you," he said. "Now I know you to be Murphy—a dog from somewhere that I don't know that came to me and kept me company. Maybe you are an angel since your owners have not come to claim you. Maybe you are a dog from the strange world of the Zong sent to watch me. Whatever you are, you have been a good friend. But it's time we go our separate ways unless you can save me from what I am about to do."

The Reverend stood on his feet and walked away. Murphy followed. The Reverend walked to Mercy and galloped away, riding east towards the Forbidden Land, where Maïrah and Uda had warned him never to venture.

Murphy followed a little longer and stopped when the Reverend entered the forest. It barked a bit, whined and then stayed at the entrance of the forest where it watched the Reverend until he was no longer in view.

The Reverend never glanced back at Murphy, but continued on until he was frightened by what he saw crossing the road. It was a harmless Sadomrah of the forest. The Sadomrah of this kind were the mothers of the forest and only became violent when threatened. However, the one the Reverend saw had inspected him from afar and knew he was no threat. It crossed the road, only giving him a quick glance.

The scenery gave the Reverend a cold sweat and somehow altered the reality he knew. It chilled him that he saw a naked woman with human flesh and legs of sheep crossing the road, a hair-rising experience. His heart pounded and he questioned his motives as to what he was really prepared for. He stood still for a while, afraid to move. Even Mercy was reluctant to go further, for the beast passed very close ahead. After a moment of deep breaths he tapped Mercy and they moved on.

As he reached the crossing point of the Sadomrah, he turned his head a bit and there it stood along with many of its kind breathing and watching the Reverend. His eyes never left the road as he and Mercy passed quietly and the Sadomrah and the others followed him with their eyes. A moment later, when he knew they were no longer near him, he tapped Mercy and galloped with a rushing speed.

The Reverend had no concrete idea what to expect ahead. All he desired was to see people, living beings.

"Lord, I hope I have all necessary preparations, for I have no idea of the direction I am taking now." This was a prayer of his heart, for he knew not if the Sadomrah were after him, or if they had set up a trap ahead for him.

With enormous paranoia, he looked back and sped away. A few miles later he was still alive and Mercy was exhausted. By then he was in a plain of brown grasses. Then he saw smoke ahead of him. "A town is close by," he convinced himself and his confidence was restored once more. "The Lord is with me. That's why these aggressive beasts froze in their tracks." He encouraged himself and looked back at the empty road. "I bet I had thousands of angels along that road ready to bring these beasts to dust." The Reverend laughed with confidence and continued his travel to the town ahead. He knew not what to expect, but hoped to be free, and perhaps, find some dignity somewhere. The lurid sunset over the horizon by then, and the shift in the animal kingdom was taking shape. Nocturnal creatures were emerging and the Reverend was close to the town ahead. It was unnaturally quiet for the hour he arrived. Being accustomed to how the Zong lived, when the harvest season was a few months away, in such a town as this he expected a flock of inhabitants moving about gaily. But on the contrary, it had no one roaming the entrance roads. Strange, he thought.

The Reverend was soon distracted to read the sign hanging at the entrance, "The Town of Poe," it read. Below it was pasted in bloodstained letters that seemed to have been written by a troubled hand, "The dying town of Poe. Come again N'Daygmong, come again."

Poe was almost a desert land. The roads were covered with black rocks. The houses were built of wood and the roofs were covered in dusty palm thatch and tree bark. Each house was built in a position that faced the other from left to right, with large roads in between for traffic. It was not a scattered arrangement, but had organized patterns and formations that left open spaces to look further beyond the outer landscapes and plains. The outer stretches, which were mostly dusty and dry, had small grasses and burnt fields, which, were caused by the scorching sun. Poe was a small town that sat not far from a volcanic mountain, which clouded the horizon with dense smoke and debris.

The mountain constantly erupted and poured out pools of lava and emitted heat day and night. As the Reverend approached the town, the scene changed. At least seven miles before he saw the entrance of Poe, he travelled through lush grass, dense forests and valleys of rocks with gushing springs and wet soil. But from where he stood at the entrance to the town, he could see a straight path that ran through the town to the volcanic mountains ahead. This road was parched and desolate with dust, sand and rocks.

The inscription he had stumbled upon was covered with dust even though it had bloodstains with the chilling call to N'Daygmong. Poe was almost a ghost town with empty houses and wagons that seemed to have been abandoned suddenly. A few tools were scattered about as if they had been deliberately dropped out of fear. The Reverend felt a surge of panic but continued his walk.

Before he could interpret the inscription, however, he was suddenly surrounded by a number of people curiously surfacing and mumbling from burrows in the ground. Their eyes widened and they appeared to be frightened as they stared at the Izeonah. As the dust rose from the ground, a dusty head was followed by either a man or a woman, staring curiously.

"Izeonah gapuh, Izeonah gapuh," they said among themselves.

The Reverend understood the language, and he smiled and walked between them as if he were a special being. "Izeonah gapuh. Yes, I am a Izeonah walking the streets." He said loudly with conviction that he had made the right choice of leaving Uda and his Zongy miles away. He was hoping that these Zong were the primitives Maïrah talked about. These people, he had learned, had a different lifestyle and were less violent. But as he continued to enjoy the attention, a swift trumpet sounded from the distance and sent the people scrambling back into their burrows. The

Reverend had no time to comprehend what had happened, and before he knew it, a large group of Zongy and a Gomrah encircled him. They had large chains and huge steel weapons and arrows on wheels. The men were all well shielded and carried deadly weapons as if returning from a fierce battle. Poelboe the Gomrah burst through the group and asked with a tight face in the Zong language, "Izeonah, haven't you heard, have you come to torture us as well?"

The Reverend, hearing the word torture, thought of it as an opportunity to instill fear in the trembling people. Somehow he felt that they did not know who he was, and since they showed signs of fear, he hoped to take advantage of that. He then smiled wildly and shook his head.

"Yes," he said in the language, "I have come to produce extreme fear until you heed to what I have to say."

"Hahhhhh," the people gasped in fear, looking at the Izeonah over his horse. Feeling that he was in control of the situation, the Reverend waved his hands as if to secrete a certain power, and his gesture made some Zong in the crowd duck their heads. Then, he made a fist. "I have power and all of you must listen unless you want me to unleash..."

" Blam!!" A wooden ball, tied to a chain came out of a Zongah's hand and struck the Reverend on the head. It knocked him off his high horse and into the dust. An echo remained in his head and he was dizzy. The Reverend first hit the earth with his chin, and it was as if the actions were all in slow motion. He first saw the earth coming up to meet his face, then his face struck the earth and his jaw quivered. There he lay struggling from the dust, spitting out sand, his face covered in dust. He looked up and a group of Zongy already hovered over him. They grabbed him and tied his hands to his back. While they took him away, an extremely deep and menacing voice, with riveting sound, blared from the forest, and they nearly dropped him out of fear.

"Quickly into the pit," the Gomrah screamed at his men.

The Reverend looked about from between his carriers and saw many Zongy running about as if gearing for the worst. They were all in a battle mode and began to roll big wheels, catapults, and large steel arrows toward the direction of the frightening voice that echoed from the valley ahead. From their demeanor, the Reverend understood why the people lived in burrows. The cry, which caused the panic, was unlike anything he had ever heard. It was filled with aggression, and it was clearly understood.

"Gomrah!!! I shall have the flesh. It is mine," screamed the voice.

"No," the Reverend heard the Gomrah respond. "It is ours. Return to your dwelling this hour, and leave us alone,"

"Then we must spill blood for I shall have it..." the beast roared again.

"It will be blood that we shall spill, hahah!!!"

Boom, boom, boom!!! The sound of fireballs followed by excruciating cries of men as if they were in a fire, followed by the beast roaring.

The Reverend was already in a deep dark pit of mud with his hands tied. The mud was up to his neck and the rope, which they used to lower him to the pit, was attached to him. It extended out of the pit. Looking from below, the Reverend saw the narrow spiral path above that the dimming daylight came through. The rope was extended that far and tied to two poles standing above the pit.

The pit became darker throughout the night as the battle raged on. It was a long night of cries of men, along with cries of the beast that continued into the morning hours.

At some point of the night, the Reverend wished Uda would come and save him again, for the night was long and filled with wailing of all sorts. He was cold and missed his bed. He missed Uda and Nicaso's angry face. He missed Murphy and wondered if Mercy was alive. He missed the sound of the people walking by his house and the sweet smell of the bread, which his neighbor baked every morning and gave him some. All of the things he missed now made the night even longer, the cold grew chillier, and his body gave up. He was becoming numb and wished he could rest.

Then suddenly the ground shook too heavily for his comfort. He had awakened from what he realized was a nightmare. While in the pit, when he fell asleep, he dreamed he was back in Europe during the War.

Standing in the camp, smoking a cigarette that night, Frederick asked him to go with him and visit the wounded who had made their way back home. He remembered how these wounded soldiers described the violent front. It was merciless they said and unlike anything they had ever seen or heard. The sounds of rockets lacerating the sky, bullets missing their targets, bodies exploding from tank shells, these men were wounded in devastating ways. Their description of the tools used in the war was so vivid that the Reverend had a nightmare about them the following night and awoke in hot sweat.

Nora was present then, and wrapped her soft arms and legs around him and whispered tenderly to him throughout the night. The Reverend then expressed his fears that if he went to the front, he might return wounded like them. Subsequently, his nightmares became a reality, for four days later he received the letter ordering deployment to the front. Unwilling to see it through, Nora procured a way and they escaped to West Africa. He had failed to save his people and now his life would turn for the worse if he went to the front.

Frightened by the letter, he knew this time it was absolutely imperative that he do something to release his conscience from the already growing guilt. Going to the front then not only promised more failures, and the likelihood that he would not return to Nora again. The allies were gaining the upper hand. Furthermore, he said to himself, if he were ever to fight, it was to be for the Allies and not the Nazis. So, after he and Nora talked that night, she found a way for them to escape and she took her frail husband away from his guilt and the coming promise of rains of fire from the bombs of the Allies. It was a brilliant plan, one that made the Reverend's heart melt with love for his strong-willed wife.

Sitting on that desert camel in Gambia, and looking into her eyes, he knew life would never be the same in her absence.

"We are one now," Nora said with certain softness. "If you go to war, it means I must come along," She smiled in a gloomy yet passionate manner. "But I am not a soldier, which means, you would have two lives to protect."

By the third day after the discussion, the Reverend was sure their plans were the right idea, and he endeavored to pay some debts before his departure. Thus, on that cold night up the hills, he bashed in Fredrick's head and then went to the other officer's house. There he stabbed him outside and screwed the sound suppressor on, heading into the house and killing the officer's family. Nora was displeased with the idea that he killed the woman and children. And though the Reverend cried after he had killed them, to him it was minor in comparison to the hills of bodies in the camp that reeked for miles.

The odor from the camp was what he smelled even after showering. He also ate it in his food and that made him starve. For not only was the smell too overwhelming, but also it was on the spoon and everything else he touched. By the time he left for West Africa, he had lost almost one third of his body weight.

These moments from his past that haunted him were perhaps

vanishing sorrows. Yet, they were not remedies to what he faced now, especially in the little town of Poe when he was thrown into a dark pit. The pit he was placed in was deep and perhaps they might forget him there. Though noises and vibrations from above removed some particles from the walls of the pit, he was sure his voice was not strong enough to reach the people above. The Reverend managed to contemplate his past once more in that dark pit. These gloomy recollections may have been caused by the cold streaming through his veins, but who cared to investigate? He was only a gloomy man, anyhow. The night was gone and fighting raged on. He would just have to endure for another day.

Chapter Twenty-One

Miracle Spear

"Affliction"
Over the brook, the songs of rooster
Blasting through the early sun,
I stretch out my mouth and
Cry for release.
The dawn of my infliction,
I see vile and disgraced men hiding,
Bound by the mire of desire, death, greed
And for my blood.
I am afflicted!

*T*he Reverend was awakened the following morning by the pulling of the rope, which brought him to the surface. When he came out, he saw the town with a few more people scrambling about frantically, accomplishing their chores and daily duties. The Gomrah from the night before, by the name of Poelboe, stood at the entrance with his Zongy. When the Reverend laid his eyes upon the Gomrah, he immediately became furious and screamed, "Let me out of this rope or you will beg for your life from Uda. I am his slave! I am a precious slave of Uda, and he will go to a great extent to kill whoever harms his slave. Do you hear me?" The Reverend was serious in his narrative until he heard a voice calling sternly.

"Izeonah quilah kah nue!"

The Reverend turned his head and saw a large group of Zongy and Gomry gathered. They all carried armor, metal plates, defense shields, helmets, horses dressed with steel, iron caps huddled in piles, furs and men. In their midst the Reverend cast his eyes about searching for the voice which he heard. He was sure it was familiar. He recognized it as Uda in his state of anger. He became silent and stared at the Gomrah Poelboe with surprise.

The Gomrah Poelboe smiled. "Slave," he said, "Proceed and meet your master."

The Gomrah signaled that they should take him to his master. The Reverend's eyes remained ahead of him, anticipating Uda's face. They were at the center of town where two men were tied to a pole with nooses above their heads ready to be executed.

It was a tense crowd of both Zongy and their Gomry. Uda, Gomsug, and other Gomry were all discussing the fates of the two men. As the Reverend approached, he saw that Uda's back was turned toward him. Uda remained engaged in the matter at hand.

"They are good and then, now, here we are," A man said with a bit of regret and bowed.

"They are disobedient and shall be hanged," the Reverend heard the voice and saw Uda waving his hand, dismissing the man's explanation.

"Feed them to the beast and he shall have his fill. Besides, it can be the last image imprinted in their disobedient eyes before they depart for the ancestry realm," Gomsug spoke, climbing on the platform and swinging two strips of his whip at the tied men.

"The beast is never filled until it has what it wants," Poelboe spoke loudly from behind the groups carrying the Reverend in their hands.

Uda turned and his eyes met the Reverend's. In their eyes,

unspoken words projected fervently. In Uda's eyes there was indignation. In the Reverend's eyes, there was hope for forgiveness.

The man holding the Reverend began setting him loose, readying to turn him over to his master. "The beast has terrorized us for three days with no rest. It wants Shumlah and Poe needs Shumlah," Poelboe added.

The Reverend was still staring at Uda who, by then, had removed his eyes and was looking at the Gomrah speaking.

"Shumlah?" Uda asked.

"Shumlah," the Gomrah responded.

"There is blood on the ground because of Shumlah," Uda said with contempt.

"We need Shumlah," the Gomrah responded sternly.

All the while the Reverend remained attentive, listening to the men building up with the tension.

Gomsug stepped into the picture with a big presence. "Poelboe," he pronounced with indignation, "You have given half of your town in three days because of Shumlah, the weakest Sadomrah of all." He turned and looked at the group with a look of confusion. He turned again, and looked at Poelboe. "I fight Mebzongbre. It is a war against men. But a war against a beast, this is new. Where did he come from and what is his name?"

"Brother," Uda interrupted, "We are not here to fight this war. Give him Shumlah and the beast returns to his world and leaves the town."

"Camphus is his name." Poelboe explained, "And we need her to put an end to this massacre."

"How are you sure Camphus will return without Shumlah? She is the reason he left the dark Damned Forest and caused such chaos?" Uda asked sternly.

"I have no insight." Poelboe responded, "but she offered eternal peace to my land, and I am ready to give my life to protect my generations to come. I am ready to listen to…"

"It is a Sadomrah from the world of lust," interrupted Uda angrily.

"Shut up," Gomsug screamed at Uda and smiled as if he saw something pleasing. "I would rather live in a world of lust than of death. Your only concern is your Izeonah pet."

Gomsug walked toward the Reverend sternly and grabbed his hand. He stared at it for a moment then he set it loose. "He is still your Izeonah pet, alright!" He said laughing rudely.

"Can I help you," the Reverend asked, giving Uda the side of his eyes.

"Can, can I, can I help, he said," exclaimed another Gomrah, lightly passing his slimy tongue through his widely opened teeth. "The Izeonah speaks Zong now. Hey, look, he thinks he is one of us."

Gomsug pushed the man out of the way and firmly stared at the Reverend again. He touched his hair and then pulled at his shirt. "You are not one of us. You can never be!" He stared about the Reverend, who remained stern giving a somewhat condescending look. "Friends, the Izeonah is a Zong now! He needs his shield and he can join us in the forest! Are you ready Izeonah? We want no wimp or a man that never needed a woman. Why are you strange, Izeonah? Are you a man? Hahahahah!" Gomsug turned and stared at the crowd.

They laughed. Even Uda twisted his face with a smile. Gomsug stole the attention from everyone as he continued to ridicule the Reverend. "Izeonah, I'll tell you something. Have a woman tonight and feel a little better and this gloomy face will disappear between her thighs, yeah?" He turned to the crowd again and they laughed. Then he became serious. "We must liberate Poe from her darkness. You can help, heh? More men are required, hahahah!"

"I am not one of you," the Reverend responded as if trying to defuse the shameful manner in which Gomsug had spoken to him, "I can never be."

"You left Zuxbaha, Izeonah, and came to the east. This is a place of forbidden venture for you, as I, Uda have spoken." Uda interrupted.

By then the noise was becoming high and out of control as the men ridiculed the Reverend from where they stood. Uda yelled angrily, trying to shut them up. The crowd became silent. "You disobeyed me," he said as if looking at the face of his son. The Reverend nodded in agreement. He was about to speak when Poelboe interrupted.

"Good friends, I must know if your hand will extend beyond these borders and help me. The sun will set soon and Camphus will make his demands again, or kill my people."

"Well, we shall help you and then fill ourselves with lust before our return with Uda's lover here," Gomsug added, jokingly and grinning at Uda.

The Reverend was in their midst, and now the dry mud gave his face a funny appearance.

"Return him to the pit," Uda added. "Let us get rid of this monster."

They began to carry the Reverend away again, but he resisted and screamed that the pit was cold.

"Uda!" He called out as they took him away, "Don't let them take me into that cold."

Uda turned his back on him and resumed the discussion, as if he were never present. The Reverend's voice was so stern and terrifying that it woke Camphus who came with a blunt force and swiftly ran through the pole where the two men were made ready for executions. It ripped away the poles and the podium, along with the men who were tied to it. Their voices were heard fading away into oblivion. The crowd ducked to the earth and began readying for attack. The town was in panic again, and ran for the burrows.

The Zongy holding the Reverend ran with him and threw him into the pit and they rushed in the direction of the beast. Fortunately for the Reverend, he was not tied. He sank into the mud up to the ears and nose, and he could barely breathe. He tilted his head and fought to stay afloat.

Above, he heard men running about and making war cries as they prepared for Camphus. It was clear to the many Gomry present that the matter was grave, and that the beast in pursuit was of great strength. Its footprints were about sixteen inches long and two feet wide. It was a monster with the most ferocious nature they ever encountered.

The people of Poe had disappeared by the time the Gomry and their Zongy were prepared to face the beast, and they discussed among themselves what was needed to defeat the beast. They eventually planned to drown it in volcanic lava, but first, they had to feed its appetite by bringing Shumlah to it.

The group split in two. One group led by Gomsug ran toward Camphus while the other led by Uda headed to the dwelling where Shumlah was kept. The group led by Gomsug began to set up their defenses by sharpening some sticks made out of poisonous roots and thrusting them into a wide open valley of dense dry trees just below where the lava stopped. Strong ropes were tied to trees and long chains with sharp objects were attached to their ends and hooked up to wheeling catapults.

Gomsug was in full armor and pulled out a long whip, calling out to his best Zongy to follow him. Without hesitation, he ran toward the sound Camphus continued to make.

Uda, on the other hand turned to Poelboe and commanded, "Show me the dwelling of Shumlah now."

"This way," Poelboe responded as he led them toward the shrine in which Shumlah lay.

"We must draw Camphus out here. The smell of Shumlah is enough," Uda said with intuition.

The echo of Camphus was by then loud, and its roars sent chills down the spines of a Young Zongah within the crowd. However, they pressed on desperately trying to ignore their fears.

The shrine lay open. Shumlah was within, making creepy noises of unbelievable magnitude like a chicken that was about to lay egg, but her tone was riveting, loud and unkind. There were guards of Zongy hiding about with sharply projecting objects as a trap if Camphus ventured there. They could hear Shumlah's scary cry, like an angry rabid dog. At first, when the men entered, she lay peacefully with a face of a girl. Her pretty eyes, like those of kittens, stared lightly at Uda. Shumlah had taken on a form of a woman in order to create sympathy. She was calm and naked sitting in the corner with her legs crossed in order to hide her private parts. With dark, wet hair and tender fat lips, she was a beauty to behold.

Sitting piteously before the door and gazing upon the men, she seemed very vulnerable and desirable. With her soft, blissful batting eyes, arms crossed about her exposed breasts, legs folded in a mild manner she was even a tempting entity to some men's lusty imagination. However, as simple as she was in her own nature, the men were aware of her Sadomrah capability and they knew her potential for violence. She was a beast by nature and could lash out.

Uda saw through her disguise and disregarded her apparent beauty. He wanted to end her madness and restore the dying town of Poe. Tears welled up in her eyes when she realized her attempts were not convincing the Gomrah, Uda, who suddenly frowned and demanded that she come out.

"Put on your true identity and join us out here," He ordered.

Shumlah suddenly stared at him fiercely and changed to her true identity. Soon a coat of fur began to slowly grow upon her soft skin and she released her arms from her breasts. The breasts were no more. What was left was only a dense white fur and she rose to her feet and completed the transformation. It was the first time, for many Zongy present, to witness a true Sadomrah display her power. And with astonishment, they watched until she waved her hand in a perturbing manner.

"You have given up on your promise, Poelboe. Your father will definitely find you incompetent when you return to the ancestry world, after we are all devoured by Camphus."

Shumlah was completely transformed into a strange creature by then. The head and neck resembled an alpaca but the body was that of human with the same fur, which covered her head. Her five fingers had the claws and sharp nails of an eagle. Her feet remained exposed, still retaining the beauty they had before she was transformed.

Her face had developed some frightening features, and her mouth was large with teeth like a domestic cat's. As she grew weary of the Gomrah's demands, her teeth showed sharply behind her lips and her toes suddenly became longer like a chicken's. She began to beg Poelboe, promising to marry his son and create giants to defend the land.

A Gomrah by the name of Esmondeh, who was perhaps disgusted by her smell, pulled out his blade and screamed, "Refrain from your offer. Men are dying out there, Shumlah!"

Shumlah swung her head out of frustration and pounded against the wall and she exclaimed with a bit of sadness and a hint of aggression, "I will not be eaten, Gomrah!" She screamed violently and her face and eyes became as red as beets. She turned to Poelboe; "You must not let him take me out of there. I can save Poe! I will produce children to defend her land. I will give your son extreme happiness in bed and in the streets, in offspring and duties."

"Camphus killed my son yesterday! I have only a daughter now," Poelboe said sadly.

"I must have you then, and bring you the same promise and more," Shumlah said, stretching her arms and almost transforming into the beauty she was when the men walked in earlier.

"A folly is what you are," Uda interrupted. "That folly which led you here. Camphus wants nothing more than to lie with you, why resist him and cause him to become angry at us?"

"Perhaps she is a folly and has caused him to inflict his great anger on us," another Gomrah said.

"I believe it," another added.

"What do you know about the dark world I come from, Gomrah? Nothing! Speak not of what you have not experienced," Shumlah stretched her neck.

"I know nothing of your world, but this I know. I saw you streaming through our town with him chasing you about. His large figure breaking through our houses and causing great disturbances is what matters to me. Now give in to his needs so that he kills no more," Esmondeh said.

Poelboe was about to speak when Uda interrupted by brandishing his blade and pointing to Shumlah, intimidating her. "Shumlah, I will not repeat myself again. Come out now."

She paused in her pacing and gave Uda a look. She knew he was ready to strike her. Holding her claws against her mouth, she turned to the men standing at the door, dropped to her knees, and clapped her hands, pleading, "Please, Gomrah, have mercy on me. I ran from the forest for my life. I offended no one. I am a girl full of youth and bliss. Why must I be eaten so soon?"

"He is your husband," Esmondeh screamed in her face and she fell back into the corner, fearing ever more for her life.

"He is not!" She screamed.

"Well, I am not of your world," Uda said. "You came to the living for help when you were condemned in your own world. You did no wrong. Who am I to protest? Either way, you are a beast. Now get up on your feet!"

Shumlah sat on the ground and then rose to her feet while coating herself with more fur, preparing to leave with the men.

All a while, there were violent screams and roars coming from where Gomsug and his men faced Camphus. By then, it was a fight for life, for the first view of Camphus was terrifying. However, his strife was brief. Gomsug and the rest of the Gomry had already slaughtered the beast before Shumlah arrived. Camphus crashed into the hot volcanic lava with some sharp tools sticking out of him. Surprisingly, he was obedient and less violent than expected.

His size and movements made him a monster to fear. In comparison to other monsters who escaped to Damned Forest to frighten Poe and other towns, Camphus's damage was the least they had seen. It was said that when a beast with such magnitude left its native realm, only a *Gamrah* or a true hunter who had killed many transforming beasts was capable of taming or killing it. Never before had such a beast from its world left a town with so few casualties as Camphus had in Poe. Usually when such beasts left their world, until they returned willingly, they left the corpses of their victims lying in the streets until the reeking smell of cadavers brought flocks of vultures to town.

Surprisingly, Camphus had done little damage for his size. He resembled an enormous Tasmanian devil, and was a very large beast that stood about eighteen feet in the air and weighed over two tons. His fur coating was thick, black and oily. His mouth was appallingly large with sharp teeth that projected out fiercely. His walk shook the earth and he was quick on his feet. But now, he lay there, succumbing to his wounds. Camphus actually was unwilling to surrender. He wanted Shumlah, and tried with all its strength to remain alive until Shumlah was his. But the Gomry who attacked him had strength and wit, which they used and brought him crashing into the volcanic lava.

He was very civil at first, and wanted to reason with the Gomry, mainly Gomsug. Although Camphus saw the future, he remained aggressive in an effort to show his dominance when he approached the Gomrah.

"Camphus!!" Gomsug screamed as he signaled to his men for a prepared attack. "Show yourself."

"Hah, Gomsug the great *Gamrah*, return to Zuxbaha, for I refuse to eat the flesh of my father." Camphus screamed from beyond the trees and valley of lava.

"Then heed my call now and obey."

"No, I want the Shumlah," hollered Camphus.

"Why the flesh of Shumlah," another Gomrah spoke from beneath the dying shrubs. His voice stirred up Camphus and he ran from within the valley and roared.

"Gomrah of Lubland, speak no more!! Speak not!! Who are you to utter words? I am a Sadomrah, violent and merciless. Give me Shumlah!!"

Camphus was now above the valley where the volcano stopped. Steam came out of his nostrils as he breathed, staring intensely at the group of armed Zongy standing against the other end of the valley. Between them a pool of lava flowed steaming and emitting intense heat. At the right, the volcanic mountain boiled. It was a terrifying sight that was covered in ashes and the clouds were dense and dark.

Camphus's mouth was full of blood and he gagged constantly, as if choking on something. Looking beyond, he saw sharp steel blades projecting from the earth and men camouflaged in the dust all readying their weapons. Camphus moved his head and cringed, aware that traps were set for him below. Laughing in a menacing way, he called out to Gomsug who, by then, stood with a long whip in one hand and a blade in the other. "*Gamrah*, take your men from the fields and remove your sharp tools," Camphus called out. "My aim is to get Shumlah." Camphus breathed deeply, gagged and yelled. "Give me Shumlah!"

"No!" Gomsug screamed and swung his whip.

Camphus then opened his mouth and let out a screeching roar, jumped above the valley of traps, and shook the ground where he landed. Rocks rolled from the mountain and fire erupted, sending particles of debris into the field. The dried grasses began to be consumed by the fire, and the beast set out on a rampage. Men ran from the heat and cried from the burns. Gomsug swung his whip and ran up the hill toward the beast, which stood firm, pounding against the earth, making a terrifying noise.

"Give me Shumlah!"

"Leave the people alone," Gomsug responded, striking at the beast with his whip.

Camphus grabbed the whip in one hand and began to pull Gomsug toward him, taking one step at a time toward him and staring intensely so that Gomsug was frightened. However, as Gomsug looked back at the blazing flames and men in turmoil, all eyes became fixed on him. It seemed as if that was a challenge he must overcome. The beast called him the *Gamrah* several times this night. It meant that the beast was no match for him. And the faces, which gazed upon him, projected the hope that he, Gomsug, had become the wedge standing between them and the beast.

One step at a time, Camphus walked briskly, his eyes fastened on Gomsug and his mouth open, making terrifying rattling sounds. The closer he got to Gomsug, the louder the sounds. His mouth leaked thick red slime, and his nose became greasy. He pulled at the whip with eyes still fixed on Gomsug. The earth beneath Gomsug's feet began to move but he stood firmly staring back fervently at Camphus. Fear came and went. Regret settled within him and questions arose, but Gomsug never released the whip as he hauled him ever closer.

Camphus slammed his fist to the earth and sent Gomsug sprawling into the air. Quickly Gomsug sprang back on his feet and stood his ground. They were close against each other, breathing intensely. The beast stood high above the giant, while Gomsug appeared to be just a tiny entity that could be crushed with a step. In between the two the whip dangled like a stick beaming from the pulls on both ends. The fire consuming the brush increased in intensity and the men's effort to find a solution intensified.

More Gomry began climbing up on the hill to rescue Gomsug. However, Camphus seemed paralyzed and did not lift his big jaws or use his large limbs to crush the Gomrah beneath his feet. It was a tense moment as the two were not more than ten feet apart. Camphus slammed its fist against the earth again, for the men were coming in waves and its strong jaws ground heavily.

"*Gamrah*," Camphus croaked, "Move!" He then pulled Gomsug towards him. But Gomsug pulled back and leaped into the air, coming down toward his antagonist's face. Camphus, seeing that Gomsug had lifted his blade for his neck, released the whip and swung his big arms. Gomsug, saw the move, dodged the arms and threw the blade with might against the beast.

Camphus's reaction was late, and perhaps he was preoccupied with the Gomrah now coming in range, appearing fierce and brutal. The hand, which he used to hit the Gomrah, was away from his face and put the bushes asunder with blazing fire scattering into fresh grass terrain. The sharp edge of the Gomrah's blade came against Camphus with a violent sound, reached his neck, and plunged in.

Camphus removed his hands and pulled out the blade, and blood leaked from his neck like an open pipe. In his agitation, he attempted to strike Gomsug. But Gomsug ducked and used his whip, which he swung onto a tree and flew away. Camphus's fist hit against a large log lying on the ground and sent it swiftly into a group of Zongy coming with force under the dry brushes. Men rolled about wounded and screaming. The noises became louder and louder.

Frantically, the men ran about swinging spears and sending their arrows toward the wounded Camphus. The blade that was used against Camphus' throat was dipped in poison and it weakened his nerves. He wobbled on his feet. Though the poison had not yet impaired his entire body, his head was becoming lighter. He attempted to pull back into the valley away from the rushing warriors. But they gave him no chance to get away, and they charged at him with screams and continued the deadly assaults where catapults threw sharp steel into the air, striking the beast.

Camphus became enraged and screamed in pain, pulling away. The weapons used by his attackers had chains attached to large objects to keep Camphus from escaping. As he attempted to jump from one end of the valley to the other, the chains strongly hooked him and kept him within a short distance. He soon dashed wildly into the valley of lava.

The fire then blazed with a mind of its own, and Camphus' legs were thrust into the hot lava and began to burn. He roared and pulled with such might that even the chains that attached the heavy objects to his body were ripped apart from the cores. Pieces of wood and steel swiftly swung into the air causing many Zongy to fall on the ground. Some went flying into the air like dead leaves in wind.

Camphus turned toward the men with all the strength that was left within him. About five men with whips swung them to entangle him to stop his movements but his strength, motivated by his anger, was overwhelming. The men held tight to the surrounding trees so that they were not ripped apart by the violent pulling. Nevertheless, the magnitude of Camphus' strength was underestimated, and he pulled the men from their stance and ripped the smallest man into two. A piece of his body was attached to the whip, which was now in the air, while the rest remained glued to the tree where he had made his stance. Their faces tightened with terror and the men pursued Camphus with all that was left, for he was becoming weaker, even though he had spilled so much blood, and spread so much fire about the scene.

Another Zongah with a whip fell into the lava and was in range of the enraged beast. Camphus scurried toward the Zongah and submerged his face completely in the molten lava and wailed out violently. His echo vibrated for miles and even those in their burrows prayed to N'Daygmong for their lives. The Reverend heard the echo and it was loud and menacing. The echo was followed by screams of men finishing the assault on the beast. The poison by then dominated Camphus's entire body, and his neck leaked. He was becoming weaker and weaker.

Camphus turned and his vision became blurry. He wiped his face trying to clear his sight. As he looked about, men defending their lives knew he was succumbing to his wounds. Suddenly multitudes of axes and spears were approaching him at an alarming speed. He tried and dodged some, but many struck his body and he staggered backward. As he tried to sustain his balance, Gomsug rose in mid air with his axe and landed another deadly blow on Camphus' face between the eyes. The axe became so deeply imbedded in Camphus that Gomsug left it in his face and somersaulted away before Camphus could fall.

Like thunder blasting through the air, Camphus fell into the lava and swiftly rolled away. The chains attached to him hung loose and the lava paste made him twitch. He tried to stand again, but soon, two fiercely approaching spears from the catapults, struck him in the back of his legs and the men locked the attached chains behind two giant trees. Camphus staggered wildly and fell into the valley of the sharp objects and surrendered to his wounds. Dispersed body parts and blood dripped from rocks and hanging logs. Dried leaves lay moistened with blood. The beast was defeated and the fire blazed about, giving a fiery victory to Gomsug and the town.

The people lifted their voices in the dark air and shouted victoriously. The fire and heat were ignored and the popping sounds of roasting bodies and dried wood were replaced with applause.

Camphus lay flat with sharp tools piercing through him. From beyond the plain and dried grasses being consumed by the flames, Uda and the remaining men arrived with Shumlah. In her eyes despair was settling. She leaped like a wild tiger on all four legs and approached the wheezing Camphus. She grunted with sorrow and stared at his fading eyes, which were closing slowly and pushing back into his head. When he laid his eyes on Shumlah, he strained so that he saw her one last time; and he saw her tears and how sad she appeared.

With her alpaca face coated with white and brown fur, nose leaking with slime, soft eyes now drenched in tears, she was a lovely sight. He opened his arms, calling her to him. Suddenly she ran down into the valley and held onto his hand. Camphus' breath was softened instantly and her touch was like a soothing remedy in his painful wound. He breathed slowly now, looking into her sad eyes.

"Camphus! Camphus! No! No!" She whispered and laid her hand on his leaking wounds while touching the spears and poisonous arrows projecting out of his body, now surrendering to death.

Shumlah, perhaps, had some regrets as she looked into Camphus' fading eyes. They opened and closed with pain while they appeared almost slipping into his skull. The noise from above, men rejoicing and others ridiculing her because of her crudeness to have orchestrated the death of Camphus, irritated her. She opened her mouth, lined with slime from the upper to the lower lips, her tongue continuously secreting more slimes, and she wailed.

"My lover, cry no more," said Camphus. "It would have been one last time. I am sorry I only thought it as a joke."

"No," she said and gave Uda a disgusted look, for his words upon the hill had been harsh, poignant, and abusive. He had taken the lead in expressing his reason why protecting her from the start was a vain effort. She cried, looked about sadly, pushed herself into his wounds and hugged him tightly. "It was not my intension Camphus!" She said and lifted her head and heard the harsh words descending from the hill.

The flames beyond had consumed more plains; and they were barely contained by the hardworking Zongy. It burned still, and the men standing on the hills showed a certain color, as if they stood in the flame itself and were not burned. The yellowish light of the flame, like tall phantoms resisting efforts to put them out, mixed with the screams of men, became a sight she no longer could bear.

Slowly she caressed Camphus and pushed her mouth into the air, her face changing, she yelled in the loudest tone. Her eyes became red as fire, and her teeth began to project from her mouth. She became a very angry alpaca with heavy arms like a puma, and the laughing men accusing her and grimly describing Campus' demise made her impulse for blood slowly dominate her judgment.

"They are lovers," Uda said. "His big cock was for her small legs. Beasts, I say, are not to mingle with."

They laughed and gazed at Shumlah whose head by then remained down concealing her plan. Gomsug had not taken his eyes from her while the men talked among themselves. A certain feeling, which had not left him, was suddenly proven right when Shumlah pulled away, with a ferocious speed towards Uda. She cried out in the most menacing tone and sprang to remove Uda's head from his shoulders. However, Gomsug was attentive to what she was planning, as she looked upon Camphus with tears. Gomsug pulled out his whip and grabbed her by the neck before she reached Uda's head.

Uda was quick to react. He opened her stomach with one stroke of his blade as she remained in the air entangled by Gomsug's whip. They reacted so quickly that before she could bat her eyes, Shumlah lay by Camphus with her stomach's contents spread across the drying lava, some being roasted, and emitting foul-smelling smoke.

There was silence, astonishment, surprise and speechlessness. The men were in awe at what had happened. Shumlah quivered slowly. She began to convert herself into the same beautiful girl she was earlier when the men arrived to get her. Her silky hair slowly dragged across the dry lava. She cringed and pulled towards Camphus so that she died in his arms, and that they were united once more in the afterlife. With the spilled contents of her stomach lying on the ground—intestines even dragging alone—she moved her dreary eyes across the men still in awe. She grunted and rattled terrifyingly, making sure no man came close to her as she moved toward

Camphus.

Even Uda found it difficult to believe for a moment, his life flashed oddly before his eyes. He glimpsed all that could have happened in his absence. He saw his wife's faded beauty and her face shriveled after she was reduced to an old prostitute.

He then gaped piteously and saw his daughter in the Forbidden Land Her arms and legs broken and the mouth of Monshung opened with gladness, ready to swallow her body. He heard her scream and no man came to her rescue. And the snake crawled and took her into the water. There, he vividly saw her eyes open with contempt and fear beyond imagination, as Monshung laid his teeth into her flesh. In his mind he watched helplessly, until she disappeared into the snake's belly.

How she tried at first to withstand the torture and to resist the snake, but her arms and legs were broken and gave her no leverage or strength to hold onto the roots growing at the verge of the river. There, he saw Nicaso and she was no more. The fattened snake with contorted belly slid back into the river and swam away.

Uda turned his eyes left, and saw his fallen sons standing upon the mountains. They stood idle and alone. The wind blew fiercely against them. Dio had chosen a path and abandoned Niejon. And Niejon shivered coldly as he called upon his brother to save him from the brisk wind. But Dio turned his back on him and walked away.

In all this, Uda saw no Izeonah. He was perhaps, dead and the land was liberated. A certain feeling crawled within him. It was not pity but rage and disgust scattered through his body in a fashion that made even he, Uda, afraid of himself. He shook himself from these awful thoughts.

He must alleviate such feelings at once, for he smelled death in his nerves and tasted abandonment on his tongue. It was bitter like black gall from a poisonous and mysterious animal. He would have run across the fiery plain to quench the feeling. But, somehow, it would have been insufficient. Something even more poignant had to give way to those feelings. Was it, maybe, killing the Izeonah? No, the Izeonah was a wimp who, perhaps, had not even an ounce of deceit in him. If anything, the Izeonah was nothing more than a hindrance, and the rage and disgust he felt now could not be quenched by his death. These feelings were beyond any pain he could cause the Izeonah.

Furthermore, oddly, perhaps only the Izeonah understood what he felt at the moment. Yes the Izeonah, the foreigner, the alien, the man who one day he must kill—this man that he had continued to lure into a place where the Prophet could find a way to his soul to destroy him. Yes, it was this Izeonah who was alone in the land of the Zong, and had cried many nights wishing he had never come to this land. It was this Izeonah who understood what he, Uda, was feeling now.

Uda flinched and dismissed the ambivalent feelings toward the Izeonah. Get out of my head! He screamed to himself. The Izeonah was no friend. Yes, one day Uda, kill him. But then he grimaced. Where had the magnitude of such anger come from? Get it out! He could scream until his larynx flew through his mouth. But then it was not the end. His heart pounded in his chest, standing on the hills. Would he have an epiphany then? No! But something must give!!!

These feelings persisted until they became like poisonous venom Uda wished to rid himself of. His body trembled and tears streamed down his face and his mouth remained closed. He looked down into the valley and saw Shumlah gliding towards Camphus. His blade still gripped in his bloodstained hand. His vision became blurred and cleared immediately. Shumlah still glided across the dry hardened lava that had turned into hot stones, approaching Camphus. There, redemption! He snapped to reality, and recognized Shumlah's plan to touch Camphus, in order that they live together in the afterlife. Not in my presence! Impossible!!

From the hilltop, Uda leaped into the valley with his blade still dripping blood. As his chest shook by the intuition of the two being attached in the afterlife, he hacked Shumlah's head away with an enormous blow. It rolled down the valley and into the lava and began to cook. He swung his blade several more times until he knew that as Shumlah stretched her legs weakly and stiffened her toes, she was only releasing her last breath, and her dream to be with Camphus was no more.

This action was more than just the throwing of his blade. The events that were about to unravel were even more challenging. Though throwing his blade on Shumlah had quenched his rage to a certain extent, a part of the rage was being converted into something more sinister. It was shame. Being downtrodden in the eyes of many, his life was once again rescued by Gomsug. Those who stood about them, then, knew it and believed that Gomsug was truly the legend and the competent *Gamrah*. The gods might as well come and crown him, for his strength was present and it overwhelmed everyone.

Gomsug gazed at Uda and saw shame riddled over him. He lifted his head and tension filled his eyes. He stared at all who could be a threat to him. Many Gomry present suddenly feared him. One by one he stared at each Gomry, making sure they yielded to him. There was no man, not a Zongah or Gomrah, that was brave enough to lift their eyes up to his level. They were all submissive. His presence was felt. The people were almost in the position to bow to him. Many had already pledged their absolute allegiance, in their facial expressions and demeanor. Gomsug knew it was time to act. He was emotionally crowned. He pulled his whip and wrapped it around his hand and raised his fist.

"*Gamrah*!!!"

"*Gamrah*!!" The crowd responded.

"Meheyassahapunawa!"

"Meheyassahapunawa!!!"

The zeal was enough for Gomsug to give Uda a final condescending look and pulled away from their midst with confidence and went toward the town. Many other Gomry, who also had claims to the *Gamrah* throne felt paralyzed as Gomsug took all the glory and praise. They followed him as he headed hastily toward the town.

The town of Poe, by then, was now overwhelmed with darkness. The almost invisible Milky Way sat in the heavens and the moon was covered by the moving clouds, caused by the reeking smoke that was evaporating from the ground, where Camphus and Shumlah lay. The smoke, which went into the air, made the cloud heavy and hazy. Behind that hazy fog sat the bright moon refusing to surface. From where it shone, it appeared so distant it seemed to isolate the heavens from the town. One could assume, perhaps, the moon was glad to have shut its eyes from so much anguish for one night.

The wind was propelled to a new height and sent the warmth of the night in all directions. The volcano roared softly and the body of Camphus, along with Shumlah, lay in the valley drained in blood and abandoned. The hot rock dried the blood as quick as it came from their veins. The brooks and grasses within the plain were opened to men returning with torches and victory songs. It was as if the fire walked and made noises from the popping and roasting of matters it consumed. The news of Camphus's death had already produced mass celebrations that the people went to meet the coming warriors with zeal. They returned from the valley, where Camphus was slain, and spread the news across the plain with their jubilant voices, and they met the people of Poe at the entrance to the town.

The warriors returned in a large group led by Gomsug. His walk was filled with confidence and his demeanor projected total dominance. He spoke to no one nor did he smile. The now defeated Gomrah, Uda, also followed him behind the frenzied crowd of happy Zongy. In his hand the blade remained.

When the crowd came out to meet the returning men, they realized that everyone was following Gomsug. Thus, they too became involved and made the crowd even bigger. They wondered where Gomsug was taking his followers. He went across the town to the pit where the Reverend was thrown. Gomsug stood over the pit staring down. "Izeonah," he screamed. "I am here to put you out of your sorrow." He began pulling the rope and the crowd gasped.

Below, the Reverend looked up and saw the beaming lights and the man with the glimmering blade pulling at the rope. There, the people murmured, is the end of the Izeonah.

"Such a suffering man," someone piteously exclaimed, "Oh well, his demise has surely come. How long has he been a slave to Uda and never received such a threat? Many years now and some months—no almost six years—no, today he receives it all at once, from this Gomrah."

Gomsug pulled the rope until the end was on the surface and the Reverend was still in the pit. He grabbed the rope and stared at it in surprise.

From the way the rope was pulled the Reverend knew he was in danger. Perhaps he was finally meeting his end. The man standing above the pit with the glimmering blade was the man he dreamed about—the taker of his life, the man who would bring peace to his remorseful soul—the man to end his suffering and reunite him with his Nora and in the arms of God. Finally, he had come. Surely it was an escape from this body of his. His life was over before it ever began. There was no one to blame and nothing to feel.

The angry shouts from above the pit were of those he came to tame. He came as a lamb—a pure lamb with a kind heart searching for peace and tranquility. But, he found nothing more than despair, which was added to what he already suffered. Yes, he came to save the Zong, but at this present moment, he was the one that needed saving. The Zong must release him from his earthly duty with the blade.

The world was full of sorrows anyhow. It was filled of

unsustainable suffering, death, human atrocity, bloodshed, arrogance, war, false religions, the devil, dark days, unknown futures, bullies and killers. Yes, this world was possessed by the devil and the Reverend wanted none of it anymore. It was time he returned home to Heaven to be with God and his love, Nora.

Nora was the life he felt beating in his chest. He was even surprised to have survived this long without her. Truly, to be absent from the body is to be present with God. It was time to be present with God, indeed! Peace at last!

Though the narrow pit only exposed a bit of the dark heavens from where he was, the Reverend saw lights beaming from the celestial realm that made Gomsug seem like an angel of death with his blade shinning above.

From the dark pit the Reverend's voice echoed, vibrating like noises coming from a hollow tunnel, "Angel," he said in Dahnkka, "Have you come for my life? I am ready to let you have it. Get me out of here and be quick about it."

Even though Gomsug could not make out what the Reverend said, the impertinence of this Izeonah speaking in the Zong language ignited Gomsug's fury.

"I want him out of there, now!" Gomsug screamed and pushed a Zongah into the pit. "Get him out by all means, now!"

The man who came from above splashed into the mud and fainted. Gomsug gave him no time to hold on to the rope. The Reverend saw him involuntarily swinging and rappelling through the air with a trembling voice that croaked like a dying prey. He dashed into the mud and the Reverend lay against the corner and watched as the mud splattered on him and other parts of the pit. The man submerged, for he was shorter than the Reverend, and then he held on to the corners and surfaced with a mouth full of that, which was in the pit. Then he jittered, became alive and screamed terrifyingly and began to curse the day he was born.

There, against the wall, the Reverend watched sullenly as if the sound which the man made had no effect on him. Then there was a rushing sound, and they stared above and saw a man descending at an alarming rate. In one hand the man held firewood, and a rope was tied to his waist. The man with the rope to his waist spread his arms frantically while descending. As he descended, the Reverend lifted his muddy hand in order that he would be taken up first. But the Zongah who was with him fought and shoved him deeper into the mud, and held on to the fellow descending so that he was the first taken out of the mire.

The Zongah became feisty and behaved aggressively, even after the Zongah hanging by the waist used the firewood to drive him away. At first, the Zongah hanging by the waist tried to calm his friend by telling him that he was next. However, the history of such pits sent chills down his spine, and he refused to listen and became even more desperate.

The Zongah hanging by the rope was being pulled so hard that he suffocated. He then thrust the firewood against the misbehaving Zongah. The Zongah in the pit was beyond anguish. He paused, gulped for breath, and released a long and terrifying cry, like a baby in unbearable pain.

The pit became extremely dark, for the night had become even darker from the smoke and fire that consumed matters in the field where Camphus and Shumlah lay. The Zongah in the pit had heard terrible stories about those who came from such pits, so he cried and scratched with vicious noises. The man hanging by the rope was so deep into the pit that he was not heard clearly by those above. He decided to pull the Zongah up first. Hanging by the rope, he risked dying from suffocation from the unceasing pulling of the rope by the misbehaving Zongah.

All the while the Reverend removed himself to the side and watched as the two Zongy fought each other. Finally, the hanging Zongah took the distraught man up first. As he was being pulled up, the Zongah thanked his friend and then turned to the Reverend.

"Stay here, Izeonah, lest my master think you are me and strike me. I hope you die and leave us for good! Wait for your turn, Izeonah!" The man covered in mud said with a crying voice as he was slowly pulled up. His mud-clad face resembled that of a clown, and his lips, almost untouched by the mud, sat in the middle of his face as he spat and cursed the Reverend.

Above the pit, Gomsug walked about refusing to stand still as his nerves jerked with insolence. The man being elevated met his demise suddenly. His head was removed before he surfaced entirely. Gomsug thought he was the Izeonah, and he swung his ax and severed the man's head, which bounced about the walls of the pit until it fell back into the thick mud below.

The Reverend heard the sudden exclamations of the crowd, followed by spilling of pasty fluid from the top and then the bouncing sounds of the head hitting the left then the right sides of the wall of the pit.

Splash! The head submerged with open eyes. It had a horrifying stare and the mouth still moved, as if saying the same words, which the owner spoke earlier when it was still attached to him.

The Reverend lay on the side of the pit as if he did not see the head sinking and being swallowed by the mud, and air bubbles popping on the surface. His eyes remained sullen and his face seemed subtle and cold. He looked above and saw the Zongah descending again. This time he came swiftly and forcefully, impelled by the urgency and rage of his master's voice.

The man suddenly dashed into the mud. His eyes shone in the darkness when he grabbed the Reverend. "Izeonah, it is time that you meet your demise." His voice was calm and pitying. He stretched his hand forth and the Reverend held on to it. Their eyes met and the man's hands trembled. He was speechless and sweated profusely.

"Fear not," the Reverend said in Dahnkka. "It is not your blood that must be spilled tonight but mine."

"How are you sure?" The man responded looking down into the Reverend's eyes. A moment of silence passed and the man continued to stare in puzzlement. He had questions he wanted to ask. He looked above and they were close. "Why are you not weeping coming to such a terrible end?" He burst out finally.

"No my friend," the Reverend responded, "I am not weeping for I know where I am going. Only my body will be harmed tonight, but my soul is eternally grateful."

"Your soul?"

"A part of me that lives after my body is turned to dust."

"What? There is nothing grateful about death. Have you not seen Jobemong's head bouncing to you?"

"Yes, I did. It was a terrible mishap. I know his soul weeps eternally. But not for me, my savior lives and I shall be with him soon."

"Your savior?"

"Yes. And his name is Jesus Christ. He is the only master that can raise you from the dead because he rose from the dead."

"Jesus Christ?"

"Yes, Jesus Christ."

"Izeonah! Izeonah! Is this true about your Jesus?"

"Yes, and when I am dead, I am going to the land filled with milk and honey, where there is no pain, no suffering and I can live forever. I will be happy and never die."

The man looked up and heard angry voices. He stared at the Reverend and his eyes widened. "I want to come to Jesus," he sighed strongly.

"Tell him yourself."

"How, Izeonah? How?"

"When you are alone, call him."

"I don't have time, Izeonah."

"You have heard of Ixeonah, the people who believe in what I believe. Find them. I cannot help you now that I go up to be killed."

"Izeonah…" The man said as he watched the Reverend close his eyes, preparing for what was ahead and begin to pray in Dahnkka. The man, understanding the Reverend's prayer, closed his eyes also and repeated the prayer. Deliberately, the Reverend prayed the sinner's prayer, and the man repeated after him. And the Reverend thanked God for his life and asked that he be received in heaven.

Slowly the man pulled the Reverend to the surface. They both closed their eyes tight so that the pain from the ax would be reduced. But they came to the surface and met no ax swinging towards their heads. Instead, the Reverend saw the Zongah's body lying in the mud and a clamor, by which he understood that Uda was present and had hindered his death.

"This Uda," he muttered, "When will you release me of my suffering? Can't you see what I have done and will continue to do? I am a man of sorrow and of unfortunate happenings."

He lifted his head and slowly he began to comprehend his surroundings. He looked to his left and saw the man who brought him out of the pit untangling the rope from about his waist and joining the astonished crowd with a face full of joy. There, he realized, the Lord is surely a mystery. "You gave me life, again, just for one soul," The Reverend muttered some more and bowed his head. "It is the Lord's doing, though I wish to die. Apparently, he still has work for me." He dropped to his knees and raised his hand into the heaven and screamed in English.

"Jesus!!" He fell to the ground. He then turned and laid a cheek against the ground. From that angle he saw Gomsug approaching with the glimmering blade. Gomsug stood above him and stared.

"Brother!!" Suddenly a desperate scream ejected from the group and Uda made his way toward the Reverend. His body almost bowed with obedience, his palms remained opened and his eyes were red and fervent. He walked slowly. When he made his way between the Reverend and the

Gomrah, he spoke softly, almost in a hopeless tone. "I am here bewildered, defeated and afraid, but not tonight. Not while my fate hangs upon his life." He pointed at the Reverend still sprawled on the earth. "Let me punish him."

"No! I shall do the honor!" Gomsug pointed his hand at Uda. "You are weak! How long have you waited. How long? He must bleed by my hand!"

The spectators standing about began to move backward slowly, giving room for the two Gomry now in full tension. Gomsug lifted his blade as an attempt to frighten Uda. Yet, Uda remained fervent with eyes fixed upon Gomsug. "Do not stand in the way Uda!" Gomsug screamed.

"No, his life was given to me to keep, you are aware!" Uda raised his voice, "I am afraid your anger is impulsive."

"Impulsive?" Gomsug said turning abruptly toward the crowds, displaying his manliness. "I am to be the *Gamrah* of this land and you called my wit impulsive? I saved your life just now!" His scream was belligerent. "You heard what Camphus said, I am to be the *Gamrah*!"

"Camphus is a beast!" Uda responded harshly.

"So is he!" Gomsug said and released his ax that missed the Reverend's head. The ax struck the ground and made the crowd gasp. The Reverend remained calm when the ax struck a few inches from his neck. Even Uda turned to see the Reverend; his face was pale and drained. He breathed like a dying mule and wheezed and grunted.

The thick smoke, which blocked the moon, had now given way to the starlight from above and the two Gomry stood facing each other. No man was willing to give up his power. Gomsug prepared to strike, but a call came from the crowd defused the tension.

"Our *Gamrah*, enough blood for one night! Enough blood for one! Enough blood for one night!" It was a continuous shout until the crowd became larger, louder and they shouted in unison. "Enough blood for one night!"

The man who spoke with the Reverend from the pit had started the shout. His voice saved the night from more bloodshed. The shout grew so overwhelming that Gomsug knew better than to ignore the crowd. The future *Gamrah*, which he was not yet but claimed to be, needed support to convince the Fathers that he was competent to lead his people and show restraint when appropriate, thus possessing the true identity of a *Gamrah*.

He heard the first shout, which called him a *Gamrah*. That

softened him. Then, he knew the future was more promising. Regardless of what Uda did this night the time was coming that he, Gomsug, would have his satisfaction, and then Uda would bow to him. He was willing to give up this fight again to maintain his prowess and fame. Gomsug looked into Uda's eyes once more, and smiled. "One day, my friend, one day. And when I lick your blood from my blade, I shall eat and sleep with the gods." Gomsug turned angrily and walked away into the night with many of his Zongy following him.

Uda looked about and the shout continued. He knew that his fame was reduced once more. He became aware that he was pushed to the bottom. The race to the *Gamrahood* had slipped even further from him. He turned and saw that the Reverend was sitting and staring vaguely in a confused state.

"What do you want from me, huh? What do you want from me," the Reverend screamed in English and then Zong.

Uda rushed toward him furiously, yelling in the most vicious tone. He grabbed him by the head and neck and tossed him into the mud. With enormous anger, he rushed and kicked him in his stomach and grabbed him and tossed him again. It was as if Uda had no intention of stopping and he continued to pound the Reverend's body with punches, kicks, slaps and tosses.

The Reverend saw himself lifted up several times and thrown about. He saw how he was dashed harshly to the hard earth. He saw Uda's foot landing on some painful places and then the beating was over. The Reverend lay on his back and stared into the heavens sadly. The night was dark now and only those with firewood in their hands were visible through the night. He turned his head about, dizzily, and his eyes settled upon a Zongah rushing towards him with a nearly naked slave girl waving her legs above his shoulder. He dashed the girl before the Reverend.

"Here," he said brandishing his sword wildly. "You want company, have her. She is of your kind, an Ixeonah. Have her!"

The Reverend paid no attention to the slave girl who began to huddle herself away by a small rock. He looked toward the heavens and watched as the soft moonlight hid once more, behind the dense dark clouds. For some reason he hoped the moon would shine, and that he would receive a sign as to why the Lord had delivered him to such inconsiderable cruelty. He was ready to die. He was ready to go home and death would have been the sweetest experience for him. But no! Out of the unknown a man cried to him and asked for Jesus. Then the Lord spared his life. Tears streamed down his face. Where is the man who was the reason the Lord saved him? He looked about and the crowd was thinning out. Uda was also gone.

The Reverend's lungs quivered painfully in his chest, and his body was weak. He heard many unrecognizable voices.

"I want you to be hanged by the morning—or I want you to fuck until your penis erodes away and then you die. Either way die, Izeonah, die."

The crowd burst into laughter and began to disperse. The Reverend was on the ground breathing vehemently and trying to reconnect with his surroundings.

"His back must be scourged with fire the next time! Leave him for now." A Zongah who was exhausted from laughing called out while holding on to his knees.

"The Izeonah is just lonely. That's why he tried making friends with a boy like Niejon," another uttered lightly over the laughing crowd and he walked over to the slave girl. "Here, take her for the night," The Zongah pulled the slave girl and pushed her. She fell over the Reverend. "Make sure you are empty by the morning and that you are moody no more." The Zongah stared at his spectators. His mouth devoid of many teeth, and he passed his slimy tongue over his upper lip. "Hahahahaha." As he was moving away, another Zongah walked over to the now petrified slave girl and ripped her clothes apart; showing her flat breast.

"Sharpen your penis for a deep night." He said with ridicule, looking at his fellow Zongy for approval. They all laughed again, filling the air with noises.

"She is a prostitute, she is wide and rough like the ocean you came over. Make sure you find your penis by the morning, hahahahah. It might disappear in there," A voice echoed from beyond the laughing crowd.

"Or they might rot out like Nubin's," another man added.

The men laughed some more. They departed while talking among themselves, laughing in the night and ridiculing the Reverend.

"No, wait, wait," A voice amongst them, who seemed to have wanted to say the last word, "You mean to tell me my penis is his friend? Because, if a boy like Niejon is his friend, then I better leave my penis here and save it from aggravating my wife."

"You should.'

"Hahaha…"

"What would be the chance tonight that she might not get pregnant by the morrow?"

"If you wrap it between your legs and hand it in to the Izeonah for safekeeping, or tie it with a banana leaf from Usula's forest."

"Hahahahaha!"

"No, that will not do. Even the time we used blight plants and the bitter roots I chewed..."

"She still got pregnant!"

"Hahahahah."

"No more running away from her. Just dump the weeping babies at the Izeonah's house."

"Then he will have more friends and speak good Zong."

"Yes! And he will leave Master Uda and his son alone."

"Hahahaha."

"The boy is not fully man yet. Foolish Izeonah..."

The voices of the rambling men faded in the end, as the Reverend lay down helplessly. He was now alone with the girl. She stood up and looked around. The crowd was gone and the crickets and nocturnal creatures were echoing from the woods and about them.

On the other side lay the decapitated Zongah who was by then completely drained of blood. The girl inched slowly away until the night made her invisible from where the Reverend lay. He tried getting up but he was weak and he fell back to the ground.

An hour went by and then he heard noises. This time it was of hogs. Perhaps they were wild or domestic, but they came in groups and began to eat the cadaver of the dead Zongah. A few more approached the Reverend, and he moved. They were frightened and stood by as if awaiting his death.

The Reverend looked towards the sound of the groaning hogs and saw that the man was being devoured and that some bones showed from where the hogs had eaten. Then, suddenly a woman with a donkey came and drove the hogs away. She stood over the Zong's body, then knelt and wept. At first she thought she was alone, but then the Reverend moved. She stopped and became suspicious. She looked about fearfully, and approached the Reverend.

"Izeonah," she called, "Who else is here with you?"

In the Reverend's heard her voice only echoed and was fuzzy. She came and stood above him. In the dark the pigs waited, groaning. She pulled out a short knife and knelt to the Reverend and she was about to stab his side when an arrow came from the dark and struck her through the neck. She grabbed her neck and gagged, gasping for breath and quivering vehemently. She dropped to her face with knees folded under her.

Then the same man who spoke to the Reverend earlier from the pit appeared. From the Reverend's point of view, he was tall with his bows and arrows standing above him. The man was suspicious and stood up to make sure he was alone. "Izeonah," he called out and grabbed the woman by the legs and dragged her with face against the mire, and threw her into the pit. He stood there listening to the tumbling sound of the body, hands on his waist. When he was contented, he turned and smiled. He took the Reverend and put him on the donkey and disappeared into the darkness. The pigs returned to finish what they had started on the dead Zongah.

Chapter Twenty-Two

The Alter Child

"Dear son..."
Close the door of your ears from
Fears and the poisons of the earthly
Matters, and let the passion of
Your heart served as wisdom
To contemplate the ideas
Between needs and desires.
Let the will, which set you free
Stand as a cornerstone to preserve
Your reality from truths and
Lies, make you believe in the
Choice that makes everything

In and around you beautiful
Like the roses of your mother's
Garden, and the unwavering teaching of your father's
Understanding.
When you are free to
Your choices, all the decisions
That drags the sentiment of
Fear of earthly matters
 To the door of your
Heart will vanish like the vapor
Of water on the street after
A sunshine, then you are the
Key to your righteous destiny.

A few hours later, the Reverend regained consciousness and realized he was in a house made of mud and wood and was cleaned. A fireplace with boiling pot illuminated the room and cast a shadow on the other side of the room. The doorway, which opened into the outer region of the house, was pitch black from the darkness outside. He could hear a woman talking outside. He lay on a high bamboo bed that stood firmly on the ground, which was positioned at one end of the room. Above him was an attic covered by a ceiling. A staircase made from wood and wild ropes extended into the ceiling and came down by his feet. The wall of the room was gray with white marks of chalk made from handprints.

As he looked towards the door, he saw his clothes in a pile. His face was swollen and he was without energy. His body trembled as he tried to sit up and he fell from his bed and screamed from the pain.

The woman came in and helped him back to the bed. She stood above him and spoke. "Haven't you had enough trouble for one night? Where can you go this night this frail?"

The Reverend gazed at her face. When she knew that he was trying to get a better look at her, she turned and ordered him, "Focus on your wellbeing, Izeonah."

The Reverend turned his face away. The woman was heavy but with soft visage and long dark hair, which had braids that landed on her back. She had a stomach as if she was pregnant. Her eyes were large and white. Her eyebrows were heavy and her cheeks were embedded with dimples. Her face also dropped downward in an oval-shaped contour. Her nose was round and fat as would be that of a bear. She was also tall with fat fingers. She wore no shoes or slippers.

"Where is the man that saved me?" The Reverend asked, face against the wall.

"No man saved you, Izeonah. Forget what happened."

"What do you mean?" The Reverend turned. "I was saved by a kind

252

man. At least that's a first…"

"Izeonah!" The woman interrupted. "This is Poe, the land of blood and violence. Nobody saved you."

"Fine, then," The Reverend said and positioned himself on the bed. "How do I explain if I'm found well then?"

"You say nothing. Nobody saved you. When you gained consciousness, you found yourself this way. That is it!" She stood by the door and stared into the dark.

The Reverend, who was even more curious, asked the woman, "Who are you?" He queried with a fervent face and a searching tone.

"Long ago," The woman said without taking her eyes from the dark, "We lived in peace, and then came the Izeonah, and he promised peace and redemption beyond what we knew. He brought with him great tools and showed us the way…for a while."

"An Izeonah came and showed you the way?" The Reverend asked.

"Izeonah, have you just slipped from your mother's womb?" She asked, walking back into the room and sat by him. There were many scars on the woman's face that resembled marks as if she once escaped a fire. "What are you made of," she asked firmly, looking into the Reverend's eyes.

"What am I made of? I don't understand."

"Are you the light that will shine forever or are you here to brighten the day and leave us when darkness comes?"

The Reverend countenance suddenly changed. Somehow it was as if he knew what she meant.

"I am the light that will shine forever."

"Hold your thoughts and think before you speak, Izeonah," The woman was stern again.

"Who are you?" The Reverend was very inquisitive now.

"The question is not who am I, the question is who are you, Izeonah? Are you surely what you proclaim?"

"I don't understand."

"Well I will ask you of one thing. Remove yourself from harm's way and live a while for us." The woman got up and walked to the boiling pot. "You must be hungry." She poured some potage and brought it over. "Here eat and be filled." She walked to the door. "I must take my leave now. I was never here."

The woman was about to exit and the Reverend called. "Wait!" She stopped at the door and faced the Reverend. "Whoever you are, an angel or a commoner, whoever you are, thank you." The Reverend put his hand over his heart, "From the bottom of my heart, thank you. I am sure by now you will not give me your name, but I assure you woman, whoever sent you, tell him or her I am the light that shines forever. I will not give up. I will not fall. The God I serve is greater then the roaring beasts of this land. I am hopeful that my better days are ahead. Thank you again."

The woman smiled and bowed. She knew that these words of a wounded man lying on the bamboo straws drinking soup were from his heart, and the sincerity in his voice made her even more cheerful.

"There will be a time for graceful words. We are in a time of turmoil. Until we are once again free, so long Izeonah. May the God who brought you here keep you safe." She walked into the dark. "You are not alone," her voice echoed.

The Reverend fought and got to his feet. He was determined to see the direction she went. However, when he made his way to the door, the woman was gone. The night was even darker and bleaker, that all he saw were houses with lights within. Yonder, he heard sounds of pleasure, men laughing and voices of women singing and making sensual noises.

She was an angel, he said to himself as he returned to recline and drink his soup. An angel from God sent to strengthen me, even now that I need him the most. Lord, I am still in the fight. The fact that Uda put his hands on me and I am not dead is a sign that I have survived the worst. I am still in the fight.

He looked to the door and there stood Murphy staring at him strangely. The night had made the dog's eyes glow and it made crying noises. At first it was unrecognizable. Then the Reverend took his face away quickly because he thought he was hallucinating due to the blood lost. But Murphy barked again and came into the room. He lay by the fireplace looking straight at the Reverend.

"Murphy," the Reverend exclaimed softly. "You are...here!"

The dog wiggled its tail. The Reverend then retracted his excitement suddenly. He remembered that Murphy stayed in Zuxbaha. That was strange, he thought. That same dog he left in Zuxbaha miles away was once more with him in Poe, lying by the fireplace. He felt a cold feeling running through his body and he was frightened.

Murphy continued to stare at him and wiggled its tail even more joyfully. The Reverend slowly turned his head as if expecting something, but was not sure what it was. Maybe, he thought, the dog would change into something he hoped not to see. Somehow he thought the dog would speak to him and reveal its true identity. No, he assumed, the dog was from the witches of the land sent to watch him. Perhaps the dog was the woman who had just disappeared into the dark. All sorts of thoughts ran through his head and none was comforting for there lay the dog that he was sure he had left in Zuxbaha. He was alone and vulnerable. Without rehearsing his thoughts, he stared at Murphy.

"Remember how malnourished you were and I fed you? What have you come to do to me now?" The dog was silent but it continued to wag its tail. "Murphy," he called and the dog got up, shook its tail and came toward him. "No!" He screamed and frightened the dog away. It returned to the doorway. "Yes, go," he said with a bit of hope. "Go away and leave me alone!" This time his voice was loud and Murphy was out of the house. "You witch, stop watching me! Go away, you devil!" This time, his face was turned toward the ceiling and he was lying on his back as he spoke. He turned his head toward the doorway again, and Murphy was nowhere in sight. He breathed a sigh of relief and whispered, "Yes, go away."

The noise, which he heard earlier, was now increasing. A beautiful tone echoed and soothed his nerves. It was a song from a girl singing about the vulnerable butterfly.

"It is a man's world.
This brief bliss fooled you to give up your nest.
Eventually you became man's mess.
Why haven't you looked for signs, my dear butterfly?
To hide your innocent smiles?
Haven't you heard of flowers who only blossom in the spring?
And man only gives you things when your love is in the spring.
Haven't you heard of heartbreaks?
The scorching draughts the summer makes?

It is a man's world.
I said to her fading beauty,
It is a man's world.
I said to her sorrow,
Come let's cry,
I said to her wrinkled face.

Stop chasing vain things, dear butterfly,
Find a way; return to your nest.
Be not fooled by his admiration of your breast.
It is only but brief.
Soon you are no more his flower but a dying reef.

It is a man's world.
I said to her fading beauty,
It is a man's world.
I said to her sorrow,
Come let's cry,
I said to her wrinkled face.

She said to me, "I couldn't remain a child forever.
I cannot live in solitude forever.
Stop questioning my growth.
Haven't you heard of the soft wind in autumn's brook?
Haven't you heard of the sweet budding flower in spring?

I witness to love and carry its sweet message with my lips?
Wherefore this is a man's world or some more...
He is my slave; controlled by my fingertips.
With my wit and comfort, in my arms, he will be mild..."

The voice from, which these words echoed were kind, sweet and made the Reverend cleave to his life even more. As he lay on the bed he remembered Nora; this time it was not in a gloomy fashion, but as the beautiful girl who sang melodiously. She sang when he was sick, and sang when he came from the camp after watching bodies being pulled from the gas chamber. She even sang in the choir on Easter Sunday.

He found out this talent of hers on his first visit to her home. He was nervous. It was already terrible that he was a Jew and that his mother had warned him that he must take a Jewish girl as a wife. He was not sure if Nora's parents had the same idea. To his surprise the visit was beyond his expectation.

"You are a man easy to love, Isaac. They will love you," Nora assured him when they walked in.

"Even a Jew?" He asked sarcastically.

"Even a Jew."

"What if I were a Negro?"

"They would love you still." Nora then shook her head as if remembering something, perhaps his silliness. She looked into his eyes and showed a lovely smile.

At the dinner table that evening, as the aroma of fresh gingerbread, baked ham, asparagus, oily pottage, creamy soups and marinated tomatoes steamed the air, he was glad to have made the trip. Though before coming, he was asked a few questions about what he would eat and when he answered, they made it for him and left him alone. Nora's father looked from the corner of the table and smiled. The Reverend was often shy and Nora had already warned her father. But on that Sunday afternoon, after he watched Nora sing "At the Cross," he was sure his life would be altered for the worse if she were no longer in it.

The night came and he entered the father's sitting room and boldly asked for Nora's hand in marriage. Staring from the piece of glass covering his left eye the father said.

"You are a Jew."

"Yes, sir."

"Have you talked with your parents about marrying her?"

"Yes, sir."

"Well?"

"My father is pleased. He is happy when I am happy...and so is my mother, though she's a bit weary."

"We are Christians, Isaac."

"We serve the same God, don't we, sir?"

"Well to a point."

"Yes, yes, I know Jesus. I am a Christian, sir."

"A Christian?" the baffled father asked.

"I believe in Jesus as the only way."

"Well then, Jesus's way it is." The father stared at the young Isaac and smiled. "Are your parents aware of this startling change?"

"Not yet, I am sure my father will approve. My happiness is his happiness, sir."

"And your mother?"

"My mother will join in the end."

"Well Isaac, I hope this is genuine. I mean it has to come from your heart. And you know what I mean."

"Sir, maybe. Nora makes me very happy. And she is teaching me all I need to know to get to the place of total conversion."

"You are doing this because of Nora or because of your soul?"

"If I say both will my answer be wrong?"

"Isaac," the father called out as he pointed to the empty chair. "Sit down, please."

The young Isaac hurried to the chair and gazed at the father.

"You are a fine young man," the father said. "Now, I am sure you are in love. But have you considered..."

"Sir," Isaac interrupted and his face lightened. He glowed and blushed. "I believe every man must experience love before he dies." He pressed his palm against his chest, "I have found love in two places: Nora and Jesus, and there is no regret for me. Both of them own me forever."

"Hum," the father said and glanced at him, as if he had just learned a lesson from the youth. He saw the sincerity in Isaac's eyes, and he knew he did not need to continue the lecture to the young man filled with love to the brim. He smiled, "Well son, you have my permission to marry my daughter."

"Thank you, sir," The Reverend burst out of the room and found Nora sitting on the banister in the backyard, staring over the trees.

The young moon had just risen and the stars glimmered from space. The wind blew softly and the tree branches waved.

Nora was wearing a white satin dress with a pair of blue slippers. Her hair was knobbed in the back with a bow, and she drank a glass of milk.

They met at that meeting place every evening since his visit. He knew she was there. With the excitement streaming through his nerves, he grabbed her from behind and held onto her tightly. She smiled and gave him a kiss. There were no words spoken between them, but the feeling was strong and it conveyed every word necessary.

The soft wind made the leaves emit frictional noises as pleasant background music to their romance. The next summer she was ready to be his wife and he was ready to be her husband. Those romantic times, looking back, never in his mind did he dream life would turn out the way it had. Not only was Nora in heaven, but also he was frail, wounded, and somehow he could not grasp the meaning of all the agony that they had both endured.

The Reverend began to recount his life and ask some basic questions about his existence. He thought, was this all that was promised for a Reverend, a follower of the living God? If this was it, then he would have none of it any longer. He was sick of being beaten and treated in this fashion. He was sick of violent people and careless minded men who considered the world and its people tools to be battered and used. These were violent men who caused the world to remain in turmoil and death, who caused many to flee across lands, cities and seas, suffering starvation, homelessness and vile maladies. They turned beautiful countries and cities into ghost lands. The marks of their bullets, deceit and greed transformed buildings into deserted domains, crippled or filled with the corpses of those who once inhabited them. They were selfish men with disgustingly pompous egos, cold, arrogant and mindless characters empty of remorse. Their evil dimensions were repulsive to him and he wished to end it all! But he had tried with all his strength. From Flossenburg's reeking stench of bodies, to the Ebola-ridden grave of his wife Nora, to this now dark land of Meheyassahapunawa. What a vain world! What a distasteful humanity! Come Christ, come! End this misery! End this sadness! Indeed man was lost, and even he, sacrifices after sacrifices, silently trying to show that there could be reasons for man to embrace the truth and beauty of his existence, he was pushed to the end—this brutal end where all that was hopeful now was death and disgust for the world he so dearly loved. Come Christ, come! End this misery! End this sadness!

The Reverend turned his eyes to the doorway beaming with nothingness and the obscure velvet bleakness from outside only reminded him of the hearts of those arrogant men he had described, surfacing in his mind. His heart pounded with anger, and the perpetuated thoughts created a sudden secretion of sweat into his wounds and it burned. This called him back to his present state, and he abandoned his contemplation.

The melody echoing from beyond the walls from where he lay soon began to dominate his mind. He tried to fill his mind with sadness again, and remember all the pain and suffering he had endured until now. Yet, it was as if the singing woman's voice became a place of solace and soothing comfort. It called him in a strange fashion that actually aroused him a bit. It was a mild erection and then it was over. The entire thought about pain and suffering made him laugh lightly.

The woman's soothing voice soon sounded like Nora's voice, calling him through the song, inviting him to live and forget his sorrow. It was her voice soothing him once more in a time of agony. He was sick now, but then he was healed. Nora's voice came breaking through the hut and gave him strength. He arose to his feet and looked around dizzily. The voice continued to call. The owner of the house had not arrived. The woman he spoke to earlier seemed like a stranger. Maybe, he began to think, he must wait for the person who looked after his injuries to come before he departed from the house. However, it was as if the voice outside demanded, in a luring manner that he leave immediately. The fact that it reminded him of Nora caused even the dizziness and pain to recede and dissipate. He felt he could walk out of the house toward the voice rekindling his memory with rewarding imageries without the pain or sickness

The Reverend walked toward the firewood soaked in oil, which was used as a lamp. It hung at the entrance of the doorway. He grabbed it, lit it and staggered into the night.

Ahead, where the noise came from, was a large house called the Naked House. It was a house of pleasure where men and women gathered in orgies and vain displays of their fantasies. From dusk till dawn the traffic into the Naked House never ended. It only ceased abruptly when Camphus and Shumlah terrorized the people. But now it was vibrant once more with all sorts of pleasures, and the Reverend walked hastily toward the voice calling him softly through the song.

Along the way he met a few people heading in the same direction. Some were surprised to see him walking along, and they made noises, talking among themselves concerning him, "This Izeonah walks ever so calmly after being slammed to the ground several times, this night. Yea, he never dies. He's a sorcerer. Hey, Izeonah you are still alive!" A few more drunkards lay by the way side. A lady vomiting to the grass while her lover sooths her was seen as the he walked passing them. The singing sound still echoed to a point that it overpowered the sounds and voices of the people walking and talking about him. It was as if their voices were dimmed and all he saw was their moving lips as he hurried to the singing echoing ahead. He pulled his clothes over his body properly, and made his way into the Naked House.

The entrance was a revolving door that extended about fifteen feet tall. The house itself was a large building with multiple apartments of large rooms, which were arranged according to the social class and type of pleasure one sought. Each room had its own bar where men and women gathered and made loud noises of pleasure.

Because the place was constructed in this fashion, the deeper one went into the Naked House the deeper the class and pleasure. The entrance was for mostly the low level men and women who were the wildest and most carefree. It was filled with laughter: naked women in men's arms, unnecessary quarrels, vile language and brute behavior.

A man with eroded teeth saw the Reverend opening the door. The dark inner part of his eyes spanned in his head as if he had no control over it, and when he looked right, it was as if he was looking left. His complexion was somewhat yellowish, his hair color deep brown and purplish. He lifted his head from between a woman's breasts as he heard the door squeak. He yelled "Effina! Hahahahaha!"

A few men took notice and paused from their pleasure and they stared at the door. The Reverend was somewhat nervous but smiled anyhow. There was the voice on stage, which, until now, had made him forget to contemplate what would happen to him in a place such as this. Nevertheless, he was already present, and the voice, which brought him so quickly to such a place, was on stage, and still as beautiful as when he left the place he had been kept for care.

The men resumed their pleasures after taking notice of the Izeonah. Every individual within the house was intoxicated beyond coherence. He who had the eroded teeth struck his head back between a woman's breasts and she lifted her head and laughed with ecstasy.

The Reverend zoomed his eyes to the stage. The girl singing was light-skinned and was naked beneath her net-like attire. She had long light-dark hair and soft eyes that were easy to gaze upon. She was beautiful in every way and the net-like attire shaped her body in a lusty manner that accentuated her body. Her eyes met the Reverend's and she knew her voice was beautiful. With the same wit she had used to entice the men, she spread her arms and moved about the stage as she continued her wanton gesture towards the Reverend, her soft breasts with nipples projecting strongly quivering with warmth beneath the attire.

Still swollen in parts of his body from his wounds, especially his eyes, he had forgotten the risk he took, yet, his eyes were still focused on the girl. It was as if she was calling onto him. He stood captivated by her, and then he regained his stance and walked into the crowd. He was unsure of what he was searching for, but his heart beat and he moved deeper into the crowd towards the girl in stage.

Suddenly a man thrust his hand forward and stopped him. "I have sharpened my penis for her, Izeonah. Get your own piece."

Suddenly the Reverend was disrupted from his fantasy and brought to reality. "Hum," he asked, taking his eyes away from the girl for the first time since he entered the room.

He stared at the man who held his hand over his chest. The man was lying against the bar and held a cup of alcohol. His hair was combed stylishly and clipped softly to his back almost touching his neck. His face and mashed nose were filled with scars. He removed his hand and stared at the girl who was at the end of her song.

"I want no problem," the man said, and pointed his hand downward at his erected pants. The Reverend's eyes followed and saw that the man was fully erect. Quickly he looked into the man's face shockingly, and then at the girl. The man lay his head backward laughing.

"I have no problem, sir," the Reverend said, "I simply admire her voice."

"Yes, then, move along." He waved his hand gesturing that the Reverend move.

The Reverend stared once more, at the man's private parts between his legs with a disturbed face. The man spread his legs apart and laughed again in a stupor. He removed his eyes slowly and then stared at the girl as she descended from the stage. The man suddenly left the Reverend and ran toward the girl who was already in the arms of five men.

"She is mine!" A man shouted.

"No, she is mine!"

"She is surely mine!" The Reverend heard the man who stopped him scream.

"Let's fight, then," another said, raising his fist.

Fighting erupted and they began throwing punches. In the midst of this commotion the Reverend saw the girl's face. She was fair and smiled with great pleasure, her eyes staring at him as the men worked out their feelings with punches. She looked once more at the Reverend and her face suddenly changed. She no longer was Nora, but a crafty witch causing mayhem.

"Ouch, you bit me—yes—I will fight you still!" The two men who remained standing resumed the fight.

On the floor a man laid flat on his back with his eyes wide open and blood oozing from his nostrils, draining on both sides of his cheek. Above him laughter roared.

A man came and touched the Reverend. He turned around and recognized that it was the man from the pit.

"It's...you!" The Reverend exclaimed.

"Yes, it's me, Izeonah," the man said. "Master Uda is in the back room."

The man walked into the crowd and the Reverend followed. When the crowd became larger, the man disappeared. The Reverend forced his way and found himself in a long, dark corridor. From his left to the right extended other corridors and rooms occupied with people engaging in all sorts of deeds. Women exposed themselves, standing at the doorway waiting for anyone who cared to come. In other corners men and women were naked and acted vilely in open sight.

The Reverend walked even faster for he saw two men in an act of sexual intercourse. He removed his eyes quickly, and pretended not to have seen them. His walk led him to a much quieter corridor where the noise was more controlled and had some hints of dignity. So far he had no thought of what he had seen. If anything, he still had not figured out his reason for abandoning his bed of healing. He was still sore, and even then, the dizziness was beginning to dominate his body so that he wobbled on his legs. Furthermore, he was unsure of what would happen if he fell in these hallways and fainted. He pressed on until he came to an open room once more. There, the celebrations continued.

Uda was in the corner, and the Reverend's eyes caught him. He had a few men and women all about him. The same man from the pit was on stage, and made jokes, which made the people laugh. It was a good entertainment that even Uda was entertained and had not seen the Reverend standing by the entrance.

The man on stage saw the Reverend and his demeanor changed. Suddenly the laughter stopped and they turned and saw the Izeonah. His swollen left eye was still unable to open, and his body wobbled, with both arms holding on to his cotton shirt. He was bent over and trembling.

Uda's eyes looked welcoming, but his face remained firm. The Reverend smiled. He looked about and the crowd was silent still. He smiled again. There was no change in Uda's demeanor. It would now be odd if he returned but he felt it would be dangerous to approach Uda at the moment. He smiled again. There still was no change in Uda's demeanor.

"Dear, Lord," he said and walked toward Uda and took the empty seat next to him. Then he gazed straight into his eyes. He smiled. Yet still, there was no change in Uda. He looked on the table. Uda's eyes followed. An empty glass and a bottle of a drink called the Seven Heads sat before them. Still, there was no change in Uda.

The Reverend glared about with all eyes upon him, watching. Uda's demeanor was still the same. Silent. The Reverend observed Uda once more, and laughed, hoping to create a different mood. No change. Silence.

Suddenly the Reverend began to act gaily and poured a glass of the alcohol and drank it. He removed the glass from his mouth and gave Uda a strong look. Uda's face had not moved from him yet. It was blank with a bit of curiosity. The Reverend poured another glass, lifted it up like a toast and glared about his surrounding so that all could see. He drank again, and closed his eyes, for the drink was strong. He stared at Uda.

Suddenly Uda stood up and the chair fell from his back. He looked down at the Izeonah who gagged strangely. The Reverend looked up at Uda and their eyes were strong. Mystery? He poured another drink and swallowed it. Uda turned roughly, and walked out of the room without saying a word.

The Reverend sat for a while and watched until Uda disappeared into the corridor. He then poured and drank, poured and drank, and poured and drank some more. He became intoxicated and was gayer than before. He stared about and smiled at those watching him confused and surprised. He took another glass and showed it to the astonished crowd, "Tonight let us drink and let us not remember tomorrow if it will bring us but another misfortune." He said in Dahnkka, and stared at a woman, "To you," and at the man from the pit, "To you, too." The Reverend gulped down the drink.

The man from the pit suddenly burst into laughter, "I will drink to you too Izeonah, especially in the morning when the weight of N'Daygmong's mountain is upon your head hahahahaha!" The man lifted his glass, "Surely let us drink and forget our sorrowful demise, heh Izeonah?"

His friends gave him a strange look. He set his glass back on the table and pulled away. The Reverend lay back in his chair extremely dizzy, but he was not about to give up. He cleared his throat.

"I challenge any one of you to a drinking contest," The Reverend lifted a bottle and showed it about. His hand trembled and his head floated lightly. "Are you all cowards!?" He screamed. His demeanor seemed hilarious and made another man laugh. Then another laughed, and then the man from the pit laughed harder.

"Izeonah, hold your bottle first, your sight second, and then your challenge," the man from the pit said.

The crowd roared with laughter. The man from the pit mimicked the Reverend's gestures and the crowd laughed again. The Reverend stood on his feet and fell to the floor. The man from the pit also mimicked the gesture and fell to the floor. The crowd laughed louder this time. He walked over to the Reverend and picked him up, "Sit up Izeonah, I am your first challenger. If I win, you change your skin color, hahahaha!" The crowd laughed in frenzy. The Reverend laughed and fixed his clothes about him. He was in pain but he concealed it all. His eyes dimmed but he squinted and he became sarcastic.

"I can never lose," he said with a big grin.

"Yes, in the morning we all lose," The man from the pit sat as he poured a glass for himself.

More men came and took over the crowd resuming the entertainment with the Reverend in their midst. Led by the man from the pit, the celebration continued until the Reverend fell to the floor. The morning came and many talked about the Izeonah's strength with his liquor, though he was being carried in a wagon back to Zuxbaha.

It was a sunny morning and the Reverend was still intoxicated from the night before. He was in the wagon with his face covered so that the sun did not irritate his eyes. The long line of Zongy and their Gomry returned to their respective destinations. Poe was liberated from the claws of Camphus. The people rejoiced and said their farewells to the men leaving their land. The crowd gathered, clapped their hands, sang songs and praised the many Gomry who brought down the beast.

The Reverend was awakened by the noise and realized he was in a well-cushioned wagon, and he was comfortable. He removed the cloth from his face and saw Uda above a horse beside him.

"Put on your face mask Izeonah," Uda ordered lightheartedly, "Unless you wish to suffer from the seven mountains many more nights." The Reverend was surprised at the manner Uda spoke to him. For the first time Uda's voice was light, friendly and with a grin.

"Where are we heading," The Reverend asked.

"Home, Izeonah, home," Uda said, looking ahead at the people waving and clapping. Then he stared at the Reverend once again, still in a light mood. "The people are glad to be free."

The Reverend smiled in return and covered his face. The Wagon sped as the horses galloped away. The Reverend heard the noises until they thinned out from his ears. Under the cover he smiled.

"Life," he said, "Surely you are a mystery. I wait to see what is next for me in this land. But for now I thank you for this experience." For the first time the burden of his heart was lifted and his body felt at ease. For the first time he felt safe. Under the cover, he smiled again. "Thank you lord," he said, and laid his head to the side safely. He was soon fast asleep.

❋❋

❋❋

END OF BOOK ONE

The journey continues into book two. Coming soon…

Visit **www.africtimes.com** for more info

About Author

McNonwuun

McNonwuun (PRINCE MADISON NONWUUN) was born in Monrovia, Liberia and moved to the United States along with his family in 2000. He attended Central High School in Providence Rhode Island and after his graduation he went to Rhode Island College. While at Rhode Island College, McNonwuun majored in English and Psychology, and minored in creative writing. He also had the opportunity to take some courses in other disciplines including, political science, film, acting, music (Jazz 1900) and Philosophy. After graduation, McNonwuun set out to do other things including film production, scriptwriting, while continuously working on perfecting his passion, which is writing. He produced his first film called *Temperamental* in early 2013. Although he had been writing long before college, *Hills Of Exile* is his first novel available to the public. This is also the beginning of many other novels that are on their way. McNonwuun is the founder of Africtimes Multimedia. To know more about McNonwuun and his future endeavors, please visit **www.africtimes.com** or follow his blog at **http://mcnonwuun.wordpress.com**